ABOUT THE AUTHOR

A native New Yorker, David V. Forrest, M.D., is a graduate of Princeton University and received his medical, psychiatric, and psychoanalytic training at Columbia University College of Physicians and Surgeons, where he is now clinical professor of psychiatry. He was chief of the largest U.S. Army psychiatric clinic in Vietnam at the peak of American involvement there and received the Bronze Star. He is a past president of the American College of Psychoanalysts and the New York Clinical Society, and is a fellow of the Explorers Club.

In addition to writing hundreds of scholarly articles in psychiatry, neuropsychiatry, applied psychoanalysis, literary analysis, anthropology, and artificial mind, he has coauthored an educational videotape series, was a consultant to the television show *Star Trek*, has created a slang dictionary for foreign doctors, and, with his wife, Lynne Stetson, has developed a board game called The Ballet Company, based on her career in the New York City Ballet. He lives in New York City and has two grown children.

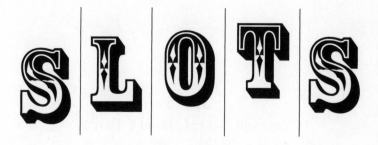

PRAYING TO THE GOD OF CHANCE

··

DAVID V. FORREST, M.D.

Illustrations by the author and Tara Jacoby

DELPHINIUM BOOKS

HARRISON, NEW YORK • ENCINO, CALIFORNIA

SLOTS

Book design by Greg Mortimer

Library of Congress Cataloguing-in-Publication Data
is available on request.

ISBN   978-1-883285-48-7

12 13 14 RRD 10 9 8 7 6 5 4 3 2 1

ACKNOWLEDGMENTS

Thanks to all who provided assistance and encouragement and inspiration; first, to Nick Gardiner and Charlie Scribner, who made the Tinker to Evers to Chance play to Glen Hartley, who represented the book, with the legal help of Lynn Chu. I count myself lucky in much more than a casino sense to have had the support of Christopher Lehmann-Haupt as my distinguished editor. It has been a pleasure and an education to work with him, and with Delphinium Books. I am also indebted to Julian Bloch, Nancy Blume, Sandy Choren, Molly Connors, Scott Cooper, Tina Compton, Sarah Christina "Babs" Curley, John and Janice DeMarco, veteran slots player and my medical building's receptionist, Linda "God don't want you gambling" Eferstein, Ralph Eovino, Daniel Forrest, Paul and Adrienne Forrest, Michael Forrest, Nick Gardiner, Allan Goldman, Erik Johnson at W. W. Norton, Susannah Forrest Karajannis, the Karajannis family, Carl Lennertz, Paul Liebowitz, Dave Marsh, Pietro Mazzoni, H.M., Allan Mottus, Mary Murray, Kerry O'Connor, Open Road Integrated Media, Hilda Pedersen, Farah Peterson, Ted and Caroline Robbins of Trafalgar Square Books, Neil J. Rosini, Esq. and the copy editor Ellen R. Feldman. The annual Interdisciplinary Colloquium on Psychoanalytic Methods in Anthropological Fieldwork, led by Werner Muensterberger, M.D., and Daniel M. A. Freeman, M.D., and hosted by Joseph Lubart, M.D., and myself at The Explorers Club and other locations, provided inspiration by enabling me to hear decades of presentations by the leading anthropologists of our time. Anne Allison's participant observation of cocktail waitresses in Tokyo may have been the most directly applicable. From his extensive library on gambling, Rich Pell recommended anthropologist David M. Hayano's ethnography, *Poker Faces: The Life and Work of Professional Card Players*, another participant observation study that is a gambling classic. Finally, most thanks are due my wife, Lynne Stetson, without whose participation this book would not have occurred to me.

By way of disclosure, I am indebted to Mr. Donald Trump—although he had no influence on this book—because he threw the only cocktail party for returning Vietnam vets that I knew of, at least for those of us who contributed to the book *Dear America: Letters Home from Vietnam*, edited by Bernard Edelman (New York: W. W. Norton, 1985).

No tax deductions were taken for casino visits made during the development of this book.

CONTENTS

INTRODUCTION

Almost 40 million people play slot machines in the United States every year, according to an annual survey by the gaming company Harrah's Entertainment, Inc. The money fed into slot machines in North America exceeds $365 billion, of which the casinos keep about $30 billion. The rest (or at least 90 percent of it) is redistributed—randomly of course—back among the players. In an article that appeared in *The New York Times Magazine* in May 2004, titled "The Tug of the New-fangled Slot Machines," Gary Rivlin offered the comparative perspective that all the movie tickets sold in North America in a year at that time totaled a mere $9 billion, and an expert estimate of the money spent on pornography in all forms totaled only $10 billion. *The Wall Street Journal* reported with surprise that "gambling was the best performing industry of the year" in 2004. Late-night funnyman Jay Leno once joked that Starbucks coffeehouses were multiplying so rapidly that they are opening new Starbucks *inside* old ones. The same might be said about the profusion of new casinos, in many of which Leno will be performing. It seems that municipalities everywhere are deciding they can solve their fiscal problems with a casino—and that if they do not, the money will flee to another state or to a casino run by a Native American tribe. Even Kansas, whence Dorothy was whisked off to Oz, has a casino resort. It was the thirteenth state to legalize gambling, a bid in the zero-sum game of trying to attract more money from other states than is lost to them, in this case, to Missouri riverboats. Even tribal casinos like Foxwoods and Mohegan Sun, in Connecticut, which earn about $800 million to $900 million a year from slot machines, are expanding by running casinos in other states for less-experienced tribes.

Slot machines provide 70 to 85 percent of casino income. A machine costs about $12,000, and the casino may clear as much as $250 to $2,500 a day from it. The market has seemed inexhaustible, and most of its growth has been recent. As gambling—sorry, make that *gaming*—has become increasingly respectable and has emerged into the mainstream of recreation, slots are leading the way, displacing other forms of wagering, including horse racing. In fact, New York, Pennsylvania, and other states have lately passed laws permitting large slot installations, called *racinos*, at racetracks in the hope of reviving interest there. Compared to scratch-offs and other types of lotteries, these new machines have been the fastest-growing form of gambling in New York. The *New York Post* of April 30, 2010, reported that New York State "generated a record $1 billion in revenue from video slot machines last year despite a shaky economy and a scandal [involving New York's governor] that has blocked a plan to put slots at Aqueduct Raceway," which "would be the state's first casino located within the five boroughs." Slot machines appear to be America's newest growth industry. While there has been some falloff during the recent financial crisis, this decline has to be viewed in comparison with larger contractions in spending, visible in the retail sector and even the patronage of Starbucks.

There are many possible reasons for this recent bubblelike expansion. The "new economy" of dot-com offerings rose and crashed, making the stock market look like a casino. This is not just my analogy but one also used by the founder of the Vanguard Group, John Bogle. The highly leveraged housing bubble made people feel flush. Once it had burst and the focus shifted to the bets investment bank Goldman Sachs had offered on it, the casino analogy became commonplace in the media. For example, in April 2010 *The New York Times* ran an editorial titled "Wall Street Casino," and an article by Andrew Ross Sorkin titled "When Deals on Wall Street Resemble Casino Wagers." The title of Vicky Ward's 2010 book, *The Devil's Casino: Friendship, Betrayal, and the High Stakes Games Played Inside Lehman Brothers,* clinches the point. In the wake of these revelations, many aging baby boomers with disposable income have looked elsewhere to "invest."

The casino metaphor has also long been applied to our legal system. Disparities between the average and the highest incomes in the United States have become huge. Controversy and scandal have afflicted religious institutions, weakening or discrediting their interdictions of once prohibited individual pursuits of pleasures. Immigrants have arrived from cultures in which games of chance offered the only opportunity for achieving success. According to a 2003 Pew Research

Center poll, Americans traditionally have led the world in *not* subscribing to the idea that success in life is determined by forces outside one's own control. But the balance may be shifting between two long-standing American archetypes: the hardworking self-made man and the gambler the cultural historian Jackson Lears describes in his book *Something for Nothing: Luck in America* (2003). Also, I prefer to reserve the term *gaming* for what one does strategically, even in a Machiavellian way, to maximize rewards in a system, such as a bureaucracy or a corporation. In our complex world, what is often referred to as "gaming the system" has become increasingly fashionable. In his book *The American Religion* (1992; reissued 2006), Harold Bloom, Sterling Professor of the Humanities at Yale University and arguably our preeminent literary critic, wrote a classic interpretation of what is unique about the creeds that have emerged on our continent since the founding of our nation. He noted that we as Americans stand out in our conviction that we are loved and favored by God and that we feel ourselves to be part of God. This could be another way of saying that our American exceptionalism is based upon a feeling that we are charmed and blessed with being lucky.

All of the above may be cultural factors in slot playing and might be considered elements in a top-down approach to understanding slot play. As a psychiatrist, I prefer to study the behavior of individuals, so you might say that I have taken a bottom-up approach to gambling. People joke about psychiatrists that we can never do anything without thinking about what it means, and I am no exception. I first played slots decades ago in Las Vegas as a recreation. In the early 1990s, one of our children was studying math at Brown University, and our trips there took my wife and me past the burgeoning Native American casinos Mohegan Sun and Foxwoods. Visits to them as they grew led me to become curious about what we and so many other slot players were doing and why. I began to talk to people on the slot floor, and to examine the slot-play experience as a mental phenomenon. What follows is intended as a user-friendly guide to playing slots, or what one might call, in fancier terms, an introduction to the psychoeconomics of slot machines.

PART 1

THE WHY
of
SLOT MACHINES

SLOTS AS MERCHANTS
OF RELIGIOUS AWE

MINDLESS AND MINDFUL SLOTS

Slot players are often maligned as mindless because there is little or no strategy involved in pressing a button to initiate a spin of the reels. When I proposed this book, a number of editors at various publishing houses told me that they assumed slot players don't read books and people who do read books don't play slots (never mind the bookstores at casinos such as Foxwoods). I have found the opposite to be true. Slot players are avid readers who love to lose themselves in books. The really smart gamblers, it is said, noisily play games with complicated betting rules, like craps, or are busy using math skills to count cards at blackjack. My first reaction to the skeptics was that their unfavorable depiction of slot players is not valid because they have defined the mental realm of intelligence too narrowly. Who is smarter, an options trader shouting bids around the pit at the stock exchange or a monk in meditative prayer on a mountaintop? It is a contrast between apples and oranges: The two are as different as raccoons and skylarks. Slots are not at all like poker, which is a zero-sum game in which winners enjoy taking from losers, and even professional players may get into physical fights. Slot players, like the skylark singing silently in their inner flight, have none of the competitiveness, boisterousness, and braggadocio of other gamblers. They play quietly and individually, but they root for one another to win and often congratulate a nearby winner, even if they inwardly feel envy or have just left that winning machine. Call it what you will, but there may be a bit less of the slob factor, too. Slot players are mannerly. They tend to be gentle, thoughtful, and pleasant folk. Although one plays slots elbow to elbow when the casino is crowded, unlike my experience at table games, I cannot recall ever moving away from an objectionable slot player, except to avoid secondhand smoke.

The Indian philosopher Jiddu Krishnamurti said that to cultivate the mind, one should not emphasize concentration but rather attention, because concentration forces the mind to narrow down to a point, while attention is without frontiers. Spared the need to strategize or count, and cloistered from the madding crowd's ignoble strife, the slot player's mind is set free, as in meditation. The repeated ritual mantra of the melodically spinning reels of the slot machine, like so many Tibetan prayer wheels being spun again and again, is the slot player's communion with Immensity, and by this I do not mean merely an immense win. The Immensity found in these machines is the force of chance that drives the world and rearranges the winds and the universe of stars. It is a connection with the possibility of fortune in the form of enormous and smaller sums of money, and with Fortune itself, which governs us all. For the slot player, play is no less than a stairway to one's lucky stars. The point is not that slot players are consciously aware of their cosmic prayers but precisely that they are not, and that they would benefit by knowing the nature of their need that is fulfilled by their play. It is commonly said that many activities other than explicit prayer—like one's work, for example—are also prayer. But slot play, as we shall see, has special claims in this regard.

WHAT EXACTLY IS A SLOT MACHINE?

For those who are unfamiliar with them (or the Martian readership, as my editor puts it), slots are gambling machines with three or more cylindrical bandlike reels, part of whose circumferences appear side by side in a window to display three or more of the symbols printed on them. When a button is pushed or a lever on the side of the slot machine is pulled (hence the nickname "one-armed bandit"), the reels spin vertically and independently, stopping automatically. If three like symbols line up on a horizontal midscreen pay line, the machine records a payout for the player. To play the slots, one feeds coins into slots on the machine, hence the name; now, more commonly, the player feeds currency or tickets with winnings or balances cashed out from other ("ticket in–ticket out") machines. Video slot machines (as opposed to electromechanical ones) simulate the appearance of reels and often have "features" or "bonus rounds" typically offering free spins or animated touch-screen choices that reveal one of an assortment of higher-payout credits. One credit is worth the denomination of the machine, be it a penny, a quarter, a dollar, or five dollars. A jackpot payout results from the machine's highest valued symbol combination, as listed on the machine or available onscreen. A progressive jackpot progresses or mounts up as a succession of players play until one wins it, whereupon it resets to a predetermined base level and begins mounting again. Usually several linked machines in a row, or bank, contribute to the progressive amount so as to make it higher, and sometimes the machines are even "hyperlinked" to identical machines in other casinos across the land to make an astronomical win possible.

WHY DO WE PLAY SLOTS?

Our clergy and our parables tell us that religious faith and devotion are not the same as logical reasoning, calculation, or cerebration. Although people may study the human records of their faiths, when it comes to matters of worship and prayer, the rational has very little to do with them and can take a person only a very short way to a spiritual destination, no matter how smart he or she may be. In fact, having to think, strategize, or figure gets in the way. This is part of the reason that the slot player, who is after bigger things, avoids the noisy craps table and the constant strategic decisions of blackjack and poker. Even the simpler bet placements of roulette and baccarat are distractions from the pursuit of pure chance that the slots offer. All religions agree—in theory, if not always in practice—that both one's IQ and the money one has at life's end are irrelevant.

Some gambling games require a modicum of thought or strategy, and some do not seem to. Blackjack, craps, and pok-

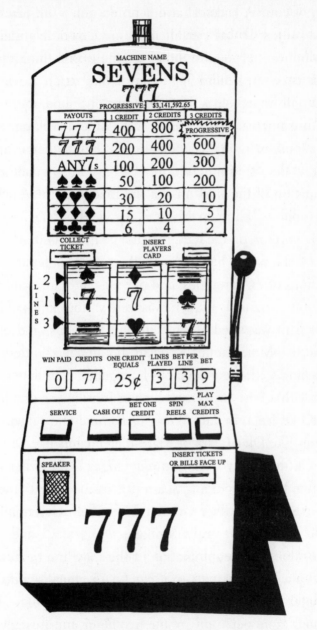

The essentials of a slot machine.

er do, of course; baccarat and keno do not. With few exceptions—only a Trivial Pursuit machine comes to mind—slot machines do not require thought. One would think that this would leave one's mind free to daydream, much as computer games with repetitive action like Tetris or Snood or Zuma do, but this is not usually the case. Most casino slot players experience a total focus on the automatic play before their eyes. That is to say, they are immersed in an expectant, vigilant state of anticipation of the next turn of the machine, to see whether the symbols will line up this time and yield a win.

The symbols on the reels may not be much help in figuring this out. They can be almost anything, although various presentations of 7s, diamonds, and playing-card rank symbols are common. Originally the symbols were various kinds of fruit,as actual fruit was used as early machine payoffs, and cherries still persist. More exotically, cigars, hot peppers, cartoon characters, and Chinese ideographs have made their appearances, along with a host of licensed themes from masscult television shows like *Jeopardy* and *Wheel of Fortune* and television celebrities like Dick Clark or Elvis or characters like Dana Carvey's Church Lady from *Saturday Night Live*. Other images are quite banal, including Spam (the canned meat) and S&H Green Stamps. Bally's Golden Times self-referentially uses classic slot machines as its symbols.

Nor does the denomination of the machine matter much in the player's anticipation; it can be 25 cents or a dollar, or multiples of pennies or nickels or quarters that may amount to much more per "pull" of the handle or, increasingly often, push of the SPIN REELS or the adjacent (and easily accidentally pushed) MAXIMUM BET buttons. Even practice play on a casino simulation can elicit a similar anticipatory intensity, based on the pleasure of winning in fantasy. This is not to say that the monetary reward is unimportant, but many players will (for example) continue to play an attractive penny machine that pays out a poorer percentage, even wagering less than the amount necessary to win the progressive, because they are entranced by the experience itself.

SLOTS AS REWARD CONDITIONERS

In one sense, the reward is everything, and so the slot machine is a perfect example of what the behaviorists call a variable reinforcement conditioning Skinner box. B. F. Skinner was an experimental psychologist famous for putting animals in boxes with a lever to press that might or might not reward them with a pellet of food. Skinner found that he could alter the animal's behavior by changing the reward schedule. If a reward comes every time the animal presses, it doesn't bother its little head much about the lever, pressing only when it is hungry to get a pellet. But if the reinforcement schedule is variable, the animal cannot predict when it will get a pellet and therefore must press the lever more times. Even more pressing is necessary if the reinforcement is variable and infrequent. The animal presses madly and constantly, and it searches for patterns in the reward-giving so it can predict how much pressing it will have to do in order to be fed. And when the reinforcement is variable, very infrequent, and based on a random-number generator like a slot machine, the animal—or the slot player— can find no pattern. We humans tend to develop superstitions about what is making the rewards come. This is because the mind finds true randomness an incomprehensible mystery that it must attempt to grasp and master. Also to be considered is the disconnect between the pressing behavior and the results. Some of Skinner's pigeons were placed in a box with no lever to peck. Instead, an automatic mechanism delivered food at regular intervals—for example, every fifteen seconds—with no reference to the birds' behaviors. Six of the eight birds placed in the box developed all sorts of ridiculous mannerisms that Skinner termed "superstitious," like tossing their heads or hopping around in a circle, apparently to influence the lever to give pellets. When the behavior was established, even rewards at one- or two-minute intervals maintained it. When the incomprehensibly timed pellet did come, the animal appeared to Skinner to misinterpret its spontaneous movements as influencing the rewards. The slot player, whose actions do not affect the randomly delivered rewards, may also pull the handle in a certain way, wear a lucky charm or article of clothing, or— as I shall discuss—develop religious feelings about the rewards.

Slot rewards are coins, tokens, or credits, not pellets of food. The reward needn't be concrete. Casinos have learned that players do not need actual coins, and most have converted their machines so that when the cash-out button is pressed, tickets are disgorged. These tickets have printed on them the amount won—or remaining from what one put in; their disbursement is often accompanied by a simulated coin-like clattering and the sound of a whistle. This mechanizing of the payment process has the great advantage for the casino of reducing the number of slot-service attendants necessary to refill empty coin hoppers, and—more important—the wait for the attendant during which the player could be gambling. Although coins are no longer concretely necessary, other rewards can be substituted, like bursts of music, lights behind the reels, and the obsessive satisfaction of seeing one's ducks lined up in a row (or whatever symbols the machine permits one to line up).

For heavier playing, other tangible rewards are available if the player registers for and uses a casino reward card often called a players club card. Once inserted in a special slot higher up on each machine, the card records the amount of money fed into the machine, regardless of wins or losses. At Foxwoods, for example, if you run $80 through the machine, you get $1 in complimentary credit that can be used elsewhere in the casino. If your point value is 20, that means you ran $1,600 through the machine, much of which was in the form of smaller paybacks you recirculated. In short, for these points it does not matter whether you win or lose, nor does it matter how much money you insert; it is the money played that counts.

As it happens, a tremendous amount of money gets recirculated through the machines because winnings tend to be replayed. The machines take their bite during every period of play, but they also kick back a certain amount. Points earned can be applied toward casino restaurant bills (making them almost literal equivalents of Skinner's food pellets) or reducing one's hotel bill—unless, of course, the player was "comped," or invited to stay free, an effective loss leader to attract players known to spend heavily.

Such rewards are sensory accoutrements that do not get to the heart of the matter. The payout schedule on a slot machine is connected to a random-number generator and cannot be predicted by either the player or the casino. Skinner, a behaviorist who considered the inner workings of the mind an impenetrable black box, never investigated *why* random variable reinforcement is so compelling Or why rewards unconnected with behavior prompt pigeons—and humans—to invent behavior in the belief that they are influencing the payout. While pigeons may toss their heads or gyrate in anticipation of a reward, humans may invent all sorts of ways to pull the handle, push the button, or even choose which machine they play. And, because humans are able to conjecture, they can indulge in magical thinking regarding their influence over the next pull.

PRAYING TO THE GOD OF SLOTS

As I've said, the slots *require* no thought. No symbols or words need to be manipulated and occupy the mental stream. What we do is communicate wishfully with the power and process behind the ribbon of events that the machine is revealing to us in a microcosm of our fate. This is a state of mind that can be compared with prayer.

Prayer seeks a state of grace in connection to a deity. Wishes are made and their fulfillment requested of the deity. For religious people, the deity is a familiar Other. What slot players connect with—the god of slots—begs to be explored. To play is to pray, but to this stranger Other.

CAPTURING THE SENSE OF AWE

The sense of awe and mystery that is inherent in modern science, especially physics and cosmology, competes with the sense of awe previously possessed exclusively by religion. A case in point, as Rod Serling was fond of announcing on *The Twilight Zone*: I open the journal *Science* of June 19, 2009, and read, "Distant quasars harbor at their centers black holes as massive as 10 billion suns." Contemplation of the vastness of the universe's expanse or the complexity of the quantum realm, as well as mastery of the atom and the genome, all threaten to upstage some of the more modest claims of religions like the parting of waters, the transformation of the sick and the dead, the multiplication of loaves and fishes, and the transmutation and transubstantiation of water and wine. But miracles are now scarce, science seems impersonal and out of reach, and people continue to yearn for accessible experiences of wonder.

OLD WORLD CASINOS

When they were first introduced, slot parlors were dark, cramped, low-ceilinged hideaways. European slot parlors still are. True, Monte Carlo, dating from 1863, was and is intimidatingly rich-looking, but if you take a cab from Lugano, Switzerland, to visit Campione d'Italia in the Lombardy region of Italy, where there are 225 slots, you will feel claustrophobic in the small, dark space. The slot room in Casino Municipale in the Palazzo Vendramin Calergi in Venice is also modest and low-ceilinged. It upholds some standards, however. Wearing sneakers, I was refused entry and referred a few doors down to a conveniently located shoe store to buy appropriate footwear. The largest casino in Europe is in Estoril, Portugal. It, too, *looks* like a casino. Although large in area, with a lovely plaza in front, it is low-ceilinged and dingily lit.

The casino at the Kurhaus in the wealthy German spa city of Baden-Baden claims, perhaps with justice, that it is the most beautiful casino in the world. Dostoevsky set his novel *The Gambler* there. Its halls for table games opened in 1855, and comprise four rooms, paid for by Edouard Bénazel, founder of the Baden-Baden Racing Association, and designed by the stage decorator Séchan in eclectic Second Empire style. Its opulent interiors are masterpieces of design that Klaus Fischer, author of the guide to the casino, compares to the "fairytale castles" built shortly after by Bavaria's "Mad King" Ludwig II. The Florentine Room, called the Hall of a Thousand Candles, is now electric. Today the dress code is strictly adhered to; in an atmosphere of near silence and restrained refinement, elegant patrons place their bets on roulette and chemin de fer. Fischer learned from their instructor that even the croupiers are required to have "a natural elegance of movement." I saw the number 33 come up a remarkable four times in thirteen spins of one roulette wheel, and twice at the next wheel. That number became piled high with chips, all without disturbing the hushed atmosphere. (Imagine the noise if something comparable happened at a Caesars Palace wheel!) In the decades before 1870, Fischer remarks, Baden-Baden attracted "Russian councilors of state, English lords, plantation owners from Java and the members of the Paris Jockey Club with their girlfriends from the opera ballet."

The dark cellar contains a modest installation of slots. No dress code here to play an automatic roulette wheel. The air seems stale under the low ceilings. Reminiscent of a crypt, this grubby setting offers nothing in the way of religious inspira-

Something religious is happening at the slots.

tion, and does not appear in the lavish guide. Whether this amounts to truth in packaging or just a failure to catch the wave of American casinos, Baden-Baden keeps its slots in their former place. I saw some unfamiliar machines there, including Grand Roulette by Admiral, Swampland by Unidesa, Bingo by Atronic, and Dracula by Orion, but there was also a row of familiar Aristocrat machines, with a hyperlink connecting them with other identical machines elsewhere, so a larger progressive jackpot could be built up among them.

Estonia, too, built casinos, following the Singing Revolution of the late 1980s, which led bloodlessly to the country's independence from the Russians. Just after entering the old town gate in Talinn, one finds a table-game parlor next to a slot establishment. Both are small and unobtrusive.

THE CASINO CATHEDRAL

In our own nation's history, the first slot machines were rudimentary appliances with small screens resembling the Dumont televisions of the 1950s (replicas of these machines have been offered in some casinos, such as the Borgata in Atlantic City). They were limited to displays of fruit and 7s, without today's bells and whistles or bonus-play features. Since the time of the first slot machines, American casinos have grown more magnificent and beautiful, with soaring architecture as awe-inspiring as cathedrals. Given the now gigantic size of these establishments, the original literal meaning of the word *casino*, "little house," has become ironic. Many of those in Las Vegas have impressive travel destination themes. Some featured models of structures like the Brooklyn Bridge and Statue of Liberty at the New York New York Casino, which, despite its rich iconography, remains somewhat gloomy inside, simulating Greenwich Village streets at night. Others have striven harder to inspire with such wonders as the half-sized Eiffel Tower that one may ascend at the Paris Casino, and an elaborate canal system with gondolas and gondoliers in the Venetian. Both the Paris and the Venetian have discovered the awesome effect of a vast indoor sky, far enough away to seem real; variable lighting reflects different times of day and allows the *rues* and *stradas* of upscale Parisian and Venetian shops to be shown off against the dreamy crepuscular glow. The magic of *l'heure bleue*, the twilight hour for which a marvelous perfume was named, is almost as lovely in the Paris Casino in Las Vegas as in the city of Paris itself. The Venetian relegates its slots to a glittering floor below the canals, but the Paris sprinkles them through the enormous city square right beneath the artificial sky. Notably absent in these models of cities, known for their churches and cathedrals, are houses of worship. They are unneeded—we all know what we have come to worship, as we dedicate our hearts once more, under these artificial heavens, to the veneration of the god of slots.

The Bellagio, Steve Wynn's masterpiece, transcends the romance of travel. Although it may well be the most beautiful casino in the world—it has been rated the most beautiful *building* of its decade—it does not compete with the real town of Bellagio, way up on Lake Como, whose lovely waters are surrounded by mountains on the border of Italy and Switzerland. In Bellagio, Italy, the Grand Hotel Villa Serbelloni, with its enormous windows looking out on the lake, its incomparable food, and nightly violins, is as close to heaven as one can get on earth. But if we are talking of palatial splendor, the Bellagio in Las Vegas is even richer and more palatial.

Shortly after September 11, 2001, my wife and I flew to Las Vegas to stay at the Bellagio, in part to recover from the trauma of the day. More than a hundred conventions had canceled because of a widespread fear of flying, our cabdriver told us, and *The New York Times* had run a feature stating that Las Vegas had been the hardest hit of American cities, because just about all of its economy depends on air travel. Las Vegas and the Bellagio were happy to have us. We were able to get into Cirque de Soleil's fabulous aquatic show, *O* (homonymous for the French word for water, *eau*), itself worth a transcontinental flight; even then the house was packed. We dined at Bellagio's Picasso restaurant and were seated at the best table, where George Clooney and Julia Roberts sat in the film *Ocean's Eleven*, and viewed the spectacular water-fountain show just outside our porch window. All around us were paintings by Picasso, enough to turn the heads of even New Yorkers like ourselves. We did put some money in the slots, but the Bellagio "comped" us for all the gourmet meals we ate during that visit. Such opulence made us feel quite royal. But amid all that elegance, we found other slot players worshipping not in their Sunday finery but in the traditional garb of vacationing Americans—shorts, T-shirts, baseball caps, and sneakers.

In his classic novel *Erewhon*, Samuel Butler satirized churches as "musical banks" in which people deposit but cannot withdraw money. Fittingly, a television advertisement for Mohegan Sun Casino suggested where the new churches are by employing music suggestive of the hymn "O Come, All Ye Faithful." The point is clear: Casinos, flaunting their beauty and wealth, are new places of worship.

INSOLENT CHARIOTS OF THE GODS

In 1958, the freelance reporter John Keats wrote *Insolent Chariots*, a book devastatingly critical of the American auto industry. For years Detroit had assumed that it held America's psyche in the palm of its hand. Motivational research by psychologists had concluded that Americans were highly status-conscious and in need of self-assurance, with men—who at that time supposedly made most of the decisions about buying cars—particularly insecure about their masculinity. Detroit assumed it had the remedy for this vulnerability: the automobile as an instrument of status therapy. Not only were the cars that were produced for us large and wide, but they were also festooned with all manner of protruding edges and gimcracks, often with phallic shapes. The most characteristic feature of 1950s cars was their tail fins. Atop the rear fenders soared triangular projections, at the base of which were two side-by-side ball-shaped red brake lights. The family auto had been reborn as a sex symbol and fantasy mistress.

The extinction of these tail-finned dinosaurs has since become ancient history, with foreign-designed compact cars having taken over from those insolent chariots. But good sense comes and goes in cycles, and recently an era of gas-guzzling SUV's prevailed, mercifully minus the phallic protuberances. These might well be called the new insolent chariots, and they have survived the bankruptcies and revival of the American automobile industry, while the appetite for smaller cars of the America that bailed it out remains to be seen.

CELESTIAL TRANSPORTATION

Just as the auto industry grew out of proportion, casinos, too, have now gone beyond audacity into grandiosity and insolence. The insolence has been to festoon casinos not with phallic symbolism, but with the appurtenances of religiosity. In our leisure time, on our days of rest, or upon our retirement, we are driving, taking buses, and flying in droves to casinos that are over-the-top in their opulence and grandeur. With expanded size has come audacity. Actual automobiles and motorcycles may be parked as tempting jackpots atop circles of linked slot machines. But the casinos have aspired to become vehicles of another sort, chariots of celestial splendor to transport us to another dimension of the spirit. And not satisfied with attracting only gamblers, they have also become family mega-centers, appropriating the wholesome image of the upscale shopping mall and encouraging people to bring their children to practice at large video-game centers, in preparation for the day when they turn twenty-one.

Just as we once rose up against the insolent automotive charioteers, we must now realize what we are buying in the package the casinos are selling us. Freud famously once said that sometimes a cigar is just a cigar, but casinos today are seldom just casinos.

SLOT SHRINES AND ALTARS

Slot machines themselves have become ever more like shrines as the eye-catching displays of the superstructures mounted above them have become increasingly elaborate. These gleaming constructions draw the eye upward in supplication to the more rarefied progressives and bonus rounds that may reward the faithful. Some even feature the celebrity-saints that players have chosen as intercessors in their quest for fortune. Is it far-fetched to consider their play as praying to the god of slots?

At times the religiosity is blatant. One video slot called Pearly Gates is almost mockingly sacrilegious. You line up harps or doves for 500 credits, cherubim for 200; line up images of clouds and lightning or of the Good Book or of Gothic stained-glass windows with 7s, bells, or cherries for 100. Should three Hand of God symbols appear on the video screen, you pick one of the three by touching it and receive a number of halos tossed by a Godly hand like Frisbees at the heads of your choices from nine assorted characters standing on clouds in a heavenly scene. If the halo lands on a head, the character gets a harp and wings and ascends to heaven and the player receives more rewards; if it misses, the deprived figure drops down a black hole to hell for no reward bonus. The characters offered include a hard hat, a cowboy, a teenager, a black man, a little old lady, and so forth. One of the characters is a dog, which has an equal chance of ascending to this slot heaven. But then some churches actually do bless pets. As Mark Twain said, "Heaven goes by favor. If it went by merit, you would stay out and your dog would go in." He also wrote, in a letter to William Dean Howells, "The dog is a gentleman; I hope to go to his heaven, not man's." Another slot machine from the designer Atronic, called Angels & Devils, has angels and devils, harps and pitchforks, a heavenly gate, and 7s with halos and fire. In the casino at the San Juan Marriott, the *Saturday Night Live*–derived satiric Church Lady slots were winkingly positioned amid a bank of "sinful" Playboy machines.

THE WEALTH OF THE SPIRIT

Throughout recorded time, religion, despite disavowing any link between wealth and spirituality (the meek shall inherit the earth; sooner a camel will pass through the eye of a needle than a rich man enter the kingdom of heaven; the parable of the talents; the prodigal son), has often intentionally confounded spiritual power with the worldly concepts of royalty and riches. For countless people throughout history, the impressive edifice with the immense wealth of gold and other precious materials has worked as a concrete metaphor for spiritual clout and as an inducement to faithful obedience. Everyone understands wealth, it seems, and in an age when the only royalty left are mostly silly excrescences of their now mostly democratic countries, everybody still understands what royalty means. Children continue to be enthralled by stories of kings and queens in their castles with their princes and princesses. So spiritual glory—transparent, weightless, ideal, and deeply real—becomes material stuff, the word made not human flesh and blood, but flash and gilt.

The expropriation of the religion-associated themes of royalty and wealth is inescapable in the casinos of slots, which, like the sites of early religions, once more closely resembled subterranean caves. Donald Trump did not hesitate to dub his Atlantic City casino the Taj Mahal, a monument to royal love. The splendid chandeliers and marble of some casinos promise the inheritance of wealth on earth, and the commissioning and collecting of glorious art rivals that of Rome and St. Petersburg. More casinos seem to be tapping into a natural American reverence for the lavish trappings of wealth, if not religiosity.

As the slot palaces for the worship of chance expand and grow ever more luxurious, leaving nearby bed-and-breakfasts and restaurants abandoned, and nearby denizens all the poorer, one asks oneself where one has seen this before. It is the picture of the poor all over the world, a sea of low buildings surrounding an edifice of worship filled with gold and art beyond the reach of any of the populace, but so necessary to sustain the hope of these poor people for a better, celestial life of wealth and ease. Worship is worship; in the same way, the football stadium looms as a classic coliseum over the low academic buildings at, say, Texas Christian University. Although the casinos argue that they are usually built in poorer areas and provide jobs, most of those jobs do not pay very well, and municipalities that have sought to encourage development by building casinos have found little economic stimulus except at the casinos themselves.

SLOUCHING TOWARD BETHLEHEM

In Bethlehem, Pennsylvania, home of Lehigh University, where Lee Iacocca, the former Ford and Chrysler honcho, went to school, Las Vegas Sands opened a new $743 million state-sanctioned casino on May 23, 2009. In its architecture, it attempts to pay homage to the previous era of steelmaking, when the city's twenty-story blast furnaces, cold and rusting since 1995, were active. Architectural elements like structural steel supports, enormous ducts, and factory windows above the slot-machine floor, coupled with the gunmetal tones of the exterior and a sign made out of a heavy railroad bridge hanging over the entrance, reminds sad locals of former glory days. This casino is oddly sepulchral and constitutes a bittersweet and ironic shrine to the former strength of American industry. A central serving bar sits beneath a huge coil of three-foot-wide rusty steel bands, and rows of hundreds of glowing rods like molten steel ingots hanging from the ceiling resemble votive candles. Beneath them, the recently hired, mostly fe-

The casino as cathedral.

male beverage servers in brown sequined skirts are so fresh-faced (they need only be eighteen years old, and new casinos seem to hire the young and beautiful) that they seem to be acolytes to something they never knew. At the Moravian Book Shop, established in 1745, Mary Lou Shade, whose husband taught American history at Lehigh, reminisces about the hey-day of steel in Bethlehem and its sad passing, beginning with the first Black Monday, October 19, 1987, when world stock markets crashed. She said that the Sands Casino, together with the Smithsonian and the National Museum of Industrial History, is planning to develop the graveyard of American steel-making into an attraction, anchored, of course, by the casino.

Bethlehem and its surroundings were already preoccupied with ghosts. Besides the Holy Ghost Church and Preschool, there are ghost walks and ghost masters for tourists, proudly haunted colleges (Lehigh and Moravian), and haunted hotels, one from 1758 and another that advertises "A Room With a Boo." In *The Wall Street Journal* of April 7, 2010, Alexandra Berzon reported that "the jury is still out" on Bethlehem's casino, and that "revenue from the slots parlor . . . has been disappointing because of the economic downturn." Although it has helped the tax base and has not led to an increase in crime, its presence is "a divisive issue." "Many feared the casino would change the image of a place that calls itself the 'Christmas City,' a reference to the city's biblical namesake," Berzon found.

A proposed casino in Gettysburg, Pennsylvania, has been similarly divisive. In one poll of Adams County residents, 42 percent were in favor of the casino, 35 percent opposed, and 22 percent had no opinion. In this case, it's partially a battle between the economic developers and the Civil War preservationists and reenactors, who feel a casino would be a "desecration" of a "sacred place." In March 2010 local blogs reported fear of increases in drug abuse, alcoholism, and prostitution. Some bloggers lumped casinos together with brothels. (At least they didn't equate them to investment banks! Can a comparison with oil companies be far behind?) Others suggested checking out what the big casinos failed to do for the surrounding area in Atlantic City. Another fear is that building a local casino removes the "destination" aspect, promoting problematic everyday patronage that risks becoming habitual instead of something special. Another blog pooh-poohs all this and aptly lumps casinos with a different set by pointing that neither church-going nor casino patronage is mandatory.

MONEY OVER THE FALLS

On the American side, Niagara Falls has a casino run by the Seneca Nation. On the Canadian side there are two, both government-operated. The older Casino Niagara has a more intimate feel, while the five-year-old, billion-dollar, 2.5- million-square-foot Fallsview Casino complex has a fourteen-story CASINO sign attached to its hotel tower. At night it bathes the area around the falls in a neon red glow. This casino and the towers of surrounding hotels owned by Italian Canadians trap more of the mist arising from the falls. Under the solarium panes of the glass dome at the entrance to the casino resort there is a tall gray central construction called the Hydro-Teslatron, named in honor of Nikola Tesla, the visionary Austrian Empire–born inventor of alternating current, which is used to carry the electrical energy generated by the falls. Simulated electrical cables rise to the dome from the Teslatron, which has a waterfall, simulated turbines, and a glowing blue core reminiscent of the "dilithium" power drive of *Star Trek*. Although the Hydro-Teslatron was only years old when I visited in July of 2009, it was partially broken and unable to deliver its continuously changing light and water show. Contemporary postings now show it functioning. The three-thousand-slot-machine Fallsview Casino itself was packed with players. It is an elegant venue, its Roman architecture replete with white and gold features. It abounds with faux alabaster statues (not quite up to Bernini's *Daphne*) reaching heavenward for rewards.

LABELING RELIGIOUS

One need not be a theologian or a religionist to make certain observations about what is religious. Psychoanalytic anthropology, which compares cultures, best equips us for evaluating whether a particular institution or activity in a given society is religious; in this theory, if it *functions* as a religion, it may be considered one. Abram Kardiner, M.D., the great proponent of psychoanalytic anthropology at Columbia University, was one of my mentors. He designated as *projective systems* those forms of imaginative devotion in which people express the tensions, hopes, and fears that their culture produces in them but does not deal with fully. Mythology and religion are such projective systems. People embrace them in order to project onto them their wishes and hopes. They are willing to sacrifice effort and wealth to them, not for immediate reward but for an eventual state of grace and a sense of being rewarded. Simply hoping is a positive experience and an influence upon their lives. It is as real as anything in our experience. The popular writer Dan Brown, in his book *The Lost Symbol,* writes that religion requires the ABCs of assurance of salvation, belief in a precise theology, and conversion of nonbelievers. Anthropologists tend to use wider and more inclusive definitions, characterizing religions by their practitioners' preferences in prayer, ritual, and meditation.

PAGAN SPIRITS

The religion one finds in casinos is often freely pagan. Indian casinos—which seem to shun the politically correct term Native American—capitalize on harnessing as much of the Great Spirit as they can. Mohegan Sun, in Uncasville, Connecticut, established in 1996, is a three-hundred-thousand-square-foot casino with 6,400 slots, comprising two subcasinos and a third newly opened forty-five-thousand-square-foot Casino of the Wind. The Casino of the Earth is a huge circular array of subareas dedicated to the cycle of the seasons; it surrounds a Wolf Den of animatronic wolves lifting their heads to the heavens and a nonsmoking Hall of the Lost Tribes. Near the entrance to the Casino of the Earth there is a striking mural, perhaps fifty feet high, of a Mohegan brave reaching up with his right hand toward the light streaming down from heaven into the Connecticut woods. His extended left hand ends in tree branches (much like Bernini's *Daphne,* at the Villa Borghese), and his lower body is a tree trunk. Close behind him is a turtle.

What has all this to do with gambling? Absolutely nothing, it would seem on the face of it. It depicts no less than the creation story of the Mohegan religion, and their Adam and Eve. The tribe believes that its male and female forebears sprouted from a tree. The turtle is the Grandfather Turtle, on whose back the world was formed. A turtle rug leads from one subcasino to the other, and bejeweled Turtle Award pins are given to the employees of the year. Pass by the shopping area and next to it the sixty-foot, seven-story Taughannick Falls, which the casino's website describes as adding "to the breathtaking Mohegan Sun experience," and one enters the Casino of the Sky, which resides, with its mountainous Wombi Rock cocktail area, under "the Sky Dome, the world's largest, most spectacular planetarium dome," as one of the casino's brochures puts it, "decorating the casino with an ever changing display of sparkling constellations." Everywhere such stunning architectural designs draw the eye upward to behold the sky. Can the Great Spirit be far beyond? The Casino of the Wind, displaying a 35-foot-high by 50-foot-wide electronic and animated waterwall that acts as a projection screen, "draws," according to a casino pamphlet, "inspiration from solar phenomena" and "the spirits of the four winds: north, south, east and west." An unabashed fifty-four-page promotional catechism titled *The Secret Guide* documents and illustrates the omnipresent and elaborately developed Native American religious symbolism. A birthday card from Mohegan Sun to previous players begins with a devotional message: "Each year, our Mother Nature sends four Seasons to Grace the earth with Bounty beyond measure. May your Year be filled with all Great Things. Best wishes from your friends at Mohegan Sun." The card has celestial and flower motifs and what looks like a symmetrical Star of Bethlehem or cross symbol on its front. T-shirts are available with MOHEGAN SUN and the same star cross printed on them. Though this symbol is authentically Native American, it may send a message to clientele who happen to be Christian. (One notes with some relief that the Native American broken cross symbol, which looks like a reverse swastika, is nowhere to be found.) Along with the motto "The Wonder of It All™" of the 1992 6,400-slot Mashantucket Pequot Foxwoods Casino in Ledyard, Connecticut (with its $55 million expansion), and its signature "Rainmaker" statue of an Indian brave aiming his bow and arrow hopefully skyward, the message of all this is clarion: our Indians are holier than thou. Maybe they are; only God (a.k.a. the Great Spirit) knows. But do these sacred symbols and icons belong in a casino? And should the word *sanctimony* come to mind, or is it all just misplaced piety? And yet....

All this gorgeously represented nature worship just may relate to the slots, though in a way that the tribes and designers may not have fully realized. For nature is more than turtles. The natural world is fundamentally statistical. The order of its physics is made of mathematical chance. Caesars Palace expresses the pagan grandeur that was Rome. The one in Las Vegas also boasts a giant replica of Michelangelo's *David* (from a Cinquecento Italy, actually Florence, positioned to direct a warning glare at Rome). In Atlantic City, as one enters the casino from the Caesars Atlantic City hotel area, one encounters an enormous templelike room with a forty-foot-high ceiling. Up a wall to the right, nine female statues in goddess gowns stand in nine arches halfway up to the ceiling, and to the left, Roman statesmen are similarly elevated.

A gigantic statue of Caesar Augustus (63 BCE–14 CE), the first (but not yet Holy) Roman Emperor, looms nearby. Directly ahead is the Temple Bar, set off by monumental classic columns, with a painted mural of daily Roman life on its ceiling. At the rear of the bar, behind a wall of glass, is a tall wine room complete with a ladder to retrieve bottles. A waiter named Michael serves you a worthy Caesar salad encrusted spectacularly with golden brown Parmesan cheese. (I shall not get distracted by the celestial food at casinos, which itself could be a subject for a book. But if you wish to celebrate food, try Paragon at Foxwoods or the Alta Strada at the MGM Grand, next to Foxwoods. In Las Vegas, try Michael Mina at the Bellagio. Attention to detail at the restaurant Alex Wynn included correctly pronouncing the names of foreign guests and providing for milady's purse its own miniature chair at the table.)

Classical gods abound on slot machines. In the New Orleans Harrah's casino, WMS Gaming's Neptune's Kingdom features blessings from that god like "Mighty Neptune grants you good fortune," and "May my extensive powers bring you wealth and riches." Pegasus, also from WMS, depicts Zeus and classical icons like a temple, chimera, coins, a vase, and a sundial. Thai Treasures, from WMS, has a temple image as its highest pay line. Inca Sun, from Aristocrat, shows pyramids, statues, pendants, and golden birds. Atronic's Dancing Spirit features "Mystic Journeys" with animal spirit guides. Aristocrat's Easter Island displays the statues (and a fleeting flying saucer for those who believe extraterrestrials made them). Patriotic themes also flourish, as in American Reels from Sigma Games Inc., which flaunts Uncle Sam, Ben Franklin, the bald eagle, Liberty Bell, fireworks, baseball, and, yes, apple pie. God, gods, and country together add up to a new casino sanctimony.

The Tropicana in Atlantic City has a "Nickel Heaven" deco-rated with devils and hellish red flames; upstairs from it is a pen-ny-slot area named Pennies from Heaven, with cherubic angels against a blue sky. The Spotlight 29 Casino in California's Coach-ella Valley sports a celestial ceiling-to-floor cylinder of rain streams surrounded by walls of undulating sky blue juxtaposed against hellish red light discernable through rising generated smoke.

PARADISE LOST AND REGAINED

The Atlantis Casino on Paradise Island in the Bahamas is the unavoidable center of the "World's Largest Resort," claims Sol Kerzner, its South African developer. The theme of this resort is carried out with such imagination, aesthetic taste, and excru-ciating attention to detail that it invites participation in a collec-tive delusion—that it is the unearthed eleven-thousand-year-old lost land of Atlantis first mentioned in Plato's dialogues. In a sunken network of tunnels surrounded by a mammoth salt-water aquarium with fifty thousand sea animals representing two hundred species, one may visit The Dig, an archaeological reconstruction replete with an abandoned Indiana Jones–like archaeologist's office, displaying all aspects of the lives of the Atlanteans. There is an observatory and a laboratory. Around a bubbling cauldron, there are diving suits with which the Atlan-teans presumably entered the boiling waters to study the volca-no that one day would cause Atlantis to sink. Upstairs from this sunken area, around the top of a dome that rivals many Euro-pean ecclesiastical *duomos* and resembles the pagan Pantheon in Rome in its circular vent to the heavens, authentic-looking murals display the imagined history of the people of Atlantis. Restaurants are named according to Plato's legend of Atlantis. But if one is in search of the Atlantean religion, one need only repair to the centrally located casino itself, which has a Temple of the Moon and a Temple of the Sun situated in the main aisle. The latter temple rather appropriately proffers not eternal reward but the casino-rewards desk, where people who pass substantial sums though the slots can receive discounts off their hotel and restaurant bills. Once again, a celestial religiosity prevails. A promotional letter touts "mythical surroundings, godly events and world-class casino action," assuring potential visitors that "paradise awaits." It concludes, "After all, why should the gods have all the fun?" Following the Reef expansion, the tag line read, "Welcome to Atlantis, Playground of the Gods." Appropriately, the letter informs the reader, "Spirit Air begins daily service from Fort Lauderdale to Nassau."

Must we conclude that a majority of slot players are consciously aware of the majesty of the firmament as they spin their slot cylinders over and over? Most are probably no more conscious of the luminous and numinous beyond the reels in front of their noses than amoebae swimming in a drop of water between a microscope slide and its cover slip are aware of the dating life of the high-school biology student peering down her instrument at them. And yet, they feel the magic (the slot players do, that is; the amoebae will have to await decipherment of their complex chemical logic, and any thought that they practice can now be described only in terms of elementary tropisms).

No one doubts that the surroundings matter in real churches. The architecture critic Catesby Leigh, in a Houses of Worship column in *The Wall Street Journal* titled "What the Structure Says: How Architects Treat the Sacred," contrasts two Milwaukee examples. One "undermines the idea of worship as something focused on a reality that transcends the self." But in the other, "the guiding principle here is the church as the consecrated house of God. With its sky-blue walls, central dome with plasterwork ornament, nave and aisles separated by paired ionic columns, and Byzantine columns flanking the apse, the chapel has attracted visitors of varying faiths unaccustomed to such beauty—let alone to such orthodox liturgical design—in a new church building." I wonder what Mr. Leigh would say about some of today's casinos.

QUALITY AND COMPETITION

That "quality sells" is an adage of marketing, and there is little question that the avenues of slots are a quality presentation, an entertainment with production values like ever more slickly designed machine cabinet housings, repertories of sounds, on-screen indicia art, and animated performance. One's experience with the machines has been honed by evolutionary competition into an ever more perfect seductiveness. Machines compete with one another for the fickle favor of slot players. Although classic three-reel machines persist vigorously, the *Las Vegas Review-Journal* noted in January 2007 that games with TV and board-game themes tend to have a short life cycle of only six months or so. Those that receive little attention are removed and replaced, and new features, especially in the newer generation of video slots, keep upping the ante to remain on the cutting edge. Technical advances in computer games quickly reach the slot floor in the form of more complex programming, higher definition video displays, and better sound. When *The Wall Street Journal* rated the most inventive towns in America by patents issued—excluding major high-tech centers like Boston and Santa Clara, California (the home of Intel)—Las Vegas headed the list, with 132 patents for new slot games. Game manufacturers like Reno-based International Game Technology (IGT), WMS Industries, Bally Technologies, and Sydney-based Aristocrat do well when a new technology, like ticket in–ticket out, or the newer server-based downloadable slots, initiates waves of replacements. Between 1997 and 2008, the number of slot machines grew from 500,000 to 800,000, according to a 2010 American Gaming Association white paper, and more than a million new machines were projected between 2007 and 2010.

Scott Cooper, manager of development at the Agua Caliente Casino in Rancho Mirage, California, has described the pace of slot machine change as "scary." It takes only about a year to bring a new game from inception to the market. The goal is to develop machines so engrossing that people will want to keep playing at lower payouts. In the lush environment of our free and affluent society, these electronic creatures evolve like a fecund form of parasitic life. The reasons for their success are not easily or fully understood, even by their makers, especially because their interface is with the complexity of our human minds. Computers are evolving rapidly to the point that it will be difficult or impossible even for their human designers to comprehend the functioning of their programs. And no one completely grasps how markets work.

THE ART OF THE REEL

Adding to the lure of slot machines is their visual appeal. At the corner of Lexington Avenue and Sixty-third Street in Manhattan, the Museum of Illustration Gallery of the Society of Illustrators exhibits more pieces of art each year than the Museum of Modern Art and the Guggenheim combined. As a frequenter and friend of that museum, I get to enjoy the finest examples of past and contemporary illustration. Judging from this experience, I believe that the graphic art and animation now used in slot-machine screen design—as in video games—are state-of-the-art, based as they are on ever-improving computational platforms. *Strictly Slots* magazine featured some of the talented and often young artists who work in this field. While they strive to attract and delight the eye, as all artists do, they work within the conventions that succeed, without needing to know precisely why.

THE IMPORTANCE OF SOUND

The MGM Grand Hotel that opened in May 2008 at Foxwoods offers an unbroken view of Connecticut woods as far as the eye can see, a dramatic vista, especially when it is steeped in the morning mist. Hotel guests may take a break from gambling in the large shell-shaped pool, and if you forget your bathing suit, you can find one across the walkway in the Grand Pequot Tower spa shop. The casino is more intimate than the vast halls in the rest of Foxwoods, but it offers a soaring vision of spiral columns and filigree in gold, gold, and more gold, with none of that old-time Indian religion. It contains many of the latest machines, like the Wizard of Oz, with its Flying Monkey bonus and its Oz Pick of Emeralds feature (choose an emerald on the screen and win bonus credits). Particularly appealing is this machine's Bose three-dimensional audio system, underscoring the important contribution of slot sound systems. Many players avoid machines that are inaudible.

KINGDOM FOR THE HORSES

Saratoga Springs was once a quiet upstate New York town of restored Victorian houses, home to Skidmore College and, in July, the summer home of the New York City Ballet at the Saratoga Performing Arts Center down the Avenue of the Pines. The town is also home to Saratoga Raceway, and in Augusts past the thoroughbreds displaced the harness-racing trotters and Saratoga bustled with horse people and their hangers-on. Rates rose at the Adelphi Hotel and Rip Van Dam on Broadway, relics of lodging in an earlier golden age of Saratoga's original casino, which had been renovated since the days of the 1960s and 1970s when the ballet corps stayed at the Rip and swatted at real bats numerous enough to populate the artwork of the cartoonist Edward Gorey.

But now, though the horses still run, the ballet comes less frequently and the Rip Van Dam has turned into business offices. When one searches the Internet for places to stay in Saratoga, one turns up Casino City. At the Holiday Inn, the concierge said there was a lot of local feeling against the new 55,000-square-foot gaming facility that had been installed at the harness track in January 2004. In fact, she said, the Chamber of Commerce, where her mother worked, didn't even like to give directions there; though the casino is easy enough to find on one's own. Although slot machines are still illegal in New York State outside of Indian reservations, a law has been passed to permit "video lottery terminals" at state raceways. Instead of being based only on a random-number generator, these "class II" machines are centrally connected and work like an electronic stack of lottery tickets. The total payouts are controlled in the aggregate, and a result cannot be hit again until the whole sequence is reloaded—at electronic speed. But playing them feels like playing ordinary "class III," or "Vegas-type," slots. Enter the "racino," a phenomenon serving to reinvigorate flagging horse racetracks, with their aging and diminishing habitués. New York State has opened machines at a number of its other racetracks as well, including Monticello and Yonkers. The goal is to recapture some of the $3 billion spent at gambling casinos outside the state. Needless to say, the new casinos compete for the same population of players, which is rapidly growing if not inexhaustible.

If I were to choose one slot palace that is *not* spiritual (and moreover looks like a place one ought to play slots), it would be Saratoga's racino. Built under the old harness-track grandstand, it is except for one entry hall a dark, even Stygian, place. The low ceiling is hung with pipes and huge, evil-looking air-conditioning ducts so low that in places you can touch them;

the whole complex is painted a matte locomotive black. The machines are so crowded together that one can't get one's bearings. The low ceiling amplifies the clanking and bleeping of the machines. The spectacle of the players, who seem nice enough local folk but are dressed as unimpressively as vacationing Americans everywhere, reminds one of the Morlocks of H. G. Wells's novella *The Time Machine* toiling in their subterranean factories. Many of the machines betray their true purpose. Granted, there are Pearly Gates slots, and nostalgic tributes like The Lone Ranger, L'il Abner, and Betty Boop, the latter offering the progressive of a paltry $10,000. There are many penny and two-cent slots and the machines take single dollars. Texas Tea (oil) and Cleopatra also make appearances. Personality slots are notably missing. But most are unshrinelike in theme and seem to be only altars unto Mammon. There is New York Gold, which must certainly have been the New York legislature's idea. Flipping Chips depicts discs of various denominations that flip to reward you—or not. My favorite in its candor is Money in the Bank, from Konami Gaming, The images one tries to assemble on a pay line include a $1 gold coin, stacks of gold coins, bags of gold coins, stacks of green cash, and an unabashed Piggy Bank Credit Card with a pig on it. The feature or bonus round, which is added free spins, is announced by a very pale, nasty-looking banker who points menacingly at the player as it begins. Konami is an originally Japanese game manufacturer that has an Australian subsidiary, which perhaps explains the kangaroos on the gold coins. The Player Extras Club at the Saratoga racino must rank among the least rewarding of all such players clubs. If you put $50 into the machines, you get 1 point; if you assemble 25 points, it gets you only a $1 coupon to be used for dining or buying items marked with the Saratoga Gaming and Raceway logo at the gift shop. The club does give you a long green plastic cord to attach your players card so you don't leave it behind when you change machines. The other advantage of gambling at New York State racinos is that if you actually win something—all wins above $600 must be reported, instead of the $1,200 limit elsewhere—you can deduct all your losing lottery tickets and scratch-offs (if you saved them) from your win. For relief from all this, you can simply move upstairs to Chariot's for a dinner overlooking the harness track, where there are betting windows to continue one's wagering—on horses.

The racino at the Monticello, New York, raceway is similar to the one in Saratoga but has higher ceilings and a more open array of machines. Many have nostalgic themes, like Frankie and Annette Funicello's Beach Party, Funky Times, and Ray Charles's America and Felix the Cat. from Bally Gaming. From Spielo there are generic themes like Roman VIIs, Crank's Bash, Cashsquatch, Pinchin' Pies, and Free Spirits. Konami Gaming's African Treasure provides vistas and lion bonuses from that continent, and Horses for Courses seems especially appropriate to the raceway. This racino has ambitions to become a real $60 million Las Vegas–style casino for the St. Regis Mohawk tribe, according to a 2007 pact signed by then-governor Eliot Spitzer.

The racino at Yonkers Raceway in New York opened in October 2006 with 1,870 machines, and by early the next year had 5,500 both upstairs and in a long extension building. The ground-floor installation is a large rectangular space with dim lighting and low ceilings, and it was bustling but not packed on the Saturday of its opening weekend. Horse racing had been suspended for fifteen months during the installation of the racino, but a restaurant with a view of the track was part of the development. The machines take bills as small as a dollar (usually they require $10), and the largest jackpot I saw was $26,000, though higher jackpots came later. After a year of slots, attendance at Yonkers had risen from just 116,000 visitors in the pre-slot year of 2004 to 90,000 patrons a week in 2007, healthily rejuvenating the raceway. One may now dine sumptuously at the bright, enclosed Empire Terrace restaurant, overlooking the track, where video monitors show other races for wagering when the horses aren't being put through their paces. Reflecting the intent to tap the metropolitan New York City market, in February 2007 the interior of the subway shuttle train between Times Square and Grand Central Terminal had been turned into a simulated slot casino, with every square inch plastered with images of Empire City at Yonkers Raceway, and each seat a different slot machine. Advertising for Empire City depicts elegant men and women in formal attire around a table lit by a candelabra, with slots visible in the background. One searches in vain at the casino for such sartorial splendor! Another TV ad shows an astonished man hallucinating a courthouse square populated with slot machines. "Play off your mortgage," the ad proclaims, at "the casino next door."

Slot racinos may serve to revive racetracks, but they are already being blamed for a sharp drop-off in lottery-ticket sales in New York State. People simply do not have unlimited money to gamble, and the attraction of the slots prevails. In the wake of the racinos and lacking its own horses, Mohegan Sun fielded a TV ad in which a woman claims, "I can spot a great machine—this one is a champion, a thoroughbred, a giant clam among mollusks!"

Slot racinos are being introduced to support racetracks.

THE RABBIT WARREN VERSUS
THE MEGA-CASINO

The noted gambling authority Bill Friedman, who wrote the classic book *Casino Management*, surveyed Las Vegas casinos to 1999 and in 2000 published *Designing Casinos to Dominate the Competition*. This nonstatistical survey found a greater intensity of slot gambling in casino architectures that are mazelike (like the ground floor of Bloomingdale's in Manhattan), with no long sight lines and no high ceilings or structures to draw the eye upward. Friedman argued for an intimate, congested, quieter, dimmer, carpeted atmosphere, one that as a psychiatrist I might deem more womblike. He also distinguished the so-called walkers—the droves that gawk at awesome casino decors—from the real players, who need to be diverted from empty lobbies, raised landings, and thoroughfares into multiple small, noncontiguous gambling areas emphasizing the machines themselves. His controversial opinion ran contrary to the growth of the cathedral-like architectures of the mega-casinos and still remains to be validated. The popular, upscale Borgata Casino, the newest in Atlantic City, has somewhat lower ceilings. Even newer, The Quarter, a dining a addition to the Tropicana Casino there, with an (ironic) Castro's Havana theme, including a Red Square restaurant, has opted for a lofty blue sky. The previously mentioned Saratoga Gaming and Raceway, while meeting Friedman's recommendations, has not met earnings expectations. It may be that the most habitual gamblers are oblivious to their surroundings and focused on their chosen machines, while it's the growing crowds of new gamblers who have been drawn to the impressive cathedral-like casinos. But an attraction to slots in smaller spaces does not preclude the religious metaphor. It may be that some prefer to pray at a shrine in the smaller confines of a less-pretentious alcove or chapel that is connected to nearby magnificence and majesty. Indeed, a slot machine in a dark corner of a casino has the welcoming glow of votive candles.

LET THERE BE LIGHTS

Light has been a central metaphor of major religions since humanity first took up farming. Holidays around the winter solstice emphasize the bright light of Christmas trees or menorahs at Chanukah, which like pagan bonfires celebrate the beginning of longer days with their promise of a new cycle of planting and harvesting. Candles are lighted for services and prayers around the globe. Enlightenment is literally a goal of Eastern religions. Light can cure a depressive condition termed seasonal affective disorder, and contributes to the uplifting effect of winter vacations on white beaches or bright snow. Whatever the grandeur factor of casinos, they seldom lack a display of thousands of lights reduplicated in mirrors and crystal chandeliers. Casino players see no reminders of time or windows to take note of nightfall, allowing them to dwell in these houses of eternal radiance forever, as if in perpetual celebration. And none of the mirrors are positioned to reflect their faces.

COMMUNING WITH THE OTHER

The state of mind as one plays the slots varies with the individual. Some curse aloud at their machine and rail at each bad spin. For them the slot is personified, and they engage in the pathetic fallacy—that is, they attribute personality or feelings to an inanimate object. Interestingly, few of the demonstrative players express gratitude to their machines when they pay out. They proudly announce what *they* have accomplished, as if they were performers on an instrument. For most slot players who are not hemorrhaging a significant portion of their net worth and who can afford to venture to play awhile, the state of mind is more meditative. Their state of tranquillity approaches a trance.

But the worship is more inherent. It is worship of chance, of Fortune, but now that the slots are electronically random, it is a worship of the fabric of modern physical reality, of the universe that Einstein feared, in which God really *does* play dice. This is an appropriate religion for our age of scientific realization and of wonder and helplessness before complexity. It is no accident that casinos are frequented by the senior population. Unlike the young, we know our mortality and wish to be in supplicant contact with the godhead of randomness that will deliver our fate. We are not gambling for money, which we often seem to have enough of compared to younger segments of the population; we are gambling for life and confronting the danger that our luck will inevitably run out.

Why do people choose to play slots rather than other games? Perhaps the best odds are at twenty-one, or blackjack. Other games grant more company, as in the boisterous quasi-mob of the craps table and the togetherness of playing roulette. If one desires a game of passive dumb luck, baccarat offers it, because there are way too many cards in the shoe to count. One answer lies in the brain.

THIS IS YOUR BRAIN ON SLOTS: THE PSYCHIATRY OF SLOT PLAY

YOUR BRAIN'S MONEY BELT

The right and left hemispheres of the cerebral cortex (or outer part) of your brain and mine are connected by a large bundle of white nerve fibers called the corpus callosum, which goes from one side to the other inside the brain. Wrapped partly around this bundle, in a semicircle on top of it running from front to back on each side of the brain, is a fiber bundle called the cingulum, a Latin word for girdle, and immediately above this is the part of the gray matter called the cingulate cortex. The front part of the cingulate cortex (the anterior cingulate cortex in anatomy-speak) is what "lights up" in gamblers when the activity of their brains is studied by functional brain imaging. Functional imaging shows regional activity as well as structure by displaying how much glucose fuel the different parts of the brain are burning.

I find this anatomic location easy to remember because it

is poetically just. A girdle is the ancient equivalent of a belt (and here I am not speaking of grandmother's type of girdle). So I think of the anterior cingulate as the money belt in your brain, reacting when you gamble, as it appropriately should, to your wins and losses. It says "ouch" to the rest of your feeling brain when you lose, reacting more to a loss than to a win, as the recent Nobel Prize winner Daniel Kahneman pointed out, explaining why people bet more desperately when they lose, doubling up their bets in blackjack, or chasing losses on the slots by playing faster, for more credits, or on a higher-denom-ination machine. This brain-based risk aversion favors slots, which have it all over the other ways to gamble in a casino because one can win big without having to take a large risk, as in doubling down in blackjack.

Furthermore, the Princeton neuroscientists Jonathan Co-hen and Alan Sanfey and others have demonstrated the chem-ical basis of the reaction to being rewarded when gambling. This involves the neurotransmitter (chemically connecting) substance dopamine, which does not make you dopey but rather active in the pursuit of gratification and able to enjoy it when you get any.

When one makes a bad bet or loses at gambling, the ante-rior cingulate registers the losses, and a small structure called the insula ("little island") assesses whether to trust the game.

When both the front and back ("anterior" and "posterior") parts of the cingulate gyrus (cortex) are underactive—that is, when their metabolism, or "burning," of the glucose that fuels brain cells is lower—it correlates with the hoarder type of ob-sessive-compulsive behavior that inclines people to keep every-thing and have trouble letting go of things, even things of little or no value. It makes sense that the cingulate gyrus is involved, because the anterior (front) part handles executive decision-making, especially between several competing or conflicting options, and the posterior (back) part monitors visual and spatial events, orientation to spaces, and the processing of emotional events. Hoarders also procrastinate or get distracted from discarding things. When they play the slots, people with this tendency may be more attached to their machines, and they may have trouble deciding whether to stay or to quit playing.

To be sure, the network in the brain is more complex and cannot be reduced to a modern version of phrenology beneath the skull. Nora Volkow, M.D., director of the National Institute on Drug Abuse, includes also in the brain's weighing of emotional salience the orbitofrontal cortex, which controls impulses; the dorsolateral frontal cortex, which is involved with executive memory and decision; and the nucleus accumbens, which is connected to the ventral tegmental area where dopamine is synthesized.

PLAYING SLOTS WITH ONESELF

Some Freudians might say that playing the slots is onanistic, that pulling or jerking the lever is symbolic. To counter this facile metaphor, one might argue that, given the alternatives of buttons to push, almost no one uses the levers anymore. But since a slight majority of slot players are female, the button may be symbolic, too. Couples or friends often play side by side when space avails. Nevertheless, playing the slots is primarily a solitary activity: one is alone with the god of slots, much as one is ultimately alone with God. Thomas W. Laqueur argues in his book *Solitary Sex: A Cultural History of Masturbation* that there are three reasons that during the Enlightenment, early in the eighteenth century, masturbation, which had previously been accepted as natural, was judged to be perverse and unnatural. First, it is irremediably private; second, the masturbator encounters not a flesh and blood partner but a phantasm; and third, the addictive urge is insatiable. These three characteristics—privacy, fantasy, and insatiability—could easily be applied to slot playing. You play the machines alone, you indulge in fantasies, and you don't want to stop before the payoff.

TRANSCENDENTAL SLOTS

Choose any slot, feed a bill into it, and play it by pressing the button as fast as the latency of each spin will let you. You will find that the rate at which you play will be less than about three spins every ten seconds, or about sixteen to eighteen spins per minute. Let us call this the basal slot-play rate. Now time your respiratory rate when you are relaxed, and you will find it to be about the same.

One of the most remarkable aspects of this basal slot-play rate is that it mimics the rate of breathing of a normal, healthy adult at rest. The reason this is interesting is that if the player times the button pressing at that rate, doing so may exert a suggestive effect upon the player's breathing so that it times itself roughly to the basal slot-play rate. If this synchronization occurs even approximately, the effect resembles a breathing rate common to induced meditative states. Herbert Benson, M.D., an internist from Harvard Medical School, has pointed out that the effects of transcendental meditation can be achieved with a simple breathing exercise. One relaxes, usually with the eyes closed, breathes in, breathes out, and says the number "one." Then one repeats this, always saying "one" rather than getting involved with counting. If any thoughts drift into the mind, one says, "Oh, well," and lets go of them. This induces a meditative state that Dr. Benson calls the relaxation response, which is very good for the blood pressure and pulse rate. If practiced twice a day for twenty minutes or so, it will enable one to reap benefits in peace of mind and creativity, much as has been claimed for meditation. Relaxed lap swimming, once one gets into reasonably good shape, can have the same effect. My point here is that slot playing may induce this same relaxation response and escape from worldly pressures that religions around the world have claimed as a meditative, prayerful state. Of course, one might conclude that there are less expensive ways to achieve that soothing state than playing a slot as fast as it will let you.

ARE YOU HYPNOTIZED BY THE SLOTS?

Some slot players say they are hypnotized by the machines and find themselves playing much longer than they intended to. They feel they must be in a trance of some sort, caused by the attractive power of the slots. They are correct that any prolonged focused activity can lead to a trance state, but the idea that the machine is causing them to enter this state is a misunderstanding of hypnosis. The answer is that one may be hypnotizing oneself by playing the slots.

I had the privilege of being trained in hypnosis during my psychiatric residency at Columbia University by Herbert Spiegel, M.D., one of the world's preeminent authorities on its clinical use. He taught that hypnosis is not a power in the hypnotist, but rather a capacity in the hypnotic subject to go into a trance. The hypnotist helps the subject to achieve what trance capability he or she possesses, in order to help the subject to achieve a particular objective, such as giving up smoking or escaping pain. Thus there are two important components to hypnosis: the ability to achieve trance and the desire to do so for some reason. The abilities of the subjects vary. Some people have almost no trance capability. Some have trouble concentrating on anything, for a number of reasons, including brain afflictions and having extremely rigid personalities that make them unwilling to throw themselves strongly into any alternative state of mind. On the other end of the spectrum are people with great powers of concentration who can enter a very deep trance and use it to control their bodies or to perform in some extraordinary manner. Hypnotic or self-hypnotic training techniques are popular with athletes who have the gift of trance capability. For some people with great trance capability, the gift is a mixed blessing. If they don't watch themselves, they may find themselves caught up in things they might not otherwise do. Often easily persuadable, they may be unusually vulnerable to financial scams.

Hypnotizability is graded by psychiatrists on a 0-to-5 scale by asking the subject to perform a few simple exercises. One of them, called the eye-roll test, requires the subjects, without moving their heads, to attempt to look up at the top of their own heads and slowly close their eyes. If the person's irises be-

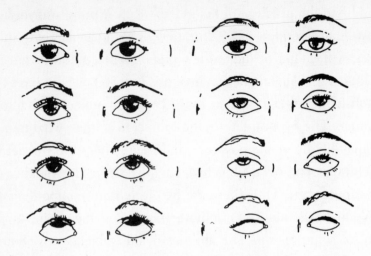

Eyeroll Test for Hypnotizability from Herbert Spiegel and David Spiegel,
Trance and Treatment: Clinical Uses of Hypnosis, American Psychiatric
Publishing, Washington, D.C., 2004

gin to disappear under their upper lids and even become slightly cross-eyed with the effort, this is a sign of hypnotizability.

The eye-roll test is but one of several that assess the subjects
ability to concentrate. I find it interesting, however, that playing the slots involves moving the eyes up and down—up to
catch a glimpse of the falling symbols, moving too fast at first
to see before coming to a halt, and then down to the pay line to
see if anything has lined up.

MOVING THE EYES

Movement of the eyes has been used also in a form of treatment for the effects of severe trauma called the Eye Movement
Desensitization and Reprocessing, or EMDR. A wand with a

white disk on one end is moved up and down rapidly before the eyes to capture the attention and help the person escape the intrusion of remembered images of the trauma. EMDR is used in conjunction with cognitive talk therapy, and its success may be due to the therapy that is given. We also move our eyes when we dream, in REM (Rapid Eye Movement) sleep. But there is an even more basic way in which movement of the eyes affects us. Raising the eyes is what we did as small children to look up at our parents and other authority figures, and looking down is what we do as adults when we show respect to or fear of superior authority or strength. The movement of the eyes so immediately betrays who is the top dog that short politicians, when positioned next to their taller opponents, studiously avoid moving their eyes up or down. Not just fear and deference, but love and worship can lower our eyes.

We look up to the heavens where early humankind placed our gods. At the time of the ancient Sumerians, a supernova in the constellation Vela X became visible very low in the sky over the water of the Persian Gulf. According to George Michanowsky, an archaeoastronomer, in his book *The Once and Future Star: The Mysterious Vela X Supernova and the Origin of Civilizations*, this celestial event became associated with the Sumerian god E-A (pronounced "ay-ah,"), who became known as "he who walks on water"). E-A also embodied the idea of an intercessor deity who came to help humankind. My particular interest in the Sumerian supernova story is the difference in eye position between looking up to the heavens and looking on the level at the horizon for Vela X. It is the difference between submitting to the heavens above and relating at eye level to a spiritual presence who becomes one of us and encourages us to revere our own humanity. In the slots, the symbols on the reels keep descending, seemingly from all the possibilities inherent in the enormous cosmos above, and then settle at eye level on the "horizon" of the pay line, where they may become friends that intercede in our lives to grant us our wishes.

Or more often, not! While the traditional machine either comprises actual descending reels or simulates them, some video slots, like WMS Gaming's All That Glitters, display cascading reels of gems. As the gems descend to make a winning formation, they then vanish to allow more gemstones to descend individually and possibly bring an additional win. This creates the illusion of an ever-bountiful source above eye level, rivaling, say, the showers of gold in paintings by Gustav Klimt as such as *Danae* or *Adele Bloch-Bauer*. George Basalla, a historian of science, has pointed out that celestial beings have been thought to be superior and godlike since the time of the ancient Greeks; Michael Schermer, a scientist, has stated that any sufficiently advanced extraterrestrial intelligence would be indistinguishable from God. Indeed, Steven Dick, another historian of science, has argued that the vast, lifeless void of the mechanical Newtonian universe, which replaced the spiritual world of the Middle Ages, has now been replaced in the minds of many once-religious scientists with a belief in extraterrestrial intelligences. In her book *Abducted: How People Come to Believe They Were Kidnapped by Aliens*, Susan A. Clancy calls these intelligences technological angels. Psychologist Robert Plank proposed that humans need to believe in imaginary beings; the scientists' extraterrestrials are likely imaginary, too. Erich von Däniken's *Chariots of the Gods* (1968), which was later debunked by Thor Heyerdahl, claimed aliens visited

Meditating to the rhythm of the slots.

Earth and created our ancient civilizations. Major and minor cults have included such beings in their theology. My point is simply that divinity descends from above eye level, as on the slot displays. (There are very few slot machine displays that don't descend; one exception is Bally's new Quick Hit Platinum 1-cent machine, which I encountered at Harrah's in New Orleans and oddly moves up.) Perhaps those who worship at the slots are participating in the developed world's version of the cargo cults, which grew in Melanesia when so much cargo was being dropped during World War II. Just as cargo cultists built landing strips of bamboo in the hope of luring the planes by sympathetic magic, slot players try to entice a winning array of descending symbols to line up and pay off. Perhaps the biblical term "manna from heaven" is apt for slot winnings.

THE BIG CRASH IN THE BIG EASY

Speaking of Harrah's in New Orleans: On April 19, 2005, months before Hurricane Katrina, while my wife and I were visiting that casino, shortly before one o'clock in the afternoon the computer controlling the electronic paper-ticket system crashed. This was a particular problem for Harrah's, because the entire casino operates on electronic tickets. As a result, although the machines could still be played with cash, they could no longer accept tickets or read player cards, and they could no longer print tickets enabling one to redeem one's winnings. People could continue playing only if they didn't mind not being able to remove whatever money they had won before it was all gone. Needless to say, moments after the crash the call-for-assistance lights atop the machines began blinking like so many fireflies. The few attendants still employed in the wake of automation hurried around hand-paying everyone who wanted to exit or change machines. Having to wait did not sit well with some of the elegantly coiffed elderly Southern ladies there, one of whom volubly complained to me that the casino made enough money not to allow its computer to crash. Although there was a major exodus, what impressed me was the number of people who went on playing despite not being able to withdraw any winnings. After an hour strolling the nearby Riverwalk, we returned to find the system fixed and all back to normal. One attendant told us this was their first crash, though she considered it ridiculous that it had happened at all. In the wake of Hurricane Katrina, the New Orleans casinos were resurrected, and thanks to the infusion of federal and insurance money, and fewer competing diversions, Harrah's earned nearly 14 percent more in 2007 than it had in a comparable period in 2005, before Katrina—with 20 to 30 percent fewer players.

ON THE WAY TO THE CASINO

Like many of Jerry Seinfeld's monologues, his account of having to pay for something after we've consumed it is an oh-so-true observation. He describes and mimics the expansive, generous attitude of diners at a restaurant while they are ordering food. We'll have some of this and some of that, and, oh yes, that, too. Then he mimics the more reserved attitude of the same diner scrutinizing the bill afterward. Are you sure we ordered that?

Similarly, traveling to the casino is an exhilarating ride,

filled with possibilities and the anticipation of play and winnings. One's allotted stash seems limitless, especially since
winning seems all but inevitable, and losing, if it happens at
all, will be minor, tolerable, and reversible. The casino looms
as a cornucopia of sensory treats and emotional thrills. A jackpot seems likely on the first pull of the first slot, or if not the
first, surely the second. Travelers to the casino are talkative and
cheerful, optimistic about the state of the world, even if they
aren't thinking much about it. They are full of dreams of paying off mortgages, buying all manner of goods, and making
contributions to both their near and dear and charities around
the globe. And it goes without saying that one will reserve some
of one's haul to bankroll future visits to the casino, in an end-
less progression of happy days into the far future. Brain studies
show similar activations during the anticipation of winning to
those produced by actually winning.

ON THE WAY HOME

Returning home usually follows the depletion of one's stash, or
at least a significant enough reduction to sap any joy. Some will
emerge a little ahead, and a very small number will experience
a windfall beyond their expectations. But most will return
thinking of economies, of making money the old-fashioned
way—by earning it. Some begin the countdown to their next
Social Security or dividend check.

The around-the-clock buses that deliver the mostly less-
affluent gamblers prescribe a specific return time. This is no
small kindness to such riders. For example, the driver of the

8:00 a.m. bus out of the Port Authority Bus Terminal, arriving at an Atlantic City terminal two and a half hours later, will announce that "your return bus will depart at four-ten pm" from the same casino and that the riders should arrive at least fifteen minutes prior to departure time to assure themselves a seat on it. In fact, both driver and riders know they may return on the same ticket any time in the next two days, but a targeted breaking-off point is both merciful and wise.

BIPOLAR MINOR IN THE SLOT PLAYER

The two moods on the casino round trip, seen through the eyes of a psychiatrist, mimic in miniature the different states of patients with bipolar disorder (previously called manic-depressive illness) because of its two states of mind, one high and one low. Bipolar patients in their manic phase are unrealistically confident, tactless, grandiose, talkative, senselessly expansive and extravagant in their undertakings and spending, and uninterested in sleep. They are exhilarated and see no obstacles to pleasures of all kinds. They also cannot connect to a memory of feeling otherwise.

In their depressive phase, they are dejected, sad, disappointed, angry with themselves, with delusions of poverty and the impossibility of getting satisfaction. Most characteristic of the pessimism is the grave doubt that life will ever be better or that they themselves will ever feel cheerful, up, or, much less, manic again.

Some slot gamblers are similar, not just in their mood shifts before and after playing, but in their tendency not to envision their downward change of mood after playing the slots and in their return to an exhilarated mood when they have recovered from their losses, amassed another hoard, and are heading slot-ward once again. We all have this lack of insight when in the grip of a mood, but some of us experience it more profoundly. The up-and-down mood changes I am describing in slot players in no way match in severity the disabilities of bipolar illness, one of our major psychiatric disorders, which I do not mean to trivialize by the comparison. But gamblers have a taste of it.

SLOTS AND FOLKS: VARIETIES OF CULTURAL AND RELIGIOUS EXPERIENCE

WINNING

Winning at the slots is a thrill that varies with the amount of the win and the winner's experience. The Betty Boop and Blondie slots even label their jackpots "Thrillions." Large wins once were accompanied by the loud and persisting clanking of coins that the machine would spit out from its hopper, which is the container where the coins that are immediately available for payouts are held, into its tray; whether or not the machine's hopper would empty before the machine finished remitting, payouts of more than one thousand coins required an attendant's hand pay. The advent of International Game Technology's cashless machines, which issue a printed ticket instead of coins, has changed the rituals of winning. After scurrying to find enough plastic containers to carry off the nickels, quarters, half-dollars, or dollar tokens of an unexpected win, the player may find the abbreviated ticket experience a bit of a letdown.

Wins of more than $1,200 require an attendant, while the temporarily unplayable, or "frozen," machine insanely pipes the tune to "We're in the Money" over and over. The slot attendant must get your Social Security number for large wins to tell Uncle Sam. Winners have been known to "play down" winnings by continuing to play and losing a bit, rather than cashing out on a slot machine, if it has not frozen, to keep the win amount below $1,200 and thus below the tax radar. Others will cash out any large win for fear that another win might push their total cash-out over the tax-free limit. The tickets remove the pleasure (and the effort) of lugging the large cups of coins to the coin-redemption windows, where they could be redeemed for more manageable currency, but from both the casino's and the gambler's viewpoints, they offer the advantage of immediate resumption of play without waiting for the coins to spit out or, worse, run out, necessitating a wait for a roaming attendant to refill the depleted hopper. The tickets allow you to accept fairly large payouts inconspicuously, if not in complete privacy. This helps avoid the (rare) evil eye of envious strangers to one's right and left, often playing an identical machine that isn't paying them squat. Ticket-redemption machines have now been installed so even the human contact of the redemption windows can be avoided. Whether redemption in this automated manner brings one symbolically closer to redemption in the religious sense—that is, being saved from sin—depends on the beliefs of the individual player.

Winning at the slots presents a person with an undeniable but evanescent benefit. For some, myself included, it can prove that undeserved honors and prizes are the sweetest. But for many others, winning is more complex. Alice, a woman I

know well, was in her mid-fifties when she won a $34,606 pro-
gressive with her third spin of a Bally Blondie machine around
6:00 p.m. on a Saturday at Mohegan Sun Casino. Her initial
reaction was awe and embarrassment. The machine had fro-
zen in its jackpot configuration and was repeating "We're in
the Money" in its reedy electronic tones, along with a maddening doorbell sound. A youthful slot-service "associate" (formerly called a slot attendant) appeared. He had seen only one
other progressive win in his career. Casino officials were summoned, and the Bally representatives were phoned to come
to the casino. Since the machine was externally licensed and
there would thus be a wait for the Bally people to arrive, the
casino officials told Alice and her husband, who had been
playing next to her, that they would be treated to a dinner at
the restaurant of their choice. They chose Rain, then the best
restaurant, and were given chits for $200, as well as the as-
surance that evidence of their huge win had been recorded
by the omnipresent overhead video cameras, lest they were
worried about abandoning the physical source of their good
fortune. At dinner, Alice's main thought was that she would
enjoy teasing her younger sister, who had tried the casino and
had no luck. After dinner, the couple returned to the machine,
where several people from the casino and two representatives
from Bally were waiting. They asked Alice if she wanted the
money in cash. This was not to propose tax evasion, as the total
amount would be reported to the government in any case, but
because, in the casino's experience, they said, some progressive
winners chose to play out their winnings in further gambling
the same night! Her husband was not thrilled at the prospect
of his spouse hauling around that much cash in her handbag.

The casino representatives told the couple not to worry about that; they would supply a security guard to escort them to their car. The couple thanked them but said they were staying overnight at the hotel and would prefer a check for all but $4,000, which was doled out in $100 bills. They gave a $300 tip to the young attendant who had showed up first, on the advice of a nearby player who had seen the win. A photographer came to take a picture of Alice, and a giant check imprinted with images of Dagwood and Blondie, the word *Thrillions*, and the full amount of the win. The purpose, he said, was to publish the photo in her hometown newspaper. Uncertain as to whether her staid community would approve of gambling, however successful, and having realistic concerns about security, she requested no publicity. The photographer readily agreed and said he would just send her a copy of the photo. The reason Alice took some of the win in cash was not to gamble (although she won another $1,000 the next morning playing the dollar slots with some of it), but so that on the way home she could drop in on her sister and as she walked through the door, in a spirit of sibling rivalry, throw a large stack of $100 bills into the air to what she expected would be her sister's amazement and chagrin. The couple's accountant, when he was consulted about the win, suggested they immediately set half of it aside for taxes. With half of the rest she bought some furniture; the remainder she banked to invest in her business. Although the win had seemed like a lot at the time, her upper-middle-class life would not be appreciably changed. A month after she got home she was embarrassed to find that her name had been listed on the casino's website with the amount and date of her win. It was removed only when she and her husband protested, mentioning the possibility of their engaging their lawyer.

But which sister was luckier? Alice is still returning to casinos in the expectation of repeating her win, whereas her sister, who has never had a win of any magnitude, lost interest in casinos, at least until she moved to within a twenty-minute drive of one. Recently this sister went to Mohegan Sun and noticed that the machine next to her had been cordoned off. When she inquired why, she was told that a man had just won $1 million on it, and indeed, on closer inspection, the machine still displayed three "progressive" symbols. The slot attendants were buzzing about that man's lack of reaction when he won. It turns out that only a short while earlier the man's wife had also won $1 million.

Once, at Casino Niagara, the older of the two Canadian casinos at the falls, playing three quarters on a Black and White Sevens machine, I had a white 7 and two Double Jackpot diamond symbols line up. Whereas three white 7s lined up would have yielded 120 credits, that twice doubled netted me 480 quarters, or 120 Canadian dollar coins (called "loonies" because of the loon depicted on one face). The sweet elderly lady wearing a lovely string of pearls at the next machine congratulated me. I boorishly replied that it would have been nice to have lined up three Double Jackpot symbols, for 7,912.29 loonies of the progressive. "Don't be greedy," she advised. One might well say amen to that, and strive for grace and manners in both winning and losing. I cashed out and wished her luck.

VICTORY AT SEA ONLY

On July 1, 2004, Bermuda passed a law banning slot machines. Previously the island had had no laws for or against gambling. If there were any machines left, they could be played only for amusement. For instance, a place called the White Horse Tavern had five multigame machines in a corner, with names like Touch o' Luck. All were turned off. A policeman we spoke with in Bermuda was of the opinion that it was pointless to "babysit" people, that if you stop them from throwing away their paychecks on slot machines, they will bet on the horses or the Quick Draw lottery instead. But Bermuda is a very conservative island with rules for everything. This is not the case in the Bahamas. "They will do whatever they will do," an official sniffed. When asked about the banning of gambling only days earlier, he said that it had only been slots that had crept in. Another possible choice might have been to permit gambling by tourists but to ban the resident Bermudians from engaging in it, as was the case in the Bahamas. But Bermudians were concerned that "the wrong type of tourist" might be attracted. There had been "tremendous pressure from the black churches" to shut gambling venues down. Gambling ships would have to be given permission to dock, so Bermuda could control this gambling, too. Indeed, the *Seven Seas Navigator*, while docking in Bermuda, was not permitted to open either its casino or its boutiques. This is typical of cruise ships in ports. Evidently slot machines and their players are not socially acceptable everywhere, and in the microcosm of Bermuda are viewed as a social evil. Just as Prospero, at the end of *The Tempest*, renounces his "rough magic" by breaking his staff and drowning his book, pronouncing his island an unfit place for illusion, Bermuda put an end to a form of enchantment once practiced there.

LOSING

In the course of play, luck most often runs against the slot player. The vast enterprises that slot parlors have become must collect their tithes, and then some, from the faithful. Different strategies may be tried to dispel the clouds hanging over the losing bettor. The 10 percent of tithes jibes nicely with the usual 90 percent return of the slots. Some players dig in, angry at their machine and hoping that sheer persistence will empty out all they have poured in and replenish their stake. More often losers enter an agitated restless state of searching for a looser machine (a machine that will pay back a higher percentage), trying small amounts at one machine after another, and continuing to play a particular machine only if they receive a win during the trial investment. The bettor may switch to inserting a lower-denomination bill, putting tens instead of twenties into lower-denomination machines as trial balloons. Some forfeit the maximum coin advantage and play fewer credits or fewer lines on the popular penny machines, where one can risk anywhere from a few up to hundreds of penny credits. This penurious response also lowers the amounts of possible wins, risking the disappointment of a progressive jackpot roll with less than the maximum bet, resulting in a much smaller win.

Others will make the healthy decision that it is a good time to break for a meal. Few casino restaurants cost more than the amount one can lose in the time it takes to eat. Still others will stop to relax, even smoking a cigarette or cigar, as casinos are one of the few places left where those indulgences are permitted—there are even slots with a cigar theme—and the high ceilings carry away smoke that might bother nonsmokers. In 2006 the Atlantic City casinos finally designated smoking and nonsmoking areas in compliance with a New Jersey law banning smoking statewide in most restaurants. The Connecticut Indian casinos already had such areas. Smoking will eventually be banned in all casinos, removing an associated habituating factor.

As I wrote previously, the neuropsychiatry of losing has recently been established, and researchers in brain imaging know not only where in the brain the reaction to losing occurs (in the anterior cingulate cortex), but also that we are wired so that our brains react, or "light up," by burning more glucose fuel in those areas. We burn more when we lose than when we win. This can stimulate a gambler to bet more to recoup after a loss, and potentially lead the more vulnerable down a prickly garden path to gambling ruin.

In one not very strained sense, winning, continuing to gamble, and the ritual of loss to the stacked odds of the slots are submissions to the statistical laws of the universe, according to which by extraordinary chance human life originated here on this planet and by which in the long run it will probably end. While I will yield to no none in my admiration of the heroic intellect of Stephen Hawking, I won't go along with his recent sardonic comment, made on the Discovery Channel special "How the Universe Works," that "intelligent life must be very rare in the universe—it has yet to be detected on Earth." *He* has certainly been detected through his many publications, and I would say persisting against adverse or almost sure odds is one of the most endearing and successful human traits.

LUCK AND THE ASIAN NEW YEAR

Many East Asian people like to gamble during the February lunar new year celebrations, like Tet in Vietnam.. Some believe that whether or not they have luck on that day will determine their luck throughout the year. As Ling Liu reported in the newspaper *Greenwich Time*, one-third of the 40,000 daily players at Foxwoods are Asian, as are one-fifth of the players at Mohegan Sun. These numbers are growing. Many Asians play table games as well as slots. Slot machines featuring 8s are considered luckier than 7s, because *eight* is a homonym for prosperity in Chinese. And 8s, as in the eightfold way of right view, right intention, right speech, right action, and so forth, are desirable in Buddhism—as well as in particle physics, in which a theory named for the Buddhist guidelines organizes subatomic particles into octets. Lucky Fours slot machines, which can land the Irish in clover, are very unlucky for the Chinese, Koreans, and Japanese, because in those languages *four* is nearly homophonous to the word *death*.

Nancy Petry, a psychiatrist who studies addiction, found a high rate of problem gambling among Laotian, Cambodian, and Vietnamese refugees in Connecticut. In an article in the journal *Psychiatric Services*, she raised the question of whether gambling attracts them because so many have suffered severe and persisting abuse and torture in their home countries. But gambling has always been popular there. In Asian casinos in such places as Macau, table games like baccarat played in private VIP rooms traditionally have been more popular than the wide-open floors of the Vegas style of casino, where slots are the big money makers. But large Vegas-style casinos have come to Macau. A Wynn casino and a version of the Venetian with 3,400 slots joined the Sands Macau, which was the first. Seven new resorts are expected. By 2006, Macau had surpassed Las Vegas as the biggest gambling city in the world.

BIG CASINO CHEESES

The extent to which the American consciousness has been permeated by casinos is at an all-time high. Some of the most popular shows on television have been set in Las Vegas (*CSI: Crime Scene Investigation, Vegas, American Casino, The Casino, Casino Doctor*, and even an animated comedy, *Father of the Pride*, about animals who live in a Las Vegas Siegfried & Roy jungle habitat), and they frequently present a background of slot machines. The people playing them are so young, gorgeous, and elegantly dressed that one almost forgets the T-shirts, shorts, jeans, sweat suits, and baseball caps that most players wear. Championship Texas Hold 'Em poker has been a surprise hit, and the series *Lucky* was a critical winner. Even a 2006 earthquake disaster miniseries, *10.5: Apocalypse*, was set in a Las Vegas casino that falls into a giant sinkhole. The players, as in the film *The Poseidon Adventure*, have to climb up to get out of their perhaps all-too-metaphoric hole.

Major entertainers, like Frank Sinatra's "Rat Pack" of celebrities, which included Dean Martin, Sammy Davis Jr. and Peter Lawford, have always played casinos. In Lawford's case, his connection with the Kennedy family brought casinos a certain cachet. Before it became sanitized, gambling had a tough mob flavor captured in Martin Scorsese's film *Casino* and in Sinatra's smoky song "Luck Be a Lady Tonight," originally from the Broadway musical *Guys and Dolls*. (It is received wisdom in psychoanalysis that the idea of luck being a lady may subconsciously trace back to childhood, when one's mother was the main source of favor or frustration.) Frank Sinatra Jr. appeared at the Sands in Atlantic City in his father's stead, until it closed in 2006.

The connection of celebrities to casinos today has become inescapable. "The Late Night leader" of television talk shows, as NBC calls him, is Jay Leno, the workaholic comic with the FDR chin who reportedly banks his entire NBC salary of $14 million and lives on the income from his live performances at casinos across the land. Leno frequently announces during his show that he will be appearing "this weekend" at Caesars in Atlantic City, "so come on down." Such an invitation from the genial man who tucks many Americans into bed every night and whose powerful support was strongly credited during Arnold Schwarzenegger's successful gubernatorial campaign in California, seems a wholesome endorsement of casinos. Interviewing former First Lady Laura Bush, Leno asked her if she had ever played a slot machine. She rather stiffly answered, "No." He continued, teasingly, "You haven't even been tempted to put a quarter in?" She repeated, "No." I wonder if any of the First Ladies who follow her will be able to make such a claim. When slots playing came up while she was on ABC-TV's The View, Michelle Obama commented that her mother had won $17,000—"it was from the quarter machines."

One can avoid Jay Leno if one chooses not to stay up late and watch his show. But Donald Trump is another matter. His prime-time reality show, *The Apprentice*, ranked high in the ratings and many of his appearances on talk shows set viewing records. He has sold his tagline, "You're fired"—at least on T-shirts. He has hosted *Saturday Night Live*, where he has joined in lampoons of his legendary self-promotion. His name is emblazoned on glitzy buildings around Manhattan. He plays golf with Bill Clinton and, yes, Arnold Schwarzenegger. Trump is known to have launched himself with money from his family's real-estate-development business to become a major Manhattan builder with casinos in Atlantic City. There is even a Trump-themed video slot machine, Wheelionaire: You're Fired, with Trump and his employees in a feature that calls for the player to choose a team and fire people until getting fired, thus completing the bonus round. On CNBC's *The Billionaire Inside: Donald Trump*, the builder advised viewers to invest during the real estate slump and to negotiate with banks should they not be able to meet payments. *The New York Times* of August 5, 2009, reported that he raised $100 million to regain his casino business, Trump Entertainment Resorts, with an extended repayment of a $480 million loan, and it has emerged from bankruptcy. So two of the most visible and influential men of America are strongly affiliated, if not synonymous, with casinos. And Trump's friend Regis Philbin inhabits slot machines as a familiar emcee of play, a slot priest toward whom the player can direct wishes and prayers.

And how about the American Association of Retired People (AARP), that self-appointed protector and representative of senior citizens? In 2004 AARP promoted in various media what it called "Life @ 50+, AARP's National Event & Expo" where else but in Las Vegas, at the Sands Expo Center. The heading was "Get Involved, Get Entertained, or Get Married by Elvis on a Roller Coaster." Poker chips in the ad pictured a pantheon of celebrities, among them Smokey Robinson, James Taylor, the Smothers Brothers, Coretta Scott King, Arnold Diaz (the "Shame on You!" business gadfly), Jane Bryant Quinn, Roger Ebert, Mary Tyler Moore, Jerry Lewis, Mariel Hemingway, Danny Glover, Maya Angelou, and Dave Barry. With these folks behind you, how can you go wrong?

THE SLOT STAGE OF LIFE

The older set attracted to slots is also a group to whom religion has traditionally appealed, not just for marriage ceremonies for their (often non-traditional) children or Sunday school for their grandchildren, but for themselves. Whether or not members of this age group acknowledge it, they have embarked on an inner journey toward meaning and comfort in the face of death, a stage of life that the neurologist Lucien Côté and I have called Mortality, when death is more imaginable than it was earlier in life. For some it is also a stage for psychoanalytic exploration or for consulting other sages with a philosophic or religious bent. Whereas Freudian therapy focuses on younger adults, attempting to reshape the effects of childhood experience, Carl Jung preferred older patients who had solved most of life's practical problems (like making money) and were ready to explore philosophical, religious, and artistic questions. Considerably more down to earth, a dubious tribute to the advanced age of many slot players is Bally's Super Seniors machine, which features geezers battling enemies like one who says, "You missed the early bird special!" The female avatar appears to be wearing incontinence padding beneath her tights.

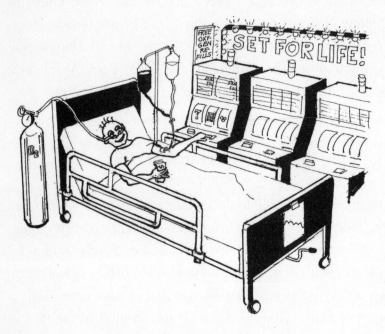

Slots are reaching out to the infirm.

ACCEPTABILITY OF SLOT GAMBLING

Mark Mayer, the editor of *Gaming Today*, in a piece on the potentially restrictive taxation of gambling, quoted Frank Fahrenkopf, president of the National Gaming Association, on the popularity of the activity: "The level of acceptability toward casino gaming has grown," Fahrenkopf said. "More Americans think of gaming as a mainstream activity. The 2003 polling showed 85 percent said gambling was acceptable, up from 79 percent. By age, the strongest was the 21–39 group at 91 percent approval." He concluded that gambling attracts "widespread industry."

Casinos find their bread-and-butter patrons among women and many of their male age-mates over fifty-five who play the slot machines, as a stroll through the slot areas in any casino will confirm. So the growing approval of the younger set may reflect its greater permissiveness in general rather than its greater participation (they have a similarly permissive attitude toward pornography and even prostitution). Young people generally play more table games. The newest casino in Atlantic City, the Borgata, is attempting to attract a younger upscale clientele with swank restaurants and fancy retail shops. There is a slot based on *Saturday Night Live*, a program that airs past most oldsters' bedtimes. The casino floor is much like those of many older hotels, and the ceilings are not very high. The lobby features living statues, mimes who freeze their whitened bodies in Grecian poses. Winners of electronic lotteries with eligibility based on inserted players cards are announced over loudspeakers, an unattractive feature that distracts attention from the slot play, although the machines also display the winners briefly.

There has been surprisingly little reaction against the propagation of casinos, though they have the potential to transform American life quite radically. The actor Dwayne "The Rock" Johnson, in his 2004 film *Walking Tall*, returns from military service to fight a corrupt casino that has taken over his home-town. In one scene, he smashes a slot machine (just one; they are expensive) with a piece of lumber.

A marvelous but unrealistically wishful 2003 film called *The Cooler* is about someone supposedly hired by a casino to cast bad luck on the players and prevent expensive payouts for the casino. When this loser, played by William H. Macy, falls in love, his luck and his effect on that of others changes: Machines now hit jackpots as he passes. Alec Baldwin was nominated for an Academy Award for his supporting role as an old-time cor-rupt casino boss. This film encourages fantasies of beating the casino. Certain traditional societies, like Ireland with its sweep-stakes, promote gambling as an important part of their social order by encouraging the hopes of their poorer citizens while relieving them of their precious dwindling resources.

Mainstream churches in America have long provided bingo nights. In the face of applications for casino licenses, nearby churches have abolished such events to conform to antigam-bling statutes, a clear admission that they previously supported gambling. "Let not the needy be forgotten," says the Episcopal prayer, "nor the hope of the poor be taken away."

SLOTS AND GENDER

The preponderance of women at the slots (my informal counts show a 3-to-2 ratio) may also be no accident. Slot playing capitalizes on one thing women do better than men: sitting still and performing a repetitive activity. Women are better at working on an assembly line while seated. They are said to be more docile and less likely to be restless. Schoolboys have always been more unruly than girls, and the possibility that boys' natural restlessness has been falsely labeled as hyperactivity and that they are being overmedicated under pressure from parents ambitious for better grades has become an issue. The image of a line of slots with women working them is not very different from that of women at sewing machines in a sweatshop. The difference is that the latter are steadily making more money than the former. One possible result of this gender difference may be that women tend to stay too long at an unprofitably tight slot machine rather than roaming in search of a looser one, as their more restless husbands might do. Contrariwise, men may be too impatient to give the machine a chance. Brain imaging—difficult to do with slot players—has shown that men winning at video games get more activation of their nucleus accumbens, an anatomical locus associated with addiction, than do women, whose activation was less intense and uncorrelated with winning.

Another gender difference sometimes proposed is that men go to casinos to find excitement, while women go to escape the stress of their daily routines. Yet, as in most things, there is clearly a large overlap of the sexes in gambling proclivities. Regional and cultural factors may also account for some differences. Raoul Lowery Contreras, a tour director in San Diego, a navy town where many Mexicans play at the casinos, told me that unlike at most slot-machine venues, it was rarer there to find a man playing the slots. In Canada, at least at romantic Niagara Falls, I found that the male-female ratio is close to 1-to-1, even with a choice of table games.

SLOTS AND VIDEO GAMES

Much as with their slot behavior, women have notably preferred repetitive home video games like Tetris and Snood. These are known as "casual games" and are in some ways more like slot machines than are the action-adventure games, which emphasize spatial orientation, penetrating levels, shooting adversaries, and competing with others, all of which appeal to the androgen-steeped brains of adolescent boys and post-adolescent boys and men, who find them more addictive than do women.

Slot machines are nevertheless increasingly coming to resemble the male-favored video games. The secondary and tertiary levels of play in video slots emulate those of video games. Although no skill is involved, slot players win more and more as they progress through higher levels. A simple example is the Addams Family machine, which can move you to a bonus round in which tombstones are among the choices—with purely random results—and horrifying dead creatures resurrect themselves with various winnings. Some games involve the accumulation of some factor, like diamonds in a bin in an overhead screen, which will pay off at some critical number. Such a feature, as well as the bonus round in certain machines' extra-spin feature, serves to keep the slot player faithfully pressed to the reels. On some machines that are set up to increase tension in the player, a timer on a big screen above shows how many seconds are left before one becomes ineligible for the bonus round—unless one bets again. A slot called Risky Business rewards with progressive disrobing by strippers of the player's choice of sex. New three-dimensional video displays resemble the virtual environments of video games.

The unending evolution of slot machines, like that of video games, is a Darwinian survival of the fittest, favoring by natural selection those machines we players stay with and return to, making them more profitable to the casino. For example, the Spam machine, with its crescendo of "spam! Spam! SPAM!" as its bonus was announced, was recently eliminated at Yonkers Raceway, owing to its decline in popularity. Like a burgeoning new robotic species, the fittest machines capitalize on the built-in reward and loss mechanisms at the gambling centers of our brains. This symbiotic evolution reveals the very nature of our brains and minds.

As Gary Rivlin reported in his *New York Times Magazine* story, manufacturers have proposed slots with joysticks and an element of competitive dexterity to attract younger male patrons who otherwise go to casinos to party. *Wired* magazine described Cyberview Technology's Glaxium as "tomorrow's slot machine" and reported that Cyberview hoped to be permitted by Nevada's regulators to offer skill-based payouts. This would radically transform the slot experience by substituting a competitive mind-set for the meditative trance induced by the random spinning and stopping of the reels.

Indeed, all themes that add a distracting narrative reference tend to diminish the meditative, prayerful state that engages the traditional slot player. In fact, many of those who have played slots the longest prefer the most basic machines, some of which have endured and topped the list of favorites (Double and Triple Diamond, Blazing Sevens, for example), while the fancier, themed slots have come, become tiresome, and gone.

CELEBRITY PERSONALITY SLOTS

The popularity of slot themes that include the images and voices of famous people reveals the slot machine's true identity as a form of altar. But in this case, instead of performing their usual roles as altars to an indifferent mathematically random universe, the celebrity slots are altars to personal gods with a small g. Here our society's celebrities function much like Greek gods, the household deities in China, and the folk gods of Japan. They are fascinating and fun because they are lofty and powerful, yet they are humanized by their vanities, their capacity for misbehavior, and their legendary escapades. They are seen as rich and generous, and many in fact are.

To the extent that they intercede between the player and the god of randomness to which the slot altars are ultimately devoted, celebrities also play the roles of priests and rabbis guiding us in prayer. The recorded voice of the celebrity in the slot machine usually sounds kind, sympathetic, and encouraging. Elvis or Regis or Dick Clark will commiserate with you on each bad spin and will congratulate you on each good one; applause for you can be heard in the background. More significant, they give you permission to play on, and in a sense even bless your play. Inasmuch as you idealize them, they inhabit your conscience. Clint Eastwood ascended to this pantheon with (no surprise) A Fistful of Dollars and Dirty Harry slots. Paul Rodriguez, the Mexican American movie star and comedian, appears on his Vegas: One Night Only slot. The one and only Duke, John Wayne, speaks to you in *that* voice on his machine. The magic touch of celebrity on these licensed slots may serve as consolation for eventual losses. The slot player has the satisfaction of having participated in combined slot and hero worship with their idols' approval. Perhaps fortunately, no slots with negative celebrity idols have yet appeared (care to license a slot, Bernie Madoff?), but there are darker-themed slots like Chainsaws and Toasters, The Phantom of the Opera, Monster Mansion, and Wild Thing, and for those with self-confidence problems, Winning for Dummies. Those with health concerns might be attracted to Nurse Follies, a video slot with icy bedpans, a mortar and pestle, a nurse holding an enema, and a bonus round of hospital charges. For the pessimistic born to crash, sink, or lose, there are Evel Knievel and Titanic slots. I've observed play on the latter many times out of curiosity to see if it would ever pay off, and it never has. Perhaps it's just because it has a high top payout.

DIVINATION BY GAMES

The history of games is the history of divination, the practice of foretelling future events or discovering hidden knowledge by occult or supernatural means. Colin MacKenzie, curator at the Middlebury College Museum of Art, told me that in the ancient culture of the Han Dynasty of China, the oldest board game found was played with an eighteen-sided die. Although the rules for this game have been lost with the passage of time, the board is identical to a divination board. Games of chance and dice have always been similar to the casting of bones (usually small joints, knuckles or carpal bones) of animals to learn the will of the gods or the fateful answer to some question. This further connects the playing of games of randomness like slots with the search for the will, purpose, or pattern immanent in the universe. The board of the ancient Chinese game models the universe. In fact, all games are reductions and simplifications—models abstract or concrete—of the world, and slots are no exception. But the world they model is not that of a revelatory deity that imparts mysterious knowledge; instead it is that of a god indifferent to cause and effect. So the slot celebrity as a priestly or even messianic intercessor remains clueless and therefore lacks the power to inform or benefit the slot player in the face of the inevitable odds of the random quantum universe.

DIVINITY AND DIVINATIONS

Stupidity and Slot Machine Players in Las Vegas, a cynical book about the foibles of slot players by David A. Goldberg, a former slot attendant, asks, "What's the difference between praying in a church and praying in a casino?" He answers, "In a casino, you mean it."

Guadalupe Lopez, age fifty-eight, of the Bronx, New York, was sitting at a Wheel of Fortune $1 slot machine at the Borgata Casino in Atlantic City when she hit it for a jackpot of $2,421,291.76. According to the *New York Post*, itself quoting *The Press* of Atlantic City, the winner had an explanation for her luck: "I have a great devotion to Our Lady of Guadalupe, the patroness of Mexico and the Americas, and had just looked up at the $2 million and had said a little prayer to her when I hit the jackpot. Our Lady really looks out for me." One cannot fail to notice the magical correspondence of names between this slot-playing lady and the particular manifestation of Our Lady. The casino denied any knowledge of the fact that Guadalupe Lopez's daughter is the megastar Jennifer Lopez, whom she had famously tried to prevent from breaking up with her star boyfriend Ben Affleck because of his gambling. A regular at the Borgata, Guadalupe usually plays the quarter machines.

Many devoutly religious people, including my former office manager Babs Curley, take some offense at the idea of the elder Lopez's use of prayer at a slot machine. "I don't believe in praying for money," Babs told me. "Some people are just lucky." A further question arises over the belief that the patron saint of Mexico and Latin America, which face such enormous social and economic problems, would focus her powers on an electronic slot machine in Atlantic City being played by none other than Jennifer Lopez's mother, who might have a more accessible patron saint in the person of her own mega-wealthy daughter. The winner declared she would set aside $100,000 of her winnings to set up a college fund for her two grandchildren.

The story has wide appeal nevertheless and made the front page of the New York *Daily News*. Many people will not consider a slot machine to be an unfit shrine for a saint, and indeed a representation of the Mother of Christ. No doubt many will simply add a prayer to Our Lady of Guadalupe to their wishful thinking as they feed the ever-hungry slots.

I decided to ask a former Jesuit priest if it was appropriate to pray for a win at a slot machine. John A. (Jack) Phelan, professor of media and politics at Fordham University, wrote back the following:

> From any standard of noble paganhood, bothering the Prime Mover with petty details is infra dig and if it

is for base gain, worse yet for you have failed to achieve Stoic Indifference. But "mechanical Christianity," as the learned Erasmus referred to the pieties of the mob, has never hesitated to pester Divinity with the quotidian; Jesus' remark about the sparrows would seem to encourage it. Intermediaries like Saints, I suppose, preserve the dignity of the Divine Court Royal. Protestants condemn gambling but Mediterranean plaza Catholics love it. So only an atheist or prig or tasteful Anglican would look down on such vulgarity. So there is no classic religious dolus (the Canon Law term for sin, sort of a cloistered tort) attached to asking God directly or through intermediaries for a new puppy, a rising stock, a good harvest, or a winning lotto ticket. From our class's point of view, it is just unspeakably common and vulgar: not the done thing—childish. But maybe Christianity is for children and perhaps even the childish. Certainly Jesus and company reserved their condemnations mostly for the proud, mighty and morally smug.

Perhaps this smothers rather than answers your query, but it's the best I can do.

Professor Phelan's skillfully worded response invites the reader to indulge in smug, superior feelings of condescension, then turns this upside down, convicting smugness, and praising prayer for a slot win as wishful, childlike, and not high on Jesus' list of dislikes.

This brings us to the blog from the online Golden Palace Casino, which reads, "In the name of the Father, the Son and the Holy Cheese." It seems that the casino's impresarios purchased for $28,000 a grilled cheese sandwich said to bear the image of the Virgin Mary's face and to have won its previous owner $70,000 at the Seminole Hard Rock Casino in Hollywood, Florida.

PSYCHIC INTERCESSORS

People who claim to be psychic sometimes offer to intercede for slot players to bring them luck. A full-page ad in the *New York Post* caught my eye with its list of wishes to be fulfilled by free psychic intervention upon the return of a coupon. The reader was asked to answer a questionnaire about wishes, most of which were for money to be delivered through gambling. In response to my own application, the psychic sent me a magnetized "talisman" (a photo of herself) that no one but me should be allowed to touch (to avoid "negative waves"). Although she noted that I didn't have money problems at present, she asked if I was sure this situation would last. Against the possibility that it might not, she sent me some lucky numbers (which presumably would help anyone playing) and said that in the personal horoscope that she would send me, she would tell me when my personal chances of winning at "the lottery, bingo, the races, the casino and other games of chance would be multiplied by 20 and even more than 30 times."

Since offering multipliers is speaking the language of slots, her pitch appealed to me, even if her powers of divination had not yet fully energized themselves, the evidence of which being her mistaken conclusion that I was out of work and spouseless. Not only did she promise aid in obtaining love and work, she also asked in her letter if I knew that "almost all celebrities turn to forecasting and astrology," as if I, too, might be counted

among their number. She further asked me to send a nonre-
turnable photo of myself or a strand of hair from my head,
and to fill out another questionnaire. While the usual charge
for the astro-clairvoyant forecast I would receive was $75, I
had been selected as an exception and would be charged only
$37.50, and only if I was 100 percent delighted by its accuracy;
otherwise, a refund check would be sent immediately. The first
question on the new questionnaire asked what games I play,
with check-offs for lotteries, racetracks, casinos, and so forth.

I happen not to believe in astrology. The simplest reason is
that as an amateur astronomer I know that the constellations
have shifted since the signs were designated. And now Pluto
has been downgraded from its status as a planet. But, no matter. Some of the people who use this psychic's numbers and
dates to guide their gambling are going to win, and a few will
win big (although the only large amount mentioned in the tes-
timonials I was sent was $30,000, far short of the $1 billion
I had requested). The fraction who do win will swear by her
powers, even as others may lose faith. The pretty lady whose
face is on our magnetized talismans, which contain "very
strong forces of energy, including a great quantity of cosmic
keys," will appeal to many as a powerful intercessor on their
behalf. Whether this psychic actually believes in her own powers doesn't matter much. Many psychics are believably sincere.
I once dined with the astrologers Arlene Dahl and Carroll
Righter. Both struck me as sensitive and sincere. The signs of
the zodiac offer a framework of personality traits so that people
who know them can remember the ways other people do and
do not fit the paradigms to which they randomly belong. Such
attention to detail is effective socially, because remembering

lots of little things about others seems to make astrology believers on the whole more engaging than nonbelievers. The point is that many people go about the pursuit of gambling luck in a manner that resembles praying to an interceding person whom they feel is on a special spiritual or cosmic level, or maybe just luckier and more famous. It's no accident that the words *divine* and *divination* are etymologically related. Almost equally relevant is that many of the casino employees who work the tables or even recommend slot machines have a poor grasp of combinatorial statistics and harbor all sorts of superstitions about the games that they work with but are forbidden to play. Magic rushes in where reason fears to tread.

WORDS TO THE WISE:
HOW SLOT MACHINES WORK
AND APPEAL TO US

THE THRILL OF SLOTS

Slots are often thought to be a quieter, more sedentary, and less thrilling form of gambling than games like roulette and blackjack, and certainly less than the boisterous craps table and the poker contests that are so much fun to watch on television because of the dissembling poker faces, the bluffing that goes on while we, the audience, know the cards the players really hold, and the strong emotions, which sometimes lead to fights. But winning in these other games usually involves tactics like doubling up, letting bets ride, or other escalating maneuvers that with increasing tension mount to a climactic win or loss resolution. To capitalize on such escalation, one must risk losing all.

With slots, however, there is a low risk per single play and the potential for huge multiples in winnings on each spin. As of April 6, 2004, when Jennifer Lopez's mother won her $2.4

million, the *Daily News* reported, the Atlantic City record had
been $8.5 million, won in 1994 at the former Bally's Grand,
which is now the Atlantic City Hilton. These huge jackpots
occur rarely. Even with the growing number of slot players, the
next newsworthy win and new Atlantic City record occurred
two years later, on April 18, 2006: $10,010,113.48 won by an
eighty-four-year-old retired waitress playing the maximum $3 a
spin on a nickel Megabucks slot. This great-grandmother with
a longtime "hobby" of playing the slots always told her family that she would take care of them when, not if, she won a
jackpot. She was given the option of a $5.5 million lump-sum
payment or a twenty-five year annuity. J. Lo's mom's win will
be paid our over twenty years at $121,000 per year—chicken
feed in the year 2024, one might fear, but a stupendous slot
win nonetheless. The world-record progressive jackpot was
$39.7 million, won in 2003 at the Excalibur Hotel in Las Ve-
gas by a twenty-five-year-old designer of computer software. A
computer expert winning on a game that is itself a computer?
And the mother of the world's one of the world's most famous
female pop stars netting the record Borgata win? Keep those
reels spinning. Your chances are just as good.

TIGHT AND LOOSE, AND JACKPOT SIZE

One strategy many slot players favor involves the choice of machines to play. A common error (akin to the so-called gambler's
fallacy, the belief that a certain roll of the dice or a number
on a roulette wheel that hasn't occurred for a long interval is
overdue) is the idea that a machine that has not paid off for

a long time is more likely to do so. Actually, the reverse may often be true. Some machines, termed "loose," are adjusted to pay more. Some may be advertised by a casino as paying 95 percent or more of the money put back in, and in the long run may be better to play. Of course, continued play results in 95 percent of 95 percent of 95 percent, and so on; one can lose one's stake from a thousand little cuts, unless one is very lucky. Usually one isn't. Overall payouts of casinos, which must include some infrequent, very high payouts, vary percentagewise from the high 80s to the low 90s for most machines. For example, in one month's tally, the total average-win percentages for Foxwoods and Mohegan Sun were 91.3 percent and 91.5 percent, respectively. The problem is that it's easy to be misled by a run of luck in judging a machine, and the point is that no one would play with the *intent* of receiving 95 percent back on every dollar ventured. People play slot machines for the thrill of the rare larger payoffs, which could happen on all machines at some time. Machines also vary in their pay tables from those whose jackpots are *relatively* small and frequent to those whose jackpots are much higher and less frequent. These varying types attract different breeds of gamblers, analogous to differences in investment styles. Some people are conservative, risk averse, and like the reassurance and apparent security of frequent small returns. Others are risk takers and are willing to pour money into a machine that is less responsive for longer periods—but then may reward them with the thrill of a larger win. Frequent large payouts would be nice, but it's the players in the aggregate who must pay for whatever the jackpots are. A looser machine can help sustain the hopes of players with minor wins for a longer period, while they pray to the god of slots for that bigger win. Overall, slots offer the possibility of larger wins with less—or at least more slowly experienced—risk than many kinds of gambling. The risk in slots is statistically sure, but comfortably slow.

OTHER SLOT SUPERSTITIONS AND MISCONCEPTIONS

Anthropologists classify superstitions as rudimentary religious thought. They consider the animistic religions that see spirits in every corner of hearth and home and nature as somewhat less developed than the major faiths. While I don't agree, because I treasure folk legends and find them very wise and rich in meaning, some commonly heard slot superstitions nevertheless are telling in their misguidedness.

A sense of *reverse favoritism* is reflected in the common belief that inserting one's players club card will result in lower payoffs. It is true the casinos collect information about your play when you use your card, but the card reader is not connected to the payout program. This worry is often experienced by people who feel guilty about something and unconsciously fear being punished for it when their identity is known in the venue of the slot casino. Rewards to players who use their cards take the form of points redeemable for comps (complimentary food or lodging), and there is no reason not to accept these inducements. Moreover, if one has a big win, one can retrieve documentation of one's losses in the same calendar year to deduct them from the win, by requesting a "win-loss statement" in writing from the casino.

Incidents of *precognition,* or advance knowledge that a win will come, are constantly reported. Players who subscribe to this believe in listening to their intuition or impulse—to choose a machine or decide to stay at or change machines. They have a hard time explaining why they win after someone else has convinced them to try a machine.

Sufficiency is my term for the belief that if you are playing a given machine and have one large win, you should leave. Oddswise, it doesn't matter. Mentally, it might be a good idea to cash out, get up, and redeem the voucher. Then you can switch to a lower level of play rather than squander your win at a higher level of play intoxicated by the idea of playing with the house's money, which is now legitimately yours.

Ownership of luck is the belief that if a person is playing and winning and another person sits down to play, even without changing the first player's card if he or she happens to be a friend or relative, the second player won't win because of a different "timing" or "touch." The instantaneous randomly generated reel results do not discriminate, and if someone sits down and wins right after you, it doesn't mean that you would have won if you stayed, unless you could time your spin to the same instant. This is unlikely, because a new possible result is generated every one-hundredth of a second. I once played an IGT Double Bucks machine that arrived oddly at a three-bar result in three consecutive spins. But even to say "consecutive" ignores all the intervening instants that my finger could have triggered.

The *empty machine* belief holds that when a slot has given a big payoff or emptied its hoppers, it is less likely to do so again. To be sure, the machine does have a memory for all that it takes in and pays out, and it remembers both the payout percentage it is set to pay on a statistical basis and the actual payout percentage, which may be different. But it has no usable memory of whether it just paid off, or whom it paid off. It is a slave to its random-number generator. Of course, a large progressive, when paid off, may lower itself to the smaller base from which it builds up again.

The converse is *the overdue machine* myth. An article in *SlotsToday* announced that IGT's Megabucks slot jackpot, having mounted to $15 million, was "statistically due to hit in Nevada." Being "overdue" to attain its long-run average payout doesn't mean that it's any more likely to hit the jackpot on any spin than it was when it was first reset to its base amount of $7 million. Some players will play on and on at the same machine on the theory that it eventually must get "hot" again.

Insignificant defects in a machine, like cloudy glass or reels that are dented, taped, or askew can trouble some players. These interfere with the desire to line things up precisely, a compulsion for many slot players, and mandate a move to another machine. And there is that ominous warning "Machine malfunction voids all plays," with its fantasy of one's jackpot being whisked away because of an incomprehensible technical flaw. If you're going to fly, you want your flying machine in tip-top shape. Perversely, some players believe that slightly defective machines may be weaker and quicker to give up their rewards.

Machine error—not! Just after Christmas 2009, at Empire City in Yonkers, I thought I had finally found a slot machine error. On IGT's Cats machine, depicting a variety of lions, panthers, and so forth, three of the cat's paw-print symbols appeared, seeming to signify a round of free spins, which were not forthcoming. It happened that a slot-machine attendant was seated beside me, replacing the paper on the adjacent machine, so I showed it to him. Studying the machine and its pay table, he could not figure out why the free spins had not taken place. With his phone he summoned a slot technician, who also could not figure it out. So, telling me not to touch the machine, he called a suited manager. These casino employees all departed and returned again. Upon reopening the pay table on the screen, the manager discovered that there were two kinds of similar-looking paw-print symbols, one with one and one with two prints. The pay table read that free spins resulted when there were three of the two-print symbols (ten free spins) or two of the two-print symbols and one of the one-print symbols (five free spins). My screen had one of the two-paw symbols and two of the one-print symbols, which triggered the 180-credit scatter pay (a payout based on two or more of certain symbols which can appear anywhere on a video screen, not just on a payline, and which may also trigger a bonus round). But it was not enough for any free spins. The morals of this story: Read the fine print closely, and what may seem to be a machine malfunction almost never is.

Good-luck rubbing, or rapping the glass of the machine, is favored by some players. This is much in evidence in San Juan, where it is also common for a player who has won a free-spin bonus to leave the machine (marking it with the player's keys in the tray) while the machine compiles whatever number of free spins the player has won. Other players will hide their eyes or put paper towels over parts of their machine's display. A twenty-one-year-old Puerto Rican woman who had been rapping not only on her screen but also occasionally on mine next to hers told me that concealing the screen avoided the influence of envious eyes. No stranger to the slots, she said she came to the El San Juan Casino twice a week, "more when I have the money." She had just graduated from college with a degree in management and was visiting the casino with her father.

Because winning combinations usually are required to start from the left, some players like to touch valuable or wild symbols appearing to the right on the screen and try (futilely) to sweep them to the left of the screen, where they would do some good. IGT's The Amazing Race has a feature that actually requires the player to rub the image of a pile of sand to discover a payoff ticket in the animation. The sooner you find it, the more valuable it is.

TIME ZONES

The belief of many people that slots vary their payoffs by the time of day deserves special attention. Lucky slot player Alice once won a jackpot aboard a Radisson *Seven Seas Navigator* en route to Bermuda in the evening, after dinner. She asked the casino host if there were any clock-related frequencies of payout on the slots. In response he opened up a slot machine to display the information it had collected for the casino. The data showed the machine was set to keep 93 percent but that its current batting average was slightly less favorable to itself, at 95 percent payout to the players. The host explained this was the difference between the statistical and actual payout percentages. All machines that pay out 93 percent, although individually unpredictable for any next spin or the short term, could be placed on a statistical bell curve over a given time period. They all would gradually creep closer to a 93 percent average, given enough time and ever larger samples of random spins. In the short run, however, one machine could pay out two jackpots in a row and another could theoretically not pay out a major win for a very long time. Thus, the answer to whether the payoffs varied by the time of day was that they absolutely do not. Moreover, the host argued persuasively that the casinos and slot manufacturers have little incentive to manipulate the slot payoff over time. There was no need to, and if the word got out that they did, it would hurt business. Most persuasively, he pointed out that the Radisson Seven Seas ships, of which the *Navigator* was just one, traveled across numerous time zones and all featured the same machines. A slot supervisor on a Baltic cruise aboard the *Crystal Symphony* pointed out that the ship had passed through four time zones, so it would have been particularly impractical to keep adjusting the machines' average payout percentages to Greenwich Mean Time. He added that, in any case, the machines' chips were changed very rarely. A more common practice was to change the "glass" displays in front and the symbols on the reels, but not the chips that control the payout schedule. For instance, the slot Triple Gold Bars could be altered to Triple Hot Ice or Triple Strike (all of them are International Game Technology games) without altering it computationally. In fact, doing so was simple and irrelevant to payout results, so that whereas such changes were previously outsourced to Caesar's, Crystal Cruises casino management now manages the task itself on their sister ships *Symphony* and *Serenity*.

One obvious example of a scheduled program change is the way the graphics differ with the seasons on some Wheel of Fortune video machines (some are at Mohegan Sun), such as for Easter, featuring chicks, bunnies, and butterflies, or for Thanksgiving. Either these machines are opened seasonally to make such changes, or they have a calendar in their chip and are allowed to swap symbols with equivalent odds.

In 2005 WMS Gaming struck a deal with Cyberview Technology for an innovation called server-based gaming, or downloadable slots. This new system, which has worried game regulators, employs generic terminals that outwardly resemble slot machines but inside do not have their own game computers and random-number generators (about which more below). The casino gets to choose from a library of hundreds of games with differing denominations and payback percentages, as well as the ability to download them to the terminals on the casino floor. This gives the casino the power to offer special bonuses to VIPs and slot-club cardholders, and also to vary the games instantly by time and day of week as well as by the characteristics of the players on the floor. Game regulators want assurances that the system will not "unfairly deceive" players about what they are getting, as David Stratton put it in his article, "Server Slots Near?" in *Slots Today*—as distinguished, we presume, from the usual "fair" amount of deception. The new machines also arouse fears of greater vulnerability to hackers than previous machines, which could be changed only by opening them one by one in the presence of a gaming official. Scott Cooper, a casino development manager at the Agua Caliente in Rancho Mirage, California, affirmed to me in a 2007 interview that the payout rates (or hold percentages) do not vary by time of day but can be reset on each machine within the brackets of the minimum allowed by the state and the maximum needed to make money. He was also wary of the effects of proposed future slots that could download the banking records of players, permitting them to make withdrawals without even the delay of having to visit an ATM.

SPATIAL POSITIONING OF SLOTS

Positioning some higher-paying machines close to aisles so that people are more likely to choose them for play is definitely within a casino's legal rights. Placement of machines to maximize business is given as much thought by casinos as supermarket managers give to the placement of products. Eye-catching new machines may be placed to draw gamblers to underperforming areas, and popular machines, like Wheel of Fortune, are commonly placed at either end of a bank of twelve machines as a so-called end cap.

SLOTS AS AUTOMATA, OR RUDIMENTARY ROBOTS

Playing slots is also considered a less emotional way to gamble than at a table because slot machines are inanimate. Technically, they are called automata, a rudimentary form of robotic life; they rank very low on the ascending scale of sci-fi humanoid androids that Isaac Asimov and the writers of *Star Trek* have so thoroughly explored. Would that slots obeyed the Three Laws of Robotics that Asimov first promulgated in 1942:

1. Robots must never harm human beings or, through inaction, allow a human being to come to harm.

2. Robots must follow instructions from humans without violating law 1.

3. Robots must protect themselves without violating the other laws.

One wonders whether slot play in general could pass these do-no-harm rules. Surely there would be some conflicts for slots as robots having to follow human instructions to spin once again when the slot player was in financial straits. But, as I'll discuss later, to compensate for this potential deficiency, slot play may offer more benefits for some than their payouts alone.

It's partly the very inanimate nature of slots that prompts us to attribute feeling and will to them. I have seen such projected feelings before, in programmers intimately involved with computers, who sometimes report that they feel they are in mystical union with their machines, in contrast to most computer users for whom the machines are just useful appliances. Perhaps because slots reward us with payouts and cause us painful losses, they became in part personified for some players long before they became equipped with celebrity voices to urge us along. After all, they have always been known as one-armed bandits (a reference to their pull handles, now rapidly disappearing).

Futurologists predict that the human race will grow increasingly dependent on robotic machines and will eventually merge with them, as the implantation of chips blurs the distinction between humans and machines. The correct prediction of Moore's law—that the number of transistors that can be placed on a computer chip doubles every two years—highlights the incredibly rapid evolution of computers. In comparison, human evolution seems to be standing still. Machines seem destined soon to exceed human intelligence, just as they have already exceeded human strength, endurance, speed, and memory. Some computer science forecasters believe that at a time referred to as the Singularity, rapid technological changes will lead to the end of the human era. Before too long, machines are likely to assume the form of more human-looking androids. The question remains as to what our relationship with them will be. Will we continue to enslave our machines, or will we gradually concede them status as humans with civil rights, as with the android Mr. Data of *Star Trek: The Next Generation* and the holographic Doctor on *Star Trek: Voyager*? Or will a darker era of machine rebellion follow, as in the movie *I, Robot* and the *Terminator* films? Will humans, like other herd and pack animals, such as horses and dogs, submit obediently to these entities when we perceive them as superior? As John Markoff wrote in *The New York Times* of July 26, 2009, it was to consider such concerns in advance of public alarm that on February 25, 2009, the Association for the Advancement of Artificial Intelligence met privately at the Asilomar Conference Grounds on Monterey Bay in California and established guidelines for artificial life created through DNA recombination. Regarding the concept of the Singularity, Eric Horvath, a Microsoft researcher, is quoted in Markoff's article as saying, "Technologists are replacing religion, and their ideas are resonating in some ways with the same idea of the Rapture" (the futurist event in Christian eschatology in which the born again are taken up into heaven).

The way many slot players respond to their machines may begin to address some of the questions raised by consideration of this subject. Those who play slots in some ways attribute superiority to the machines, which may seem strange, given that as mere computational automata they are far less intelligent than we are.

"If you're so damn smart, why aren't you rich?" the saying goes. This question reminds us that one way slots make us feel inferior is by seeming to be richer than we are. Indeed, many have the capacity to bestow on us more money than we already have, recalling humans' long history of deferring to wealth, if not worshipping the wealthy. Religion has both capitalized on and perpetuated this habit by confounding metaphors of wealth and royalty with holiness and the desirable company of heaven. I once heard an Episcopalian cleric eulogize a much-loved departed parishioner (oxymoronically) as "a spiritual aristocrat."

Slots are unpredictable rewarders. People tend to connect superiority with unpredictability because it reminds them of how mysterious and beyond our control grown-up behavior seemed when we were small children.

If the increasing attraction of slot machines is any indication, humanity's future relationship with ever more intelligent machines may bear close watching. Where the blackly humorous old joke showed the scoreboard at Caesar's Coliseum reading Lions 1, Christians 0, a similar scoreboard at Caesars Palace would show the machines being much further ahead of humans than the lions were.

Such is the trustworthiness of slots, according to the computer scientists I've spoken with, that if electronic voting machines were as reliable, Americans might eventually be willing to trust the tabulation of election results to them.

THE SLOT GOD MOVES IN MYSTERIOUS WAYS

Just how incomprehensible the ways of slots can be is illus-
trated by the following incident I happened to see. George,
a man in his mid-sixties who had been dutifully following his
slot-playing wife around Foxwoods Casino, absentmindedly
put a $10 bill into a Sun & Moon machine across the aisle
from her. This was a multiline video slot offering nine different
lines, for bets up to five quarters apiece. In other words, one
could bet anywhere from one quarter on one line, or 25 cents
per spin, to five quarters on nine lines, that is, 45 quarters, or
$11.25 per spin. He bet one quarter on each of the nine lines,
or $2.25. The machine had no pay table displayed, which is
common with complex multiline slots; one can see the pay table only by touching the SEE PAYS button, which opens a series
of screens listing payouts. The symbols on the screen appeared
to be various Mayan stone carvings inexplicably juxtaposed
with the often displayed Ks, Qs, ands Js denoting the playing
cards King, Queen, and Jack. A Mayan pyramid, resembling
El Castillo, the step pyramid at the center of Chichén Itzlá, in
Mexico, was represented as well. This is the mysterious Mayan
religious monument that, at the equinoxes of March 21 and
September 21, produces an effect in light and shadow on the
north side of the pyramid that looks like a serpent and is holy to
the Mayans. After George tried a few spins at one quarter each
for nine rows, a silver coinlike image with a Mayan face on it
appeared at the left end of the bottom row. Actually, it didn't
just appear; it manifested itself with a blinding silver glow, accompanied by a crescendo of cymbal sounds. Next to it on the

Ancient starburst brought deity down to eye level.

right was the pyramid, which then dissolved with an impressive gong sound into a similar brilliantly glowing coin face, but in gold. At the same time, additional gold and silver coin faces appeared in other columns. The machine announced in a displayed sign, "Congratulations! You have won the dream spin bonus feature of 50 free spins at a bet of 1 credit each for 9 lines. Push any feature key to start." Pressing a blinking key, George sat passively while the machine tossed off fifty spins, racking up bonus points every spin or two for an eventual total bonus of over 3,600 coins, or $900. Some of the spins even added other bonus spins. If he had paid for those spins, it would have cost 50 x $2.25, or $112.50. Astounded by the machine's largesse, and feeling flush, he then bet the highest possible wager of five credits each for the nine lines. After only a few more spins, the same silver and gold "dream spin" incredibly came up again, giving him another fifty bonus spins, but now at the top five-credits-times-nine-lines betting level. He would have had to insert $11.25 x 50, or $562.50, to gamble what the machine was gambling for him. This time the total was almost 6,000 quarters, or $1,500. So in several minutes the machine had given up $2,400. At this point, the machine froze with the CALL ATTENDANT sign, because the tax-free limit of $1,200 had been exceeded and the "candle" light on top turned on. The attendant checked George's driver's license and Social Security number, then disappeared for ten minutes or so. He returned with a casino official wearing an expensive-looking pink pantsuit, who took George's signature and doled out in cash just the $1,500 for the latter sequence of spins. George tipped the pleasant slot attendant $20, but not the official, figuring she was management. He then pressed the cash-out button to collect a ticket for the first $900, which he could take to the cashier's window.

I had been watching all this from nearby and congratulated him. He was happy with his win, but he said he remained mystified by it and in fact couldn't figure out any of the multiline video machines. He concluded that you just play them without following the workings or knowing the scoring system. The pay table is complex and not posted on the front of the machine. It can be accessed in the program, but only by means of the SEE PAYS. Even when one has seen the video display of the many possible winning lines, it is often difficult to recognize a win until the machine actually registers it. Since the Mayan codices have also resisted deciphering, the Mayan theme seemed especially fitting.

I asked George also how long he had been playing the slots before this win. He said about twelve hours, and that he and his wife had been down about $1,200, so the win would offset it and then some. Later, after dinner, I came back and found him still playing. He had had no more big wins. Some small wins had been accompanied by the message "You little devil!"

George's new persistence at the slot machine after his win reminds me of another player's persistence prior to her big slot win documented on *American Casino*, a reality show on the Discovery Channel. At the Green Valley Ranch Casino in Las Vegas, a young woman won a $143,309.74 "jumbo jackpot," the largest slot jackpot this casino had ever paid. One of the casino staff was heard to remark that it made him feel good to see a win by a local person "who is in here every day."

Video slots display much more elaborate graphics than old-style slots do, some of them as beguiling as George's Mayan slot is mystifying. One of the most beautiful to date is the Atronic game Treasures of Venice, with its views of Venice, a Rialto Bridge, and a campanile (the bell tower in Piazza San Marco). The bonus rounds show Venetian masks, accompanied by stirring musical passages. The accoutrements of this machine even include a screen adjustable to the player's sitting height. IGT's Rembrandt Riches and DaVinci Diamonds are also more than easy on the eye. WMS's Jungle Wild II immerses one in a lush jungle with all its sounds.

WMS's Dirty Harry: Make My Day machine at Mohegan Sun's Casino of the Wind offers not only lots of sound and encouraging words by Clint Eastwood but also a kidney-thumping vibration in the seat back that feels as close as I want to be to riding a Harley down to Daytona Beach. Bally's American Original machine awards up to fifty free spins in brisk succession to the sound of a Sousa march, and Bally's Hot Shot Progressive includes a feature that combines potential free spins of Blazing 7's, Diamond Line, Double Jackpot, Triple Jackpot, and Blazing 7x Pay, with progressives on a 1-cent Empire City slot requiring a max of two hundred units, or $2 per spin. At one moment when I glanced at the display, these progressive sums were, respectively, $23.70, $140.28, $816.50, $19,026.41, and $31,089.87. Vying with so many complex video symbols in other displays, this popular machine illustrates the enduring appeal of simple 7s.

BUDDY, CAN YOU SPARE A NICKEL?

On top of every slot machine sits a double-decker cylindrical light called the candle. The upper part of the light turns on when you press the button to call the slot attendant for change or assistance. Both parts blink if you hit a jackpot. The bottom part is color-coded to show the machine's denomination: white for 1¢, red for 5¢, yellow for 25¢, gold for 50¢, blue for $1, and violet for $5. For a time it looked as though the nickel and quarter slots were approaching extinction, to be replaced by the dollar slots. But the popular new multiline video nickel and quarter slots, and even penny and half-penny slots (whose advent has been called the penny-slot revolution), invite the player to venture small coinage with the possibility of much higher multiples in wagers, often with the added temptation of jackpots and progressives. Ticket-redemption systems eliminate the need for players to handle pennies (not to mention half pennies). The number of lines bet, like the number of fishing lines one puts in the water, increases the likelihood of a win on one of them, and the wins are multiplied by the bet per line. People succumb easily to the temptation of placing larger bets, or even inadvertently press the too-accessible MAXIMUM BET button. Many who would never dream of playing a $5 slot machine will find themselves pushing a MAXIMUM BET button on a nickel slot of one hundred credits, which also amounts to $5, or even on a quarter slot for twenty-five to forty-five credits, $6.25 to $11.25. To be aware of what one is betting, one needs to do some mental arithmetic, which disrupts the meditative state of many slot players. Moreover, the payback percentage of nickel slots (88–91 percent) is usually lower than those of simpler $1 (92–95 percent) or $5 (94–97 percent) machines, so by switching from the more basic slots to these low-denomination video slots, one trades the benefit of higher wins for the entertainment provided by their beguiling and dazzling visual effects. (*The New York Post* of January 18, 2011, reported a win of $3.5 million at the Borgata on a penny slot, so the unlikely can still happen.) What's more, the mojo of religious symbols is deployed with ease in the video format. Aristocrat's Queen of the Nile slot manifests double pyramids, sending a beam of light heavenward, while sacred scarabs and Tutankhamun heads abound. Hawaiian symbols and fiery displays may be seen on other slots, and for Texans there's the mythic jackalope. Aristocrat's Golden Incas displays an Incan Sun God figure that rewards the player with free spins. Bally's Gifts from the Gods shows an Aeolian harp as a scatter win (when three symbols appear anywhere, not necessarily lined up) and a reward hierarchy topped by the pagan gods Zeus and Athena, then Mount Olympus, and other Greek symbols like a sword, shield, helmet, and temple, going all the way down to a fig leaf. So much for phallic worship!

THE ALL-KNOWING GOD OF SLOTS:
THE WALLS HAVE EARS AND THE CEILINGS EYES

Most slot players know there are video cameras surveying all the play on the casino floor—in the trade they call them the "eye in the sky"—but how much will one be seen by them? The 1,000-machine Agua Caliente Casino has 480 cameras, both fixed and pan-tilt-zoom. Some watch cash registers in restaurants; some must watch for so-called slip-and-fall con artists, or people who look for an apparent loose piece of carpet to trip over, for example, and then sue the establishment for a faked injury. Casinos are a highly competitive business, yet they cannot afford the personnel to watch every play by every player. To do so would require as many personnel as players! Still, everything the cameras see is recorded and recoverable. We may assume that if as a result of unusual winnings on a given machine thievery or cheating or tampering is suspected, live cameras and video recordings will be scrutinized. Television viewers saw that being done by the security team on the hit show *Vegas*, which ran from 2003 to 2008. But how much is the average slot player, gradually going through the money she or he brought along to play, being scrutinized? Without knowing about any casino's actual surveillance, one must assume it's not much. Players' ideas of how much they are being watched reflect their images of themselves; indeed, it is a kind of projective test, like looking at ink blots and imagining their meaning. Some very retiring and secretive people seek slots that are hidden away in corners. One man plays only slots with no seats so he can stand up with his pelvis pressed against the machine, peering down his chest at the results. He reminded me of some men at urinals. A woman who had been a stage performer was certain she was being watched at all times. Less vain, exhibitionistic, or visually oriented people may ignore the possibility of scrutiny, or simply not care. One may imagine it's boring to watch people gambling, but Caesars Atlantic City Hotel Casino was fined $80,000 for using the overhead surveillance cameras to record footage of female gamblers' anatomy, and two employees were fired.

More interesting is the way people project onto casino authorities all sorts of benevolent or punitive intentions that could be considered parental—or even godlike. Being in the presence of a supposedly all-seeing, all-knowing authority in possession of technical wizardry brings out feelings reminiscent of when we were small children and could be completely supervised by our parents (or of an omniscient deity who judges our every action—and keeps a record in the Big Book in Heaven to confront us when we arrive at Judgment).

ILLUSIONS OF CLASS
AND ATTAINABLE STATUS

The subject of social class, dear to the English and rarely given a rest by them, is so un-American that we dare not mention it aloud. We often substitute notions of wealth and fame for class. The best and funniest description of the tripartite American class structure (upper, middle and lower) is Paul Fussell's book *Class: A Guide Through the American Status System*, Fussell argues that one's social class is unchangeable, no matter how much money one gains or loses.

But if Americans were simply interested in wealth and not class, some of our casinos would not be so pretentious. In fact, we go to these places not just for the potential money we can win but also to experience hanging out in a classy place for a while, possibly one beyond our means and station. Similarly, we go out to restaurants partly to enjoy being waited on; waiters may be seen as a vestige of the servant class. Some insufferable people even go out of their way to abuse the waitstaff in order to feel that they are lordly. They do not appear lordly in others' eyes, however, as most of us have more egalitarian sentiments. Like restaurant waiters, the many people who serve us while we play the slots earn their tips. Besides acknowledging the work that they do, it's a pleasure to give money to a live human being for a change, instead of the unappreciative inanimate object one has been feeding.

Our American way offers opportunity to all, but no one would argue we administer it evenhandedly. Many who patronize casinos are looking for the chance at success offered impartially by slot machines. Slots may be the most democratic way to gamble precisely because they are machines. For some, slots are actually a relief to deal with instead of people. They can't discriminate, even subtly, like a maitre d' lifting an eyebrow. No slot player is ever made even slightly uncomfortable or unwelcome. And slots can take a minuscule investment and turn you into a millionaire.

A study conducted at the University of Nevada by Dr. Coni Kalinowski, a psychiatrist, found that 89 percent of a sample of seventy-nine people with intellectual disabilities—that is, IQs of less than 75 from a variety of causes—had gambled, about the same proportion as the general Nevada population, and this sample had only slightly higher rates of problem gambling (6.3 percent vs. 2.2–3.6 percent, according to various studies). Dr. Kalinowski speculated that gambling might offer benefits for such people, such as undemanding socialization, unstigmatized recreation, and participation in an adult activity.

Fair treatment alone is pleasant for the disenfranchised. But fair treatment in an environment of elegance and grace from which they might expect to be barred or shooed out is heady stuff indeed. At each step up the ladder of bettors, low, medium and high rollers can rub elbows with their "betters," without having had a private education or needing to brave a country-club membership committee. And they have exactly the same chances of success. Whoever they are, if they gamble or, better (at least from the viewpoint of the casino), lose a substantial sum, they have an equal chance of attracting the personal attention of a casino host doling out perks. Casinos care only about how much you bet. They call a "high roller" anyone who is willing to lose $10,000 in a weekend, and reserve the term "whales" for those willing to risk a great deal more than that.

THE CASINO DEVELOPER

Scott Cooper, casino development manager of the Agua Caliente in Rancho Mirage, California, was in the midst of building a $200 million hotel expansion when he took the time for an interview and comped my wife and me dinner at the casino's restaurant The Steakhouse. Two months later, a floor was being added every ten to twelve days, and an additional $100 million investment had been approved, to include the building of a 2,000-seat showroom, an additional parking garage, and a more extensive remodeling of the casino. In the past twenty-five years, Scott has opened more properties than any other developer, building twelve casinos from scratch at sites including Las Vegas, Saratoga, the Finger Lakes, Buffalo, West Virginia, Illinois, Missouri, and on Louisiana riverboats. That is, at each location Scott was the first employee to arrive, and it all unfolded from him. I asked him why the Agua Caliente was undertaking a $300 million Bellagio-like expansion, especially given that it is one of five casinos in the Coachella Valley around Palm Springs, which offer so many places to stay, including the sprawling Westin Mission Hills Resort only five minutes away. He answered that the Agua Caliente was expanding because in a casino everything but the gaming is a loss leader. Eighty-five percent of the profit at the Agua Caliente is made on the slots, and only 15 percent on the table games, because they are labor intensive. Having its own hotel would permit the casino to save the money it would have spent rewarding its whales with expensive rooms elsewhere (including the upscale Mission Hills, where I was attending a psychiatric convention) and its lesser players at lesser lodgings. If the hotel, spa, restaurants, and convention space show a slight profit, it is often because these areas receive what is called comp or soft revenue that is charged back on the books to gaming profits or included in marketing costs. In other words, Scott Cooper's entire development project is just another loss leader for the slots.

Meanwhile, at Atlantic City, Caesars Palace had added a pier of high-end shops, Harrah's was expanding its hotel upward, and the Borgata added another tower. There was also to be a new $2 billion 3,800-room casino hotel, bankrolled by Morgan Stanley, on the former Sands site, with twin towers (the tallest buildings in Atlantic City) and 150,000 square feet of new casino space. One begins to sense the enormous financial muscle of slot machines.

BUBBLE TROUBLE

The recession of 2008 exposed the tremendous overbuilding of casinos to competitive pressures. On January 10, 2010, the *New York Post* reported the worst Atlantic City results since 1997, a drop of 13.2 percent in profits. *The New York Times* of January 30, 2010, noting that New York State had secured a casino operator for Aqueduct Raceway in Queens, that the Shinnecock Indian Nation expected federal recognition to build a casino at the Belmont Raceway a few miles away from Aqueduct, and that there was a push to build two Vegas-style casinos in Monticello, suggested the danger of diminishing returns for the state from market saturation. Profits at the Buffalo–Niagara Falls Seneca casinos had dropped 7.2 percent, prompting enlargement plans to be dropped, and there were worries that an Aqueduct casino would steal business from the state's top performing Yonkers Raceway Empire City Casino. The two enormous Connecticut casinos, Mohegan Sun and Foxwoods, already had seen declines in profits and were vulnerable to plans to approve casinos in 2010 in Massachusetts, which supplies 40 percent of their gamblers (*The New York Times*, January 11, 2010). Morgan Stanley dropped out of the Atlantic City Sands site project in the summer of 2010 claiming a $900 million write-off. The site was put up for sale to international investors at 30 percent of what this last available site along the Boardwalk originally cost.

Against such recession and saturation problems, the baby boom generation (those born from 1946 to 1964), the wealthiest American generation yet, is now aged forty-seven to sixty-five. This generation can continue for some time to supply players of the prime ages for the slots. As Andy Rooney reported grumpily on the CBS-TV program *60 Minutes* of May 16, 2010, our casinos earned $32.5 billion in 2008, and their earnings dropped only slightly, to $30.7 billion, in 2009. Despite this small decrease, the expansion of casinos seems to be resuming, even in the current jobless recovery, as more politicians are promoting gambling as a potential fiscal fix.

NONPATHOLOGICAL GAMBLING

Despite the enormous growth of casino gambling in the United States, it is probable that a majority of those who gamble do not do so pathologically. While the total number of problem gamblers may be up, the proportion is likely down compared to the days when slot gambling was more marginalized and seedy, a definitively downscale activity compared with the elegant, trendy, and family-friendly activity it is increasingly considered to be today. A white paper published in 2010 by the American Gaming Association says that pathological gambling hovers at one percent of the population—the same as in 1976, when there was only Las Vegas—and is not increasing, nor is the average amount spent on casino visits. Healthier people are coming to the slots. Ordinary families bring their children and drop them off in convenient babysitting programs or video-game parlors that the casinos provide. Such is the growing appeal of gambling (and gambling today is overwhelmingly slot machines) that it invites closer examination. The majority of heavy slot players I have spoken with have engaged in the pastime seriously only in the past several years. The results of this trend are only now starting to trickle in, and psychiatric studies of various vulnerable populations are just beginning to emerge. On the one hand, I'm reminded that heroin was thought at first to be nonaddictive. Then again, such an apprehension may be too dire. The explosion in slot playing and casino overbuilding has been sensitive to rational recession-inspired belt-tightening.

GAMBLING AS A NATIONAL REFLECTION

Traditionally, prevalent gambling in a society is not a good sign from a psychoanalytic/anthropological point of view. It may reflect widespread poverty, a large disparity between the rich and the poor, and a sense of hopelessness regarding the possibility of achieving economic advancement by other avenues. In some third-world societies, it is seen as an opiate of the masses. When I conducted a psychoanalytic/anthropological analysis of Vietnamese society in 1975, I found that gambling in the national lottery exceeded the country's gross national product. While there is some evidence that the United States is sinking towards third-world status with respect to income disparities, a lower level of occupational opportunities, and the decline of educational standards, this does not seem to correlate with the greater participation in slot gambling by our senior population, which is at present the most affluent segment of American society and the wealthiest generation we are likely to see for the foreseeable future. Younger people who buy multimillion-dollar-prize lottery tickets, often driving many miles and across state lines to brave the steep odds, may be hoping to transform their lives with a win. But this motive rarely applies to slot players. For one thing, the payouts are generally too small to be radically transforming. The highest progressive jackpots on machines like Wheel of Fortune or Betty Boop's "Thrillions" may reach $1 to $2 million, but these are exceptions; most machines have no progressive and a top rating of only several thousand credits or coins, which may be quarters. True, there are very high payouts on some hyperlinked machines. But overall, as I pointed out earlier, there is a predictable loss of money for the player; though casinos may advertise a certified rate of return of 95 percent or 97 percent, this is deceptive if one assumes one will bring home 95 percent of the money one puts in the machines. Rare high wins must be figured into the total return, and they are most likely to occur to another player on another day. Players forget that money played again and again results in a percentage of a percentage—say, 95 percent of 95 percent of 95 percent—until eventually the gambler's limit is reached. Usually the slot player does not come home ahead.

PLAYING PERFECTLY

Harvey, a forty-four-year-old with nine years' experience, plays only what he considers a game of skill, Double Bonus Poker. You get a hand of five cards on a spin, then get to replace as many of them as you would like. He has a favorite machine that he plays for a double $10 investment each hand. He chose this machine carefully for its higher pay table and plays it exclusively for the entire time that he's in Atlantic City. Does he get bored? No, he says, because he considers it gambling,

All Harvey has to do is play perfectly into eternity.

he is interested in the money, and besides, there are other things to do in Atlantic City (I didn't ask). He prefers one of the card-playing machines that do require skill. The payout actually exceeds 100 percent with perfect play. Harvey considers himself a professional gambler. He has model casino habits: He watches his wallet and never drinks a drop while he is playing. Obviously, he ventures large amounts at $20 a hand. His largest win has been $80,000. His play must not be quite perfect, though, because he remains more than welcome at the casino. In fact, the casino finds it profitable to reserve for him the particular machine he plays when he is in town, and to shut it off when he is asleep or doing something else, so that when he returns it will be free. (Of course, when he is not in Atlantic City, the casino frees it up for anyone else to play.) His arrangement is not unique. He cited a female player who plays the $100 two-coin slot exclusively; the machine is roped off for her. They might as well put her in a room and point a camera at her, Harvey added. This is what was famously done with William Bennett, our former secretary of education, who was publicly embarrassed by the revelation of his high-stakes slot playing in a private room (and just as publicly said that while he did not believe his habit set a good example and that his "gambling days are over," he still wanted to place a bet on the Super Bowl).

Harvey evidently feels he has his machine figured out. He concedes that it's statistically possible the machine will *never* hit with a royal flush or that it will hit one continually, but the odds are against both occurrences. All you have to do is play perfectly and play forever, and you will approach your machine's advertised greater-than-100-percent payout. Part of his confidence comes from his conviction that he has the mathematical odds of his machine down pat. He knows the machine has a random-number generator, but he thinks this means each of the five cards has an independent 1-in-52 chance of coming up. Even if this were true—and some gaming authorities require it to be—if a poker machine simulated a single deck and the same card could not come up twice, then the cards after the first one would have successively a 1-in-51, 1-in-50, 1-in-49, and 1-in-48 random chance of coming up. What Harvey does not think about, though, is that there are no real cards in the machine, only a computer algorithm that generates their image. And the algorithm can do whatever it wants, as long as it observes the state payout minimum of 80 percent. It controls the hands that can be drawn according to preset averages. It may be set at 100 percent or even above 100 percent payout with perfect play, counting on imperfect players (the so-called dead money in poker tournaments) to make up the difference for a casino profit. The chip program dictates combinations, not individual cards. The ideal frequency of each winning hand is set by the program. Two pairs will obviously occur more often than a straight, and so on. The random element just governs when those combinations will appear before Harvey's eager (and eventually tired) eyes, in the preset ideal frequencies. He may miss the big wins if they occur at another time, like intermittent investors and market timers who miss history's big upticks. He may not always play perfectly. And ideal preset win frequencies do not equate with actual realized frequency on a given machine. It is just a statistical target that no one—not Harvey and not the casino—can count on.

For example, Donald Trump once accounted for some of his casino's poorer quarterly performances by a lower "hold percentage" or what is raked in from losing gamblers. This was from the table games, but big machine wins could throw off the hold percentage, too. Whatever the cause, the next month Trump announced a bankruptcy reorganization of his casinos.

SPEAK EASY OF ALCOHOL

A psychiatric colleague, Jeff Kahn, M.D., sent me an admonitory cartoon of a slot-playing woman receiving an intravenous alcohol infusion, implying dual unrelenting addictions. It is rare to see an obviously intoxicated slot player—one exception being a scotch-drinking senior whom I saw slip off her stool at Mohegan Sun. Her physician husband and I attended to her and ascertained it was just alcohol. Most players seem little interested in the roving servers. The other exception I can recall was at the Borgata in Atlantic City after 11:00 p.m., when a group of young people dressed for disco dancing burst boisterously onto the slot floor. While they were clearly intoxicated, they were not experienced slot players, at least to judge by their noisy inability to figure out where to insert money into the machines.

SUFFER THE CHILDREN

For families who bring along their children, casinos like Mohegan Sun provide care at an hourly rate of $7.50 for children over the age of three and $8 an hour for children aged six weeks

Some games in the children's area have gambling themes.

to three years. Descriptive brochures are printed in English, Chinese, and Vietnamese. There are many supervised activities, from jump rope to karaoke, Barbieland, and Lego building. The video arcade has the latest games, including a Motion Theatre simulating rides. But there are also games with gambling themes. One promises jackpots every play. And there is a kiddie version of Wheel of Fortune, played with 25-cent tokens (which cannot be refunded) and offering payoffs in tickets that can be cashed in for toys. A sign outside the Kids Quest arcade reads NEW HORIZON HOURLY CHILD CARE. As I watched the children feeding their tokens into their slots, I wondered whether the new horizon referred to their future outlook or their future as marketing targets for the casino's adult slots.

Although our society is strict about the legal age of consent for sex despite many children being sexually active, I wonder if we shouldn't be equally strict with respect to gambling. There are children all over the casinos except for on the gaming floor proper, where they are denied entry by guards. This prohibition is strictly enforced; casinos have been fined more than $100,000 in cases where minors were caught playing. But the message being sent by some of the children's games is that youngsters are being groomed as future slot players. Admittedly, I'm sensitive on this issue. On the reality television show *Deal or No Deal*, which involves taking chances on the differing amounts of money in various closed briefcases, I'm bothered that the contestant's children were often present and asked to advise their parents about whether to continue gambling.

CASINO SURROGATES

A profusion of online gambling sites offer "practice play" (probably the only sensible approach to them, as they are offshore and often unregulated), and there are game disks available from Masque® Publishing, Bally, and Phantom EFX that are similar or identical to the games on the casino machines. These permit one to separate monetary rewards from what for many are the obsessive delights of lining up like symbols and other non-monetary pleasures of slot gambling. Some people will be surprised to discover they enjoy the surrogate experience as much the real one. For others, there will be no comparison; they will find it like playing Tetris or Snood. There is probably some sensory carryover from the real casino to the substitute, at least for a time. Evidence of this is the boredom one can experience with a particular slot machine upon returning to a real casino after overplaying the same slot in a surrogate game. Also, one's interest in surrogate games falls off more rapidly if one hasn't recently been to an actual casino or doesn't expect to visit one in the near future. Certainly such software provides an inexpensive alternative for some players—a form of methadone for slotoholics, so to speak, or perhaps decaf for coffee fiends.

THE NONHUMANITY OF RANDOMNESS

Harold Searles, a renowned pioneer in the use of psychotherapy to treat schizophrenia and another of my favorite teachers of psychiatry, has emphasized the complexities of our relationships with both other humans and the nonhuman environment. Perhaps the least human aspect of that nonhuman world is its characteristic randomness. Just as nature abhors a vacuum, our minds hate randomness. Defined as any sequence in time or space totally lacking pattern, randomness is so alien to our minds that we don't believe in it emotionally even if we know intellectually that it exists. Our brains themselves are the most highly organized matter in the universe that we know of, and nothing we produce with our minds can be random in sequence or pattern. Where there is pattern, there is predictability, so we see predictability everywhere, even when there is none, as in the slots.

To obtain a random sequence that can be used to make a completely fair slot machine, one must derive it from some physical phenomenon. For example, a corporation called Silicon Graphics patented a method for generating random numbers by taking digital photographs of the swirling patterns in lava lamps. Some excellent physical sources of randomness, like the radioactive decay of isotopes, are cumbersome to use, and one would need to amplify the output so it could be detected and converted into a digital sequence. Other methods, like the numbered balls blown by air that are used on television to select winning lottery sequences and in the feature in the Slotto casino machines, are too slow to give slots all the numbers they need to keep pace with your play. In the 1950s, the RAND Corporation made a million-number table by electronically simulating a roulette wheel. The University of Geneva began a website application on March 18, 2004, that anyone can use to download random numbers, as I have done partially below. Johnson-Nyquist noise — or the electronic white noise generated by the agitating effect of heat on the electrons in a conductor—is a practical quantum mechanical source of randomness.

The stream of digital ones and zeros that emerges from such a source is totally unpredictable, but it also has an unpredictable bias toward more ones or more zeros. This is not to say it has a pattern, but any bias over the long run is not fair to slot players. A way to eliminate this bias was invented by the great Princeton mathematician John von Neumann (the pioneer of game theory and computer science, among a host of other mathematical contributions), who also invented our undetectable nuclear submarine routes. The mathematical elegance of his solution is delightful. It simply takes the ones and zeros as a sequence of pairs. Then, whenever a one precedes a zero (1,0), the number one is derived. Whenever a zero precedes a one (0,1), the number zero is used. This eliminates sequences of repeated ones or zeros in between the used numbers and results in about one-quarter of the uncorrected output; this is still enough because random numbers can go on to infinity. (To mimic this digital process, extract just the first twenty-two 1s and 0s as they occur from the beginning of the random number table that follows, or 0111111011101001010110. Then, by von Neumann's method, reduce this to 01110001. We have already reduced a ratio disparity of eight 0s to fourteen 1s to an even ratio of four 0s to four 1s. If the process is continued, it would always tend to yield a 1:1 balance.)

HOW SLOTS WORK: THE RANDOM-NUMBER GENERATOR

Slots work by coupling a computer algorithm to what is called a random-number generator. In the simpler, older machines,

three reels with twenty symbols on each appear to spin randomly. Actually, they do spin randomly until called upon by a frequency algorithm (mathematical program) to stop at prear-
ranged frequencies at variable intervals determined by the random-number generator. From a random-number generator
available online, I requested one thousand random numbers
between 0 and 1,000 and got the following:

669 689 501 361 645 545 882 626 415 592 585 91 396 776 585
881 693 188 767 701 313 473 106 697 149 27 740 907 146 601
693 65 201 268 272 845 234 482 669 585 476 133 360 663 570
35 998 291 186 269 731 76 225 85 531 206 402 334 396 398
729 276 966 198 38 606 586 360 715 995 567 78 79 517 765
833 189 700 885 774 606 962 653 169 589 56 974 364 871 456
794 264 369 123 727 851 155 766 573 91 330 823 377 578 649
77 748 809 48 234 470 498 864 847 872 634 904 685 431 362
711 202 454 114 114 497 717 904 574 993 266 965 91 337 40
681 207 449 887 879 962 328 955 429 535 344 947 236 359
800 937 101 69 268 919 572 304 590 78 392 852 538 954 29
807 519 320 176 299 794 229 394 570 791 38 781 104 392 149
975 757 481 387 139 655 852 451 387 389 684 361 545 934 96
547 21 173 533 588 202 671 916 119 358 649 16 455 390 486
440 642 786 474 847 370 1,000 722 301 318 802 27 801 172
74 541 239 583 67 39 495 424 468 62 306 558 774 494 837 728
824 793 163 779 113 71 19 993 243 101 30 670 419 8 321 433
110 163 180 667 386 967 74 128 788 52 447 877 489 152 440
399 901 991 596 922 910 594 959 207 347 380 10 630 479 693
158 435 260 84 899 340 3 493 981 362 305 588 68 136 119 122
198 882 340 932 690 418 368 731 535 507 34 626 701 759 535
156 730 72 263 602 99 838 592 27 902 401 766 639 873 925
91 263 680 598 423 804 728 262 555 493 922 408 744 962 31

291 611 294 84 592 291 729 88 396 756 589 483 823 871 365
774 824 835 748 472 738 368 965 189 638 792 413 173 604
706 90 743 590 367 236 54 941 866 237 277 17 874 153 844
752 354 671 24 355 660 424 90 74 682 698 266 940 63 856 668
967 721 834 387 382 171 963 129 689 385 898 888 98 385 290
719 784 667 537 704 844 880 430 264 492 433 425 389 769
124 329 658 327 725 754 954 468 449 982 49 27 250 784 306
677 922 998 829 346 446 276 569 870 619 762 305 902 774
872 343 162 201 177 939 696 507 269 15 844 367 656 279 364
832 108 503 107 769 882 835 342 163 948 778 868 195 850
908 21 664 141 453 610 6 960 637 788 115 21 58 58 914 989
402 869 23 280 791 998 305 971 739 358 377 548 845 38 697
493 981 797 441 60 964 695 946 699 96 178 628 339 919 870
695 903 398 407 240 150 548 223 895 841 777 550 739 732
443 716 599 754 58 458 601 401 147 189 99 307 23 407 976
338 619 558 986 884 151 301 542 685 524 704 157 644 343
831 525 406 47 496 423 710 91 564 809 230 42 283 877 170
439 50 740 836 854 623 665 413 218 754 732 147 350 892 871
742 758 750 11 463 16 804 474 684 365 247 819 608 644 184
234 295 563 497 899 746 55 317 848 542 274 134 91 661 122
422 611 442 291 312 659 44 84 524 820 289 664 598 450 888
51 555 710 716 858 140 173 458 998 613 612 855 503 865 193
575 936 940 488 204 843 429 350 684 648 203 363 943 475
733 219 343 590 635 382 200 792 320 951 216 552 570 481
498 524 296 520 514 363 803 824 247 459 878 700 407 381
464 343 337 153 796 731 147 799 139 202 418 628 664 243
380 720 32 427 797 530 294 244 274 202 260 829 967 710 548
650 895 665 757 521 426 236 103 141 227 412 706 77 702 388
482 185 140 694 560 705 202 88 756 614 931 202 6 533 504
520 877 311 648 436 229 690 797 356 541 529 259 728 384

268 901 604 390 410 486 619 409 721 164 188 717 894 78 496
305 266 444 251 454 333 721 166 621 349 64 548 605 804 830
406 348 339 777 474 48 539 117 320 834 677 859 797 575 754
598 927 14 147 510 330 943 62 475 74 470 693 928 887 793
84 119 747 799 976 688 156 819 922 914 990 657 409 677 324
258 519 907 224 563 441 634 27 997 669 451 927 52 924 998
447 304 396 417 946 455 823 701 167 946 13 541 187 323 458
476 409 106 382 554 313 267 168 642 650 812 131 50 228 325
722 491 433 939 598 437 671 75 84 205 736 914 501 903 442
924 462 569 761 995 122 71 336 840 871 519 668 731 793 549
648 564 219 222 102 516 794 596 347 142 560 606 161 539
401 211 995 496 367 370 404 589 380 155 653 260 26 825 931
345 448 177 189 168 707 374 145 524 469 996 767 638 472 82
726 176 605 900 146 545 908 445 412 533 750 834 689 965
110 282 388 173 522*

Assume that the random-number generator in a given slot machine is generating the above random sequence of numbers over one thousand spins of the reels. Assume also that the jackpot in a particular slot machine is three 7s in a row. How can the chip in the machine be set to pay off once in one thousand spins? It can do so by assigning a particular number to that machine configuration (of three 7s). It could, for example, display three 7s only when the number 777 comes up. This number in fact does come up in the thirteenth row from the bottom. The number 777 would not *have* to come up in one thousand spins—there are some repeats, and all the numbers from 0 to 1,000 do not occur. On average, though, they all will occur about once in one thousand spins. But the designated number need not be 7s at all. It could be three 6s, or 381, or 892. For a payoff frequency less than 1,000, the program could say the number had to be 542, but only when the last digit that preceded the 542 had been an 8. This would make the odds 1-in-10,000. That's more like it, the casino would say. It is too easy to roll the reels one thousand times. Playing three quarters one thousand times would cost only $750, and a top machine payout of 4,000 credits would amount to $1,000, meaning the casino would lose money. Besides, there are all those lesser wins to pay out. The program also spells out when these payouts will occur. Winning and losing spins can all be connected to some random sequence. For example, a display of three bars for a thirty-coin payout could be programmed to result whenever any number ending with 59 came up, or ten times per thousand spins. These are all hypothetical examples. In practice, three-reel machines may take three nine-digit random numbers (one for each reel) from the stream of hundreds per second, divide these by a divisor from 64 to 512, and take the remainders left over from that division to select stops on virtual (mathematically constructed) reels, which are converted by the program to stops on the physical reels. But whatever a machine is programmed to do (and it must monitor and limit the lineup of the reels), it does it autonomously, controlled by a chip that is installed inside and that is independent of any outside control from the casino, which can only observe and take feedback, not alter play. And the machine does it absolutely impartially, in complete ignorance of who has sat down to play.

In theory, there is nothing to prevent the program from installing a clock and calendar so the payout ratio varies according to time and date, because this would still be true for all players. But casino managers I have asked about this say that slot payouts do not go by the clock. Machines arrive from their manufacturers (IGT, Aristocrat, WMS, Bally, Konami, Atronic, etc.) ready to be plugged in. The theoretical payout ratio may be set or changed by opening the machine in the presence of a gaming commission official. The ratio is bracketed between a lower limit allowed and an upper limit dictated by the casino's need to make a profit. Then the machine runs, only statistically approximating its preset payout percentage.

Charles Fey, an American, invented the slot machine in 1894 and the prototypical three-reel bell slot machine in 1898. But Basil Nestor, in his fine article "The 10 Most Influential People in the History of Slots," in *Strictly Slots*, includes Inge Telnaes in his list of innovators. She patented the virtual stop in 1984. This got rid of the limitation of only twenty-two stops on three physical reels per machine, which allowed only 10,648 possible winning or losing combinations. Reels with more stops and extra wheels weren't popular. Telnes devised a computer simulation of the reels, connected to a random-number generator, which could create a hundred or a thousand stops per reel, which are mapped in some ratio, like 3-to-1, onto the limited physical wheels. This made huge jackpots possible, because a freer computer program, and not the physical reels, determines the outcome and can be set for many more probable spins before a jackpot occurs. Many players are fooled by the simplicity of the reels into thinking a big jackpot will soon be theirs. When one plays a mechanical slot machine, one intuits that if the three reels spin freely in a balanced way, the jackpot will come up sooner than it does. This would be true if the reels were not slaves to a clever program. But the three reels are not independent of one another, and the configuration they arrive at seemingly independently can be thought of as a more elusive, single-directed combination. In this sense, a simple modern three-reel machine controlled by a computer chip is fraudulent in the way it is likely to be interpreted by the intuitive mental mathematics of a player who views the three spinning physical wheels and gauges the mechanical probability of three 7s lining up. The trade-off is the possibility of a more attractive, but rarer, jackpot. Some players have told me they prefer the reel machines with a handle one can pull to the video slots because they feel that they somehow have a more direct connection with the outcome. This is untrue; in both types of machines, a random-number generator comes between their playing action and the result. The other development that further enlarged the jackpot amounts was the Megabucks machine, introduced in 1986 by IGT, which enabled machines at a number of casinos to be linked by phone lines (a hyperlink), thereby rivaling the possible wins in state lotteries.

There is nothing to prevent the program from specifying how often those annoying "teasers" occur, when there are two 7s on the pay line and a third 7 visible just off the pay line, either above or below it. Such teasers are built in. In some machines, one will see no 7s for a long time and then see three of them with one askew. The programs are proprietary (that is, owned by the machine makers), but a game designer from IGT, quoted by Gary Rivlin in his previously mentioned 2004 article, both admitted the planned inclusion of near misses and noted how effective they are at keeping people spinning the reels. Teasing near misses seem to occur so often it may come as a surprise that one game, a predecessor of the enduring Bally game Blazing 7s, was outlawed for a time for including too many of them, according to Frank Legato, in the April 2006 *Strictly Slots* magazine. Near misses are supposed to emerge from the random-number generator, not from other programming. In the same magazine in April 2005, Legato reported on another controversy involving machines that on every spin paused for a split second at a jackpot before stopping. When these machines were yanked by officials, the brief stops were explained by the manufacturer as a software glitch, not an attempt at subliminally influencing the players. These teasers may be a sensitive issue, judging by the reaction of a leading game manufacturer from whom I had requested permission to print a photo of a jackpot win that included one of their machines. After initially giving approval, they balked when they gleaned from a summary of this book that I would discuss randomness and near misses.

Machines in casinos operated by the Canadian government have a printed message on the control panel that reads: "The game display does not indicate how close you were to winning, and cannot necessarily be used to determine your chances of winning or losing if you continue to play." This warning probably has about as much effect as do those on cigarette packs, but it would be an improvement in honesty to have it on slot machines in the United States as well.

PART

2

RETHINKING
YOUR SLOT PLAY

RAISING ONE'S CONSCIOUSNESS ABOUT SLOTS PLAY

YOU CAN'T AVOID GAMBLING

Risk is an inevitable part of living. One's very presence in the physical world creates a slight chance of an unfortunate occurrence. We tend to overlook the small but real statistical risk of travel by trains, planes, and automobiles. We ignore that bad things can happen when we climb out of bed in the morning, take a shower, or drive our car. We take risks when we eat out, fall in love, have a baby, buy any product, choose an occupation, or pick a doctor, lawyer, or accountant.

Our wealth is always at some risk as well. Even the investment of money hazards its devaluation. If you put your savings in the safest possible investment, you will usually lose some money through inflation. And any more promising venture carries a higher chance of risk as well as of reward.

In a sense, then, we're all gamblers, whether or not we think of ourselves as risk takers. So we might as well accept it and try to manage it.

One way to do so is to avoid extremes. We don't have to smoke or drink if we find ourselves inclined to do such things excessively. We don't need to abuse drugs. Hard as it may be, we can cut out such activities completely, if necessary. We can avoid dangerous avocations like solo mountain climbing, decompression scuba diving, or hang gliding. It is especially easy to avoid certain extremes if we can keep the activities involving them at a distance. It is easier not to smoke cigarettes when not confronted by them. The cigarette ban in public places has helped us New York City doctors get our patients off cigarettes. Even casinos now have smoke-free slot rooms with, we hope, machines that pay off at a rate equal to those in the smoking sections (where ideally—to support abstention from tobacco— they should pay out less and advertise the fact). Alcohol is harder to avoid, but one doesn't have to drink at all if to do so is risky to one's well-being.

Certain other activities that are harmful when done to excess—like eating, shopping, or exercising—cannot be given up altogether, for obvious reasons. One can only hope to minimize their risks by doing them in moderation.

Slot-machine playing offers its own set of challenges when it comes to risk. The very fact of luck may inspire slot play, not to speak of other forms of gambling. Slot playing is no more physically hazardous than daily living and presents no unusual challenges to those with special physical limitations. True, the unavoidability of risk in life is not a justification for adding slot playing to one's recreation, but just because slots are risky is not a reason to renounce them.

One way to moderate your slot play is to keep casinos at a distance. Simple proximity and ease of access are major factors in an individual increasing his or her slot-machine gambling. Psychiatric studies of the effect of a new casino sometimes use a fifty-mile radius as a limit of nearness. Avoiding casinos has become more difficult as they have begun to sprout up everywhere. Because of ease of access, online gambling may be the most risky for gambling addiction: It is a casino in one's home, on one's personal computer. Many online gambling companies are based in the Caribbean and have London offices. They were doing $5.4 billion of business a year at the time of a Bloomberg report in 2009, and regulating them has been problematic. In September 2006, as part of a safe port bill, the U.S. government moved to make it illegal for banks and credit-card companies to process Internet gambling payments. This comes as no surprise, considering how this prohibition benefits our brick-and-mortar (or should I say gold-and-marble) casinos.

One should endeavor to travel some distance to indulge one's slot-playing pleasures. Distance is a deterrent—and a moderator. If one must endure the temptation of a casino next door, one might try to convince oneself that there is something boring about it and that another gambling venue at a respectable distance is preferable or a special treat. Even with inflated gasoline prices, one can drive a great distance for far less than one can lose in the time it takes to do so. And just as with cocaine or cigarettes, the longer a gambler spends away from gambling, the more the urge to return is reduced. Unlike addictions to fast-acting drugs, in which a stimulating rush occurs when an addict returns to them after abstaining, with slots there seems to be no initial rush, and some time is required for even a formerly habitual player to get back to his or her previous state.

THE PLEASURE OF THE LESSER MACHINES

The slot-machine experience by design encourages one to gamble larger amounts in the hope of bigger wins, which can eventually bring an intoxicating rush of adrenaline. The feeling can resemble the effect of cocaine or the autointoxication of the manic phase of bipolar mood illness. This can and should be avoided. One way to do this, if you have smaller amounts to play or have been losing too much, is to switch to a lower-denomination machine or one with a lower top payoff. Instead of those with progressives, find one with a top payoff of 2,500 credits or less. Play a Purple Passion two-credit machine, for example, in which the top wager is 50 cents, with a top yield of 1,600 25-cent credits, or $400, if three Purple Passion doubling logos come up. With a small investment, the more penurious slot fan can play such a 50-cent machine so many times that the odds for the machine are overwhelmed and some semblance of a large win can result—such as triple bars and a doubling logo for 160 credits, or 2 doubling logos and a 7 for 640 credits. A big loser can rescue some dignity at such a machine, feel relatively flush, and play longer with a reduced stash. But playing lesser machines long enough, will eventually empty any hoard, just as dripping water eventually wears away the substance of a rock.

Continually playing as fast as one can result in approximately 3 spins per ten seconds, or 18 spins per minute, or 1,080 spins per hour, minus the time required to feed more cash or coupons into the machine, the time for the machine to count up winning spins, any bonus-round delays, and the slowness built into some machines like the Triple Diamond Deluxe, in which certain symbols that land above or below the pay line move on to the pay line in a secondary motion. Not counting these subtractions, which delay monetary input, machines can differ greatly in their payout, depending on what they demand in the way of the denomination and number of coins played. Many players may not notice there is a CHANGE BET key, usually to the left on the control panel, with which one can bet as little as one credit. One may switch around among different bets if one finds that amusing. One should note on multiline machines that in lowering the bet one may be sacrificing possible wins on some of the lines that crisscross the screen and can be visualized only with the SEE PAYS display. Inserting fewer than the maximum number of coins is usually not recommended, because certain jackpots, bonuses, or higher rates of payouts are then missed, and players can't take full advantage of the precalculated statistical payout rate. An exception to this rule is machines with no third-credit jackpot and with linear—that is, exactly proportionate—payoffs for playing the second or third credit. To put this another way, machines in which the possible rewards for the second and third credit are, respectively, simply twice and three times the possible reward for playing the first credit do not penalize submaximal spins. An example is the IGT Double Diamond Haywire two-credit $1 machine on which hitting three double diamonds is rewarded with $800 when playing with one credit and with $1,600 when playing with two credits. One might as well play twice as long on one-credit spins or invest half as much. Even on a machine that pays a premium for that second or third credit, the markup may not be that spectacular and may involve only the extremely unlikely topmost spin. Of course, if there is a large progressive, part of the attraction is playing the max while fantasizing that you'll win it. It's always a good idea to read the fine print of the pay table carefully, even if it's not immediately visible and must be opened up for display on a video screen. For example, the Bally Stars & Bars Quick Hits Progressive machine at the Yonkers Raceway Racino announces, "All Wagers Contribute to Progressive." That's great, but on opening the pay table one learns that one must play the maximum credits to have even a chance to win the progressive.

The following table shows the average hourly tab required to play various machines, taking into account the 5 percent net cost of feeding credits through a machine with a 95 percent rate of return:

Name	Denom- ination	Max. Coins Played	X 1080 spins/ hour	95%	5%
Purple Passion	$0.25	2	$540	$513	$27
Triple Double Diamond	$0.25	3	$810	$769.5	$40.50
Five Times Pay	$0.25	5	$1,350	$1,282.50	$67.50
Purple Passion	$0.50	3	$1,620	$1,539	$81
Triple Double Diamond	$1.00	3	$3,240	$3,078	$162

The percentages in the right-hand columns are statistical averages that obtain only after long periods of play, longer than it would be practical for anyone to persist. But they give some idea of the ratios between the types of machines. Also, keep in mind that 95 percent is a very good machine return and, unless advertised, is unlikely to be found. In the short run, much less money is likely to be retained, although highly unlikely big wins could occur. Big jackpots, when offered, must also be factored in.

Intelligent management of your resources would include playing the less-demanding machines. Thrilling bigger wins will usually be a lot more expensive to arrive at, and longer in coming.

Rob, an affable retired pipe fitter who has wondered whether he should consult Gamblers Anonymous about his twice-a-week slot playing at Mohegan Sun, is grateful that he can play the Atronic Magic Woods penny slots game "all day" for 21 cents a spin. Rob likes to talk about other people's superstitions, like touching the screen in various ways before a spin. Equating superstition to religion, he adds that "all religion is man-made," that it "has caused a lot of trouble in the world," and that loneliness is a big problem for many slot players. He says that people should balance their trancelike focus on the machines with socializing with one another.

ALTERNATING BETS

Another way of economizing and breaking the trance by focusing one's attention is to place one forefinger on the MINIMUM BET button and one on the MAXIMUM BET button, or at least a somewhat larger one, then alternate bets on succeeding spins according to one's whim. This will not increase your chance of winning, but it creates some self-imposed drama, allows you to relish when a win occurs with the larger bet or doesn't with the lesser, and balances somewhat your chagrin when a win occurs with the lesser bet or doesn't with the larger.

AVOID PLAYING ALONE

Much like drinking alone, playing slot machines all by yourself should be avoided if possible. This may seem a contradiction, as slot play is so individual and, some would say, so self-stimulating. The play's the thing that's so compelling. But the presence of a spouse, sibling, or friend nearby provides a beneficial deterrent to isolation and excess. With a companion, there is twice the chance that one of you will become bored, tired, or hungry, and will want to leave, taking the other along. The isolating power of the slots is so great that many do not observe the play of others, even companions. Some arrange to meet at intervals and have a fail-safe rendezvous if they lose each other, thus avoiding the lost-guest paging booth. Cell phones are not always audible on the slot floor. A spouse who is winning may be willing to share with a partner who is losing, if only to forestall unhappiness and the desire to head home while the winning spouse wants to continue playing. They can agree ahead of time to stop when either runs out of a preallotted stake, although this may be hard to stick to if one runs out of money much earlier than the other. Another way of cutting losses is for one member of the couple to watch while the other plays, a strategy one sees practiced by young lovers. Often this doesn't last, because it's less fun to watch than to play, even when one is sharing the winnings. Another trick is to switch places frequently, although doing so means resisting the superstition that changing players means changing the luck on the machine. One can feel guilty taking over when a machine is "hot" and has had a run of luck, or resentful when it's "cold." It may be wiser to switch machines as one changes places with one's partner.

Because you are alone in a crowd when playing slots, slots can be a refuge for the lonely. You can strike up fragmentary conversations with your neighbors, but these seldom last long because slot players are so . . . busy. On the other hand, players never mind helping one another understand a machine. If the solitary player comes and goes on a bus, conversations may be possible, but most buses from the Port Authority in New York to Atlantic City are silent in both directions, whatever the variations in mood, and the operator usually insures the lights over the seats can't be turned on so as to permit most passengers to sleep on the way home. A casino outing for the assisted-living crowd is somewhat more communal because the riders know one another. Whether or not they remain together during their slot play, they lunch together and compare war stories on the way home.

In some circumstances, though, gambling with a friend or relative can work against sensible play. Should one's companion win big, this may stir up feelings of envy or competitiveness that may cause one to play less sensibly.

PLAY OUT YOUR TIME, NOT YOUR MONEY

When you consider your next visit to the slot casino, think of setting a time limit. This will enable you to have as much fun as possible and little in the way of painful losses. It swaps a positive goal for the unsaid one of getting rid of the money you brought with a preplanned limit or, worse, hitting the ATM for more cash to lose. Casinos provide alternatives to gambling like fine dining, spas, and exercise facilities, together with entertainment that, while pricey, is a bargain compared with gambling. At Foxwoods, the aptly named Paragon Restaurant, on the twenty-fourth floor, offers first-rate cuisine and a pleasant atmosphere. When my wife and I dined there, I had the peach soup and the Australian abalone special, and she had a crab salad and tournedos. We each had wine and coffee, and shared a lemon soufflé. With attentive service and the chef's extras, this took more than an hour and a half, and cost, with tip, $277.64. A year later we returned and for a similar amount had a Caesar salad prepared at our table, a rack of lamb, and a Kobe steak filet. Two people playing 25-cent slots could easily exceed what we spent in the same amount of time. Equally tasty are the young chix lobsters at $25 each offered by the Summer Shack at Mohegan Sun. I usually order two, an indulgence to be sure, but eating them is labor intensive and takes a long time. I figure I could keep eating chix lobsters on and on and spend less money than I would playing slots for the same amount of time.

Once, when I was driving from New York to Boston, I decided to stop and take advantage of a $59 overnight room offer by Mohegan Sun, where Billiards International was presenting the Challenge of Champions in the Wolf Den Arena. There was no charge for this event, which lasted all evening, with the Taiwanese player Fong-Pang Chao finally defeating the German champion, Thomas Engert. I was rapt watching these players run the table against each other with impossible shots once either gained the slightest edge out of the break. The prize was $50,000, winner take all. Their steely calm was impressive. There is, by the way, a Run the Table slot where you can simulate that billiard feat—or not—in the bonus round. I didn't play a cent that night, ate dinner very late, and went to bed. After an early swim in the pool the next morning, I was back on the road, having dropped a token $30 into the machines on the way to my car.

Another way to manage time is to look for slower ways to play and still enjoy it. Video poker games deal hands that require deciding which cards to hold or discard. This small piece of strategy means waiting for the discarded cards to be replaced and slows play by at least half so that playing takes twice the time. It also interferes somewhat with the meditative quality of the slot experience. Play can also be slowed by using machines that take coins rather than tickets, if you can still find them. Yet another way is to keep a log of what the machine is doing over time. Enter a record of each row of symbols that appears, and of the amounts won and lost. Remember that no machine subtracts your wager from the amount of the "win."

BREAKING THE SPELL OF SLOT PLAY

Reflecting on one's play—along with analyzing and recording its results—not only slows things down; it also breaks the spell. And it changes you from the guinea pig into the experimenter. This small difference gives you an exhilarating sense of control over your fate. That's one of the points of this book—to empower yourself. Even with slots, the truth shall set you free.

HOW MUCH SLOT PLAY IS TOO MUCH?

Like alcohol, gambling and slots play have become part of the fabric of American society. True, only a small proportion of slot players become slotoholics, so to speak, just as only a few consumers of alcoholic beverages become problem drinkers. Still, addiction to slot playing can be a real problem. Both the American Psychiatric Association and the American College of Psychiatrists have traditionally refused to hold their annual conventions in Las Vegas for fear of seeming to endorse a behavior that can become pathological. Perhaps there is also concern that having succumbed to the charms of Las Vegas, fewer would attend the meeting's sessions. Many other medical associations do meet in Las Vegas, however, and in light of the growing popularity of casinos, the psychiatric associations may have to change their stance. After all, there are casinos in New Orleans, Vancouver, Montreal, and Palm Springs, and on ships that cruise out of Port Everglades in the Miami–Fort Lauderdale area, all recent sites of major psychiatric meetings. And, if present trends continue, slots will be harder and harder to avoid.

Psychiatrists are concerned about pathological gambling for good reasons. Like James Caan in the premonitory film *The Gambler* (as opposed to his sober return as the patriarchal casino owner in the hit television series *Las Vegas*), pathological gamblers can bring ruin to themselves and their families. The most severe cases are easy to identify by their deficit financing. ATMs provide easy access to cash and casinos offer credit lines. But no casino wants the reputation of encouraging a social evil, especially when already they are said to have a license to print money. They don't want to end up like the tobacco and liquor companies, having to speak out of both sides of their mouths in commercials simultaneously encouraging indulgence and warning against its ill consequences. Casinos even allow problem gamblers to elect voluntary self-exclusion, relying on the casinos' facial recognition software to be refused admission if they have a weak moment.

OF MACHINE BONDAGE

A number of signs indicate that one's slot play has gone too far. The first, the last, and every symptom in between is failing what can be called the human relations test. If slot play (like video gaming) has become a substitute for human connection, it has become too intrusive in one's life. Common examples are a couple on the way to visit one of their grown children who opt to patronize a casino instead, or anyone who skips an important family gathering to play the slots. In fact, excessive gambling is often linked to unsatisfactory relations with one's children. I've even heard of seniors who would rather give money to the slots than to their kids, reminding me of an elderly patient of mine many years ago who said she was so angry at her daughter that she would rather throw her money in the deep blue sea than leave it to her.

MENTAL SYMPTOMS OF OVERPLAYING

Looking forward to slot playing as the best thing in your future is not a good sign, either, suggesting that you need more in your life. Diminishing pleasure in gambling may be another bad sign of habituation, although it may also mean that you're ready to move on to some other activity in a healthy way. But I do not want to reduce involvement in slot playing to a simple pleasure principle, or to pathology. As I have described, the attraction to the slots is more complex.

Intrusion of visual imagery into everyday activities is another symptom. This was unabashedly—and supposedly lightheartedly—portrayed in Mohegan Sun television ads in which a man experiences a slot flashback while watching the numbers add up on a gasoline pump. He may be in trouble, as intrusive imagery of this sort can be a symptom of traumatic overexposure to the slots, much as for veterans of combat intrusive flashbacks are often a symptom of post-traumatic stress disorder (PTSD). The assertive tag line of the Mohegan Sun commercial, "You'll Come Back," is a little scary in its suggestion of a narcotics dealer who knows his customer is hooked.

FINANCIAL INDICATIONS OF OVERPLAYING

Here are some pocketbook symptoms of being addicted to slot machines:

- Bringing increasing amounts of money along on each successive trip and raising in one's mind the tolerable loss per trip.
- Not knowing or caring how much one has gambled, and misrepresenting the amount to others.
- Becoming jaded with lower-denomination machines and moving up to higher-limit slots that one previously would not have dared to play.
- Increasing the amount of cash and the denomination of the bills one is comfortable carrying around and willing to spend without inhibition.

- "Chasing wins," or compulsively continuing to play on until one wins again or loses significantly. (A Canadian brain-imaging study found that pathological gamblers activate a special area in the right frontal area of their cerebral cortex more often than do nonpathological gamblers.)
- "Chasing losses" compulsively, until one loses significantly or wins. (Brain imaging at Oxford University has shown that excessive loss-chasing activates motivation-and-reward areas in the brain, and that deciding to stop when one has chased and lost activates the anterior cingulate—what I've called the brain's money belt). Near misses (7, 7, and 7 off the payline) activate the brains of pathological gamblers more like a win, and non-pathological gamblers (correctly) like a loss, according to a 2010 Illinois study.
- Deteriorating self-care or hygiene. (David A. Goldberg's *Stupidity and Slot Machine Players in Las Vegas*, the previously mentioned misanthropic book by a former slot attendant, describes players who would rather urinate in their clothes than leave a machine.)

IT ISN'T ALWAYS ABOUT THE MONEY

Although money is important, for many slot players other criteria matter more. Most slot players are relatively affluent, especially if they're seniors, and they're unlikely in any case to gamble away the last of their Social Security checks. While many will run out of energy first, because very attentive slot playing can be as tiring as driving a car and emotionally taxing as well, others find it relaxing and conducive to meditation. They don't seem to care whether they win or lose; it's the action that amuses them, and they are as happy with the lowest-denomination machines. An article in *The New York Times* of June 24, 2010, by Douglas Quenqua, describes the slot machines called pachislos in Japan, where gambling is illegal. Often featuring American pop themes like Harley motorcycles, Sylvester Stallone's character Rambo, or President Obama, they evade the gambling prohibition by having a manual stop-wheel button that suggests a skill may be involved. Token operated and not played for cash, these machines appear to be as hypnotic to their glassy-eyed habitués as were pachinkos, their predecessors.

SPENDING ONE'S TIME

Another symptom of excessive slot play might be considered wasting one's time. But different players attribute different significance to time. Many older people have too much time—although time goes much faster when one is older—and nobody worries about them watching too much television or in general wasting their dwindling time on Earth. So what's the harm if they're occupied by slots? Younger players may say that slot playing is a recreation that takes up no more time than they can spare from their busier lives. But many of us might profitably ask whether we could do something better with the time spent on slots. We might advance our careers if we are still working, continue our educations as "lifetime learners," or devote ourselves to charitable service or to creative activities like writing memoirs or painting. We might even travel. Most satisfying is figuring out how to be good company for other people and of use to one's community.

MEDICATION CAN HELP SEVERE CASES

Two large national surveys discussed by Wendy S. Slutsky, Ph.D., in *The American Journal of Psychiatry* have shown that pathological gambling is rare in this country (it affects just 0.4 to 0.8 percent of the population), and that 36 to 39 percent of this group reported that they no longer had gambling-related problems in the year prior to the surveys. Only 7 to 12 percent had ever sought formal treatment or attended Gamblers Anonymous meetings. So one may conclude that natural recovery occurs in about one-third of pathological gamblers, for reasons that are not understood. Howard Shaffer, a professor at Harvard cited in a special report on gambling in *The Economist* of July 10, 2010, stated that the rate of pathological gambling in America has remained stable for thirty-five years, despite a spike in the early 1990s and all the new opportunities to gamble. This is not to deny that many more folks are gambling. Shaffer and his collaborators have made a number of interesting studies of gambling behavior, including on the Internet, which favors slot gambling. They have found evidence that exposure to casinos increases gambling, but that with time a mitigating adaptation also occurs. Progression to pathological gambling is predicted by emotional instability, by gambling to escape problems, and by getting others to pay for one's gambling. There is no evidence that pathological gambling cannot be ameliorated. Those who quit often showed higher losses just before quitting, but also a tendency to favor shorter odds rather than chase longer ones.

Very severe pathological gambling may be helped by psychiatric medications that treat what psychiatrists call obsessive-compulsive behavior, which entails excessive focusing on things and feeling compelled to act in certain ways in relation to them. The behavior defies all inner resistance, is repetitive, and tends to be rigidly limited to certain activities. An example would be continually washing and scrubbing oneself or one's home, or counting involuntarily and ritually, so that the obsessive person has difficulty paying attention to a conversation because he must, for example, count the slats in the venetian blinds. Obsessive-compulsive people may suffer terrible anxiety if prevented from completing their ritual behaviors. Freud once said that while paranoia, or viewing the world suspiciously, is like a parody of a philosophy, obsessiveness, in its ritualistic devotions, is like a parody of a religion. Once again we are reminded that slot gambling, as it approaches obsessive-compulsive behavior, becomes more and more like the practice of spiritual rites.

The medications we psychiatrists use work in the synapse, or gap, where one nerve cell in the brain connects to another and transmits thought activity by releasing little packets of a signaling chemical called, not surprisingly, a neurotransmitter. This chemical crosses the gap and is received by other specially shaped chemical molecules on the surface of the next cell, thereby completing the circuit. Because this transmission is not a one-shot deal—thought and feeling must go on, after all—following transmission other chemicals called enzymes clear away the neurotransmitter so that the receptors are open to await another transmission. In people with obsessive gambling problems or a host of other out-of-control habits that are hard to stop, one of the signaling neurotransmitters, called serotonin, is in too-short supply in the synapse.

The medications used to treat this problem are called selective serotonin reuptake inhibitors, or SSRIs for short. They inhibit or decrease the effects of the enzymes that clear away the neurotransmitter serotonin, so that it can stay in play longer. There are other medications that work on other neurotransmitters, but serotonin is an important one for a sense of well-being and for avoiding harm. Without enough of it in play, people may become searching, yearning, disconsolate, unhappy compulsive gamblers. Some of the medications are Prozac (fluoxetine), Paxil (paroxetine), Zoloft (sertraline), Remeron (mirtazepine), Celexa (citalopram), Lexapro (escitalopram), Anafranil (clomipramine), and Luvox (fluvoxamine). You must consult a physician to get them, and they do not work until taken for a week or so, or sometimes even for months. Chronic gamblers have low levels of the neurotransmitter norepinephrine, too, and norepinephrine reuptake inhibitors are also available. A current experimental approach, reported by J. D. Grant, M.D., a psychiatrist at Brown University, in *The American Journal of Psychiatry*, employs nalmefene, a long-acting medication that opposes the opioid receptors in the brain that are active in addictions, including alcoholism. A low 100-milligram-a-day dose is recommended to avoid side effects, including damage to the liver.

If there are medications that reduce pathological slot playing and other gambling, a curious person might wonder if there are substances that can cause or increase pathological gambling. And indeed there are. Generally they are biologically active substances that increase another neurotransmitter, one associated with novelty seeking, pleasure enhancement, movement motivation, and risk taking. This is dopamine. Amphetamines and other stimulants boost this substance. While hyperactive children paradoxically are quieted by such stimulants and helped by them to concentrate on their schoolwork, if you are an adult with an adult brain, you are better off not taking an amphetamine before a big test, because, although your brain may be sped up, you may find yourself unreasonably confident and feel encouraged to guess wildly. Cocaine users, too, get amped up because of an amphetamine-like effect. Pathological gamblers show frontal-lobe functional impairment similar to metamphetamine-dependent persons. I have even seen patients complain of mildly excessive gambling while taking the antidepressant Wellbutrin (bupropion), which has a slight dopamine-stimulating effect. Perhaps dopamine's most dramatic effect is on people with Parkinson's disease, a condition in which insufficient dopamine is produced in the brain. Parkinson's patients are slow and stiff in their movements, and they are notably sober and risk averse. A paper by Dr. Erika Driver-Dunckley, a neurologist, reported that one class of the medications they receive, called dopamine agonists (Mirapex, or pramipexole; Requip, or ropinirole; and Permax, or pergolide), when taken in high doses produced a remarkable effect on people with Parkinson's. Within a year of the time casinos became available to them, these normally sober and temperate patients experienced an increase in both casino gambling and single-day money losses. The agonists work by stimulating the dopamine receptors. In this study no patients on only Sinemet (levodopa), which is converted into dopamine in the brain, experienced this symptom, but many patients today receive a combination of levodopa and an agonist. Dr. Valerie Voon, in a similar 2006 survey, found that patients taking dopamine agonists preferred slot machines to table games, and each lost an average of $100,000. Dr. Oksana Sucherowsky, in another 2006 study, echoed Dr. Voon's finding that 6 percent of Parkinson's patients exhibited pathologic gambling (compared with 1 to 2 percent of the general population). Dr. Sucherowsky recommended warning patients about gambling when prescribing these medications. Because dopamine agonists are also helpful in treating the sleep-disturbing restless legs syndrome, a recent television ad blitz on this common disorder is likely to yield a new group prone to gambling as a side effect—as may a proposed new medication to enhance female sexual drive, which also focuses on dopamine as one of its neurotransmitter targets.

Jaak Panksepp, a prominent neuroscientist with psychoanalytic training known in the popular press for his studies of laughter in nonhuman animals, has linked the brain's dopamine system with the basic human phenomenon of seeking. Seek and ye shall find, the saying goes. Seek in excess and ye shall find yourself gambling. In any case, if it is risky to drink alcohol while gambling, taking stimulants may be much more risky.

Most medications work better when you are undergoing some sort of treatment, especially psychotherapy that specifically addresses your problems. There are many types of therapy that can be helpful. The suggestions that follow are largely cognitive-behavioral, a form of therapy that tries to help people to alter their ways of thinking and behaving.

The machines are winning.

GIVING ONE'S INNER CHILD
SOMETHING ELSE TO DO

BREAKING DOWN THE SLOT EXPERIENCE INTO ITS
ELEMENTS TO FIND SUBSTITUTE ACTIVITIES

Psychiatrists and psychologists often suggest activities to replace one that has become troublesome because of its pathological intensity. This happens because of the tenacity of our minds. Slot gambling sticks there. We have seen that its visual aspects even recur as flashbacks. It's hard to stop thinking of an elephant once its image is suggested. But it's easier to stop thinking of an elephant by substituting a giraffe. The best substitute activities are those that resemble as closely as possible what they replace. In order to find substitutes for the slot experience, we need to dissect it. One element is the obsessive pleasure of lining things up and thus establishing order out of chaos. Another is the discovery of something rare and valuable. Casino trappings and the prospect of jackpots prompt fantasies of royalty or wealth. Many people see a gambling machine as an authority and view winning and losing as a judgment. Still others, in search of love and community, seek comfort in the slots' reward systems and promises of entry into elite slot-gambling circles. Some feel enhanced by association with celebrities and by the sense of wonder and majesty that casinos try to inspire.

I shall discuss each of these elements and suggest activities to replace them. Among them will be slot-simulating computer games, hobbies and pastimes that offer similar mental rewards, and places and things in the world with more genuine value. Most important, by fully comprehending the components of religious worship in slot play, one can render unto Caesars Palace the things which are Caesars Palace's and keep for one's personal religion that which rightfully belongs to oneself. I would not urge people into therapy or toward medication, although those possibilities exist and may be helpful, too.

WHY BRIDGE IS DIFFERENT

First, let me give an example of what you are *not* looking for as a substitute for playing. The game of bridge is diametrically opposed to slot playing in many ways, even emotionally. With slot machines, there is minimal strategy; deciding how many credits to play or moving to another machine often has no basis in logic. In contrast, bridge is all strategy, based on a multitude of mathematical probabilities. When I asked Gail Greenberg, a bridge world champion, about the mental state of bridge players, she emphasized how vigilant and busy one is with the many simultaneous tasks that must be done, among them having a sense of the cards played, assessing the probabilities of which cards lie in your partner's and the other team's hands, and judging the many directions in which the play may go. Gail never gets nervous while playing, but many beginning and even experienced players do. They describe the sort of tension you might feel walking a tightrope. One false step drops you drastically "down," or below your contract, especially if you have made a risky bid. Often when you lose, the fault is yours or your partner's, and this may lead to a meltdown, or blaming. Some consider it a mistake to play with your spouse as your partner. By contrast, people playing slots are relaxed. They don't have to perform or compete, and whether they win or lose, they are not judged except by themselves—and, of course, whatever divine powers they choose to believe are acting upon their slot play.

ORDER OUT OF CHAOS

For slot players who take visual satisfaction in seeing the symbols lined up, a substitute activity might be collecting something that involves forming patterns or filling in spaces, like toy soldiers, sets of dishes or silverware, coins, or postage stamps. While any such hobbies can be reasonably priced, they can get as expensive as gambling, even if considered investments. Many video games, like Tetris, feature fitting things together neatly. Bowling is also about order, aggressively knocking the neatly arranged pins down. But then they are all set up again, so one's aggression is safely erased and can be expressed again. Table setting, flower arranging, gardening, and topiary can be satisfying forms of patterning—as can watching chorus lines, drill teams, and marching bands.

REPLACING THE RHYTHM OF THE REELS

Slot players often become spellbound by the rhythm of the play. Some casinos, such as Atlantis on Paradise Island in the Bahamas, take into account a player's rate of slot play in doling out complimentary rewards. The speed limit is obviously the maximum at which the machine can be played, which is about equal to the rate of relaxed breathing. A long losing spell or switching to a very high-limit slot may slow play or even grind it to a halt. But usually play assumes a monotonous rhythm punctuated only by the machine's rewards, whose amount and frequency can vary enormously. This repetition, with its waterfall-like cascade of symbols, is soothing. As I noted earlier, few machines have symbols that spin upward, although some games from Aristocrat depict a spectacular fountain of coins shooting up at payouts and cash-outs, and Houdini has a bonus feature that revolves like a lock. Many older people do not raise their eyes easily, so it may be both unexpected and reassuring that something coming rapidly from above stops straight ahead on the pay line.

The pleasure one derives from the soothing rhythm can be replaced in many ways. Sound-generating machines can help one relax to the sound of ocean surf, or a waterfall, or raindrops, or the human heartbeat, which we all heard in our mothers' wombs and is known to be soothing even to the adult ear. All music has a rhythm, and with those ever-shrinking gadgets one can go around with one's ears plugged with sound. The repetitious slot action can be reproduced at home with simulations and a host of other computer games that have monotonous repetitive play.

Nonelectronic repetitive pastimes like knitting may be best of all. A surprising number of men find knitting relaxing. The ancient activity of weaving is repetitive, creative, and satisfying.

Members of Pennsylvania Dutch Amish communities find solace in rhythmic chores that do not involve electric power, such as stitching quilts. What reader of Tolstoy's *Anna Karenina* can forget the pleasure Levin takes in mowing with the peasants when he stops thinking about how to work his scythe and gives himself over to the "unconscious" rhythmic pleasure of the task. Weed whack manually, rake leaves, or shovel snow.

In slot tournaments the participants pound the button madly for five minutes because there is no cost for each press, and they want to trigger the machine the moment its latency from the last spin ends. These contests reward the highest score along a bank of machines that have been adjusted to an unrealistic tournament mode in which many high-paying results occur. Slot tournaments are frantic and tiring, and they subject their players to the risk of repetitive stress injuries. Their pace does not permit meditative play.

REAL WORLDS AND ARTIFICIAL WORLDS

Earlier I compared Bellagio the casino and Bellagio the truly Elysian municipality on Lake Como in Italy. Casinos, like theme parks before them, and like Ripley's Believe It or Not! and P. T. Barnum's before *them*, seek to bring home the faraway, exotic, and truly valuable things on Earth—but in predigested and prefabricated form. Many Americans prefer these *Reader's Digest* condensed places to the real thing. Their proximity and lack of need to know a foreign language also appeals to them. Whether adventurous citizens of the world like them or not, ersatz environments are poised to expand enormously. Virtual environments built upon the technologies of video-game computing will allow players to participate with a much greater sense of reality. Casino machines have already begun to employ these technologies, and ever more seductive machine environments are on the way. (Meanwhile, we have the paradox of the casinos' exotic exteriors and their interiors filled with machines whose retro themes often reassure senior players who are familiar with television programming.) As a physician devoted to healing, I am among the first to grant that a life in front of the slots, as in front of the television, can be enriching for those who have trouble getting around or who might elsewhere be preoccupied with their infirmity and mortality. And who am I to deny that the real world these days, with its economic uncertainty and threats of terrorism, can be unbearably daunting? But from time to time mightn't it be worthwhile to divert one's gaze from both TV and the slot wheels and to consider the world's many other pleasures? Don't forget that numerous travel destinations have casinos, too, and if you choose to sail to them, you can enjoy the casinos on board en route to more real things in other interesting places.

That new-car smell that greets one at the entryway to some casinos is pleasant to be sure, but let the memory of fresh air and the brightness of the sun help draw you to the exit, especially toward evening, when the rooms get smokier and the corridors more fetid. Casinos are most pleasant in the early morning, when there are more free machines and fewer people to block your way to them. They advertise morning play to

The air in casinos smells sweet, but outside it is sweeter.

seniors. The staff is fresh and more open to make small talk as they serve you coffee and hot chocolate, or as they pay out large winnings. In the sparsely populated rooms, even a smoker of cigars doesn't impose on others as much. One feels unhurried and flush with the stake one has brought. And the press of the crowds that arrive by the afternoon may lead you to play less wisely, especially at popular machines, where others wait their turn behind you while you play them.

SLOT-MACHINE SIMULATIONS

If you are unfamiliar with slot machines or want to cut back play, simulations can be useful. If you are trying to learn, you can play simulations to get a feel for how slots work, free of people watching you, the tension of the casino, or the fear of losing money. Compact discs simulating either traditional electromechanical reel machines or video slots in various denominations, including nickel slots, are available. In Appendix I I have compared the results of simulated and actual slot play. Yechiam Yemini, a professor of computer science at Columbia University whose graduate course on neural networks I audited, says one should always choose the simplest demonstration of a principle. When you look at the comparative tables, you might say with justice, "Ho hum," given that not much happened with either the simulation or the real machine trials—because neither netted a spectacular big win. Boring results like these are relatively probably and typical, and the few play sequences undertaken here were the only ones I did for the demonstration. In other words, I didn't do a lot of trial sequences, and then select unsurprising ones to make a point.

Many actual casino slots are available in simulations, and they mimic very closely what the player experiences on the casino floor, except for the paying in and paying out. Some also offer the option of adjusting the payout rate to "True" or "Extra High," so you can either get a feel for the actual game or have the fun of seeing more of the features and of winning the payouts (and even the jackpots) more frequently. The simulations are pleasing if you just like the rhythm of play or are interested in experimenting with what you could expect if you played the real thing. They can also be sobering if you keep track of how much imaginary money you are betting. Another benefit is that you can learn a great deal about yourself even if the money involved isn't real: how cautiously or rashly you're inclined to bet, whether you escalate your limits, and how you feel about losing. Some may keep playing just to activate some feature available only at a secondary level of play to see what it is like free of charge. Whatever the reason for your simulated play—to learn what slots are like, to feel more in charge of your play, or to help you withdraw from the real thing—remember that the difference between the real and the pretend experience can be deceptive and that returning to a real casino can affect you like real coffee after decaffeinated—or gin instead of water! Play the simulations as a substitute to your heart's content.

COIN OF THE REALM

Sandor Ferenczi, a member of Sigmund Freud's early circle of Viennese psycho-analysts, described how all of us as children become interested in money. He started with the observation that all animals, including baby humans, are fascinated with their bowel movements, even with the smell. But civilized society demands hygiene in toilet matters, so, as Ferenczi pointed out, under the pressure of civilization personified by our parents, we sublimate our interest in feces through a sequence of substitutions. Our parents say "ugh" or "yucky" or "dirty" so many times that we adopt their attitude of disgust. We first reject the odor and warmth of feces and substitute a love of mud, which may resemble deodorized, cold feces that can be played with. Next to go are the brown color and the moisture; with them gone, the era of the sandbox begins. The child is then sifting deodorized, decolorized, and dehydrated feces.

Stones and other objects like buttons, bottle caps, and badges are the next substitution, in which softness and malleability are given up for hardness. The final transformation is to coins and jewels, which symbolize feces deodorized, decolorized, dehydrated, and cold—even icy cold in the case of diamonds which are able to shine and reflect light away from themselves. What is worthless to society and valuable to the baby has become, by means of this series of symbolic substitutions, valuable enough to the adult to be kept on one's person rather than gotten rid of. The denial of the infantile interest in feces is now complete and disguised as the valuing of something seemingly opposite in every way. In Freudian psychoanalytic theory, opposite extremes of the same qualities are recognized as having in common positions on a single continuum and therefore considered symbolically the same. Even when abstracted into credit-card payments or casino slot tickets, money retains this residue of the sweet smell of (potty) success.

Because they are still the baby's first possession and first loving gift to its parents, feces remain the model for all subsequent possessions of value. I once made a study of attitudes toward money in suburban children and found that they equated it largely with love. In older people with senility, psychiatrists commonly observe excessive concerns with losing money or even wasting electricity, which may be a departure from a more generous younger self and a regression to a more infantile state. People who save all manner of useless things are sometimes called "anal retentive." This term recognizes an early childhood stage of regret over losing one's first bodily products. In its extreme form, this may manifest itself in a demented horror of flushing.

While plastic credit cards and other tokens have increasingly replaced coins and paper currency in everyday life, slot machines, at least until recently, emphasized the tangibility of money by dealing in coins. They all still take crisp paper currency.

One night not long ago, I handed a taxi driver a $10 bill that I had been given in change by another cabbie. As soon as his fingers closed on it, he said, "It's no good." I was amazed at his ability to detect in the dark what indeed turned out to be counterfeit, since I couldn't tell that it was different from any other $10 bill. Neither could my friend Kevin O'Connor, a bond dealer who collects rare currency. Nor could my brother Paul, who has served as the chief financial officer of several corporations, and used to dole out cash to clients at a talent agency. But when I took the bill to one of my favorite Chinese restaurants and asked the manager to examine it, she and the staff were amused that I would have any trouble detecting that it was phony. They showed me numerous ways they could tell, from running it between their fingers, snapping it with a fingernail and hearing the sound it made, and smelling it to all sorts of printing details, and finally the color a line of special ink turned when it was drawn on with a pen. I sometimes tell this story to medical students to teach them the value of careful observation in making diagnoses.

My point here is that people who handle money all the time become aware of its tangible qualities. Slot players become particularly sensitive to coins and tokens. This can lead to strange attitudes. While some grow to like touching the coins, others begin to abhor them, particularly because their fingers may take on a grayish discoloration from the silver. Many even begin to notice impulses that psychoanalysts refer to as the return of the repressed. They begin to attach to the coins the disgust they were taught to have for their feces. They then find themselves paradoxically wanting to get rid of the coins that have collected in their pan by putting them in the slot, almost as if they were flushing them down the toilet like a good child seeking parental praise.

The electronic tickets that now are rapidly replacing coins in about 90 percent of the 900,000 North American slot machines, allowing players to avoid the touch of coins, have produced mixed consequences. Practically, the tickets are rendering slot attendants and change persons obsolete. At Foxwoods, the slot attendants now appear only for a hand pay, when the $1,200 tax-reportable limit is reached. Mohegan Sun sets a lower limit of $500, presumably to keep more attendants working receiving tips. For whatever reason, some players cling to the coin machines, and so some casinos retain coin machines for them. Atlantic City's oldest casino, Resorts, is cautiously reintroducing coin-operated slots in the hope of pleasing those who remember and prefer them. I saw one lady clutching a bucket of quarters and groaning when she saw a ticket come out of a Wheel of Gold machine. She told me that play with the tickets "goes too fast" compared with manually feeding coins. In any case, coins, gold, and jewels remain as featured symbols on many reels, and the machines that cash out in tickets still make a simulated coin-clanking sound.

Whatever you think of the theories of Freud and Ferenczi, it's a good idea to avoid real dirt by remembering not to touch one's eyes or nose with the same fingers you use to press the slot buttons or feed the coins. And wash your hands periodically, especially if *you* already have a cold. A study many decades ago in *The Lancet* found that lucre is really filthy with germs (the author generously offered to take any of the dangerous stuff off readers' hands).

COIN COLLECTING AS A SUBSTITUTE FOR SLOT PLAY

One of the better substitutes for slot playing may be coin collecting. My advisor on the fascination of coin collecting is the noted collector Allan H. Goldman. He says that that no matter how much one spends amassing a valuable collection, one gets to keep the coins, which is not true of the inveterate slot player. This virtue of collecting may be particularly appealing to slot players still attached to the unique feel of coins, especially now that it's hard to find a machine that accepts them. Slowing down and looking at the coins one handles can be a pleasant way to pursue the hobby. Moreover, it's a less-remote possibility than winning a jackpot that the coins you collect may have greater than face value, either because their value has increased over time or because they turn out to be rarities. For instance, until well into the twentieth century, the dollar slots were kicking Morgan silver dollars, issued from 1878 to 1921 and known to some as the "King of American Coins," some of which are now worth tens to hundreds of thousands of dollars, depending on their condition. (The American Numismatic Association grades coins from Damaged, through About Good, or heavily worn, all the way up to Mint Uncirculated and Proof, or specially made.) The 1893 San Francisco mint silver dollars are especially rare.

The point is that one need not go near a casino to engage

in prospecting with coins. One gets them in change all the time, one can order rolls of them from banks, one can buy brilliant uncirculated and proof examples from dealers or the U.S. Mint, and one can attend coin shows and "cherry-pick," or search through the boxes of miscellaneous coins that dealers often put out at their stands for that purpose, and with surprising frequency find the odd rarity. (Combing your fingers through these piles will remind you of raking the winnings in a slot pan.)

For more about coin collective, see the Appendix.

FOR THE BIRDS

I once thought bird-watching was a pastime for anti-social people. I couldn't have been more wrong—as it turns out, some of the most sociable people I know do it. Fifty million Americas watch birds, among our fastest growing outdoor activities. While it can be pursued in magnificent solitude for the meditating slot player, it can also bring people together in clubs and informal groups, to commune with nature and share the pleasures of the hunt—with a guidebook and camera in hand. Birding can be viewed as a form of gambling one's time with the very rarest birds as the jackpots. The quest for them can be sought near and far in the world on a shoestring. I particularly like the notion of bird-watching as a substitute for slot playing because it's in the nature of slot players to search for rare experiences. A related new pastime is geocaching. Using a global positioning system (GPS), players follow coordinates listed on a website to find cached logbooks (to record your discovery) and symbolic rewards that have been hidden in tins somewhere in the world. Once the rewards have been found, they are then replaced for other competitors. Geocaching is like a global treasure hunt. One warning to participants is that police have been aroused to suspicion by players turning up in out-of-the-way places with no apparent practical objective.

THE WHEELS GO ROUND AND ROUND

If your attraction to slots is the machines themselves, with their wheels that go round and round, you might take up model railroading as a replacement activity. This is another pastime that can bring you closer to God, in a sense, except that as a model railroader you don't so much commune with God as get to play God's role by assuming power over a world you've created. Your hands have shaped the dry lands, as the Scriptures put it. You decided where the tracks go, and you make the trains run on time. As the creator and prime mover of this world, you not only have power over it but also responsibility for its welfare. So, in a very limited sense, you get to understand God's problems. This may explain why some railroad modelers share their godliness, so to speak, by connecting with other modelers, exchanging trains with them as if they were connected by tracks from basement to basement across the country. For some possibly non-theological reason model railroading still attracts more men than women.

SEARCHING FOR AUTHORITY AND JUDGMENT

Life offers various substitutes for the authority some players attribute to slot machines. For those seeking judgment of their behavior that they findplaying the slots can confer, there is *Court TV* and the many other television shows featuring judges pronouncing guilt or innocence. The blind capriciousness of the courts, often referred to deprecatingly as casinos, has been portrayed by the blindfolded female figure of Justice holding her scales, a vivid metaphor that could be appropriated for slot machines. For those addicted to competitive winning and losing there are professional sports to follow: the Chicago Cubs baseball team for losers and the Boston Celtics basketball team for winners. Watching as well as participating can be stressful. When urine samples from male fans of the losing team have been analyzed right after a game, the amount of male hormone turns out to have dropped compared to that of winning fans. We suffer such deeply felt losses and testicular indignity because we learned to accept the absolute rules of games and sports when we became school-age children, a phase of development called latency because we shelve our romantic strivings (until puberty) and accept games as simplifications of the complexities of life. For those slot players who remain stuck emotionally at this stage, playing can be invested with portentous meaning out of proportion with real life.

FILLING THE GAPING HOLE

Max, a fifty-four-year-old clothier from the Detroit area who was playing slots beside me at the new Aria casino in Las Vegas, likes to discuss the machines. No wonder. He plays the slots four days a week and told me he was one of MGM Grand's top one thousand players. He has gambled since he was twenty-one, only on slots, and is "not a table man." Only in the last two and a half years, since his parents died within months of each other, has he become such a "driven" slot player, to use his term. He said he likes the "solitary confinement" of the slots. A single man, he compares a good slot experience to a good sexual response in a woman. Max wonders what it is about slot machines that so grips him. The youngest of three, he has an eldest brother who is a rabbi and not a gambler, but Max takes after his mother, a Holocaust survivor who played $5 and $10 slots for the last twenty years of her life. For Max, life was "all about work." He was "a successful retailer for forty years until the recent fall off." He describes himself as a driven worker both in business and in "gaming," which, since the death of his parents, makes him feel as if he is "filling a gaping hole." Max says he is a sensible gambler and knows "when to get off a streak, when the tumblers are not aligning." This metaphor suggests he views slot machines as safes, and indeed he thinks of them in rows he calls "banks." I found Max in the Aria, Las Vegas's newest casino, located in its ambitious City Center project, which President Obama visited while we were there in February 2010. The Aria is the most banklike casino of those I have visited: dark, gray, and metallic with rectangular columns of dark brown wood and steely accents under a high ceiling. Max prefers "urban" settings and describes the also recent, very up-scale Encore extension of the Wynn casino in Las Vegas, with its warm décor of red carpets and chandeliers, creamy pleated cloth and white slatted panels (an "encore" of Steve Wynn's successful new Macao venture, according to the manager of its distinctive Society Café), as "refined, stunning, elegant, for the quiet gambler—it lacks gambling energy and I wouldn't gamble ten cents there." On this visit Max had found the Bellagio casino to have "bad energy" and avoided it, except for its fabulous restaurants like Michael Mina, Picasso, Circo, and Yellowtail. Max feels he can intuit the energy in a slot machine or a "whole bank" of them. He believes slots "hit" most from 10:00 to 11:30 a.m., in the early evening hours, and especially from 2:00 to 3:00 a.m. When I asked why at those particular times, he said, "Because they got to pay out [sometime]." It is at this hour, he believes, that the gangsters come in to launder their cash, at least in Detroit. Although he agreed that slot players are nicer than craps players, he has seen a darker side of slot behavior in Detroit, where there is a frequently paid $750 fine for breaking the glass of a disappointing machine.

Max's biggest single win was $15,000, but in 2009 he fell and broke both his right shoulder and right arm, requiring surgery and a sling for six weeks, during which he had to switch to playing slots with his left hand. In a two-week period, he won $10,000, $8,000, and $4,000. "People asked me why I don't always play with my left hand," he said, "but I'm a creature of habit."

YOUR PERSONALITY AND YOUR PLAY EXPERIENCE

When a psychiatrist meets a new patient, the first few minutes reveal two dimensions of the patient's mind. One is the strength of personality organization, which shows whether the person is preponderantly normal, neurotic, borderline, or psychotic. From this the psychiatrist can judge the person's vulnerability to breakdown and assess how severely ill that person might be. The other dimension revealed is the individual's personality style, sometimes referred to as character *armor* because it involves the habitual defense in the face of new experiences that a person first develops in childhood. Both these dimensions are relevant to slot play. The first, personality organization, affects how reasonable the person's expectations may be, ranging from realistic to delusional. The second, personality style, shapes the player's interaction with slots and the casino personnel. Together they produce, as in all walks of life, a variety of playing types. Brief descriptions of the several types follow. The nicknames I've given them, obviously informal, are followed by the psychiatric terms.

- **The Fussbudget:** People with an *obsessive* personality meticulously control their feelings. They like precision, neatness, and order. They are often preoccupied with dilemmas of their own making that lie between two alternatives of their own making. They can spend hours playing in a retentively tight way, then bet rashly enough to squander their funds. Methodical and scientific in their approach to all things, even buttering their bread, they can be secretly superstitious, often about numbers. For them the slot machine is both a mysterious altar and a precision instrument, which leads them to devise complex rituals of play. They develop elaborate strategies, but favor simpler machines, especially ones with threes—three reels, triple 7s, or diamonds. They give tips that are either too small or too big. Many doctors and scientists are fussbudgets (among them the author, in case you hadn't guessed).
- **The Soap Star:** *Histrionic* people are as emotionally expressive as the fussbudgets are throttled down. Wishful,

dreamy people looking for love and romance, they see winning and losing as being favored or disfavored. Often charming and alluring, they can get petulant. They do not care much about money and can be extravagant, especially if caught up in the drama of the moment. Nor do they sweat details or care about small change. They see slots as shrines to celebrities or bottles containing genies, and prefer machines that refer to romantic tales or are centered on people with whom they can identify, like Betty Boop, *I Love Lucy*, Elvis, Cleopatra, and *I Dream of Jeannie*. They tend to be generous tippers unless they feel the waitperson is more attractive than they are.

- **The Sleuth:** *Paranoid* people are wary, vigilant, afraid of being cheated, and concerned about the casino surveillance system, even though they are law abiding. They consider themselves both rational and realistic, but they may focus too much on tiny details. They suspect that plots may be hatched against them. Slots to them are devices invented and controlled from afar to gyp them. They are often humorless, unsympathetic, and poor tippers.

- **The Poor Soul:** *Depressive* personalities fear poverty, expect losses, and hoard their small stake. The slot machine is a lofty altar where people superior to them go to play and pray. The Titanic slot machine suits them, and they would just as soon play for pennies. They feel they don't deserve their winnings, and tend to forget them, focusing instead on their losses. They're poor tippers unless they've just won, in which case they feel unworthy of the money.

- **The Big Shot:** *Hypomanic* people are the opposite of depressive; they are overly confident, sure of victory, and willing to squander large sums. Their mood is high, and the slot machine is ready to hand out blessings that seem boundless, especially since they disregard their losses. They are big tippers.

- **The Clinging Vine:** *Phobic* people are timid and use their fears to attract supportive people to cling to. The slot machine is an altar on which they may well be sacrificed bloodily. They may be drawn to scary themes but prefer harmless ones like Jackpot Party. They are reluctant to venture much, and fear becoming separated from whomever they came with—not difficult to do in the larger casinos, which have lost- guest stations for them (as well as for those of any personality type who have lost their memories to dementia).

- **The Daredevil:** *Counterphobic* players are the opposite of phobic, obviously—daring, fearless, venturesome, and risk taking, often more to prove they are unafraid than to garner monetary rewards. The machine Evel Knievel and video poker may appeal to them. They tend to view the slot machine as a worthy adversary and challenging god, and will risk high denomination slots as if on a dare. They are poor to fair tippers—they feel people should *earn* their rewards on the battlefield of life, tested for grace under fire.

- **The Con Artist:** *Sociopathic* people are antisocial schemers, crooks, and cheats who like to get their hands on other people's money to exploit it. The slot machine is a safe to be cracked. Of all the personality types, they are the least likely to have a religious experience at the slots, unless they should undergo a sometimes convenient conversion in prison. Chainsaws and Toasters or Wild Thing may be the machine for them. They may stiff waitpersons rather than tip them.

- **The Oddball:** *Schizoid* people are eccentric and idiosyncratic loners. They may live in fantasy and relate to the machines as strongly as to people, an autistic trait. Antisocial and oblivious to conventional behavior, they may be shy and retiring and prefer to withdraw into a corner to play. But they are acute observers. The slot machine is a robotic friend with whom they can commune in imaginary conversations. Tipping or other appropriate manners may not even occur to them.

- **The Showoff:** *Narcissistic* people feel entitled to wealth and special attention. They seek admiration and the fealty of others to bolster their self-images, but instead of giving of themselves emotionally to others, they prefer to lavish gifts. The slot machine and the casino are their servants and admirers who are supposed to worship *them* as royal or earthly demigods. If they are wealthy—and wealth often breeds a sense of entitlement—they are especially good at becoming the "whales" the casinos court with special favors, fulfilling their grandiose fantasies of themselves. Vulnerable to injuries to their self-esteem, they may take their marbles off the table, so to speak, and leave at some perceived slight. They tip well if they identify with the waitperson's attractiveness or are surrounded by an audience.

Perhaps you recognize yourself, or some of your traits, among these types. Their manifestation among slot players suggests that the machines can function like a Rorschach test: By being surprising and undecipherable, they can provoke people to react according to type.

SLOTS AND OUR FATE

SLOT PLAY AND BRAIN DISORDERS

We Americans seem now to be on the verge of a slot-playing craze. Like most products, slots are designed according to what sells without the manufacturer knowing quite why. Medical studies will eventually disclose what propensities make people more vulnerable to play. Certainly those with a tendency toward alcoholism are at risk, and perhaps more so if they are binge drinkers. Chronic alcoholics may be less likely to blow a fortune than people unaccustomed to drinking and with little tolerance for the freely flowing alcohol with which casinos ply receptive slot players. Worst off may be pathological alcoholics, those who undergo a transformative personality change after a fairly predictable number of drinks. I don't think that in general slot players are big drinkers. Servers' trays seem to be filled with lots of coffee and soda, as alcohol usually has to be ordered. Table-game players exhibit much more of the gregarious and boisterous behavior associated with alcohol. Many slot players are smokers, perhaps because the rhythms of the slots are like breathing. Nevertheless, as more casinos become smoke-free, players go on spinning the reels.

In my psychiatric experience, some of the most defenseless to the excesses of gambling have been bipolar patients in the manic phase of their illness, marked by extravagance, unrealistic appraisals of possibility, boundless confidence and expansiveness, unlimited energy, and no need to sleep. Does this sound good? It isn't when the inevitable mood crash occurs, together with the need to face what one has squandered destructively. When they are also alcoholic, bipolar people are all but unstoppable risk takers, especially if they have gone off their mood-stabilizing medications. A research study led by Dr. Eric Hollander, of Mount Sinai Hospital in New York, showed that treatment with lithium helped people with even mild forms of bipolar disorder limit their pathological gambling.

Given that slot players tend to be older, the question arises of the risk to those who have lost some intellectual function, like memory, judgment, or the ability to calculate. Certainly many such people are at risk, especially—as is often the case—if they're in denial of their illness and lack the ability to recognize they're impaired. A frequent symptom in such older patients is a concern about losing money, often symbolic of a loss of cognitive awareness that they subliminally sense but prefer not to acknowledge. These patients, who may have Alzheimer's disease or other senile dementias, may become extremely pinchpenny (though, paradoxically, they are easily swindled into writing large checks). Their niggardliness may protect them from playing slots irresponsibly. If those with poor memory do play, they may lose track of what they have spent (although, if they remembered to insert their players cards, the casinos keep track for them and their loss of money can be reviewed). Some non-demented people are innumerate and gamble more than they want to because they don't do the math—multiplying credits bet by denomination—or carelessly hit the MAXIMUM BET button.

It happens that I'm a psychiatric consultant to a group of neurologists at the Neurological Institute of New York who study and treat movement disorders. Like them, I see many patients with Parkinson's disease, a fairly common disorder in later life evidenced by stooped posture, slowness of movement, and tremor. I have been struck by the scarcity of this often obvious disorder among the many older persons I have seen playing slot machines, further evidence that the pleasure of slot play is related to the dopamine reward system I discussed earlier, which is lacking in Parkinson's patients. The exceptions are those receiving replacement dopamine, who may gamble more. Such patients are overcorrected, so to speak, with regard to their movement disorder, and are unlikely to display the trembling and stiffness that are the motor symptoms of the disease. A study led by Sabrina M. Tom, a psychologist at UCLA, has ascertained that the dopamine systems of the brain are increasingly active when a gambler anticipates wins and decreasingly so with losses.

Another possibly vulnerable group are those who have the high-functioning form of autism called Asperger's syndrome. Such people can have difficulty socializing with others and often compensate by engaging their strong technical or mathematical abilities to connect with a nonhuman, mechanical environment. If all of us personify slots to some degree, these people may view them as their brethren—as dear to them as any person of flesh and blood. This possibility and its implications await study as slot play expands.

TAKING A STAND ON SLOTS

A famous speech about alcohol delivered by Judge Noah S. "Soggy" Sweat Jr. in 1952 could be applied to slot machines, as the following paraphrase—in which I have substituted *slot machine* for *whiskey*—will illustrate:

> If when you say slot machine you mean the devil's device, the deceiving scourge, the bloodless monster that defiles innocence, dethrones reason, destroys the home, creates misery and poverty, yea, literally takes the bread from the mouths of little children; if you mean the evil play that topples the Christian man and woman from the pinnacle of gracious living into the bottomless pit of degradation and despair, and shame and helplessness, and hopelessness, then certainly I am against it.
>
> But;
>
> If when you say slot machine you mean the source of conversation, the philosophic altar to chance, the time that is consumed when companions play together, that puts hope in their hearts and a prayer on their lips, and the serene look of entrancement in their eyes; if you mean the holiday getaway; if you mean the stimulating wins that bring a thrill to the old person's state on a tedious, tiresome morning; if you mean the play which enables one perhaps to magnify one's wealth, and one's happiness, and to forget, if only for a little while, life's great tragedies, and heartaches, and sorrows; if you mean

that slot machine, the play at which pours into our treasuries untold millions of dollars, which are used to provide tender care for our little crippled children, our blind, our deaf, our dumb, our pitiful aged and infirm; to build highways and hospitals and schools, then certainly I am for it.

This is my stand. I will not retreat from it. I will not compromise.

THE POLITICS OF SLOTS

A clear national consensus on the slot phenomenon has yet to emerge. Broad bipartisan support for slot expansion is implicit in the willingness of so many politicians to support the legalization and construction of slot casinos or the installation of the slot machines themselves (technically, and face-savingly, renamed video terminals) at racetrack casinos (or racinos) in exchange for a percentage of earnings going to the state. In the future, look for the national debate over gambling to model itself after the one over tobacco, pitting conservatives supporting individual responsibility and the freedom of a growth industry against liberals calling for a safety net to protect the weak and foolish. How this will play out may hinge on how the casinos handle their seemingly irresistible appeal. Again, the history of the tobacco industry is instructive, particularly its arrogance in marketing a risky pleasure. If casinos overplay their hand and try to capitalize on people's needs for worship and awe, they may provoke a backlash. Innovations like downloadable slots, portable wireless devices for gambling around the hotel pool, electronic check cashing, and access to customers' bank information are invitations to abuses by slot management. The atmosphere of surveillance could be amplified, reminiscent of Big Brother in George Orwell's 1984. Gamblers accept that the house must have an edge, but there are limits to what they will tolerate. The slot-palace majesty that breeds dreams of riches can too easily smack of arrogance and rub against our sense of egalitarianism. Gambling needs to know its place.

BECAUSE YOU CAN

Still, one can't overlook that the grandeur of casinos is what appeals to many gamblers, not to speak of the inspiration they provide to spend more than they can afford. After all, throwing away money is one way to feel you have more than enough of it. In the men's room at Harrah's Atlantic City, I once heard two men bragging to each other about how much money they had *lost*. The figure of $15,000 seemed to win the argument. I was reminded of potlatch duels in which Native Americans in the Pacific Northwest tried to impress one another by destroying their possessions.

There can be a thrill just in risking large amounts, and even people who have not declined into pathological gambling can enjoy it. Handling a lot of cash and throwing it into machines makes some players feel like the last of the big spenders. That's why there are high-limit areas and $100 machines.

Allan J. Mottus, the retail industry analyst who publishes *The Informationist* about the beauty industry, told me a few years ago that gambling men like to objectify their winnings by purchasing trophies for the women in their company, which is why casino stores are so lucrative for retailers. Mottus also recognized then that we were in the denial stage of an economic recession in which the American middle class was refusing to acknowledge that it has lost real wealth. Gambling is a way of showing we still have money and can spend it.

Indeed, while gambling is often called a regressive tax on the poor and helpless, it can extract a toll from the rich and powerful as well. One of my college roommates, Bob Mc-Cracken, a former a management consultant with McKinsey & Company who lives near the Mohegan Sun and Foxwoods casinos in Connecticut, told me that certain public officials in the area have been caught embezzling money to cover gambling losses. Patrick Kelly and Carol Hartley have chronicled this sorry trend in *Management Research Review* (2010). This is an ironic reversal of former times, when casinos were run by organized criminals and surrounding communities wanted to clean them up. Now casinos are squeaky clean—run by people who must withstand rigorous perusal of their backgrounds—while local officials are often the ones who are corrupted. The surrounding municipalities have become addicted to their cut of gambling proceeds, which would have to be replaced by unpopular rises in property or sales taxes.

SLOTS GET SENIORS TO SPEND—AND WORK

Many senior citizens, fearing that they'll outlive their money, become overly cautious and hoard it, a habit exacerbated by their loss of mental agility. While their saving is preferable to overindebtedness, their gambling puts some of their money into circulation and loosens their inhibitions about spending in general. Just as important, gambling keeps some seniors engaged in productive work to replace what they have spent, which is good for their health and independence..

Fifty-nine-year-old Clara is a delightful example. She was pulling the handle on a penny In the Money machine at the maximum $2.50 per spin when I interviewed her at Mohegan Sun's Casino of the Wind. Each week, she drove two hours from another state to visit the casino, and she took two vacations in Vegas each year. She had been playing the slots for eight years, and her biggest win had been $3,000 six years ago. She worked sixty hours a week as a nurse's aide to support her slot play. She was one of the most energetic and talkative slot players I met, cheering on her own machine and those of her neighbors in a generously good-natured way. She was lively proof that the benefits of slot play go beyond mere enthusiasm.

HOW SLOT CASINOS MIGHT BECOME MORE RELIGIOUS

Still, if people insist on turning to casinos as places of worship, then the casinos might as well accommodate them. Why not? Since, as I've been at some pains to point out, many have already transformed themselves architecturally from dark dungeons into magnificent cathedrals, they might as well go whole hog. After all, most of the themes of slot machines that derive from pop culture trace their origins back to the classics of Western literature, not excluding the Holy Scriptures. Just as Disney's *Lion King* is a retelling of Shakespeare's *Hamlet* with a happier outcome, *Star Trek* and Patrick O'Brian's sea-adventure novels derive from the true story of eighteenth-century seafaring explorer Captain James Cook. *Star Wars*, insofar as it tells of an elite band using a special power (the Force) to fight for good in the universe, can be related to the legend of King Arthur, which in turn, like so many legends, has roots in the stories of the New Testament. Other "degraded" versions of the Christian myth include Mary Wollstonecraft Shelley's *Frankenstein*, which relates a form of resurrection, as do H. P. Lovecraft's creepy "Re-Animator" and C. S. Lewis's *The Chronicles of Narnia*. The story of Count Dracula derives from the historical figure Vlad III, Prince of Wallachia, better known, because of his cruelty, as Vlad the Impaler. Dracula in particular and vampires in general comprise debased versions of the ritual of Holy Communion and eternal life, not to mention a metaphor for the defloration of virginity in the sexier versions for teens. Comparative mythologists such as Sir James Frazer (*The Golden Bough*) and Joseph Campbell (*The Hero With a Thousand Faces*) point to recurring mythic themes of Osiris, Prometheus, Buddha, Moses, and Christ—the "monomyth" in which the hero answers the call to journey into another world to face trials and return with some boon for the ordinary world. Many slot machines I have already mentioned have recycled Egyptian, Greek, Roman, Asian, Meso-American, and American Indian religious elements, and the boon becomes the possible payout reward for the player's trials. George Lucas has acknowledged a debt to Campbell as inspiring *Star Wars*, which has a popular slot version, as does *Star Trek* and, for that matter, *Frankenstein* and *Dracula*.

These and countless other derivative themes regularly show up on slots across our nation. So with tongue in cheek and in a

Swiftian spirit of satire, let me modestly propose where casinos might go much further in realizing the religious implications of the business they are in.

Making the slots more explicitly religious might be done in stages, with sensitivity to different religions. First, now that we're used to the ring of the phrase *Jesus Christ Superstar* from the musical, slot-machine creators might introduce a franchised series of slots for Christian players that add Jesus to the pantheon of celebrity personalities. As I noted earlier, the Pearly Gates slots are not too far from this now, and there is also, of course, the satirical "Church Lady" *Saturday Night Live* slot. Already the three-reel win on most machines echoes the Holy Trinity. Jewish players might be offered Old Testament prophets and kings like Solomon, Job, and David, and Bathsheba. These gamblers could be provided a three-golden-calf jackpot for all the guilty pleasure they need. More Confucian or Taoist themes could be added for Asian players, who surely deserve better than the Fortune Cookie slots they're now offered, which display Chinese takeout, rice bowls, exotic cocktails in multiple colors, temples, fans, good-luck characters, and a doubling dragon. As more Asian American players gravitate from table games to the slots, we have of late also seen Bally's Double Dragon and Chinese Kitchen; Aristocrat's Good Fortune, Geisha, and 50 Dragons; and IGT's Triple Fortune Dragon, Lion Dance, Choy Sun Returns, and Double Happiness.

For the many slot players who are Roman Catholics, fallen away or not, a roster of saints could be introduced first, like a Saint Francis of Assisi slot with various animal symbols. The Virgin Mary might be offered next, with Annunciation doves, the manger, the Star of Bethlehem, Joseph, Saint Anne, and the Three Wise Men as a lesser wins. It could operate much like the Dagwood and Blondie slot machines, with Mary and Blondie being of greater value than Joseph and Dagwood.

Finally, a Jesus slot could feature carpentry tools, disciples, loaves and fishes, the healed and risen dead, the crown of thorns, the cross, and a bonus round offering immortality in heaven seated on the right hand of God. Instead of Elvis singing "Don't Be Cruel" slot wins could feature a descending Jesus intoning, "Do Unto Others" and "The meek shall inherit the earth."

Some casinos already practice the charitable good work of identifying players who lose a lot and compensating them—through their players club cards, which accrue points usually based on amount of play. These points can ordinarily be redeemed for such rewards as coupons for restaurant food, items in casino shops, or free slot play. Even though the additional special interventions for players who lose heavily do not affect the secret and sacrosanct slot machines' percentage return, these rewards are still controversial and considered unfair favoritism by some. Tennis great Andre Agassi launched a slot in which a proportion of his licensing and manufacturer's take goes to Agassi's Nevada educational charity.

THE SINS OF SLOTS

One of the paradoxes of being a psychiatrist is that with the aim of understanding patients' behavior we strive to be nonjudgmental, neither approving nor disapproving of what society judges to be moral and immoral behavior. And yet the problems we try to help people solve can often be seen as relating to the Seven Deadly Sins—Pride, Lust, Sloth, Gluttony, Wrath, Envy, and Greed. The psychoanalyst Karen Horney described how "neurotic pride" is an important contributor to many neuroses. For instance, overly exalted expectations of one's self and demands for perfection can lead to feelings of inferiority and a fear of even trying to achieve something. The therapeutic solution to such problems is not to condemn the pride as a sin but rather to analyze its emotional and rational costs for the patient, and to help the patient progress to more realistic and satisfying sources of self-esteem.

Casinos function is a somewhat similar way. For instance, slot play taps into the fantasy of achieving great wealth with little effort. This could be characterized as both Prideful ambition and naked Greed, with possibly a little Sloth thrown in and a touch of Gluttony when the winners celebrate or losers console one another at fine casino restaurants. When a huge jackpot win rings out, you can cut the Envy with a knife, but I have found most slot players to be well mannered about it. Less affluent players may envy the high rollers while fearing the risks they take, but you'll see few people in hair shirts crying out to condemn all this sin. Casinos function to sanitize sin. Their forgiving atmosphere seems to intone, "*Ego te absolvo a peccatis tuis* [I absolve thee of thy sins]—and indulge your excesses, for your reward is about to come in the here and now."

GAINING ENTRY TO THE INNER CIRCLE

Slot playing is solitary, as I've emphasized. Although there is a polite camaraderie, togetherness doesn't gel. A new version of

IGT's Wheel of Fortune attempted to generate communal excitement among slot players by arranging nine stations around a bonus wheel. Shaped like a giant grapefruit juicer, it spins for several players at once. At Foxwoods and Mohegan Sun, I found the seats in front of this machine filled, but there was no interaction among the players, as there was at the craps table and the roulette wheel. Monopoly and eBay games may also be found in banks with a large screen spanning them. Bonus rounds benefit all those who are actively playing them—but in varying amounts—and this sometimes, but not reliably, can bring out joint rooting.

Psychiatrists regard membership in a religious community, regardless of the religious denomination, as a proven support for a person's resilience in the face of adversity and even psychiatric illness. And, as more than one pastor has said, the benefits are everlasting. In their way, casinos also replicate religion in their power to confer admission to the elect—meaning the saved or those in a state of grace—although, unlike some sects of Protestantism that believe in predestination, inclusion has to be earned by venturing money. In casinos, admission to the elect is based on the amounts you bet or the rate at which you play. That admission gains you free or low-fee hotel stays, meals, special areas to play in, and tickets to a variety of entertainment events, not to mention a sense of privilege and worthiness that comes with exclusivity. But this clubby sense of belonging doesn't occur at the slot machines, which are usually played in egalitarian solitude.

At Mohegan Sun Casino, at the foot of an artificial mountain and next to the high-limit slots area, a VIP lounge serves complimentary drinks and hors d'oeuvres like shrimp and clams marinara. I asked the host, a pleasant middle-aged woman, exactly how one qualified to enter this inner sanctum. One had to play table games like poker at the rate of $50 a hand for four hours, she explained, or the slots for a minimum of five hours on a $1 machine or for two hours on a $5 machine. A complicated algorithm determines a player's theoretical level of play, or "theo." This is based on money played rather than lost, but a $2,000 loss in a single day guarantees your entry. While we were chatting, a small man pushed his way past us, and the host had to ask him to produce his players club card for scanning. He was reluctant to do so, and the host, a bit flustered, told me this man spent $30,000 a day at the casino and was well "qualified," but because of his pushiness in entering the area, he had been among those responsible for her having to check everyone's card at the entry to make sure no one "unqualified" got in.

Paying one's way into the real world's inner circles may be more worthwhile. For less than some people pay for playing slots, contributions of ascending amounts to museums and performing arts institutions will buy one admission to special dining rooms, viewings, and contact with performers. Gifts to medical research can make laymen privy to the latest developments described by medical scientists, as well as VIP treatment. Donations to religious organizations help to keep you and your loved ones in the prayers of the clergy. Almost every human endeavor has its inner circle of status, and money is not the only key to get there. But gambling a lot of money will bring you to grace in a slot palace faster than a beautiful young woman can get by a bouncer, and a lot faster than a camel can go through the eye of a needle.

Another privileged community one might aspire to become a part of is that of casino owners. As Steve Wynn put it on the television show *60 Minutes* on July 26, 2009, "The only way to win in a casino is to own one, unless you are very lucky." Members of the Indian tribe that owns Foxwoods, displayed in life-size photos at the nearby multimillion dollar Mashantucket Pequot Museum and Research Center, apparently have married outside the tribe, because they resemble the general mix of folks one might find in a Manhattan subway car rather than a group of Native Americans from central casting. According to Farah Peterson, a socially aware recent Yale graduate whose mother was chief auditor at Foxwoods, racial tensions surface sometimes between the casino tribe owners and the surrounding Connecticut populace, which feels the owners have been unfairly favored. Since appearances and possibly offensive stereotypes are no guide, and life is not a Hollywood movie, DNA tests for ethnic heritage, discussed by Amy Harmon in *The New York Times* of April 12, 2006, are now being sought by droves of people hopeful of claiming tribal blood and gaining a piece of the action.

THE WONDER OF IT ALL AND
ALL OF THE WONDER

When we attempt to explain why humans play slot machines, we return again and again to an element of religious worship. The human mind seems wired to believe in divinity and to find it somewhere. I have been fortunate, as a New York City psychiatrist who has frequently been consulted about intercultural problems, to meet people from all the world's major religions, and I have been struck repeatedly by the spirituality present in all cultures and common to all humanity. Even the most atheistic or agnostic scientists are inclined to revere the infinite wonders of nature. Astronomers who study the skies and fail to find gods with stars at their feet and elbows are nevertheless awestruck and humbled by the vastness of a universe they can only begin to understand. A corollary is that religion is so inherent to humans that those who try to avoid it in one way find themselves pursuing it another. The most secular and rational among us tend to be superstitious about something in our lives, be it health or money or science itself. I am reminded of Uri Geller, the stage magician who pretended to bend spoons with his mind (and who was exposed by former fellow magician Johnny Carson). Geller said scientists were the easiest to fool, perhaps because they wanted so much more to believe. I once followed him as the monthly speaker at a chapter of the Young Presidents' Organization, and the members there, all successful young business leaders, had been impressed with his message about the magical power of the wishing and believing mind.

A main point of this book is that a person playing a slot machine is also praying to the allness of the universe, and that somehow that person senses it. Ivars Peterson concluded his book *The Jungles of Randomness* by expressing wonder at the pervasiveness of his subject. "The mathematics we use in the gambling casino also applies to much of the rest of the universe," he writes. "We are surrounded by jungles of randomness. With our mathematical and statistical machetes, we can hack out extensive networks of trails and clearings that provide for most of our day-to-day needs and make sense of some fraction of human experience. The vast jungle, however, remains close at hand, never to be taken for granted, never to reveal all its secrets—and always teasing the inquiring mind." The universe of chance that ignites the starry lights we see at night is a fabric that may be sensed and touched all about us. A movement in theoretical physics championed by John Wheeler, whose course in physics I was privileged to take as a Princeton undergraduate, holds that even the laws of physics emerge "higgledy-piggledy," or in a disordered way, from the universe's random beginning. Stephen Wolfram's magisterial yet completely readable treatise A New Kind of Science explores the order, complexity, and beauty that self-organize spontaneously out of simple rules imposed computationally on the molecular randomness of the universe. Wolfram writes that, amazingly, "an ordinary physical process like fluid turbulence in the gas around a star should rather quickly do more computation than has by most measures been done throughout the whole course of human intellectual history." The universal popularity of games of chance throughout history and the enormous growth of electromechanical and video-computational gambling in our time suggest that wagering is a way for many people to confront statistical enormousness. It is by no means the only, or even the best, way. Rarity and statistical improbability can be approached variously in the natural world. The mysterious universes of large and small, displayed weekly on the cover of the journal Science, are marvel-filled treasure houses awaiting scientific discovery. Learning about the intricate cascades of molecular memory in the human brain and contemplating the mind that is emergent from its neural networks must humble us in the face of our own complexity. When we contemplate the heavens, aided by the best astronomical photographs, we may find ourselves stunned even more with their wonders than our ancestors were when they founded religions.

In one of Arthur C. Clarke's awe-inspiring short stories, "The Nine Billion Names of God," a Tibetan monastery acquires a computer to help the monks complete what they see as their divinely assigned task—to list the nine billion names of God. They believe that the world is composed of those names and, moreover, that its very creation was intended to manifest the divinity that those names embody. Until the arrival of the computer, they have been enumerating the names manually by spinning their prayer wheels, but the computer will speed up the task and allow them to complete it. Once it is completed, they believe, the world will end. The two Western technicians, having installed the machine and fearing the monks' reaction when the computer finishes the task and nothing happens, are departing down the mountain and musing about the quaintness of the quest, which they calculate is about to be completed. As they look back at the lamasery framed by the heavens, the stars begin winking out one by one.

Could our spinning of the slot reels of chance, exploring every combination of their symbols, be similar to the monks' task and have some purpose equally profound and seemingly mystical? Whatever the answer, casinos and their slot machines seem to be here to stay and are multiplying rapidly. As the slot symbols cascade, deep calleth unto deep. Whatever society does with them, it is well to keep in mind that we shall get the casinos and gambling machines we patronize, and that they will evolve to suit and exploit the reaches of our minds. As players, whether we experience these machines as mere amusements or as altars, as inanimate things or as personifications, as apocalyptic gauges of our fates or as magical instruments that connect us with the ever more astonishing cosmos, we owe it to ourselves to become aware of what is going on in our minds and hearts as we play. Evidently something there is luring us, and it is high time for us to understand what it is.

APPENDIX I

What follows is a comparison between real and simulated slot machines. I have chosen for simulation one electromechanical machine from many on a compact disc entitled Masque Slots from Bally Gaming, because of its three-coin, three-reel, one-pay-line simplicity and its fourth bonus reel—with straight pays, multipliers, and respins—which pays when three coins are played. It contains Jackpot (JP) and Jackpot 5 (JP5) bars, and single (7), double (77), and triple (777) blazing 7s. I present the results of one hundred consecutive spins to demonstrate how closely the commercially available game mimics the casino game. If studying these results seems monotonous, remember that the lulling pace is a major part of the experience of playing, especially in the older games. Some of the newer low-denomination games have devised more action in the form of frequent smaller payouts, and more complicated play, but the sense of repetition is still there, and the total payouts tend to be lower than in the simpler games preferred by many veteran players.

The pay table is as follows:

Machine Spin Result	1st Coin	2nd Coin	Respin Pay Range (3 Coin)
777 777 777	500	1,000	2,000–6,000
77 77 77	100	200	400–1,200
7 7 7	50	100	200–500
Any three 7s	20	40	80–240
JP5 JP5 JP5	20	20	80–240
JP JP JP	10	20	40–120
Any three JPs	5	10	20–60
Any three symbols	2	4	8–24

Bonus Frenzy, a slot simulation from Masque: 100 consecutive spins, Trial 1						Bonus Frenzy, a real slot machine at Mohegan Sun Casino: 100 consecutive spins, Trial 1					
Spin #	1st Reel	2nd Reel	3rd Reel	4th Reel	Win	Spin #	1st Reel	2nd Reel	3rd Reel	4th Reel	Win
1.	0	JP5	JP5	Respin	0	1.	JP	JP	JP5	0	10
2.	777	0	0	0	0	2.	0	JP	0	0	0
3.	0	JP5	JP	0	0	3.	JP	0	0	2x Pay	0
4.	0	JP	0	0	0	4.	JP	0	0	0	0
5.	777	JP5	JP5	Pay 10	14	5.	JP	0	0	0	0
6.	0	JP	0	0	0	6.	7	JP	JP	0	4
7.	0	JP	0	0	0	7.	7	JP	0	Pay 10	0
8.	JP	JP	0	0	0	8.	JP	0	7	0	0
9.	JP	JP	0	0	0	9.	0	JP5	JP5	5x Pay	0
10.	JP	JP	0	0	0	10.	7	0	0	0	0
11.	0	0	0	0	0	11.	77	JP	0	0	0
12.	JP	0	JP	0	0	12.	JP	0	0	0	0
13.	0	0	0	Pay 10	0	13.	0	JP	0	0	0
14.	0	JP	JP	0	0	14.	JP	0	0	0	0
15.	JP	0	0	0	0	15.	JP	JP5	0	Respin	0
16.	JP5	0	77	0	0	16.	JP	JP5	0	0	0
17.	JP	0	0	0	0	17.	777	JP5	77	0	4
18.	7	0	JP	0	0	18.	0	JP	7	0	0
19.	JP5	JP5	0	0	0	19.	0	0	0	Respin	0
20.	0	0	0	0	0	20.	0	0	0	Pay 10	0
21.	JP5	0	0	0	0	21.	0	JP	0	0	0
22.	0	0	77	0	0	22.	7	0	0	0	0
23.	0	7	0	0	0	23.	7	0	0	0	0
24.	JP	JP	JP	0	20	24.	777	JP5	0	0	0
25.	0	JP5	0	0	0	25.	0	0	7	Pay 10	0
26.	0	JP	0	0	0	26.	7	7	0	0	0
27.	JP	7	0	0	0	27.	JP	JP5	77	0	0
28.	JP	0	JP5	0	0	28.	JP	0	0	0	0
29.	777	JP	777	0	4	29.	7	0	0	0	0
30.	0	JP5	0	Pay 10	0	30.	0	7	0	0	0
31.	JP	0	77	0	0	31.	0	JP5	0	0	0
32.	JP	JP5	0	0	0	32.	0	JP	0	0	0
33.	0	0	0	Pay 10	0	33.	JP	JP5	0	0	0

Bonus Frenzy, a slot simulation from Masque: 100 consecutive spins, Trial 1						Bonus Frenzy, a real slot machine at Mohegan Sun Casino: 100 consecutive spins, Trial 1					
Spin #	1st Reel	2nd Reel	3rd Reel	4th Reel	Win	Spin #	1st Reel	2nd Reel	3rd Reel	4th Reel	Win
34.	77	0	0	0	0	34.	777	0	JP	Respin	0
35.	JP	0	0	Respin	0	35.	JP	JP	JP	Respin x 4	100
36.	JP	JP5	JP	0	10	36.	JP	0	0	0	0
37.	0	0	0	Pay 10	0	37.	0	7	JP	0	0
38.	7	JP	JP	Respin x 4	20	38.	7	JP	0	2x Pay	0
39.	JP5	JP5	JP	0	10	39.	777	JP	0	Pay 10	0
40.	JP	0	77	0	0	40.	JP	JP	7	0	4
41.	0	JP	0	0	0	41.	7	JP	0	0	0
42.	0	7	777	0	0	42.	0	0	0	0	0
43.	0	7	JP	Respin	0	43.	7	0	7	0	0
44.	JP	JP	777	0	4	44.	0	0	0	0	0
45.	JP5	0	0	3x Pay	0	45.	JP5	7	JP	0	0
46.	JP5	JP	0	Pay 10	0	46.	7	77	77	0	40
47.	0	777	77	0	0	47.	7	JP5	JP5	0	0
48.	JP	JP	JP	0	20	48.	0	JP	0	0	0
49.	7	0	0	0	0	49.	7	0	0	0	0
50.	JP5	7	0	3x Pay	0	50.	0	0	JP5	0	0
51.	0	0	JP5	3x Pay	0	51.	JP	0	0	0	0
52.	JP5	0	0	0	0	52.	JP5	0	0	0	0
53.	7	JP5	0	0	0	53.	77	JP5	JP	0	4
54.	JP	JP	JP5	0	10	54.	JP5	0	JP	10x Pay	0
55.	JP5	JP	0	0	0	55.	7	JP5	0	0	0
56.	77	JP	JP	0	4	56.	JP	77	7	0	4
57.	JP5	JP	0	0	0	57.	JP	0	0	0	0
58.	JP	0	JP5	0	0	58.	JP	0	0	0	0
59.	0	JP	0	0	0	59.	0	JP	JP5	0	0
60.	JP	JP5	JP	Respin x 3	40	60.	JP	7	77	Pay 10	14
61.	JP5	7	7	0	4	61.	0	0	7	Pay 10	0
62.	77	0	7	Pay 10	0	62.	JP5	0	JP	0	0
63.	7	JP	0	0	0	63.	0	JP	JP5	0	0
64.	JP	0	0	0	0	64.	JP	0	JP5	0	0
65.	JP	JP	0	300 Pay	0	65.	0	0	JP	2xPay	0
66.	JP5	777	0	Respin	0	66.	JP5	JP	0	Respin	0
67.	JP	777	0	0	0	67.	JP	0	0	Respin	0
68.	0	0	JP5	0	0	68.	JP	JP	7	0	4
69.	JP5	JP	JP	0	10	69.	0	JP5	7	Respin	0
70.	JP5	JP	JP5	Respin x3	40	70.	7	JP	JP5	0	4
71.	0	0	77	0	0	71.	JP5	JP5	0	0	0
72.	0	0	0	Pay 10	0	72.	7	0	JP	0	0
73.	0	0	0	Pay 10	0	73.	7	JP5	0	Pay 10	0
74.	0	777	77	0	0	74.	JP	0	JP5	0	0
75.	JP	JP5	0	Pay 10	0	75.	JP5	JP	0	0	0
76.	7	7	JP	3x Pay	12	76.	0	0	0	0	0
77.	JP5	JP5	JP	0	0	77.	JP5	JP5	7	0	4
78.	JP5	0	0	0	0	78.	77	JP5	JP5	0	4

Bonus Frenzy, a slot simulation from Masque: 100 consecutive spins, Trial 1						Bonus Frenzy, a real slot machine at Mohegan Sun Casino: 100 consecutive spins, Trial 1					
Spin #	1st Reel	2nd Reel	3rd Reel	4th Reel	Win	Spin #	1st Reel	2nd Reel	3rd Reel	4th Reel	Win
79.	0	JP	0	0	0	79.	7	JP	0	Respin	0
80.	JP	JP	JP	0	0	80.	0	JP5	JP	0	0
81.	0	JP	0	0	0	81.	JP5	JP5	0	0	0
82.	77	0	JP	3x Pay	0	82.	JP	0	0	0	0
83.	0	JP5	0	Pay 10	0	83.	0	JP	JP	0	0
84.	0	0	JP	0	0	84.	JP5	77	JP5	Pay 10	14
85.	JP5	0	0	Pay 10	0	85.	JP5	7	0	Respin	0
86.	0	0	JP	0	0	86.	0	JP	77	0	0
87.	JP	JP5	0	0	0	87.	7	7	0	0	0
88.	777	0	7	0	0	88.	777	JP	0	0	0
89.	JP	0	0	0	0	89.	JP5	0	JP5	0	0
90.	JP	0	0	0	0	90.	0	JP	7	0	0
91.	JP	JP	0	0	0	91.	7	JP	JP5	0	4
92.	JP	JP	0	Respin	0	92.	7	7	JP5	0	4
93.	JP5	0	0	0	0	93.	0	7	0	Respin	0
94.	777	0	0	0	0	94.	JP	JP	0	0	0
95.	JP	JP	JP5	0	10	95.	JP	JP	JP5	0	10
96.	JP	JP	JP5	0	10	96.	JP	JP	0	0	0
97.	7	JP5	0	0	0	97.	0	JP	777	0	0
98.	7	JP	0	0	0	98.	JP5	0	0	Respin	0
99.	JP	777	0	0	0	99.	0	JP5	0	Pay 10	0
100.	JP5	JP	0	0	0	100.	JP5	0	0	0	0

Total credits won: 252	Total credits won: 228
Wagered: $0.75 x 100 = $75.00 Return: = $63.00 Loss: = $12.00, or 16%	Wagered: $0.75 x 100 = $75.00 Return: $58.00 Loss: $17.00, or 22.7%
Other trials on the same simulation, Trial 2	Other trials on the same type of machine, Trial 2
Total credits won: 214	Total credits won: 168
Wagered: $0.75 x 100 = $75.00 Return: = $53.50 Loss: = $21.50, or 28.7%	Wagered: $0.75 x 100 = $75.00 Return: = $42.00 Loss: $33.00, or 44.0%
Other trials on the same simulation, Trial 3	Other trials on the same type of machine, Trial 3
Total credits won: 226	Total credits won: 394
Wagered: $0.75 x 100 = $75.00 Return: $56.50 Loss: $18.50, or 24.7%	Wagered: $0.75 x 100 = $75.00 Return: $98.50 Win: $23.50, or 31.3%
Overall Comparison: Three Slot Simulations: Loss = 23.1%; Three Actual Slots: Loss = 11.8%. If these percentage differences were to continue, they would amount to a great discrepancy, but the probability is that given enough time they would converge, even if a big win occurred on either the simulated or the real slot machine.	

APPENDIX II

COIN COLLECTING

Peace Dollars, minted in 1921 through 1935, with Liberty looking flapper-like with her hair flowing in the wind and wearing a spiked crown, go for $35 to $45 each (at the time I am writing). Uncirculated 1971 to 1978 Eisenhower Dollars are worth from $10 to $30. And the new George Washington dollar coin, if it erroneously lacks the edge inscription IN GOD WE TRUST, is worth $50. A 1913 to 1938 Buffalo nickel can be worth $30. A Jefferson nickel from 1938 to the present can be worth $135 (1939-D, for Denver mint). A 1913 Liberty head nickel with a V on it was sold at auction in 2010 for $3.74 million. Seated Liberty half-dollars sell for $400, Walking Liberty for $4,500 (1921-S). The quarter slots could have spit out a Standing Liberty Quarter (1916–1930) worth $13–$150 (1916 up to $10,000), a 1935-S Washington Quarter at $10–$69, or a Barber quarter with Liberty in a Phrygian cap from $20 up to as much as $2,000. Like millions of new collectors, one can amass a set of the statehood quarters that were issued five per year beginning in 1999. Rare coins circulated through the machines were not necessarily screened by casino staff because of the volume and because people brought in their own coins.

The 1894-S Barber dime, of which only twenty-four were made, is worth hundreds of thousands of dollars. Classic Mercury dimes (1923–1945, except for 1932–1933) can be worth $800 (1921-D About Uncirculated condition). As for pennies, if you find a wartime one from 1943 and it is brown (rather than white), depending on the mint it can be worth $75,000 (Philadelphia, twenty coins extant), $100,000+ (San Francisco, ten coins extant), or $212,000 (the 1943 Denver penny, only one of which is known to exist). The Lincoln cent of 1909–1958 with the wheat ears on the reverse was the first regularly issued coin to portray a notable American. These "Wheaties" were bronze every year except 1943, when they were almost all made of steel coated in zinc. The 1913-S goes for $22.50 in Good condition, the 1943-S steel one for $1.55 Good, $24.50 Uncirculated. Even some of the Lincoln cents with the Memorial reverse can be $5-6 Uncirculated. Or, for $295, an amount easy to slip into the slots, one could in 2007 have bought the biblical penny, the Roman Silver Denarius with the head of Tiberius, from Coast to Coast Coins. Tiberius (42 BCE–37 CE) was Caesar when Jesus was asked if his followers should pay taxes to Rome and replied by asking whose portrait was on the coin. When he was told "Caesar," Jesus answered, "Then render unto Caesar what is Caesar's, and unto God what is God's." Coins allow one to hold history in the palm of one's hand. It is even infinitesimally possible that the coin you hold will be the very coin mentioned in the Gospel of Saint Matthew.

BIRD WATCHING

I used to think bird-watching was a pastime for eccentric people. I couldn't have been more wrong. More than 50 million Americans say they watch birds, and the pastime is the fastest growing outdoor activity in America. It is true that it can be pursued in magnificent solitude, which might suit anyone who appreciates being alone now and then. But it can also be done in company, bringing together families, and both clubs and informal groups. In fact, some of the most sociable people I know have turned out to be bird-watchers. Ask your friends, and you'll be surprised by the number of bird-watchers you find among them. The website www.birdwatching.com describes the pleasure of the activity for communing with the immense beauty of nature, and even the satisfactions of the hunt, our primitive heritage. Of course, birders, as they call themselves, don't shoot their quarry, except with a camera. Another advantage the website touts is that it gets you exercising, effortlessly and compellingly. All you need to get started is a hat, a field guide, and binoculars. Sharing this last is not encouraged, as it's easy to miss something. The Cornell Laboratory of Ornithology (www.birds.cornell.edu/programs/All About Birds/) shows you how to get started. It's easiest to start locally, in your own backyard or neighborhood park. But if you're willing to travel, the Cornell lab suggests its favorite spots across North America, as well as explains how to identify birds by field marks, posture, size, flight patterns, and habitats. Instead of playing the casino at Niagara Falls, you might take advantage of the fact that you are in the gull capital of the world (the "gulliest" months being October through December) and that along the river rare birds can be found, like the Pacific Loon that was spotted there. The information birders collect can be valuable; if you want to contribute to preserving birds, citizen science projects are offered. Looked at a different way, however, birding can be viewed as a form of gambling in which the very rarest birds function as the jackpots. A look at "The 50 Rarest Birds in the World" website (www.camacdon-ald.com/birding/rarestbirds.html) might inspire you to search for an Abbott's Booby, last seen in Australia, or perhaps the California Condor, the only bird among these fifty rarest last seen in the United States. The quest for them could take you to places the casinos in Las Vegas never thought to emulate and the James Bond movies never used as exotic locations.

MODEL TRAINS

A little less than half of model railroaders make up imaginary rail lines, while others model a specific line and the cities it serves. The truly meticulous insist on total fidelity to the real world, down to weathering all surfaces and even spraying met-al parts with rust. Model railroading is so engrossing that one railroader found it enabled him to quit smoking. With what he had been paying for cigarettes, he could buy a new locomotive every few months. A good way to start is to pick up a copy of *Model Railroader* or *Railroad Model Craftsman* and see what is going on. You'll learn that steam locomotives now have elec-tronic sound systems that chuff realistically in synchrony with their pistons as they move down the track. You don't even have to use up worldly space to enjoy the hobby. You can build virtual

"I wish God would quit running that train around
and put the lights out."

layouts with computer software and run virtual trains on them. Or you can marvel simply at the feats of other modelers. In an issue of *Railroad Model Craftsman*, Ted Culotta describes how he built a boxcar from scratch (without a kit), to which he applied every rivet individually—in HO or 1/87 scale. Sam Posey, a professional racecar driver, chronicles his development into a model railroader with contagious enthusiasm in his 2004 book *Playing with Trains: A Passion Beyond Scale*. Rod Stewart, the rock superstar, is an avid model railroader who brings his workshop along on tour. In a *Model Railroader* article, he said, "I pity a man who doesn't have a hobby like this one—it's just the supreme relaxation." If running miniature trains doesn't do it for you, the Valley Railroad at Essex, Connecticut, after some study of a manual and a friendly examination, lets you run a real steam locomotive for an hour, an incomparable pleasure. I have done it twice, operating a Consolidation and a Mikado engine.

Music Business Made Simple.

Start an
Independent
RECORD LABEL

J.S. Rudsenske
J.P. Denk, editor

SCHIRMER

New York /Madrid

Learn more about the author at MusicBusinessMadeSimple.com

Schirmer Trade Books
A Division of Music Sales Corporation, New York

Exclusive Distributors:

Music Sales Corporation
257 Park Avenue South, New York, NY 10010 USA

Music Sales Limited
8/9 Frith Street, London W1D 3JB England

Music Sales Pty. Limited
120 Rothschild Street, Rosebery, Sydney, NSW 2018, Australia

Order No. SCH 10150
International Standard Book Number: 0-8256-7310-0

Cover Design: Josh Labouve

Printed in the United States of America

Library of Congress Cataloging-in-Publication Data

Rudsenske, J. Scott, 1963-
  Music business made simple : start an independent record label / by J. Scott Rudsenske ;
James P. Denk, editor.
    p. cm. -- (Music business made simple)
  Summary: "Presents the information and tools needed to successfully start and operate an
independent record label"--Provided by publisher.
  Includes bibliographical references and index.
  ISBN 0-8256-7310-0 (pbk. : alk. paper)
  1. Music trade--Vocational guidance. 2. Popular music--Vocational guidance. I. Denk,
James P. II. Title. III. Series.

ML3790.R832 2005
781.64'068'1--dc22
                                    2004021538

CONTENTS

Acknowledgements

Thanks to my wife, Hilary, who has supported me in all my endeavors. A special thanks to my friend, editor, and, on occasion, voice of reason, James Denk, who has put as much of his heart and soul into these books as I have. Thanks to my former colleagues and friends Richard Cagle and Greg Pitzer for providing me with positive insight and encouragement throughout the years.

Credits

Managing Editor: Andrea M. Rotondo
Developmental Editor: J.P. Denk
Proofreader: Barbara Schultz
Cover Art: Josh Labouve
Production Director: Dan Earley
Interior Design: Len Vogler
Publicity Coordinator: Alison M. Wofford

J.S. "Skip" Rudsenske is an entertainment attorney practicing in Nashville. He graduated from South Texas College of Law in 1989, and has practiced entertainment law since that time. He is licensed in Texas and Tennessee. He is a current and past board member of the Sports and Entertainment Law Section of the Texas Bar. He represents both companies and artists in the music, film, theatrical, and television industries. He also represents successful published authors and visual artists.

Mr. Rudsenske represents national recording artists on Atlantic, MCA, Koch, Priority, Sony, and Universal Records, and has been in-house counsel for, and represented independent record labels such as Flashpoint International, Wreckshop, Jam Down, and Game Face Records, all distributed through major label distributors. He has represented independent film companies such as Panda Entertainment and Reptile Films.

Over the years, he has personally managed recording artists on independent and major labels, and also has started his own independent label. He was the owner of the Urban Art Bar in Houston, Texas, where he personally booked and produced events by artists such as Bush, Oasis, Jewel, Jeff Buckley, Creed, Tonic, Matchbox 20, The Goo Goo Dolls, and Better Than Ezra.

His law firm created and maintains the Website *MusicBusinessMade Simple.com*. He is a voting member of NARAS, the organization that presents the Grammy Awards. He is the author of this book and is a regular speaker at music conferences and seminars. You can learn more about Mr. Rudsenske at *www.jsrlaw.net*.

PHOTOGRAPH BY: LORI BREWER

INTRODUCTION

D o you want to start a record label or make your current label more successful? Are you an established artist or producer interested in running your own company? Perhaps you're a successful business-person seeking to apply your skills and experience to an entrepreneurial venture with an exciting, creative product. Maybe you're a music industry professional in need of solid advice on the music business and the next steps toward even greater success. This book is for you.

The fact is, every serious businessperson needs a little guidance as he or she works to build a successful enterprise. In this regard, the music industry is no different from any other. The advice and information in this book apply to every person who is interested in starting a record label, is presently running a small label, or wants to know more about how a record label operates.

WHY SHOULD YOU BUY THIS BOOK?
Almost everyone knows someone who has dreamed of success in the music industry. Every year, thousands of people take their shot at a music career. Most do not succeed. Some crash and burn spectacularly. Others simply get tired of working for pennies. But some *do* succeed and go on to have long, rewarding careers as musical artists.

It's the same with the record labels that sign these artists. Many enter the fray, but few last. Even fewer thrive. We wonder: "Why did Label A make it big, while Label B (which has talented bands) never got beyond selling records out of the back of a car?" If you can figure this out, please let me know. You've found the magic formula for which we've been searching.

In fact, there is no formula, and this book does not provide a map to Easy Street. Success in the music business is a matter of development, preparation, hard work, and a little luck. This book provides practical information and advice on how to handle situations that arise during the creation and development of a record label. It will help you to prepare, which will increase your opportunities to succeed in the music industry, and make sure you're ready to take advantage of those opportunities.

Of course, you will need a lot more than a book to answer all your questions and to get the detailed guidance you'll need as your business grows. For that, you eventually will hire an entertainment attorney, an accountant, and experienced personnel. But there are many steps before you reach that point. As they say, you can't go from the mailroom to the boardroom without education and experience. Even if you know nothing about the music business, this book can help you get out of the "mailroom" and on your way to starting a successful record label.

PART
ONE

GETTING
STARTED

STARTING A RECORD LABEL: AN OVERVIEW

Today, music is everywhere: On radio and television, in supermarkets and elevators, on the Internet, and even on telephones. It would be difficult to go a day without hearing any music. It would be equally difficult to find someone who doesn't like some genre of music. Why?

One explanation is that music has been proven to affect people's emotions. Media and businesses use music to influence our moods and habits. You probably even have some or your own favorite music to suit certain situations: Workout music, driving music, "mood music," etc.

However, before music can have an impact, the artist who creates it needs an audience. For the artist to have success in the music business, his or her audience must pay to hear the music, either in recorded form or in a live performance. Enter the record label. As the head of a label, your ultimate goal will be to find a paying audience for the records you release.

But before you get started, realize that your path and goals in the music industry probably will change over time, and that simply knowing the way doesn't guarantee you'll reach your destination. The level of success your label achieves will be based on many factors. You can control some factors, such as desire, goals, dedication, and perseverance. Others, such as musical trends, consumer buying habits, the economy, and just blind luck, are beyond your control.

Even under the best conditions, it takes years to build a successful record label. At any point along the way, outside factors might require you to change direction. This is not to say you can't achieve your goals. You just need to be prepared to alter your course and adapt to shifting trends and circumstances.

Your first assignment is to learn about the music business. It's not enough to know how a record label operates. You also must understand how different aspects of the music industry affect record companies. Many people believe they know good music and can spot talent, and that, therefore, they're ready to start a record label. However, there is much more than this to the business of owning a label. To succeed, you need to know how to sell records.

Most successful independent labels are established by record executives with many years of experience in the industry. Some are started by former recording artists, and others by people who simply have a passion for music. If you're part of this last group, you'll have to make up for your lack of experience by learning as much as you can about the music industry.

You will also have to learn what it takes to set up and run a record company. There are several ways to organize a business; you'll need to determine which one is right for your label. Then, there are city, state, and federal governmental requirements to meet. Also, it's critical to acquire—very early on—the music contracts needed to operate your record label. Finally, even if you keep your label small and simple, you'll have to address issues of funding, bookkeeping, accounting, office supplies, and employees.

Your third assignment is one of the biggest challenges for any record label. You must be able to identify marketable talent and know where to find it. As a smaller label with limited resources, you won't be able to attract fully developed artists. Instead, you almost certainly will be working with lesser-developed artists with raw, unpolished talent. That's fine. You aren't running a major record label, and an important part of your job as an independent is to serve as a proving ground for artists. You'll have to decide how best to use your time, money, and energy to develop raw talent into skilled recording and live performing artists. And, of course, you have to know where and how to find talented artists.

In addition, you must understand the primary steps involved in making your product (CDs, tapes, etc.): Recording, manufacturing, and packaging. It's crucial to have a good working knowledge of the recording process, which will help you to get the best recording for your money and to avoid potentially expensive pitfalls. The right studio—preferably one with experienced professionals, or at least a talented producer—can help stretch your resources and allow you to put out an excellent product, even if you don't have a lot of money.

After the recording is completed, you have to know how to package your product. Packaging includes creating and printing the artwork to be inserted into the plastic CD/cassette case and printed onto the compact disc or cassette itself. Packaging also includes having the compact discs/cassettes manufactured to fit into their plastic cases. The final manufactured CD or cassette should look and sound good so buyers will be satisfied with it. Remember, your name will be on your product. As with any other business, if you hope to survive and grow as a record label, you'll need to make quality products.

Finally, you'll need to understand and master the most important tasks for any record label: marketing and promotion. It does not matter how talented your label's artists are, or how great your products look and sound; if you don't inform the public about your products and provide an opportunity for people to buy them, your label won't have any sales and you won't be in business for very long. Before signing or recording your first artist, do some research about the marketing, promotion, and distribution options available to your label. I discuss this in detail in Part V, Marketing and Distribution.

Successful independent label owners understand that their labels are businesses and treat them as such. They take a methodical, careful approach to the music industry and appreciate the value of building their business one step at a time. Not coincidentally, their labels also tend to be the ones that last the longest. These record companies recognize that success and longevity come not with being the biggest, but with being the best. If you seek to establish a quality and long-lasting label of your own, follow their example. The rest of this book will help to show you how.

Things You Can Do Today To Build Your Label

1. Learn about the music industry, including the marketing and promotion of artists and recordings.

2. Read and study books and other resources about how to set up and operate a business.

3. Start doing research on how to identify marketable talent and where to find it.

What Does a Record Label Do?

A record label's sole function is to create and sell records. Except for the money a label invests in producing records, every dollar has one purpose: To sell records or, in industry lingo, "product." (Bear in mind that, for the purposes of this book, the term "records" refers to all configurations manufactured for sale to the consumer, such as cassette tapes, compact discs, and vinyl records. Eventually, new technologies and formats may make these configurations and the term "records" obsolete.) In this sense, a record label is really no different from a company that sells soap or cereal. It will conduct marketing studies to determine the type(s) of consumers that will like its product. Then, the label will promote the record to encourage those consumers to buy it. And like soap or cereal, both the artist and the record that he or she has worked so hard to create are considered products—sources of income—to the parent company.

Record companies promote their artists' records through advertising in the media, such as magazines, radio, television, and the Internet. They may hire independent radio promoters to seek radio airplay. Labels also may promote sales in record stores by paying for those posters you always see on the walls, and/or by placing a copy of the record at a listening station or in high-visibility areas of the store. A label's publicity department will send newly released records to magazines and newspapers, hoping to obtain good reviews or stories about the artists. The size of the label and its monetary resources will dictate the kinds and amount of promotion it is able to do.

Not surprisingly, smaller labels tend to have smaller promotion budgets. Therefore, they must find creative ways to promote their artists' records. If you're starting a small independent label, you may be able to do no more than produce the artist's recording, pay for minimal advertising and promotion, and provide the artist with records to sell at his or her live performances. This arrangement benefits both parties and should be acceptable to an artist who is in the early stages of his or her career. Your label is able to make a small investment in its product, and your artist gets someone else to pay for recording, packaging, and promotion.

There are some things a label should not do. The record company's job is to promote and sell the artist's records, not to develop an artist. Yes, an independent label will sign artists who are less experienced and less developed than artists on major labels. Therefore, artists will be developing their talents and gaining experience while recording for your label. But many small labels make the mistake of signing artists who have raw talent but no performing or recording experience. Certainly, you want artists with talent, but ideally, you want to sign people who also have been playing live and have spent at least some time in a recording studio. This will allow your label to devote time and money to promoting records, while your artists perform at live music venues and make appearances to promote their records further.

It may be difficult for your new label to attract developed artists, especially at first. But you should make it a priority to seek artists with some level of experience. It's very helpful to find artists who already understand the concept of "development" and will do the things necessary to develop their talents. They will utilize your record company as one resource in their endeavor, but will not rely on the label to develop them.

One note of caution: You may hear about labels, usually locally, that claim they can do it all for an artist. They'll provide coaching to help develop the artist's live performance and recording skills. They'll manage the artist and book the artist's shows. And, of course, they'll produce, promote, and sell the artist's records. This is too much. They're spreading themselves too thin, and are almost certain to fail to live up to their claims.

Don't attempt to create one of these labels. As I tell my clients, if you are going to start a record label, start a record label and leave the coaching, managing, producing, etc. to the professionals who know those jobs best. Through networking, you'll meet managers, agents, etc. who develop talent. The best thing you can do is to establish a good relationship with these professionals and introduce your artist(s) to them. Let them do what they do the best, while you focus on *your* business: Producing, marketing, and selling high-quality recordings.

Things You Can Do Today To Build Your Label

1. Understand that a record company's sole purpose is to promote and sell records, and think of creative ways to promote an artist's record.

2. Seek out talented artists who have at least some prior recording.

3. Focus on running a record label and leave the coaching, managing, and booking to other industry professionals.

QUALITIES OF A SUCCESSFUL LABEL

Most artists never have record labels lining up to sign them. More likely, only one label will be interested in signing an artist at any given point in his/her career. Nonetheless, an artist will want to sign *only* if the label is reputable, experienced, and knowledgeable about the music business. I advise artists that it's better to remain unsigned than to get trapped in a bad deal with a record company that can't (or won't) help to advance their careers.

What does it mean for a label to have a good reputation, and why is it important? If the record company is not able or willing to live up to its responsibilities (i.e., produce a good record and then promote and sell it), the artist will be out of luck, and his/her music career will be stuck in neutral. This can happen even to established artists, but it can be especially damaging when an artist is just getting started. If it happens to the artists you sign, you'll develop a bad reputation as a label that does not help to advance your artists' careers.

This reputation will have a negative impact on the quality of artists you're able to sign, since artists naturally are disinclined to work with labels perceived to be unhelpful or incompetent. Furthermore, a bad reputation will affect the terms of the contracts with artists you do sign. Entertainment attorneys who have concerns about your label will seek to negotiate contract terms that are more favorable than usual for their clients (artists) and give fewer rights to your label. In the end, a bad reputation will cost you business and income, which will make it very difficult for your label to succeed, or even survive. To avoid this, consider the following insights when setting up and running your label.

First, recognize the obvious: Every label must start somewhere, and most artists will not want to be the guinea pig. But like every other new label, you'll have to sign your first artist, whose record you will need to record, promote, advertise, and sell. Being professional and working hard to achieve some success for the first artists you sign will help to build your good reputation. This will help you attract better, more developed artists in the future.

Of course, you'll make mistakes with the first artists who sign to your label. And you probably will continue to make some mistakes as long as you're in business. This is inevitable. However, your label will develop a good reputation if you limit your mistakes, learn from your experiences, and overcome problems in a professional, efficient manner.

Most developing artists should understand that they have to start their careers early, and that they probably will sign with independent labels to make their first records. However, even a young, undeveloped artist will rightly want to know that your label can produce a quality recording. A good reputation does not mean your label can sell a million records and make the artist a pop star. Instead, it means that your label can do its job and will fulfill its responsibilities to the artist (namely, recording and releasing quality product).

The quality of records your label produces will have a big influence on its reputation, and will either encourage or discourage other artists to sign with you in the future. Therefore, every aspect of your records—right down to the artwork and packaging—should be of the highest quality you can produce. These products are your label's "resume," which you will present to other artists and industry professionals who are considering working with your label. The stronger your resume, the better your chance of signing the artists you want.

When your label is just getting started, you probably will have very limited financial resources. However, this doesn't mean you can't record and package a good record. Research and preparation can help you overcome financial limitations. The first part of your research will be to learn about the various processes involved in creating CDs/cassettes. The second part is to find the best companies and/or people to help you with this process. I have found that it saves money to use experienced professionals—even those who may charge slightly more—because they are far more efficient and make fewer mistakes than their less experienced colleagues. I discuss tips for getting the best recording and packaging for your money in Part IV, Production.

Beyond your label's ability to make a quality recording, the artist will want to know if you have the resources and commitment to promote and market the records you produce. Indeed, regardless of your label's size or budget, you should have a marketing and promotion plan in place before you sign a single artist. Unlike large labels, which can produce every style of music, most small labels don't have sufficient financing to put out more than one genre. That's okay. An independent label should strive to become proficient at producing a single style of music. The more diversified a small label is, the more diluted its resources become, and the less likely it is to gain expertise in any genre. This certainly will limit its promotion and marketing success. I discuss this issue, as well as factors to consider when deciding on a musical genre for your label, in Chapter 27, Choosing a Genre.

It will take time, but eventually your label can develop alliances with the best producers and studios for the type of music you put out. You will learn how to find, work with, and promote artists who make that music, and how to advertise to the appropriate audience. By creating a niche for yourself, your label can maximize the impact of its limited funding (and the success of your artists). Labels like SubPop, Rap-A-Lot, Blue Note, Rounder, and Alligator have shown how small record companies can succeed and have a huge influence on their corner of the music industry.

Be open to discussing your goals and plans for each artist so that he or she understands how you will promote and market his or her record. If you're trying to sign an artist who already has developed a fan base and achieved some success (through previous recordings, radio airplay, regional touring, etc.), listen to the artist and be willing to work with him/her to build upon that success.

It is also critical for you and your staff (if you have any) to do your homework and operate your label with professionalism. This is a sophisticated business. If you don't understand how it works and how record labels fit within the industry, you will appear uninformed and ill-prepared to potential artists and their representatives. Even successful label owners who know the industry can gain a reputation for being unprofessional if they appear arrogant or disorganized. Lapses such as failing to pay bills or royalties in a timely manner, or acting badly toward third parties, will inevitably hinder a label's ability to sign artists and to grow. Conversely, being competent, knowledgeable, and professional will make your label attractive to talented artists, set a good example for your employees, and encourage third parties to work with you.

Another component that is crucial to a record label's success is the contract presented to each artist. The contracts you use are necessary and important business tools for your company. They should reflect your label's business practices and adhere to basic industry standards, while delineating how you plan to deal with each artist you sign. New independent labels sometimes obtain recording agreement forms from books or the Internet. This is fine, but don't make the mistake of molding your business to the terms in those contracts, or agreeing to services you cannot provide. In other words, review and revise any contracts you're going to use, making sure they reflect how your label is conducting business and what it can do for an artist.

Unlike independent labels, major record companies usually give the artist a lot of money up front. On the other hand, major-label contracts tend to be more restrictive than those from independent labels, as they are designed to protect the label's investment by controlling most aspects of the record's creation and promotion. A small label that attracts artists by offering creative freedom and less restriction should not present a major-label contract to its artists. Instead, this label should employ an entertainment attorney to create a contract that will protect the label, yet be consistent with the label's ideals.

Finally, make sure your label can coordinate and carry out all the work required to deliver on its promises. Young, developing artists who are serious about their careers should understand that it is important to start out with independent labels, and they should not expect instant fame and fortune with their first contract. You don't have to offer a million dollars to attract talented people; artists simply want to know that you'll live up to your side of the deal. So it's important not to make promises beyond the scope of the label's capabilities.

When you start out, you may not be able to offer anything more than to produce a quality recording with quality packaging, do some basic promotion and limited advertising in local markets, try to get some radio airplay in the local market, and provide record distribution on a consignment basis in a few local record stores. This is what you can do, and you're going to do it well. It's nothing to be embarrassed about.

To make sure everyone is on the same page, you'll want to discuss the artist's goals and expectations before offering a contract. Make sure the artist understands what your label does (and does not do) so he or she will not have unrealistic expectations. Promising more than you can deliver will only cause problems with artists currently on your label and give you a bad reputation among other artists you may want to sign. It's better to have an artist walk away because you can't do enough than to lure someone with an offer you can't fulfill. Focus on building a reputation as a small, but professional and competent label that produces quality records, offers reasonable contracts, and sets realistic expectations. This strategy will help your label to establish a positive standing in the local industry, sign increasingly better artists, develop good business contacts, and grow.

Things You Can Do Today To Build Your Label

1. Be professional and work hard to achieve some success for the first artists you sign, while building your good reputation.

2. Even if you have limited resources, make sure all of your records—including artwork and packaging—are of the highest quality your label can produce.

3. Be honest with artists and promise only those things you know your label can provide.

Learn About the Business

I receive e-mail, letters, and telephone calls from people who want me to explain what I know about the music business. Unfortunately, there's no way I can do this briefly. Even if I could, my lecture wouldn't be very beneficial to even the most attentive student, because there's too much information to digest in one sitting. It takes time for it all to sink in.

Though I've been practicing law in the entertainment industry since 1989, I never stop learning about this business. I learn in two ways. First, I continually study books and articles about the music business and the law. I also attend legal seminars and music conferences each year to learn about the most recent changes in, and interpretations of, entertainment law, and to discuss legal and business issues with other entertainment attorneys and industry professionals.

As a record-label owner, you don't have to become an expert. But if you hope to sell records and succeed, you definitely need to learn about all aspects of the music business. The more your label grows, the more you will need to know.

Luckily, there are several good, basic books about the music business that can provide the information you'll need. You don't need the biggest, most detailed, and most expensive publication. It might look impressive on your coffee table, but it won't teach you much. Chances are, it will be intimidating and complicated, and probably will end up collecting dust somewhere.

Instead, buy books that are the smallest and easiest to read, like this one. Even if you have experience in the music business, you always can learn something new or reinforce what you already know. Stick with solid, user-friendly books that help you become more knowledgeable, and to maneuver through the fundamental issues of the music business. A search of your favorite local or online bookstore will get you started.

The books you purchase should cover basic legal issues, copyright and trademark, distribution, contract negotiation, marketing, the business of radio, Internet sales, etc. This information will help immensely in the day-to-day operation of your label. It won't eliminate mistakes completely, of course, but it will help you make better choices when opportunities (or potential disasters) arise.

As I said, you don't have to know everything, but for your own protection, you must know enough to spot potential problems. When an important issue does arise, or when you're not sure how to proceed, you should seek the advice of an entertainment attorney or other music-business professional.

Besides reading books, you can educate yourself about the music industry by attending classes on the subjects listed above. Numerous community colleges and universities offer such classes, many of which are very good. Other helpful resources, such as videos and audiotapes, can be found at your local library or bookstore, or on the Internet.

One excellent place to obtain solid, current information is at a music-business seminar or music conference. The panels and discussions at these events will be educational and will expose you to perspectives from professionals in a variety of fields. I discuss this topic at greater length in Chapter 7, Music Conferences.

I also recommend that you spend some time studying the history of successful record labels. These companies probably went through many of the same things you will experience, and made some mistakes along the way. Obviously, it's better to benefit from their mistakes than to make them yourself. Two good resources about the development and operation of record labels are *Exploding: The Highs, Hits, Hype, Heroes, and Hustlers of the Warner Music Group*, by Stan Cornyn and Paul Scanlan; and *Hype*, a video about the SubPop label.

It's also helpful to read or listen to interviews with successful record-label executives. A good interview will cover the label's rise to success and will usually include stories about steps the executive took early on that contributed to later success. Two excellent programs that combine executive interviews with an examination of the music industry are the MTV-produced programs *The History of Rap: The Russell Simmons Story*; and

Takin' it to the Streets.

As you watch, read, listen, and learn, you'll begin to recognize some common themes, regardless of the kind of music being discussed. You'll read or hear about the barriers each label had to overcome, such as resistance to alternative musical genres and difficulty in getting new genres distributed or played on the radio. Many labels will discuss the artists who ultimately helped put them on the map. You will learn how some labels started at the grass roots level, and how they promoted themselves to the public and the industry. Naturally, many label executives will discuss mistakes they made and successes they had. They may also discuss the importance of being surrounded by creative, innovative people and the need to have a vision for the label. Many, if not all, of these issues will probably affect your label, too, so it pays to learn from people who know how to deal with them.

Finally, give yourself a history lesson on the music business. Learning how it has developed over time will help you to grasp fundamental concepts and issues, and to understand why things are done the way they are today. Knowing how the industry has progressed to this point can help you envision how it (and your label) may progress into the future. Some excellent books on the history of the music business are *Hit Men,* by Frederick Danner; *What'd I Say: The Atlantic Story,* by Ahmet Ertegun; *Mansion on the Hill,* by Fred Goodman; and *The Men Behind Def Jam: The Radical Rise of Russell Simmons & Rick Rubin,* by Alex Ogg.

In the music business, information is power. Learning the basics up front will help you to understand the business, set realistic expectations, avoid some mistakes, and move your label forward more quickly.

Things You Can Do Today To Build Your Label

1. Read books or watch videos about running a record label, especially those that offer advice from past and present record label owners.

2. Educate yourself about the music business by taking a class at a local college or university.

3. Attend a music business seminar or conference.

THE IMPORTANCE OF SETTING GOALS

*E*veryone has dreams, things they want to accomplish. For some, that vision includes owning a successful record label. Since you're reading this book, maybe this is your dream, too. No matter what your specific music-related objectives are, a series of realistic short-term goals along the way will help you achieve them. Setting goals gives you a destination and a strategy to get there.

Before you begin, understand that your goals for the record label may change as you gain experience and your label evolves and matures. This is completely normal. In fact, you should reassess your goals regularly, making changes as needed. Knowing from the start that your goals may shift will keep you from becoming frustrated if you don't achieve the objectives you set at the very beginning of your journey.

How do you go about setting goals? First, get a pencil (with an eraser) and a pad of paper. Brainstorm. Write down any goal that comes to mind. Don't evaluate. Just write. At this point, no goal is unrealistic. You will review and revise your list later (thus the eraser). Maybe your label will not sell a million records. Then again, maybe it will. For the moment, allow yourself to dream. This will help you visualize what you want the label to accomplish. If you can't envision a goal, or can't explain it in writing, you can't achieve it.

Where do you begin? Well, your first goal should be the ultimate destination you want to reach. Start with a broad goal, and keep in mind that it is likely to change during the label's development. You might want to sign Grammy Award-winning artists and have your label's records distributed by a major distributor. Other long-term goals might include having a successful publishing company, or having all your artists "go Platinum" (sell more than 200,000 albums). On the other hand, your goal might be as simple as making a living by producing music you like. Like most record company owners, you probably will also want longevity, and to be an influence in the music industry. Keep your list of goals handy so you can refer back to it on occasion, write down new goals, and change old ones.

Once you decide on your long-term destination, you need to set a series of short-term goals to help you get there. Each short-term goal represents another step toward achieving your long-term vision. Short-term goals might include getting your label up and running, signing your first artist, and getting your first artist's recording produced and released. Maybe you want to release several artists' records in one year. Great! The more CDs you release, the more records the label will sell (at least in theory). But still, your first short-term goal is to release that first record. The next short-term goal will be to sell a certain number of copies of that record.

To achieve your short- and long-term goals, you must construct a plan and then put that plan into action. This is your road map, outlining how you're going to achieve each goal. The next chapter explains how to construct and carry out your plan.

Things You Can Do Today To Build Your Label

1. Write down any and all goals you may have as a record-label owner and organize them into a logical sequence.

2. Identify your ultimate goal for the record label and write down a series of short-term goals to help you to achieve it.

3. Accept that your goals may need to be reassessed and revised as your label grows and changes.

THE PLAN: A ROAD MAP FOR SUCCESS

*A*fter making a list of your goals, you'll need to construct a plan to achieve them. Simply put, this plan is a "to do" list that will allow you to meet your goals. When constructing a plan, it's important to write down each step. This may seem elementary, but it's important. Don't be afraid to write down the simplest or most obvious task. As the owner of a label, you'll have to see the "big picture," as well as all the details. This exercise will help you begin doing that. It will help you get (and remain) organized, and understand the relationship between one step and the next. It will also help you develop good planning and managerial skills, which will come in handy when your label has four artists in the studio, three out on the road, and two supporting new releases on a media publicity tour.

As discussed in Chapter 5, The Importance of Setting Goals, one of your short-term goals will be to release a record by an artist you have signed. What will be your plan to achieve this goal? Below is a detailed description of one possible step-by-step plan leading to the release of your label's first record. It can serve as a model plan to achieve other goals set for your label, too. As you become more experienced, you may not have to write every action into a formal plan. But you'll continue to create and carry out plans as long as your label is in business.

Obviously, you must set up your label before you can sign artists or release records. The plan below skips the steps related to the initial organization of your record company. (I cover those issues in Part II, Setting Up the Label.) In this plan, I assume you've already set up your label and are ready to begin operation. Some steps may be completed simultaneously. For example, you might begin talking with manufacturers to learn about prices even while you are negotiating a deal with your artist. A basic plan to accomplish the goal of releasing your label's first record might look like this. (All of these steps are discussed in much greater length later in the book.)

1. **Find an Artist.** Begin soliciting demo tapes from artists, attending live performances, and reading local trade magazines to learn about developing artists. Meet with various artists to discuss their goals and your goals as a label, and your plan for each artist.

2. **Sign the Artist.** Negotiate a contract that will meet the goals of both artist and label.

3. **Budget.** Create an initial budget for pre-production, recording, manufacturing, and packaging the record.

4. **Find a Manufacturer.** Find and meet with an experienced manufacturer your area. View and listen to other projects produced by the manufacturer. Discuss costs and format requirements for cover art and the CD booklet. Seek recommendations for talented graphic artists in the area with whom you might work. Find out which recording format, such as DAT, CD-R, or other configuration is required by the manufacturer. Ask about having film created for artwork and printing. Discuss obtaining a bar code. Confirm turn-around times and total costs for the entire process.

5. **Find a Graphic Artist.** If you are not using the manufacturer's art department, find a local graphic artist with experience in compact disc layout. Meet with the recording artist to discuss ideas for the record's "look." Have the recording artist write down his/her ideas about the artwork and present these ideas to the graphic artist. Discuss costs for the graphic artist to create a draft and final version of the artwork before delivering a finished product. Ask the designer about having film created for the artwork. Confirm turn-around times and total costs for the entire process.

6. **Do Pre-Production.** Find a studio in which to do pre-production of songs. Select a producer for your artist. Choose songs for the record. Pre-produce all songs before going into a studio. Discuss the songs, goals of production, production schedule, and budget with the artist, producer, and studio. Be open to new ideas, and be prepared for unexpected expenses. Based on these steps, create a final production budget. Obtain contracts for a producer and studio before production begins.

7. **Produce the Record.** Prepare a schedule for the artist and producer, based on the studio's schedule. Attend recording sessions to monitor the producer, artist, and overall progress toward meeting production goals. Communicate with the producer, artist, and studio regarding progress of the record. (In other words, make sure your schedule and budget requirements are being met, and that everyone is staying on task). Upon completion of the recording, obtain a digital audiotape (DAT) and/or a recorded compact disc (CD-R) with the fully mixed tracks. Have the recording professionally mastered.

8. **Manufacture the Record.** Deliver the recording and artwork to the manufacturer. Be sure both meet the manufacturer's format requirements. Obtain a proof copy from the manufacturer so you can review the artwork prior to printing.

Of course, your label may follow a slightly different path to complete its first record, but you get the idea. It's important to have a plan, and to set out stepping-stones along the road to your ultimate destination. This allows you to take manageable steps, rather than taking one giant leap that you miss. The small successes will help to keep you motivated and moving toward your short- and long-term goal(s).

After completing the record, you would develop a plan to release your artists' CD for sale. But that comes later. Right now, you may not have enough experience to set all your goals or develop a plan for each one. Don't be discouraged. You just need a little help. Everyone does at first. Contact experienced professionals in the industry, and educate yourself with books and articles about independent labels and the music industry in general. And remember, you can always revise your goals as you learn more.

Perhaps most important, keep in mind there is no right or wrong strategy for achieving your goals. Two record labels can take completely different approaches to reach the same destination. Only you can decide what is best for your label, based on your circumstances and resources. Today, your main goal is to get pointed in the right direction and get moving.

Things You Can Do Today To Build Your Label

1. Decide that you will construct a plan to help achieve your long- and short-term goals.

2. Write down a detailed, step-by-step approach for completing each task required to achieve your goals.

3. Contact experienced industry professionals and educate yourself through books and articles to help you prepare your plans.

MUSIC CONFERENCES

Music conferences provide one of the best opportunities to network, learn about the music business, and see great performances by some of the industry's most innovative and talented artists. Smaller conferences often are one-day events with a few speakers and performances by local artists. More established conferences usually last two to three days, feature national recording artists, include a trade show, and offer informative panel discussions.

The panel discussions can offer invaluable information for independent record labels. They might address practical issues, such as how to publicize and promote your artists, or how to get a distribution deal. Some will cover more academic subjects, such as the future of the music business, copyright law, or negotiating independent record contracts.

These panels can also be inspirational, as they sometimes include successful artists or executives from well-known labels. The panelists can help you understand the music business better, because you will have the opportunity to view things from the perspectives of the various types of professionals you may deal with as a label owner.

At larger conferences, panel discussions usually occur during the day. In the evening, there are showcase performances by some of the best artists—signed and unsigned—in the world. These musicians are rarely on major labels or heard on pop radio. I always find it encouraging to be reminded that great artists can succeed on independent labels without being played on pop radio stations 40 times a week. This should be encouraging for you, too.

Some conferences also include a trade show, where different businesses associated with the music industry set up booths or tables. These groups may represent CD manufacturers, merchandisers (such as T-shirt and poster manufacturing companies), music directories (of recording studios, radio promoters, manufacturing companies, entertainment attorneys, etc.), music magazines, and/or public relations or promotions companies. Most conventions will supply bags containing promotional items (known as SWAG, or Stuff We Always Get). If you go to enough conferences, you'll build an impressive collection of lighters, free CDs, and, of course, conference programs.

Organizers of larger, more popular conferences will print a conference book listing all registrants and trade show participants. You'll find professionals from all corners of the music industry in these directories, which are excellent resources for contact information. Whether you're looking for potential radio promoters, manufacturers, distributors, attorneys, or anyone else in the business, this is a great place to start. Moreover, conferences give you an opportunity to speak to these people face-to-face, usually in informal settings.

Many labels use conferences to promote themselves and their artists. This makes sense, because those in attendance often work with labels: Radio music directors, club and radio DJs, promotions companies, record store buyers or salespeople, record distributors, etc. All of these professionals may one day be able to help your label, not to mention buy your records. Done properly, it can be highly beneficial to promote your label and artists at conferences.

You can create a buzz several ways: By advertising in the conference directory, placing post cards or other promotional items in SWAG bags, and/or handing flyers or CD samplers of artists on your label to contacts you meet. These efforts can be even more effective if your label sponsors a showcase of your artists at the conference. (Make sure each artist has a "promo pack," as described in Chapter 54, Creating and Using the Promotional Package.) Typically, you'd pay a fee for the right to sponsor a stage at a conference. There will also be other costs, such as advertising and promotion. But the publicity of a well-produced, well-attended, and exciting performance by your artist(s) can be well worth the cost. Because each conference is different, you'll need to contact a conference representative to learn the specifics about how to sponsor a stage. However, even if you don't give out promotional items or sponsor a stage, music conferences are great places to learn about the music business, hear new music, see experienced artists perform, make important contacts, and learn different ways to promote and market your product.

So, where are these conferences? Some of the more established music conferences are South by Southwest in Austin, Texas; North by Northwest in Portland, Oregon; the CMJ Music Marathon in New York City; and the Winter Music Conference in Miami Beach, Florida. *Billboard* magazine sponsors a number of conferences, and many smaller but credible events are held throughout the year all over the country.

You can find more information by searching for "music conferences" on the Internet. In addition, several music industry directories list music conferences all over the world, along with contact information. The *Recording Industry Source Book, Musician's Atlas* or Billboard's *Musician's Guide to Touring and Promotion* are three such directories. Visit their Websites for information about how to obtain copies of these publications (listed in the Resource section in the back of this book).

Finally, if you can't make it to the larger conferences, don't rule out attending a local music conference or seminar in your own city. Your support will help them grow into more established events. Plus, these smaller conferences are always looking for sponsors, assistance, or talent to showcase. You can provide all of these things. Check the Internet and your local music publications or businesses for information about conferences in your city.

Things You Can Do Today To Build Your Label

1. Attend a national music conference to learn about the music business and see great performances by some of the industry's most innovative and talented artists.

2. Promote your label and/or your artists at a music conference by advertising in the conference directory, placing promotional items in SWAG bags, sponsoring a stage, and/or giving flyers or CD samplers of artists on your label to contacts you meet.

3. Support a local music conference by attending, sponsoring a showcase, and/or volunteering as a speaker.

PART
TWO

SETTING UP THE LABEL

SETTING UP YOUR LABEL

You may be starting a label because you love music, but remember, it's still a business. And as with any business, one goal of a label is to make a profit. Therefore, you should establish good habits and a professional approach from the start. This will make your life much easier and help your label to grow more quickly.

It isn't difficult to set up a label, and you can do some things on your own. However, I recommend hiring an experienced attorney to help. This is a good investment, because even the simple stuff can be confusing if you don't know how to do it, and any mistakes you make in the beginning will cost more money to correct later.

You'll need five primary tools to set up a label: Money, an attorney, a business entity, contracts, and an accounting program. As always, cash comes first. How much? Believe it or not, you can start a label for less than $2,000. This won't pay for employees, expensive office space, or recording time in a fancy studio, but it will get you off the ground.

You can pay some of the start-up bills monthly with income from your day job, but others will require a lump sum of cash up front. After reading this book you'll be able to put together a budget for starting your label and operating it on a day-to-day basis.

Second, when setting up your label, you'll have to decide what type of business entity it will be: Sole proprietorship, partnership, or corporation. (I explain these terms and what they mean for you in Chapter 15, Forming a Business Organization). If the label has more than one owner, you will have to operate it as a partnership or corporation. In any case, you'll need an attorney who is familiar with setting up businesses to ensure that your business (the label) is properly established. An entertainment attorney may or may not have this expertise.

I do not believe in overpaying for anything, especially legal service, but some expenses are inevitable. During the label's set-up phase, I strongly suggest meeting with an attorney to make sure you are completing and filing all the necessary government documents. An attorney can also advise you about local, state, and/or federal forms that may be needed, such as a federal tax identification number form (if you will have employees and/or your label is a partnership or corporation), assumed name certificate (doing business as), sales tax certificate, etc. Once again, the fee you pay for an attorney's time now will save you from having to spend a lot more to fix mistakes later.

Fourth, you'll need contracts. It's impossible to operate a record label without them. The music business is built entirely on the acquisition and exploitation of copyrights. Federal law says any agreement related to those copyrights must be in writing if it is to be legally binding. It is not sufficient to get oral agreements or a handshake deal with artists, producers, back-up musicians, or studios. Only written contracts are binding. Without them, you might find that you don't own the recordings you've spent money to produce, or that someone who worked on the recording is expecting more money in royalties than you verbally agreed to pay. Without a written contract, your rights in such cases will not be certain. Instead of referring to a clear written agreement to resolve the issue, you'll have to hire an attorney to litigate your rights and risk losing any or all of the rights you thought you had. Start out with written contracts and avoid these problems.

Most entertainment attorneys can provide contracts via e-mail or on CD. If you purchase contracts off the Internet or obtain them from a book or a friend, spend the money to meet with an attorney to review the contracts so you understand them and are able to adapt them to your label's specific needs. It pays to do this right the first time. After this initial one-time cost, you can use the contracts over and over. As your business grows, you will want to meet regularly with your attorney to update your contracts.

Finally, if you plan to sign artists, sell records, pay royalties, make a profit, and pay taxes, you'll need accounting software. A relatively inexpensive program like Quicken or QuickBooks will reduce your workload considerably when it comes time to prepare accounting statements, pay royalties, and do your taxes. Many computers now even come loaded with a version of these programs. You can upgrade to more sophisticated royalty accounting software in the future, but this isn't necessary when you're getting started. If you have current accounting software on a computer, just use that or buy a good basic accounting program.

What does all this cost? The fees for filing an assumed or fictitious name certificate for a sole proprietorship can run $10 to $50. You will definitely need an attorney if you are going to set up a partnership or a corporation (add $250.00 to $1,000.00). Accounting software will cost from $200 to $400. You will pay an entertainment attorney from $200 to $500 to help with your contracts, depending on the rates and specific services provided. Adding it all together, as little as $660 to $1,950 can get your label up and running—the right way.

Things You Can Do Today To Build Your Label

1. Begin saving money to pay for the start-up costs.

2. Meet with a business attorney to select a business entity for your label and file the necessary forms. Also, meet with an entertainment attorney to help with music contracts.

3. Acquire a simple accounting program and learn how to use it before you start operating.

What Does an Entertainment Attorney Do?

We've all heard horror stories about record companies battling with their artists and distributors. I've seen the aftermath, and it's not pretty. The ultimate job of your entertainment attorney is to counsel you about legal aspects of the music industry so you can avoid these kinds of disasters. Your attorney's responsibilities will commonly include drafting and negotiating contracts for you as you enter into agreements with third parties (i.e., distributors, artists, and producers), preparing your copyright or trademark registrations, and advising you on issues as diverse as goal-setting, factors to consider when choosing an artist, and your label's direction.

Most important, the attorney will advise you before you sign any agreements, and do everything possible to make sure you enter into contracts that are fair and protect your interests. He or she will make sure you understand the contracts you sign, and that the contracts are up to industry standards. The attorney can also help you understand how all these legal documents affect your business on a day-to-day basis.

Just in case I haven't been clear: *Before you enter into negotiations or sign any contract in the entertainment industry, always get the advice of an entertainment attorney.* Simply having an attorney does not guarantee that you'll get the best contract. However, having an attorney greatly increases the likelihood that you'll understand the contract you are signing, and that you won't get burned.

One thing entertainment attorneys generally do *not* do—despite the popular myth—is seek out and secure production and development or distribution deals (a process known as "shopping" a label). It is true that some entertainment attorneys perform this service, but very few succeed in getting their clients a deal. Those who do succeed are almost always working with a label that already has spent years building its business and has had some success selling records. A reputable, experienced entertainment attorney will explain this to you.

Many label owners want to hear that if they hire an expensive lawyer, they'll get a deal with a distributor associated with a major label. You can try this, but I strongly recommend that you don't. You probably will end up with no distribution deal and a lot less money.

Unfortunately, distribution companies perpetuate this myth, telling start-up labels that they need an entertainment attorney to submit their materials. Why? Because these distribution companies do not accept material directly from unknown labels (like yours). Instead, they require materials to be submitted by someone—such as an entertainment attorney—who already has a relationship with the major label with whom they are associated. They give you the impression that all you have to do is hire an entertainment attorney to present your music to the distributor. But it's not that simple. What they're really doing is leading you to someone who can explain how the business works. I provide this explanation in Chapter 51, Finding a Distributor.

If an attorney says he or she will shop your products to distributors, be cautious. Before writing a check or entering into an agreement for the attorney to send your material around, ask a lot of questions regarding his or her experience, who he or she has represented, and how many distribution deals he or she has obtained for small labels. The fact is, you can't buy success in the music industry. You succeed through development of your label, hard work, and record sales. My goal in this book is to guide you through the process.

Things You Can Do Today To Build Your Label

1. Learn what an entertainment attorney does and does not do, and what one can do for your label.

2. Talk to other industry professionals and ask if they ever have experienced music-related legal troubles because they didn't hire an attorney.

3. Before you enter into negotiations or sign any contract in the entertainment industry, always get the advice of an entertainment attorney.

When Do You Need an Entertainment Attorney?

*A*n entertainment attorney should be your first professional contact in the music industry. A good attorney can help you set up your label as a legal business entity, draft and negotiate the contracts your label signs, and help guide you through each step of the label's development. For these reasons, I recommend finding an entertainment attorney as soon as you decide to start a record label.

Most entertainment attorneys will charge a nominal fee (maybe $75 to $100 per hour) to meet with you initially. This first consultation can provide answers to many of your questions, insight into the music industry, and valuable information about the steps you'll take to establish (and later, run) a record label.

It really is beneficial to have this kind of direction, and to have someone looking out for your best interests—even if you have to pay for it—from the very start of your business. You won't have to sign an exclusive contract with an entertainment attorney, who will be available whenever you want to set an appointment. Once you become more experienced and knowledgeable, you'll be able to make most decisions about the day-to-day operations of the label, while your attorney will continue to counsel you in legal matters.

Exactly when you first contact an entertainment attorney is, of course, up to you. I don't like to set absolute rules, or say "never" or "always," because every situation is different. But as noted above, once you decide to form a legal business entity, you need an attorney. And when the time comes to enter into contractual agreements with third parties, absolutes do apply. Never sign *anything* related to your music business without the counsel of an entertainment attorney. This is not an option, but a requirement. Protect yourself.

No matter what your music-related goals may be, your label's business will be based on contractual agreements. Before signing a contract, always have it prepared, or at least reviewed, by an attorney. This will help you to know exactly what you're signing, what you are committing to, and what you will receive in return. You should always seek the advice of an experienced attorney who is knowledgeable about the music industry. Your Aunt Sara's neighbor, Frank, who practices real-estate law, is not the guy you need representing you in your distribution deal.

Some people believe that employing an entertainment attorney will hinder negotiations with other parties because the attorney will intimidate the other side or somehow ruin the deal. This is an unfortunate misconception. As described in Chapter 19, your entertainment attorney will advise you and help protect you from signing a bad deal. It is your attorney's job to negotiate the best deal for you and make sure the contract clearly sets forth the agreement of the two parties. That's all. There is no reason why this should hurt your chances of making a deal.

Reputable companies, artists, and other professionals in the music industry know this and will welcome your use of an attorney. It often helps the process go more smoothly. In fact, no major distribution company will negotiate a contract unless you are represented by an entertainment attorney. And no reputable professional will object to your having an attorney review an agreement before you sign. If the person or company with whom you are talking does not want you to use an attorney, or says you don't need an attorney, or breaks off negotiations because you sought counsel, then you absolutely should not sign a contract with that person or company anyway.

Of course, you may prefer to save money and go without an entertainment attorney. It is always your choice. But know this: During many years of experience, I have spent a lot more time trying to get clients out of bad deals than negotiating moderate to good deals for clients who hired me at the start. As the old saying goes, "You can pay me now or pay me later." Bottom line: Attorney's fees are as much a cost of doing business in the music industry as the money spent recording or promoting CDs. This will be true as long as you own a label.

Things You Can Today To Build Your Label

1. Start searching for an experienced entertainment attorney to help you get your label started and to prepare and negotiate the contracts you will use in your business.

2. Insist on having legal representation for any deal you make, and think hard and long about doing business with any company or individual that discourages you from doing so.

3. Realize that attorney's fees are part of the business, and that a good attorney will save you a lot more money than he or she will cost.

FINDING AN ENTERTAINMENT ATTORNEY

*I*t will take a little effort to find the right entertainment attorney. To start, you should look for an attorney with three qualities: A good reputation with others in the entertainment industry, knowledge of the music business, and experience with copyright law.

Some state or local bar associations (the organizations that regulate attorneys) can help identify attorneys in your area who practice entertainment law. Music-industry directories, such as the *Recording Industry Source Book* and the *Musician's Atlas,* are also great resources. And don't forget about the Internet. All of these options are more efficient than looking through the Yellow Pages, because they will identify entertainment attorneys specifically, instead of simply listing attorneys in all fields. Ultimately, your most reliable references will be trusted colleagues in the music community. No matter where or how you search, remember the three qualities noted above to give yourself the best chance of finding a good entertainment attorney.

Depending on your legal needs, an out-of-state attorney may be perfectly capable of representing you and your label, via telephone, fax, and/or e-mail if necessary. However, some legal matters require you to be represented only by attorneys licensed to practice law in your state. You will need to discuss this with the attorney up front. Finally, before placing your label's wellbeing in an attorney's hands, schedule a meeting (either in person or on the telephone) to get a sense of his or her level of knowledge, type and years of experience, current and previous clients, etc. It usually helps to talk with someone and get to know him or her a little before signing a deal.

Most attorneys will charge a fee to talk to them. Like everyone else, they're in business to make money, and their time is valuable. If they're talking to you, they can't be talking to their other clients, so it's only reasonable that you should pay for their time. I usually charge a nominal hourly fee of $75 to meet with people who are starting a label. This is a great way to get my full attention and a solid consultation for a reasonable cost. Many, if not most, entertainment attorneys operate the same way. The fees charged for services rendered afterward will depend on the specific work required, along with the attorney's experience, reputation, and location.

Remember to call ahead to schedule an appointment, and understand that you probably won't be able to speak to the attorney immediately. When you call, confirm with the staff that the attorney consults with clients on entertainment matters, explain your situation, and ask what the cost is for one hour of the attorney's time on this type of matter. You also might inquire about whether the attorney charges a different rate for general consultations than he or she charges for consultations about specific matters, such as negotiating or drafting contracts. You even might ask the staff if they can provide some information on the attorney's experience. The firm may well have a Website that answers some of these questions, so you should do an Internet search before calling.

Prepare before your consultation with the attorney. This will save the attorney's time and your money. Write down the questions you want to ask and the items you want to discuss, so you will be sure you cover them all with a minimum of wasted time. An hour can pass very quickly. I often ask the client to write down his or her questions and send me a copy in advance, so I can get an idea about what he or she is expecting to discuss during our consultation.

If you haven't been able to find information about the attorney's experience before your appointment, don't be embarrassed to ask. I welcome prospective clients to ask about this. It means they are doing their homework, and that they're probably responsible and serious. I respect that. Other attorneys should, also.

During the meeting, ask the attorney if he or she can counsel you on the development of your record label, and what his or her rates are for the services you will need. Some attorneys may charge a lower rate for consultations than for contract negotiations.

If you're satisfied and comfortable with the responses, you can begin asking more substantive questions. For example, ask the attorney to describe the best way for you to proceed in starting your label, and to identify the kinds of issues with which you should seek his or her assistance. Hopefully, by the end of the meeting, you will have found an entertainment attorney with whom you feel confident and comfortable. But if not, don't feel bad. This is an important professional decision, and you need to get it right. If you're not comfortable with this attorney, continue your search until you find one who is right for you.

Things You Can Do Today To Build Your Label

1. When looking for an entertainment attorney, seek referrals from friends, colleagues, persons in the industry, or from your state or local bar association.

2. Consult the Internet, the *Recording Industry Sourcebook* or *Musician's Atlas* for entertainment-industry attorney listings.

3. Schedule a consultation with an entertainment attorney before committing to a long-term relationship. It will cost you a few dollars, but it will give you a chance to learn more about the lawyer and help you decide if you are satisfied with his or her knowledge and experience.

CONTRACTS: THE ESSENTIAL BUSINESS TOOL

*E*ntire law-school classes are taught, and entire books are written, on legal battles related to the music business. (See, for instance, *They Fought the Law: Rock Music Goes to Court* by Stan Soocher.) Most of these problems focus on contract disputes. That's why, next to your attorney, the most important business tool available to you as a record-label owner is the written contract. In fact, you can't make money, sell records, or even exist as a label without contracts.

The copyright and trademark laws are clear: Whoever creates the vocal and musical sounds on the master recording (e.g., artist, producer, side artist, etc.) owns those sounds. Likewise, graphic artists who create the artwork for your records own that art as soon as it is created. Unless you obtain your rights in writing, any agreements you make with recording artists, producers, side artists, graphic artists, etc. are not valid or enforceable in a court of law. As a result, you could lose your rights to the recordings made—and paid for—by your label, including the right to sell them.

The only way your record label can obtain the rights to use and sell the recorded performances on the master recordings, or the artwork you have chosen for the CD cover, is for the label and the artist(s) to enter into a written contract, or agreement, that grants those rights to your label. (Note: The terms "contract" and "agreement" are interchangeable in the legal industry.) Without this written contract, the master recordings will continue to be owned by the artist, producer, and any side artists who created them. And the graphic artwork will continue to be owned by the graphic artist. This is only one of many issues to be addressed in the contracts you sign with musical and graphic artists, but it is probably the most important.

For any successful record company, written contracts are a fact of life. Over time, your label will enter into contracts with recording artists, of course, and probably with producers, graphic artists, distributors, and others. So make sure you obtain the necessary contracts (described in the following chapter), study them, and use them. This is a great way to establish good business practice from the start.

> **Things You Can Do Today To Build Your Label**
>
>   1. Accept that you will need to obtain written agreements for all the business your label does.
>
>   2. Obtain the proper contracts and adapt them to your business. An experienced entertainment attorney can help you do this.
>
>   3. Read some legal horror stories from the music industry in the book, *They Fought The Law: Rock Music Goes To Court*, by Stan Soocher.

THE CONTRACTS YOU WILL NEED

*H*ow do you ensure your rights to the recordings and artwork done for your record label? Through the use of four basic written contracts: A Recording Agreement, Producer Agreement, Side Artist Agreement, and Graphic Artist Agreement.

The Recording Agreement is the contract between the record label and recording artist. It describes the number of recordings the artist will make, the label's obligation to pay for the production of the recordings, the record company's rights to the recordings, and the amount the label will pay the artist from the sale of those records. I discuss this agreement in detail in Chapter 20, The Recording Contract.

You also will need a Producer's Agreement. I explain the role of the producer in Chapter 40, What Does a Producer Do? Briefly, the producer is a technical and creative person who works with the artist to complete the master recording that a record label will then manufacture into compact discs, cassettes, etc. Similar to a Recording Agreement, a Producer Agreement explains the services the producer will perform on the recording, the record company's rights to the recording, and how much the label will pay the producer for his/her services. It will also state whether or not the producer will be paid a royalty from the sale of the records.

Third, you'll need a Side Artist Agreement. The side artist, or featured artist, is not the primary artist you have signed to your label, but a vocalist or musician who performs on the recording. Sometimes, it is a well-known recording artist, possibly signed to another label, who provides a vocal or musical performance on one or more songs. If the side artist is a member of a union and will not receive a royalty from record sales, then your label will not provide the Side Artist Agreement; it will come, instead, from the artist's union. As you might guess, the Side Artist Agreement outlines the services the side artist will perform on the recording, the rights the record company has to the recording, what the side artist will be paid, and whether the side artist will be paid a royalty from the sale of the records.

Finally, you'll need a Graphic Artist Agreement, a written contract between your label and any graphic artist who creates artwork for your artists' CDs or cassettes, logos for the artist or label, merchandise designs, advertising, or any other original art. This same agreement might be changed and adapted for use with a photographer who takes photos of the artist. This contract covers the services to be provided by the graphic artist, the payment to be made to the graphic artist, and the ownership rights of the record label to the artwork created.

Where do you find these contracts? The basic agreements are available for purchase and download on the Website *MusicBusinessMadeSimple.com*. You'll be able to use them immediately and adapt them to your label's specific needs. The site also offers explanations of each agreement.

There also are a few excellent books that provide these contracts and explanations, such as *The Musician's Business & Legal Guide* by Mark Halloran, or *All You Need to Know About the Music Business* by Donald Passman. And, of course, you can consult your entertainment attorney to obtain all of these agreements and plenty of guidance in how to use them.

No matter where you get your contracts, you must take them to an entertainment attorney before you use them. The agreements you obtain from the resources listed above will meet music-industry standards, but you will need an entertainment attorney to help you adapt them to your business and to make sure the contracts conform to the laws of your state.

I cannot overstress the importance of obtaining and using written contracts in the daily business of your label. In addition to the ownership rights discussed previously, written contracts address many other important issues, including the creation, distribution, marketing, and sale of an artist's records. They establish a clear understanding among the parties regarding rights and responsibilities, and greatly reduce the likelihood of future disputes. Once you become familiar with these agreements, you'll find it easier than you think to incorporate them into your label's everyday business. Moreover, using these contracts and living up to the terms set forth in them will help to establish your label as a legitimate player in the music industry.

Things You Can Do Today To Build Your Label

1. Obtain the four basic contracts you'll need to form a label: Recording Agreement, Producer Agreement, Side Artist Agreement, and Graphic Artist Agreement.

2. Read more about these contracts at *MusicBusinessMadeSimple.com* or in the books, *The Musician's Business & Legal Guide* or *All You Need to Know About the Music Business*.

3. Meet with an attorney to adapt your contracts to your label's needs and to make sure the contracts conform to laws in your state.

DEVISING A BUSINESS PLAN

A business plan is a document that sets out the direction for your company and explains how you're going to achieve your goals. Every company needs one. Creating your business plan serves an organizational purpose and also challenges you to explain on paper—to potential employees, partners, and/or investors—how your company will be set up and how it will run from the start.

Your label's business plan will demonstrate to artists and other professionals that, even as a start-up label, you're organized and professional. It should address management and operations, your promotion philosophy and strategy, marketing and sales, and the label's financial outlook. I address these topics in detail below. Your business plan will also include a mission statement (a sentence or two summarizing the label's vision and purpose), and will describe in detail how the label will achieve this mission. Basically, it's a road map of how your record label will conduct business. A sample business plan can be viewed, purchased, and downloaded at *MusicBusinessMadeSimple.com*. This example can provide a blueprint and help you get started.

Do not fear the business plan. It is your friend. Your initial business plan should be simple and for your benefit alone. You need to start somewhere. Most of your initial plan will cover how you're going to achieve your label's mission statement and goals. It doesn't have to be complicated or overly difficult, but it will require thought on your part. And that's good. You need to know how you intend to get from point A to point B. Your first business plan will help your label get started and keep on track.

It may also help you attract funding. For example, you might have a friend or potential investor who believes in you and wants to invest in your new record label. He or she understands this is a start-up label, but will still want to see your business plan. Even a simple plan set down on paper will show that you're serious and that you've thought about how to run your label, including the steps you'll take to sell records (and therefore, make money).

As your label grows, you'll develop a day-to-day operating plan, and hopefully, the label will begin to show a steady income. At that point, you will formulate a more detailed business plan to attract additional investors, bigger distributors, etc. Below, I describe five main sections that should be included in your business plan (change them or add others as you see fit): Mission Statement, Marketing and Sales, Management and Operations, Promotion Philosophy and Strategy, and Financial Outlook.

The Mission Statement is a brief overview, usually no more than a couple sentences, of your company's immediate objectives. Here is an example.

> Record Company's mission is to build a record company utilizing local and regional talent, concentrating initial efforts on selling records in New York City and the surrounding regions. Record Company will concentrate marketing and promotion efforts on supporting and developing recording artists, to increase record sales in regions where the artists perform live.

This simple statement makes your mission clear. It identifies short-term goals that can change as your company grows. It will also provide a daily reminder of what you are attempting to accomplish. Once you meet the goals set forth in the mission statement, or as circumstances change, it's time to examine your business plan and write a new statement.

The mission statement explains immediate objectives and helps you to maintain your focus on achieving them. Of course, you can also include a statement about your longer-term goals in a different section of your business plan. This statement will inform prospective business partners or investors as to where you hope to take your company in the future.

It's important to develop a marketing and sales strategy early in the planning process. For example, you must decide which musical genre your label will produce (e.g., alternative or punk rock, hip-hop or rap, blues, jazz, Americana, etc.). As I mentioned earlier, I think it is important for start-up independent labels to focus on a single type of music. This makes it easier to focus your resources, establish a niche, and identify the audience or market for your label's records. Your choice of genre should be based on business (which genre will sell the most records), but also on your personal interests (which genre you love most). If you aren't committed to the music, your label won't succeed. I discuss this issue further in Chapter, 27, Choosing a Genre.

Management and Operations refers to your label's day-to-day operational structure. Even if you're going to do everything yourself at first, this section of your business plan should identify and define the responsibilities of each role you'll be filling. Specific management positions or departments for independent labels would include Label Manager, A&R (Artist and Repertoire), Publicity and Radio, and Marketing and Sales.

As your company grows, you can consider hiring other people to take over some of those roles. Until that time, you do each job yourself or use outside help/consultants on a per-job basis. No matter who does the work, your plan should define job titles and responsibilities. This will show a definite structure within your company, and will outline the operational functions required to accomplish your mission statement.

Promotion Philosophy and Strategy means your plan for informing your market about the label's artists and products (i.e., records). Some obvious promotional techniques used by major labels are radio airplay; music videos; radio, television and magazine advertisements, etc. With limited funds, you'll have to be creative. I recommend that you research and compile a list of inexpensive publicity strategies, such as those described in the Promotion section and Appendix A of this book. Identifying your options and formulating a promotion plan early on will save time later, and will make your daily publicity and sales activities more effective.

Finally, you need to explain the Financial Outlook for your company. This section of the business plan will include analysis of the costs associated with creating a label and producing the compact discs or cassettes your label will sell, and daily business operations. Identifying and understanding the market outlets available to you (e.g., small local record stores, the Internet, your artists' live shows) will give you some idea of how much income your label can expect to generate from the sale of a record. Naturally, you'll have to do some research to learn what you might be paid by these various sales outlets. But with some work, you will be able to make an educated estimate.

Your initial financial outlook will consist of a preliminary budget for costs and a projection of income from sales. Obviously, your projections will be largely speculative at first. That's okay. You need at least an estimate of your costs, compared to potential income, to make intelligent decisions about how to proceed with your daily operations. Your finances may not always turn out as anticipated. Whose do? But being proactive may allow you to foresee financial shortfalls and avoid some big mistakes. With experience, you'll be able to predict your costs and income more accurately.

The business plan is an essential tool to starting any company, including your record label. It takes time, energy, and serious thought. You'll have to identify your goals and vision for the company, do research, obtain answers, and then write it all down. It isn't easy, but it will help you "put the pieces together" in your mind and on paper, and determine what you have and what you still need to start and run a successful record label.

Things You Can Do Today To Build Your Label

1. Obtain a form business plan from an entertainment attorney, a music-business resource, or at *MusicBusinessMadeSimple.com.*

2. Research the price your label can expect to receive for CD sales to various wholesale and retail outlets, and use your findings to produce a financial outlook for your label.

3. Create your own business plan, including the mission statement, marketing and promotion approaches, operational strategies, and financial outlook.

FORMING A BUSINESS ORGANIZATION

*L*ike all companies, record labels operate under some form of business organization, which is simply a legal way to separate the business's operations from the owner or owners. In the case of a business with an individual owner, the business' name, assets, and checking account are typically kept separate from the owner's personal property. You will probably need legal and business advice to help you decide which business entity is right for your label. Because each state has different laws, I advise that you work with an attorney in your state.

The three basic types of business organizations are sole proprietorships, partnerships, and corporations. As your record label evolves, your business organization may change from one type to another. The sole proprietorship is a business with a single owner. The partnership is a business with more than one owner. The corporation is a single or multi-owner corporate entity. Each organization has different legal rights and responsibilities, which I address below.

A sole proprietorship is the easiest business entity to establish because it does not require any formal organization to exist. You, the single owner of the label, are the business. As such, you can hire employees, obtain loans, pay taxes, own property, etc.

When starting up your label, you probably won't have many legal liabilities. Therefore, it may be easiest, quickest, and least expensive to organize your business as a sole proprietorship. However, as your label and personal assets (money and property) grow, your legal responsibilities and risks will grow along with them. In addition to its increasing tax liabilities, your company might be subject to legal actions for things like breach of contract or copyright infringement. As a sole proprietor, these actions would be made against you personally. You really don't want that. So as your label grows and your personal assets increase, you'll want to consider forming a corporate entity to protect your personal assets. I discuss this further below.

A partnership is a business organization founded on an agreement between two or more owners, who operate the business for the purpose of making a profit. Although most state laws do not require partnership agreements to be in writing, I strongly recommend that you do set forth the terms of any partnership in a written agreement. This will help to eliminate, or at least reduce, disputes. The co-owners have rights to share in the profits and make decisions. Each state has its own laws governing operation of a partnership, so you'll need to talk with an attorney in your state before forming one.

The partnership is a legal entity. It owns rights to property, including intellectual property like copyrights, has the right to make contracts, and can be sued. Similar to a sole proprietorship, each partner is personally liable for the partnership's taxes, debts, contractual responsibilities, and any legal actions taken against the business. Each partner is equally responsible, unless otherwise agreed to in writing. The assets owned by the partnership, and the personal assets of the partners, may be seized to satisfy a legal judgment against the partnership, such as for the non-payment of a debt or taxes, or a breach of contract. Consequently, as your label's value increases, and as you and your partners gain more personal assets, you should consider forming a corporation to protect yourselves and your assets from lawsuits.

To establish a corporate entity, most states require applicants to complete a few relatively simple forms and pay a fee. The main form is commonly called "Articles of Incorporation." Even after the forms are completed and your application is accepted by the state, you must meet additional legal requirements to become a corporation. Further, each state defines a variety of corporate entities, each with its own requirements. So, it's important to hire an attorney to discuss the best type of corporate organization for your record label and to assure that all necessary documentation is completed correctly and filed with your state.

A corporation is owned by shareholders (or a single shareholder) and is governed by a written document, commonly called "bylaws" or a "shareholders agreement," that describes the shareholders' agreements about how the corporation will be managed. Unlike a sole proprietorship or a partnership, a corporation is a legal entity separate from its owner(s). Because it can be held liable on its own, the corporate entity protects its owners from personal liability. In the case of any legal action taken against the corporation, only the corporation's assets—and not those of the owners—are at risk.

The laws are created to allow different business formats and accommodate different types of business ownership. It's important to understand your options and know which organization is best for your label. You can set up a sole proprietorship with little or no formation costs. It is also relatively easy and inexpensive to establish a partnership among two or more people who share the same ideas and interests. Or you can protect individual assets by forming a corporation. Chances are, you'll start out as a sole proprietor. Later, you may take on partners and form a partnership. If your record label really grows, you can form a corporation to protect the owners' individual assets.

Things You Can Do Today To Build Your Label

1. Obtain legal and business advice from an attorney and/or a certified public accountant to help you to decide which business entity is right for your label.

2. Choose a business entity for your label and learn the specific requirements needed to form and set up the entity in your city and state.

3. Form your business today by completing the necessary forms and paying any required fees.

COPYRIGHT BASICS

The music business—and therefore, your label's business—is founded on the acquisition, use, and/or sale of copyrights to songs and the recordings of those songs. To understand this fully, it will be helpful to understand the basics of copyright and its relation to the music industry.

Copyright is the legal right, established by federal law, of an author to control his or her intellectual creations, and to make copies of his or her original works. In the music industry, an "author" can be a songwriter or a recording artist who records the song. The law protects a songwriter, and recognizes him or her as the song's owner as soon as the song is written down or recorded. The same is true for a recording artist, who acquires a copyright to the recording of a performance the moment that performance is recorded. Copyright allows songwriters and recording artists to protect and maintain ownership of their creations, or to transfer those rights to third parties, like record labels.

As suggested above, copyrights for written songs are separate from the copyrights for recordings of those songs. Publishing companies acquire the copyrights to written songs through a publishing agreement; record companies acquire the copyrights to sound recordings of those songs through a recording agreement. How does this work, and what does it mean for your label? Here's an example.

Say the recording artist Madonna wants to record the song "American Pie," originally written by Don McLean. As the author, Don McLean originally owned the copyrights to the song. However, he has transferred his rights to this song (and perhaps others) to a publishing company, Benny Bird Company, Inc. If Madonna is going to record this song, her record company, Warner Bros., must obtain a license (written permission) from Don McLean's publisher, Benny Bird Company, Inc.

Under the terms of this license (called a mechanical license), Madonna will record "American Pie," and her record company will pay Don McLean's publishers a royalty for each copy of her recording sold. McLean will then receive a portion of that royalty from his publishers. (This is called a mechanical royalty, which I explain further in Chapter 24, The Mechanical Royalty.) The publisher will retain a portion of the royalty, based on its ownership of the song, which Mr. McLean has transferred to the Benny Bird Company, Inc. As the original creator of this particular recording of the song, Madonna will own the copyrights to this recording, but not to the song.

However, because Madonna has a written recording contract with Warner Bros., the label would own her rights to her recording of the song, and would pay her a royalty from its use. This is the other side of the copyright equation: Record companies, like yours, obtain the rights to recordings through contracts. Although the artist, musicians, and producer create the recording, these authors will transfer their rights to that recording to the record company. (I explain why in Chapter 19, The Record Deal: An Overview.)

To extend this example a little further, assume a film-production company wants to use Madonna's recording of "American Pie" in one of its movies. The film company would have to ask Don McLean's publishers, Benny Bird Company, Inc., for the rights to use his song in its film. The film company would also have to ask Madonna's record label, Warner Bros., for the right to use her recording of the song. Either McLean's publisher or Warner Bros. could refuse to grant these rights for any reason. In this case, the film company would have to find a different song and recording for its movie.

Your label will be faced with similar copyright and ownership issues, and it is important that you continue to study and understand how copyright laws affect the industry. You can read more about basic copyright issues in *Music Copyright for the New Millennium* by David J. Moser, or on the U.S. Copyright Office Website: *www.copyright.gov*.

Things You Can Do Today To Build Your Label

1. Meet with an attorney to learn more about copyright law.

2. Study how copyright laws apply to the music industry and learn how they will affect your business as a record label.

3. Make sure the contracts you use are current and provide fair copyright protection, both for your label and for the artists and producers with whom it works.

Copyright Protection: Notice and Registration

A s explained in the previous chapter, music publishers acquire the rights to written songs, and record companies acquire the copyrights to recordings. These rights must be acquired in a written contract. I explain this process as it relates to record companies in Chapter 20, The Recording Contract. Once the record company enters into a written contract with an artist, who then makes a master recording of songs, the record label owns the copyright to that master recording for the "duration of copyright." (As of January 1, 2005, the duration of copyright was 125 years. After 125 years, the recording goes into the public domain, which means anyone has the right to use that recording without the record company's permission.)

I explained in the previous chapter that copyright laws grant legal protection to an author or owner of a copyright from the moment a song/recording is written down/recorded. However, there are two things your record company should do to protect its copyright fully: Place a copyright notice on the recording and register the recording with the U.S. Copyright Office.

One of the best ways to protect your rights to the recordings made for your label is to place a copyright notice on all copies of the recordings, which will include the year the work was published. This notice will actively notify the public that you are claiming a copyright.

Because both unpublished and published works may be registered for copyright with the U.S. Copyright Office, it is important to know if your song or recording has been published before you submit your copyright registration. Publication occurs when you distribute copies of your artists' recordings to the public for sale (or if you give copies away, rather than sell them). When a record label releases a compact disc for sale, the label will include a copyright notice on both the disc and the accompanying artwork to indicate ownership and date of publication. This notice is accomplished simply by placing the letter "P" in a circle (for "phono record," or the recording), and a "C" in a circle (for the copyright to the CD artwork), followed by the year of publication and your record label's name. A separate copyright notice is used to indicate the owners of the songs. The notice should be legible, permanently affixed to the CD and artwork, and located in clear view of the user.

This notice protects you in two ways. First, it prevents anyone from claiming that they innocently infringed on your copyright. Second, it tells the public who owns the recordings. That way, if someone wants to use one of the recordings, they know whom to contact to obtain a license and whom to pay for the use.

If the recording was created and is being released in the United States, the second way to protect your record label's copyright is to register the recording with the U.S. Copyright Office. U.S. copyright law requires an author (or owner of a copyright) to register his or her work within three months of the time it is published. (Work that was originally registered as unpublished must be re-registered if it is subsequently published.) Because your record label owns the recordings made by your artists, it is imperative that you register these recordings with the Copyright Office as soon as possible after they are released for sale.

Failure to register your work with the Copyright Office does not affect your ownership of the work. However, the law restricts your rights in two important ways if you do not register the work. First, until you register, you can't file a lawsuit against a copyright infringer. Second, if you fail to register your work within three months after publication, you will be prevented by law, even after the work is registered, from recouping attorney's fees and receiving additional statutory damages (up to $250,000) in any copyright infringement lawsuit you might file.

Copyright registration is accomplished by sending a properly completed registration form (the SR form) to the Copyright Office, along with a fee of $30 for each application, and either one or two non-returnable copies of the work to be registered. You will submit a single application to register all the recordings on the CD. If the work is unpublished, enclose one copy of the work. If the work is published, enclose two copies with your registration application.

Once the registration process is complete, the copyright office will place your application on file. This serves as public notice of your claim to copyright on your work. The information on your application is a public record, and a copy of your application will be available to anyone who wants to see it. This documented registration of the recordings made for your label will establish the proof of ownership you'd need to file a lawsuit for copyright infringement.

Now is a good time to mention the urban myth known as "Poor Man's Copyright." This is the idea that an author can prove ownership by mailing him or herself a package, making sure the dated postmark is clear, and not opening the package when it arrives. Unfortunately, this strategy does not meet the requirements of federal copyright laws for registering your work.

You may have a room filled with unopened envelopes containing all of your recordings, but if you fail to register your work with the Copyright Office within three months of publication, you will never be able to pursue attorney's fees or statutory damages on those recordings. You may also be limited in terms of the amount of monetary damages you can recover from the infringer if a court determines that the infringement was an innocent mistake caused by your failure to register the work. Even worse, if the infringer registers a copyright for your recordings, you may have difficulty overcoming that registration and risk losing your rights altogether.

The bottom line is, register your work. Protect yourself. The information presented here will help get you started. Much more help is available on the Internet. For further information and free copyright forms, visit the U.S. Copyright Office's Website at *www.copyright.gov.*

Things You Can Do Today To Build Your Label

1. Place the proper copyright notices on all of your CDs and CD artwork.

2. Obtain the proper forms for registering your copyrights with the U.S. Copyright Office at the Website, www.copyright.gov.

3. Meet with an attorney for advice and assistance in registering your recordings with the U.S. Copyright Office.

IMPORTANCE OF TRADEMARK

18

A trademark is a creative or fanciful name or design, used to identify the owner of goods or services. Whereas copyright laws protect literary, musical, dramatic, and other artistic intellectual property, trademark laws protect names, logos, or other (trade) marks associated with a business or individual.

The significance of a trademark is that it legally assures the owner's right to use (and profit from) that trademark in association with the service or product he or she provides. The trademark also allows its owner to prevent others from using the same or a similar name or design. These exclusive rights are granted via the Federal Lanham Trademark Act, or by state trademark laws.

In the music industry, trademarks are most often used for the name of a record label or of a group, band, or artist. The trademark PolyGram Records, for example, identifies the corporate owner that manufactured U2's records for many years. The trademark U2 identifies the band that provides musical entertainment services.

A record label's name is often intended to convey the vision of the owner or appeal to a broad market (e.g., Maverick, Epic, Elektra, Universal, or Giant). Other names, such as Metal Blade or Rap-A-Lot, identify, in a creative way, the type of music the record label distributes. As a label grows, its name becomes associated with the quality of the artists it signs and records. This recognition gives value to the name or logo, which the label wants to protect as a trademark.

An identifying name, mark, or design can also be a very profitable piece of property for recording artists. It's basic marketing: When consumers become familiar with a particular name and begin to associate it with a service or product they like, they are more likely to purchase the goods produced under that name. For example, it's highly likely that, based on their familiarity with, and approval of, U2's previous work, many people will purchase their next compact disc, even before hearing it. This type of blind purchase occurs most frequently with established names and adds considerable value to those names. A lot of records get sold simply by having a recognizable band name on a well-known record label.

Initial trademark rights are acquired through use of the name, mark, or design, either by affixing it to the product or by using it when advertising the product or service. Therefore, when your record label uses its label name and/or logo in advertisements for its services—specifically, the production and manufacturing of compact discs—the label acquires ownership or trademark rights to that name, mark, and/or design. This is important, because trademark laws prevent others from using a mark or name that is confusingly similar to the one(s) you already own.

You could even place the familiar "TM" (trademark) symbol in very small letters immediately following your label's name or mark on compact discs, CD artwork, and print advertising. This will indicate to others that you are claiming trademark rights to that name or mark. After your mark has been accepted for registration by a state or federal trademark office (see below), you will exchange "TM" for the traditional "R" in a circle.

A trademark owner may register that trademark in the state or states in which he or she uses it. If the owner has used the trademark in more than one state (i.e., distributed and sold albums or performed in several states), he or she may be eligible for federal registration. But don't wait until you meet federal registration requirements. Register initially in the state where you begin operation to protect your name and logo from the start.

Trademark registration in individual states is fairly simple and inexpensive; federal registration is a bit more complex and costly. In either case, use an experienced attorney to prepare your registration. If you register your mark incorrectly, you could risk losing your filing fee, registration, and use of the mark.

Before registering a trademark with the State or (if qualified) Federal Register, you are required by law to use the name and/or logo publicly, usually by putting it on manufactured CDs or on advertising for the sale of your label's products. Having done this, your label can register its name and/or other mark, which effectively and legally notifies others that you are the owner of that name or mark and are using it. Once you have registered, no other label will be allowed to register or use a name or logo similar to yours.

If another label does try to use the same or a similar name or logo, your prior use and registration would allow you to notify the user to cease using your mark and, if need be, pursue litigation to end such use and prevent it in the future. The same is true for the names and logos of recording artists signed to your label. Once those names and logos are registered, no other band or artist can use them, or anything similar. You can find further information in the book *How to Register a Trademark: Protect Yourself Before You Lose Your Priceless Trademark (The Entertainment Industry)* by Walter E. Hurst, or by visiting the U.S. Patent and Trademark Office online at *www.uspto.gov.*

Things You Can Do Today To Build Your Label

1. Make a list of possible names for your label, and logos that might go with them. Have fun and try to come up with something that is catchy and meaningful to you.

2. Begin placing your label name and logo on copies of CDs, your Website, and all promotional material, accompanied by the symbol "TM."

3. Meet with an entertainment attorney to help you register your label's trademark nationally or in the state where you do business.

The Record Deal: An Overview

A record deal is a written contract between a record label and a recording artist. Usually, it includes an agreement by the artist to record exclusively for the label for the duration of the contract. In return, the label generally agrees to do the following things.

1. Produce the artist's recordings at the label's expense.
2. Pay to have these recordings manufactured into compact discs, and packaged with printed material containing cover art and liner notes, song lyrics, etc.
3. Distribute the records for sale.
4. Pay the artist and writers of the songs a royalty, or a percentage of income from the sale of the compact discs, cassettes, etc.

Larger labels may also agree to produce a video and promote it to music-video stations to help generate interest in the artist and increase CD sales. In return for the label's services, the contract establishes the label as owner of all recordings done by the artist while under contract to the label. This means the record company can sell compact discs, cassettes, etc. derived from those recordings forever. It's that simple.

In the beginning, your label will not have the resources of Sony Music. You'll have to be realistic about what you can offer to artists and which artists you can attract, based on factors like the amount of money you have to spend, your distribution deal, and the label's ability to advertise and sell records. For example, you may not be able to pay an artist an advance beyond the recording, production, and marketing costs for his or her record. That's fine. In fact, almost every label starts this way. You just have to recognize your label's limitations and find creative ways to work within them.

At first, you're only going to be able to attract developing, unpolished talent. That's fair, since your label will be developing and unpolished, too. As your label grows, makes more money, and starts building a good reputation, you'll be able to attract more experienced and established artists, who will expect higher pay and more service. Even then, you may prefer to continue seeking out new talent instead of working with established artists.

Once you decide to sign an artist, how do you prepare, or where do you find, a recording contract? Some independent labels attempt to sign artists with a form recording agreement used by major labels. They use the rationale that if this contract is good enough for artists on major labels, it should be good enough for artists on an independent label.

But there are significant differences between giant record labels and tiny independents. For example, large labels have lots of money, well-established national distribution, and the ability to advertise and sell millions of records. You don't. You won't be able to pay a big advance or spend money making a music video, and you probably don't have a system in place to sell records beyond your city or state.

Therefore, the contracts used by major labels probably won't work very well for yours. You have to be practical and realistic. Given your limited resources, you can't expect an artist to agree to an exclusive, low royalty-paying, seven-year deal that a major label might offer. In fact, that kind of agreement with an unknown talent probably isn't in your best interest, either. Your contracts need to fit your individual circumstances, and should represent accurately what you can offer to an artist, and what you expect in return.

But where do you obtain a recording agreement? You can find form contracts in books or on the Internet, or obtain them from an attorney, a colleague, or another independent label. No matter where you acquire the contract, you will almost certainly have to consult with an entertainment attorney to help you revise and adapt it for your label. It is critical that the agreement you present to potential artists reflects what you can and cannot deliver. Nothing will kill your label's reputation faster than failing to live up to its promises. Remember, the first artists on your label will be new and unproven. They will (or should) understand they can't expect too much. An honest assessment on both sides can lead to an agreement that benefits everyone.

You will present your model agreement to each artist you wish to sign. Because you will need to personalize the contract for each artist (it's highly unlikely that any artist will accept the contract without trying to negotiate some of the terms), it's practical to have the agreement on a computer so you can make changes easily. This is much more professional than whiting out errors and writing in changes on a photocopied agreement you can't change. The next chapter, The Recording Contract, provides greater detail about major elements to include in your label's agreements.

Things You Can Do Today To Build Your Label

1. Become familiar with the essential services that a record label provides.

2. Recognize your limitations as a small label and decide which services you will realistically be able to offer to artists.

3. Obtain a form recording agreement for your label. Meet with an entertainment attorney to tailor the agreement to your label's needs and abilities.

THE RECORDING 20 CONTRACT

*I*t is absolutely necessary for your label to obtain a detailed written agreement with any artist whose records you wish to record and sell. To do this, you will use a recording contract, a record label's most indispensable business tool. The four main points covered in a recording contract are: The term, or duration, of the agreement; recording advances; ownership of master recordings; and royalties. I discuss the first three topics in this chapter. Royalties are addressed in the next chapter, How Does the Artist Get Paid?

The "term" of a contract is simply how long it will be in effect. Most often, a contract's term is defined by the number of records the artist will record for the label within a given amount of time. Generally, an artist will agree to record exclusively for the record company during the term of the contract, and to complete one record within 12 to 18 months.

As part of the term, the label usually includes a statement that reserves the label's right, or "option," to record more records with the artist in the future. The option allows the label to evaluate the income and excitement generated by an artist's previous record(s) before deciding whether or not to invest more money for another record. Typically, only the record company has the right to exercise the option, which is reasonable, since the label is paying to produce, manufacture, and promote the record.

If the record company and artist agree to a term of one record with four options, the contract could last up to five years. The first CD would be recorded during "year one," and one additional CD would be recorded in each of the following four years. The industry standard for maximum total length of a recording agreement is seven years. The length of term your label can offer will be determined by the laws in your state related to personal service or employment contracts, or the industry standard for labels at your level of success. Although the law will be the same for all labels, smaller labels tend to offer and negotiate fewer options than major labels do.

Sometimes, recording contracts will run 12 months from the record's release date, rather than from the date the contract is signed. However, this arrangement may reduce the number of records a label can agree to record and release for an artist. If the contract runs 12 months from the date of the release and the label releases the record six months after it is completed, the first term of the contract is actually 18 months. If the label maintains this schedule, the label would able to record and release only five records in seven years.

Once the label and artist agree on the contract's term, they must negotiate an advance: Money paid by the label to the artist, or spent by the label on the artist's behalf. The artist will pay this money back to the label from future royalties he or she earns for the sale of his or her records. The term "advance" is most often interpreted to mean a cash payment from the label to the artist upon the signing of the recording contract. Bruce Springsteen famously sings about getting a "big advance" from the record company in his song, "Rosalita." However, in reality, very few artists receive significant cash payments until and unless their records start to sell.

Yes, sometimes the label gives the artist money just for signing the recording agreement. If the artist is very well known or likely to sell a lot of records, a label might pay him or her a cash advance. I do not recommend this for smaller labels signing first-time artists. As an unproven talent, the artist has no reason to expect a signing advance, and your label probably can't afford to pay one anyway. That's fine. The goal at this level is to get records made and out to the public, so it's far more important to spend your money recording, manufacturing, and promoting the CD as well as possible. Besides, the small amount you might pay an artist is not enough to change his or her life. It only sets a bad precedent, encouraging the artist to ask for money each time he or she is running short on cash.

And even if they don't get a signing bonus, artists still get advances. The record company has many up-front costs associated with recording and releasing a CD, and most payments made by the label before the artist's record arrives in stores are considered advances. For example, there is a "recording advance," which is the money spent by the record label to make the recording. Other advances can include money spent on CD artwork, or given to the artist for touring, or spent to promote the CD. The recording contract should make it clear that these expenses are considered "recoupable advances," to be repaid by the artist through his or her future royalties. Until the label has been paid back and has "recouped" these advance payments, the artist will not receive any royalties from the sales of his or her CDs.

Here's a simple example of how a label recoups its advances, assuming there is no cash advance to the artist for signing the contract. Imagine that an independent label pays $15,000 for all recording and artwork expenses related to the artist's CD. In addition, the label spends $30,000 to advertise and promote the record, for a total of $45,000 in advances paid to the artist. (I do not include manufacturing costs in this example because they normally are not recoupable from the artist's royalty. They can be as low as $5,000 or as high as $200,000 depending on the size and success of the independent label and the artist.)

Now, let's say the contract calls for the artist to be paid a $1.00 royalty for each compact disc sold. (Most independent artists receive an average royalty of $1.00 to $1.50.) In this case, the first 45,000 CDs sold would result in a payment of $45,000 to the artist. However, because the contract says the advances listed above are recoupable, the record label will reimburse itself before paying the artist. Thus, the first $45,000 from the artist's royalties will be paid to the label. The artist will begin to receive his or her royalty payment of $1.00 for the 45,001st record sold, and will receive $1.00 for each copy sold thereafter.

Another main issue addressed in a record contract is ownership of the master recordings. The record label will own the copyrights to the master recordings, along with the exclusive right to sell compact discs, cassette tapes, digital downloads, etc. of those recordings. This is industry standard. However, the label's rights still must be clearly described and legally protected in the recording contract. Your entertainment attorney can help to make sure they are.

Obviously, each of these issues will be addressed in much greater detail in the recording agreements you sign with artists. You definitely will need the assistance of an entertainment attorney to make sure these points are properly covered in the contracts your label uses, and to make sure that each party in the agreement gets a fair deal. But it is important for you to have a working knowledge of these issues from the start. To see and download a standard recording contract, visit *MusicBusinessMadeSimple.com*.

Things You Can Do Today To Build Your Label

1. Research your state's laws and industry standards regarding length of recording contracts for independent labels at your level.

2. Learn about what kinds of payments are considered "recoupable advances" and how you will incorporate them into your recording agreement.

3. Meet with an entertainment attorney to make sure your contract protects your label's ability to recoup advances and protects your ownership of master recordings.

WHAT IS DISTRIBUTION?

There are various ways of getting your label's product to the market. You can sell the CDs you produce out of the trunk of your car, from a booth at the artist's live performances, through mail order (by advertising in magazines or through a Website), or, of course, in record stores. Distribution is the process of getting record or retail stores to order and purchase your CDs.

How do you get your artists' CDs into record stores? One way is to contact or meet with the store's buyer and ask him or her either to purchase some of your artist's records for the store, or to take the CDs on consignment. If the buyer takes some of your CDs, he or she may pay you right then, or may ask you to send an invoice (bill). In this case, you'll get paid in a few weeks. If the store takes your CDs on consignment, you'll get paid 30 to 90 days after someone buys the CDs. If no one buys the CDs, the record store will return the unsold CDs without payment. This all may sound simple, and, in concept, it is. The trick is getting the stores to take your products.

Even if you are marketing and promoting only in one large city, it can be very difficult and time-consuming to convince every record store to accept your label's product. As a small local label, you may have a hard time convincing larger chain record stores to take your CD at all. Therefore, smaller, independent "mom and pop" record stores are your best bet. But since "mom and pops" usually don't have extra money to risk on your (unknown) product, they probably will accept your CDs on consignment only. It is also possible that some of the independent record stores you approach may sell only certain kinds of music, which do not match the music your label produces. The only way to find out is through research and trial and error.

As you can see, it's a challenge to get your label's product into record stores. But don't get frustrated. Every label has the same problem, and distribution to retail stores is still the best way to get your CDs into consumers' hands. It's difficult to do this on your own, but you have a friend in the business, called a distributor, who can help. If you don't want to spend all your time talking up record-store buyers, you need to persuade a distributor to work with you to get your products into stores. I address the role of a distributor, and how to find one, and the specifics of the distribution deal in Part V, Marketing and Distribution.

News headlines tell us the music industry is changing rapidly, especially in terms of how consumers are getting their music. With the advent of digital technology and the Internet, many consumers are able to download the music they want, or simply go online to purchase a CD, which is then shipped to them.

As a result, the business of distribution is also changing and adapting. Yes, you need a distributor to get your records into as many record stores as possible. The distributor can also establish relationships with the online retail community to help your label sell its records in this new "virtual record store" environment. Your label can and should sell its records on its own Website and on Internet retail sites. Your distributor's relationships with online retailers will help to get your label's products on more sites, and will improve the placement and visibility of your products through various online marketing techniques.

Digital technology, such as downloadable music and CD manufacture on demand, is changing the face of music distribution, and there is much debate over the life expectancy of traditional "brick-and-mortar" record stores, especially independent shops. The good news is there will always be a market for new music. You just have to know how to reach that market.

If you hope to succeed, your label must keep up with shifts in the industry. Learn as much as you can about the different ways consumers acquire their music, so you can adjust your marketing plans to include all forms of distribution. This will increase the label's opportunities to sell your artists' music, whether on standard manufactured compact discs, via downloadable digital files, or through some other format that has yet to be invented.

Things You Can Do Today To Build Your Label

1. Determine which stores in your area carry the kind of music your label produces and determine which ones might be receptive to carrying your CDs.

2. Do some research to find distributors in your area who work with independent labels that produce your genre of music.

3. Learn as much as you can about the different ways consumers acquire their music, so you can adjust your marketing plans to include all forms of distribution.

How Does the Artist Get Paid?

*I*n their book, *Music, Money, and Success,* noted entertainment attorneys Jeff and Todd Brabec explain that one of the most important sections of a recording contract is the part dealing with royalties. Unfortunately, it can also be the most confusing section. Here and in the following chapters, I hope to shed some light on this great mystery of the record business.

A standard record contract will call for the label to pay the artist two types of royalties: A record royalty and a mechanical royalty. A basic record royalty is pretty straightforward: The artist receives a percentage of the sales price for each CD purchased. The exact percentage is set forth in the contract. However, because of some creative accounting methods devised by the recording industry, the record royalty paid to an artist will almost always be lower than the rate identified in the contract. I explain this further in the next chapter, The Record Royalty.

The artist also receives a record royalty when the label is paid for other uses of the artist's recording. For example, the artist receives a percentage of the money paid to the label for use of the recording in a movie or television commercial, or on a compilation album. Traditionally, if a film producer or advertising agency wants to use an artist's recording in a movie or television commercial, the record label will pay the artist 50% of the fee received for such use. Once again, though, the exact amount to be paid to the artist in these cases will be negotiated and set forth in the contract.

The second kind of royalty paid by the label is a mechanical royalty. Mechanical royalty rates are determined by the industry standard, which uses U.S. copyright laws as a guideline. Like the basic record royalty, mechanical royalties are paid each time a record is sold. However, these royalties go to the songwriter, not the recording artist. If the artist who recorded the song also wrote it, he or she would receive both record and mechanical royalties for each copy of the CD sold. If someone other than the recording artist wrote the song, the label would pay record royalties to the recording artist and mechanical royalties to the songwriter. See Chapter 24, The Mechanical Royalty, for a more detailed explanation of this issue.

Other than royalties, a label may make two additional payments to an artist. The first type of payment, called an advance, is explained in Chapter 20, The Recording Contract. An advance can be money paid to the artist for signing the contract, and can also include label expenses for recording, production, and promotion costs related to the artist's CD, among other items.

A label may also make a "per diem" payment to its artists. Translated directly as "each day," the additional per diem payment covers daily expenses, such as food, lodging, gas for the van, etc., when the artist is recording or touring. It can range from $50 to $300 per person, per day, depending on the circumstances. Neither a signing advance nor the per diem is legally required in most states. (However, if the artist belongs to a union, the per diem will be required during recording.)

Things That You Can Do Today To Build Your Label

1. Study the different payments that your label may make to artists, and analyze how these will affect your budget.

2. Research the present compulsory mechanical royalty rate to determine how much you will pay a songwriter for recording his or her songs.

3. Contact a local musician's union, such as the American Federation of Musicians (AF of M) or the American Federation of Television and Recording Artists (AFTRA) to determine the guidelines for making "per diem" payments to an artist.

THE RECORD ROYALTY

23

A s explained in the previous chapter, a recording artist receives a royalty for each copy of his or her compact disc that is sold, and when his or her recordings are licensed for other uses, such a film or television commercial. The record royalty rate is set by the recording contract and is calculated as a percentage of the sales price. A royalty rate of 13% means the artist gets 13% of the price for each CD sold. In the music business, royalty rates are known as "points" (as in percentage points). Therefore, a royalty rate of 13% of the suggested retail list price (SRLP) is also referred to as 13 points. If a compact disc has an SRLP of $13.98 and the artist is getting 13 points, then the artist's base royalty is $1.81. Theoretically, this means the artist will be paid $1.81 for every record sold.

However, most recording contracts will include additional deductions that reduce both the base royalty rate and the number of records for which an artist is paid. These deductions are industry standard. Your entertainment attorney can help you determine which deductions are appropriate for the contracts you offer to artists, based on your label's specific needs. Still, you should have a general understanding of how these deductions work. So step right up, ladies and gentlemen, and watch in amazement as I turn a $1.81 record royalty into $0.97.

Blame CDs. Everything changed when compact discs hit the market in the early 1980s. At the time, they sold in stores for about $18.00 to $20.00

each, compared to $10.00 to $12.00 for vinyl albums. Record labels did not want to pay higher royalty rates for compact discs, because even at higher prices, CDs had a lower profit margin than vinyl albums. Back then, it cost more to manufacture CDs than vinyl albums. Also, labels had to entice stores to purchase the new CD medium by selling it to them at a reduced rate. To cover their costs (and protect their profit margin), record companies devised three new royalty deductions which became part of the standard recording contract: A packaging deduction, CD price reduction, and free-good deduction.

Theoretically, the record company pays manufacturing and packaging costs out of its profits, and therefore, does not recoup them from the artist's royalties. But due to the initial high costs involved with manufacturing CDs, labels began to include a 25% royalty reduction in their recording agreements during the 1980s. Even though the relative costs have dropped considerably since then, this "packaging deduction" is still used today. The packaging deduction reduces the SRLP by 25%. So instead of receiving 13% of the actual $13.98 SLRP, the artist gets 13% of $10.50 ($13.98 x 75%). Thus, the $1.81 artist royalty rate is automatically reduced to $1.36.

Record companies also wanted to avoid paying higher royalties on the higher sales price of CDs. Remember, in the 1980s, CDs were selling for $6.00 to $10.00 more than vinyl records, so in some cases, the royalties paid on CDs could have been almost twice as high as those for record albums. To bring the royalty paid on a CD closer to that paid for a vinyl album, labels simply started paying a lower royalty rate for CDs. This was known as a "royalty price reduction." If an artist was receiving a 13% royalty rate for each vinyl LP sold, he or she would get 85% of that royalty rate (or 11%) on the sale of a CD.

The royalty price reduction remains part of the contracts used by some labels today, even though vinyl is pretty much extinct and CD costs have dropped. As a result, the artist's royalty rate is effectively reduced from 13% to 11% (13% x 85%), and the overall royalty paid on the sale of each CD drops from $1.36 to $1.15 (11% x $10.50).

Finally, there is a "free-good deduction." "Free goods" are CDs that the record company or distributor gives to the record store to sell, but for which the record store does not have to pay. Typically, a record store gets 15 free CDs for every 100 it buys at full price (usually $7.00 to $11.00 each). This standard practice was originally intended to entice record stores to accept the CD format at a time when LP records were far more popular. And it's an excellent enticement; the record store's profit margin on "free goods" is 100%. When a store sells your artist's 15 "free goods" CDs at $13.98, it makes $209.70. Imagine how many artists' CDs are in the store and multiply that by $209.70 (the store won't receive free goods for every CD, but you get the idea). You can see why this arrangement is very appealing to retailers.

Typically, a label's recording contract will include a clause stating that the label can automatically reduce an artist's royalties by 15% to cover the cost of "free goods." The basic idea is that if the record label isn't going to get paid for those CDs, then neither should the artist. The "free goods" clause protects the label if its distributor has agreements to provide free CDs to various retail stores. But even if the label's distributor provides fewer than 15 free goods CDs for every 100 copies purchased by the stores, or no free goods at all (which is more the norm today), the 15% "free goods deduction" will remain in the contract.

Therefore, the artist will receive royalties for only 85% of his or her records sold to retail stores, even though the record label probably will be paid for 100% of those records. Why? It's industry standard. Due to the "free-good deduction," the artist's royalty rate (currently $1.15 per copy sold) will be reduced another 15%. In the end, the artist's royalty for each CD sold—which started at $1.81—will be $0.97.

All of the deductions described above are standard in most of today's contracts. It is possible that the recording contract may reduce royalties even further by paying the artist for only 90% of the CDs that are sold. The 10% "breakage deduction" was created to pay for vinyl LPs that arrived at stores broken. The advent of CDs pretty much solved the problem of broken product. However, as the other deductions remained in recording contracts, so has this one. It is not as common as the other deductions, and certainly is not included in every recording contract. If implemented, the "breakage deduction" will reduce the artist's royalty by an additional 10%, meaning the artist will receive $0.87 for each CD sold.

One additional calculation related to an artist's royalty is a "return reserve." The return reserve is needed because, for the purposes of determining an artist's royalties, a CD is considered sold when the record store buys it from the record label, not when the customer buys it from the store. This means that an artist's royalties are calculated before his or her CDs are actually sold to the public.

So far, so good. But there's a potential snag with this arrangement. Stores often buy more copies than they expect to sell, to be sure they have enough stock on hand if the record becomes a hit. If a store decides the CDs are not going to sell, it has the option of returning unsold product to the label or distributor. Naturally, the store will receive a refund for the returned CDs. In this case, the label will have paid royalties for CDs that were not sold.

To protect itself from losing money in this situation, the label will include a "return reserve" statement in its recording contract. Through this provision, the label will hold back, or "reserve," a percentage of the artist's royalties for a specified period of time (up to one or two years) to assure that no royalties are paid for CDs that are later returned to the label. If the CDs are not returned within the agreed-upon time period, the record label must release the "reserve" to the artist.

Obviously, the base royalty rate is only a starting point; the types of royalty calculations described here have a significant impact on the amount of royalties actually paid. As a label owner, you do not have to make these deductions, and not all contracts include them. The decision is yours. Consult with your entertainment attorney and/or accountant to devise a royalty payment clause that is best for your label, based on your distribution deal, financial resources, and philosophy regarding royalty payments.

Lately, many independent record companies have begun to eliminate the mystery and creative accounting from recording contracts. Many smaller labels contract to pay the full 13% on the SRLP, with no other deductions. Other labels are calculating the artist's royalty simply on net profits. After all expenses are paid back to the record label, the artist receives an agreed-upon percentage of the profits. In this way, the artist and label share in the profits, which are calculated in the same manner for both parties. This makes it easier for a record labels to calculate royalties, and for the artist to understand what his or her royalties will be. A sample Recording Agreement that calculates royalties based on net profits may be viewed at *MusicBusinessMadeSimple.com*.

Things You Can Do Today To Build Your Label

1. Read additional resources, such as *Music, Money, and Success* by Todd and Jeff Brabec, or *All You Need to Know About the Music Business* by Donald S. Passman, for further information about how and why royalties are calculated the way they are.

2. Attend a music-business seminar that covers topics associated with royalty payments and current record-industry accounting practices.

3. Consult with an entertainment attorney to decide the best way to calculate royalties in your label's contract, including the possibility of basing the artist's royalty on net profits.

THE MECHANICAL ROYALTY

*I*n Chapter 16, Copyright Basics, I explain the difference between the copyright of a recording and the copyright of a song. As set forth in the recording contract, your label will pay the artist a record royalty for the right to own his or her recordings of the songs. However, your label will not own the songs themselves, and you won't be able to record them until you receive permission to do so. To obtain the right to record each song, you'll need to secure a mechanical license from the person who wrote it, or more likely, his or her publishing company. This license gives you the right to reproduce, or record, the song mechanically (hence the name). In exchange for this right, you'll pay the owner(s) of the song a "mechanical royalty." (You can review and download a sample mechanical license at *MusicBusinessMadeSimple.com*).

If your artist wrote the songs he or she has recorded for the CD, you'll pay both record and mechanical royalties to the artist. If the artist wrote only part of the song, or wrote the song with someone else, each person credited with writing the song will be paid a percentage of the mechanical royalty that reflects his or her contribution to the song. For example, if the artist wrote only the music, or only the lyrics, he or she will receive 50% of the *mechanical* royalties because he or she wrote 50% of the song. As with the record royalty, your label's recording contract will contain a provision through which your artist grants the label a mechanical license to the songs he or she writes. If someone else writes the songs being recorded, alone or with your artist, you must obtain a separate mechanical license from that songwriter. Regardless of the percentage of mechanical royalties paid to the artist, he or she will receive 100% of the *record* royalties, because he or she recorded this version of the song.

The mechanical license represents one way a songwriter can make money from his or her song. If a company wants to include that song on a movie soundtrack or a compilation CD, the company will have to pay the songwriter(s) a mechanical royalty. If the company wants to use the version of the song recorded for your label, it will have to pay your label, too (because the label owns that recording). Later, in Chapter 26, I provide a brief explanation of the various ways in which a song, and a certain recording of the song, can make money for the label, artist, and songwriter.

The mechanical royalty your label will pay to songwriters is based on U.S. copyright laws. Once a song has been recorded and released, anyone may legally record that song without the songwriter's express written permission. However, the label or individual who records it must notify the songwriter and pay the statutory mechanical royalty rate, as prescribed in copyright law. This rate is subject to increase in the future. On January 1, 2006, the statutory mechanical royalty rate will increase from 8.5 to 9.1 cents per song recorded.

However, this is only a benchmark. A record label will negotiate to pay the songwriter(s) less, usually 75% of the statutory rate, for each record sold. More successful artists may be able to negotiate a higher rate, like 85%. As noted above, the statutory mechanical royalty rate applies in instances where a label or individual records a pre-released song without the songwriter's express written permission. If a label is seeking that written permission (most obviously, when the songwriter is also the label's recording artist), the label will attempt to negotiate a lower rate.

Under the current rate of 8.5 cents per song, the mechanical royalty actually paid by the label would be approximately 6.4 cents per song (75% of 8.5 cents). This amount then would be divided among all of the writers. If one songwriter wrote the words and another wrote the music, the royalty would be split 50/50, or 3.2 cents to each person. If there are more than two songwriters, each would receive a proportionately smaller amount. For example, if two people co-wrote the lyrics and one person wrote the music, the two lyric writers would split one-half of the royalty (each would receive 25% of the total payment), and the music writer would receive the other half.

It is important to reiterate that royalties are paid for each song on a record. For every CD or cassette sold, the songwriter will receive the mechanical royalty (6.4 cents), multiplied by the number of songs. For a CD with ten songs, a solo songwriter would receive 64 cents per sale.

Aside from lower mechanical royalty rates, industry standards dictate other variances from the copyright law. For instance, while the law dictates that a label will pay the songwriter for all records "manufactured and distributed," songwriters typically agree to be paid only for the number of records "sold." Moreover, if the recording artist is also the songwriter, record labels will typically negotiate to pay the artist for only ten songs on a record, even though the artist may choose to write and record more. Again, the copyright law is the benchmark. But if a label seeks to obtain express permission, the label is free to negotiate to obtain the best deal possible.

Things You Can Do Today To Build Your Label

1. Learn more about compulsory licenses and copyright law at the U.S. Copyright Office Website *(www.copyright.gov)* or the Harry Fox Agency's Website *(www.harryfox.com)*.

2. Continue to study the roles of, and differences between, record royalties and mechanical royalties. Be sure to understand how they will affect your label's business.

3. Consult with an entertainment attorney to discuss the mechanical license provision and make sure this provision is included in the recording contract you will use with your artists.

Royalty Accounting

As described in earlier chapters, the recording contract gives a label the exclusive right to record an artist and sell the artist's records for a specified period of time. In return, the record company agrees to pay the artist a certain amount of money for each copy of his or her record that is sold. This compensation is called a royalty.

Traditionally, the royalties paid to an artist are a percentage of the record's sales price. The exact percentage will be negotiated and set forth in the recording contract. Some smaller labels are changing their royalty accounting, paying their artists a percentage of the CD's net profits instead of a traditional royalty. While this approach may eventually change the way record companies pay recording artists, it's still evolving and is not common practice.

Several previous chapters explain the different forms of royalties and the methods for calculating royalty payments. These chapters also describe the deductions a record label will make from an artist's royalties to cover costs related to the production and sale of the record. These may include a packaging deduction, free-goods deductions, royalty price reduction, return reserve, etc.

After all CD/cassette sales, royalties, and expenses have been calculated, the label will send an accounting statement and royalty payment to the artist, usually every six months. The rest of this chapter will explain how it works. Also, Appendices B and C include a sample accounting statement for a recording artist who also wrote all of the songs on his or her CD.

Most record labels do not show all deductions/reductions on their royalty statements. This is partly because some royalty accounting software packages show only final calculations, and partly because labels like to keep artists' royalties a mystery. I adhere to the philosophy that labels—especially smaller independents—should include all deductions and reductions in their royalty statements. This openness helps the artist to understand how his or her royalty payments are calculated and prevents the artist from thinking the label is trying to hide something.

Obviously, it is very important for both labels and artists to understand how royalty rates are calculated and how various deductions and reductions affect the amount of royalties paid. This knowledge will help you, as a label owner, make solid decisions regarding the royalty rate(s) you will offer to artists, and the reductions/deductions you'll include in your recording contracts. It will also help you to know how much of the label's income you'll need to set aside during each accounting period to pay your artist(s).

Most recording agreements call for the label to pay its artists semi-annually (every six months). Naturally, you'll have to save enough of your label's income to cover royalty payments when they are due. You may make a lot of money from sales during the first month or quarter (three months) after you release an artist's record. Be happy. You're solvent! But beware, this initial "pop" may not continue.

I've seen many labels make the mistake of getting overly excited about solid early sales of a new release. Instead of being prudent and setting aside money for upcoming bills, artists' royalties, or additional marketing and promotion to help sell more records, the labels spent their "extra" income producing new recording artists, purchasing unnecessary office equipment, or even giving themselves big bonuses. There's nothing wrong with any of these expenditures if the label owners wait until *after* the label has a steady, predictable flow of income. Until that point, hold back money to make sure you'll have enough to pay all necessary bills.

Also, be sure to set up two separate checking accounts: One for royalty payments and one for the label's operating expenses. If you see a balance of $20,000 in the general operating account, it can be very tempting to spend that money on other expenses. If you hope to survive as a record label, you *must* pay royalties. On time. The best way to ensure that you have cash available when you need to pay royalties is to keep your artists' royalty money separate from the label's money. While you're at it, open interest-bearing checking accounts so you can earn interest on the money until it's time to pay the artists.

I strongly urge that you use an experienced bookkeeper to keep your label's checking accounts in order. And at tax time, you'll need to give your books to a CPA. The label may have significant income before it pays out royalties (and maybe even after). Therefore, it is critical to keep your accounting in excellent order at all times.

And again, I cannot over-emphasize how important it is to pay your artists' royalties in full and on time. Non-payment will give your label a bad reputation and require you to hire attorneys to defend you from the inevitable lawsuits filed by your artists. That's a bad business model, and the attorneys' fees may be as much, if not more, than the royalty payments you owe. It's much better to spend your label's resources on marketing and promoting the sale of CDs than on fighting artists over royalties to which they are legally entitled.

Take the time to set up your accounting properly from the start. This initial investment will help your operations run smoothly, keep your artists happy, and help your record label build a good reputation.

Things You Can Do Today To Build Your Label

1. Familiarize yourself with the accounting statements in Appendices B and C of this book and make sure you understand how an artist's royalties are derived.

2. Learn about computer accounting programs. Select one that will help you to maintain accurate and thorough checking-account records, and will allow you to create detailed royalty accounting statements for your artists.

3. Search for a reputable accountant in your city (preferably one with experience in the music industry) to help set up your label's books and accounting system.

What Is Music Publishing?

As discussed in Chapter 16, Copyright Basics, the music industry deals with two important forms of copyright. The first form relates to sound recordings—the actual recorded tracks on a CD—which are owned by the recording artist, who may or may not have written the songs, or by the artist's record company. (As explained in Copyright Basics, the record company acquires ownership of the recorded tracks through the Recording Agreement.) The second form of copyright, for the written songs being recorded, is the focus of this chapter. The distinction between these two forms of copyright allows songwriters and/or their publishing companies to make money each time a new recording is made of one of their songs, or whenever one of their songs is used for commercial—and some non-commercial—purposes.

Imagine a common example: A car-maker wants to use a particular song in one of its television ads, hoping to appeal to a certain market with whom the song is popular. Before making the ad, the car company must obtain separate permissions from (1) the record label that owns the recording and (2) the owner of the song, either the songwriter or the songwriter's publisher. Even if the record company says yes, the publisher can say no. If this occurs, the carmaker cannot use the song. If permissions are granted, the car company will have to pay a fee to the record company and to the songwriter or publisher.

As discussed below, the same rules apply when an artist wants to record someone else's song. But that is only the beginning. Think about all the music you hear on a typical day, other than on your CD player. Songwriters and/or their publishers make money whenever one of their songs is played on the radio (including Internet and cable). They are also paid when their songs are used in films or TV programs, or in advertisements.

The music you hear on the phone when your attorney puts you on hold? Someone paid a fee to use that song. Someone also paid to use the music you hear on airplanes, in supermarkets, at sporting events, on jukeboxes and karaoke discs, in mobile-phone ring tones, and on your video games. Naturally, songwriters/publishers also get paid when their songs are printed as sheet music or in songbooks, or are downloaded from legal Internet sites.

Anyone who wants to use music in these ways must obtain permission and pay a fee, royalty, or both to the songwriter or the songwriter's publisher. Why? Because it's the law, and because it's fair. If you wanted to rent a fancy car to impress clients from out of town and seal a big deal, you would consider it fair to pay for the benefit provided by this nicer car. And like the rental car, an artist's songs are property: intellectual property.

If a business wants to profit from the use of an artist's songs, or even wants to use the songs as entertainment for its customers (which still promotes profit indirectly), the business must pay for the right to use that music. This is how songwriters and their publishers make a living. If a business owner doesn't want to pay for the songs, that individual always has the option not to use them, just as you have the option to pick up your clients in that 1984 Hyundai of yours, instead of the nice rental car.

You may be wondering how these issues relate to your record company. Well, if one of the artists on your label wants to record the song "I Wanna Be Your Lover," written by Prince, you must obtain permission from, and pay a mechanical royalty to, Prince or his publisher. As described in Chapter 24, The Mechanical Royalty, labels pay mechanical royalties for the right to reproduce other artists' songs "mechanically" on their own artist's CDs. Because Prince has a publishing agreement with Universal Music, you would have to obtain permission from, and pay a royalty to, Universal Music, which, in turn, would pay a percentage of that royalty to Prince.

If your recording artist is also the songwriter, your record company theoretically would pay the artist a mechanical royalty for each song on the CD every time a copy is sold. I say "theoretically" because when the recording artist is also the songwriter, the record company will usually negotiate to pay mechanical royalties on no more than ten songs per CD. I explain this more fully in the Mechanical Royalty chapter.

Publishing income, or income from the use of songs, can be lucrative to the songwriter and to his or her publishing company. Your record company can form a publishing company to help to administer and profit from the songs written by the artists on your label. But that's another book. If you're curious, you can view a sample publishing agreement at *MusicBusinessMadeSimple.com.*

Things You Can Do Today To Build Your Label

1. Understand the difference between the copyright of songs and the copyright of recordings, and remember that you will have to pay mechanical royalties to the writers of songs that your artist records, even if your artist is the songwriter.

2. Learn about the publishing business and about forming your own publishing company by reading *Making Music Make Money: An Insider's Guide to Becoming Your Own Music Publisher* by Eric Beall, or *Music Publishing: The Real Road to Music Business Success* by Tim Whitsett.

3. Meet with an entertainment attorney to discuss how and why you might set up a publishing company after you have created a successful label.

PART
THREE

THE

TALENT

27 CHOOSING A GENRE

A type or category of music is referred to as a "genre." Common genres of music include pop, rock, rhythm & blues, hip-hop, and country, among others. All of these general genres can be broken down into more specific sub-categories, such as punk, soul, dance, Americana, easy listening, etc. One of your most important decisions as a label owner will be to decide which musical genre your label will produce.

There are different ways to do this. Some people start record labels to sell music they like. Others choose a genre with which they have some experience, possibly as artists. Yet, others decide to produce and sell music that is popular at the time they start the label. Regardless of the genre you choose or your reasons for choosing it, select a single style of music and stick to it.

Why? Primarily because your label will begin with limited financial resources and may not even have any employees. You will probably not have sufficient funding or manpower to excel at more than a single genre of music. Instead, you'll rely upon business contacts to help produce your artists' recordings, create CD artwork, promote records, and get your CDs into stores that sell the genre of music you are selling. If you're lucky, your professional contacts will be willing to do this work inexpensively.

You'll find that many of these people specialize in a specific type of music. For example, consider graphic artists. Based upon the genre of music and the intended consumer, graphic artists must incorporate certain elements into the artwork they create for a record. That's why you can often guess the type of music just by looking at the CD cover. What appeals to heavy-metal fans may not attract hip-hop music buyers. Obviously, you want artwork that appeals to the consumers your label is trying to reach. It may take you a couple of CDs of trial and error to find a graphic artist whose work you like and who can work for a price you can pay. It takes time to establish a productive relationship. If your label is producing several genres of music, you may need to find several different graphic artists.

You'll go through the same process while building relationships with other professionals with whom your label works regularly, such as radio and independent promoters (who will contact radio to get your music played and/or provide other marketing strategies, such as club or retail-store promotions), magazine and radio station representatives, distributors, and retail salespeople. As with graphic artists, you'll have to deal with professionals in each of these fields who specialize in each genre that your label records. A lot of time, energy, and money—limited and precious commodities for an independent label—will be devoted to finding the right people, even if you are recording only one genre of music. This is why I recommend focusing your resources on a single genre, at least at the start.

Many small labels spread themselves too thinly by focusing on talent rather than genre. Your label may find a promising teen who wants to be a pop star, a talented jazz musician, and a rhythm & blues artist who is developing a big regional following. You may want to sign them all, but if you want your label to succeed, you can't, or at least shouldn't. Major labels are able to sign many diverse artists because they have a different department devoted to each genre, headed by people experienced in promoting and marketing that style of music. Until you can afford to hire the personnel to create separate divisions, stick to one type of music. If you want, you can expand your scope after you've established the label and gotten a sense of the business.

Music consumers are notoriously fickle, and their tastes change frequently. As you've certainly noticed, a band or musical style that's popular one year (or month) may not be popular the next. New artists, genres, labels, and even music-business practices arise as the industry reacts to shifting consumer demands. Some artists and labels manage to evolve and succeed; others disappear. This constant state of change can be maddening and challenging, but it is also one of the most exciting elements of the music industry. Furthermore, it's inevitable. If your small label is going to survive and grow, you'll need to stay ahead of—or at least even with—the curve. This takes research, good instincts, hard work, and of course, money. With your limited staff and other resources, you'll be doing well just to keep up with the interests of one genre's audience and produce music they want to buy.

Always remember, your label is selling a product. As in any other business, there's a lot of competition for consumer dollars, so you have to produce quality stuff. Owners of smaller labels can have a difficult time understanding that each genre of music is a different product whose consumers have different needs. Yes, country and hip-hop are both styles of music packaged on CD. Sitting on a shelf, they look similar, but in fact, they're very different products with different markets.

For this reason, it's highly unlikely that someone who knows hip-hop can jump right into the country market, or that a small label will succeed in both genres. Even some styles that are closely related, such as hip-hop and R&B, have different audiences, radio stations, and music magazines. Thus, different approaches and marketing efforts are required for each.

It always comes back to the same question: Who is buying your records? Once you've answered that question, you should apply all of your energy and resources to reaching those consumers at all times. Different consumers shop differently, read different magazines, listen to different radio stations, and watch different television programs. I discuss marketing techniques in a later chapter. The point here is that as an independent label owner, you will find it difficult, if not impossible, to define and market to consumers of more than one genre.

If you put out two or three records each year in the same genre of music, you can become an expert on selling to this genre's market. Moreover, you can work regularly—and build solid relationships—with one graphic artist, one independent promoter, one radio promoter, and one advertising executive who are experienced in this genre. After a while, they may even give you a discount for your repeat business.

There will always be talented artists in other genres. And maybe you're starting a label because you want to help artists. But the business of a record label is to sell records, and you can't help anyone if your label goes bankrupt. The best way to help the most musicians and to succeed as a small label is to choose one genre of music, do it well, and focus on marketing your music to the consumers who want it.

Things You Can Do Today To Build Your Label

1. Decide on the one genre of music that your label will produce and market.

2. Identify the promotional and distribution resources in your immediate area that deal with your genre and work with independent labels. Such resources might include public radio, independent record stores, distributors, radio promoters, graphic artists, local magazines and newspapers, etc.

3. Conduct market research to determine if there is a consumer base (market) for your label's genre in your city and region.

IDENTIFYING YOUR MARKET

As noted in the previous chapter, major labels have the budget and personnel to seek out talented artists, regardless of genre, and record and distribute those artists' records. This is not the case for independent labels. Indeed, I believe the owner of a small label should choose one style of music and search only for talented artists whose music fits within that specific genre. While you're scouting talent, ask yourself, *Will this artist appeal to my label's audience, an audience I know, and which likes the kind of music my label produces?* To answer this critical question, you must first know who your audience is. And to identify your audience, you must have a clear sense of your label's genre.

This may sound like a circular puzzle, but it's not. You just have to do things in a certain order. First, select your genre. This will allow you to take the next steps: Identify your audience and develop solid marketing and promotional plans to reach them. Only after these steps are complete will you begin to look for talented recording artists in your selected genre. It all comes down to knowing who will buy your label's records (your market) and finding the best ways to reach these customers. Inevitably, you'll make some mistakes and adjust your label's strategies accordingly, but this is the logical way to get started.

If your label produces music that is clearly part of a specific genre, like country, Americana, jazz, blues, classical, or hip-hop (to name a few), it will be fairly easy to identify your market. However, styles, tastes, and genres change over time, so you always have to remain current and in touch with your market. For example, consider country music. As a genre, country may never have been more popular than it is right now, but the music you hear on commercial country stations today is very different from what you would have heard on the radio 30, 40, or 50 years ago. These days, even country icons, such as Hank Williams, Johnny Cash, and George Jones, are almost never played on commercial radio, despite their huge popularity and influence within the genre. Such changes occur in all genres over time, either because record labels believe the market has shifted, or because innovative new artists have led the genre in a new direction. To survive and succeed, your label must keep up with these changes (and its audience), regardless of your genre.

If your label's music does not have commercial radio appeal or an identifiable market, don't worry. Yes, this will make it more difficult to find the consumers who want to buy your music, and to get your product to them (otherwise known as marketing). Also, there will be fewer labels recording, marketing, and selling the type of music your label releases, so you'll find fewer established resources to help with your marketing efforts. Consequently, it may take a little longer to obtain a distributor or radio airplay for your product (if that is what you seek).

But you should not change the music your label produces just to attract an easily identifiable market. Even if you can't categorize your music, your label *can* sell records. Further, this "road less traveled" gives you a chance to have an impact on the music industry by signing innovative, groundbreaking artists whose music may influence the market later. The commercial music of tomorrow is the visionary's music of today. If you're able to anticipate future musical trends, your label can have great success in signing "non-commercial" artists.

Of course, you still have to sell records to stay in business. I believe that everyone who starts a record label (including you) wants to sell records, and that the ultimate goal of every label owner should be to find a paying audience and get the label's music to them. You may not have to sell a lot of records, but you have to sell enough to produce and sell more. To achieve this goal, you need to know your market.

Things You Can Do Today To Build Your Label

1. Select a genre.

2. Begin market research to identify the audience in your region that buys music by artists in your chosen genre.

3. Develop marketing and promotion strategies to reach your audience before you start looking for talent. When seeing new artists perform or listening to their demos, always ask yourself, *Will this artist appeal to my label's audience?*

WHAT TO LOOK FOR IN AN ARTIST

Talent, like beauty, is in the eye of the beholder. As a record-label owner, part of your job is to judge whether an artist is really talented, or if his or her skills are only "skin deep." You may be excited the first time you see and hear an artist perform, but it's important to invest enough time to evaluate the artist's talents objectively and consider how well he or she matches up with your label's goals. As with many things in life, an artist may be exciting when he or she is new to you, only to become uninteresting after a time. That's why most A&R representatives go to see an artist perform several times before discussing a contractual arrangement. Many reps won't even tell the artist they're going to be in the audience. This allows them to determine if the artist is consistently good, or just happened to have one great performance.

Live performance skills are among the most critical factors to weigh when seeking artists for your label, but they certainly aren't the only consideration. Aside from raw musical talent, there are four primary points to consider before signing an artist: (1) songwriting ability, (2) live-performance ability, (3) recording ability, and (4) whether or not the artist appeals to your label's market.

First, it always starts with the songs. A big criticism of the music industry today is the inability of many label personnel to identify great songs without first hearing a professionally produced recording of the song. As a small label, you won't have the luxury of expensive production. You must be able to hear a great song hiding under the hiss and poor quality of a demo tape. Many elements make up a good song, including the structure, lyrics, story, and the emotions it elicits from listeners. But music is not an absolute science, and there's no formula for writing or identifying a great song. If there were, I'd be living on my own island right now. It takes experience with music, a good ear, and also a bit of a gift to know a great song when you hear it. It's a skill that really can't be taught, but can be developed over time.

Second, an artist must be able to consistently perform live at a very high level. The live performance is what separates great artists from good ones. It is also the best promotional tool available to independent labels and their artists. An artist's strong live performance will yield good publicity from media, which will encourage more people to come see the artist's shows and/or buy the record. A great live show and the attention it generates over time may prompt local DJs to invite your artist to perform live on the radio. Eventually, it will also attract the attention of promoters and booking agents, who are always looking for hot new talent to perform at their clubs and events. Again, this is the best publicity any artist and small label could want. And it's free! The greatest musical experiences many people ever have are at memorable concerts. Signing artists who can provide those kinds of experiences will give your label credibility and help you sell records.

The third factor to consider is an artist's recording ability. Like songwriting and performance skills, this talent takes time to develop. An artist who performs well live may not be comfortable in the studio. Sometimes song arrangements differ from the live version to the recorded one. And many recording artists will tell you it's difficult to capture the energy of a live performance in the studio.

Obviously, it's great to find artists who have mastered their studio skills, in addition to their songwriting and live performances. However, because it costs money to record in a studio, most developing artists are unable to record enough to develop this craft. As a label owner, you might benefit from booking time in a smaller, less expensive demo studio to allow the artist to work on his or her recording skills. The artist can work on the songs for his or her record, while also getting comfortable in a studio setting. You can even bring the producer you intend to use for the record, so he or she can get a feel for the artist's work. If an artist already has the first two qualities—great songs and strong live-performance skills—his or her recording skills are bound to develop naturally.

Fourth, you obviously want to sign artists who appeal to your label's market. You can learn a lot about an artist's "market" by attending his or her shows. The people who pay to see an artist are potential purchasers of his or her records. Note the average age, cultural background, race, and gender of the audience members. Taken together, these characteristics are known as demographics. Record-label marketing executives often spend a lot of money on surveys to determine the demographics of their artists' audience.

An artist usually knows his or her audience better than anyone, so it's important to listen. By attending live shows, you can determine if the artist's fan base matches your label's market. The important thing is not to try to force a square peg into a round hole. Be honest with yourself. You may like an artist, but if he or she does not fit into your marketing plans and will not appeal to your label's customer base, you shouldn't sign him or her. However, if the fans who come to the artist's shows also listen to the radio stations that play your label's records, read the magazines in which you advertise, and buy records by other artists on your label, this artist may be a good match.

Things You Can Do Today To Build Your Label

1. Go see live performances by developing artists in your area whose music fits the genre you have chosen for your label. Note the number and demographics of people at each show, and what you liked/did not like about each artist's performance.

2. Listen to recordings by successful and developing artists, trying to hear good songs beneath a bad arrangement or low-budget recording.

3. Contact local recording studios and inquire about their rates. If you have a talented artist who needs to develop his or her recording skills, book some time in an inexpensive studio so the artist can gain experience working in that environment.

Other Factors to Consider Before Signing an Artist

To succeed, an artist must possess talent and the other qualities discussed in the previous chapter. These attributes are strong indicators of an artist's compatibility with your label. However, there is even more to consider before signing an artist, including his or her level of development, age, and professionalism, and the personnel working with the artist. These factors may be less obvious than those already covered, but they are no less critical.

With a new label, you will probably sign artists in the early stages of development. They'll sign with you, in part, because they have to start somewhere. Similarly, your new label has to sign its first artist, and record and release that first record at some point. And just as artists are able to approach more established labels after they've demonstrated an ability to make money, your label will be able to seek out more developed artists after you've produced and released several high-quality records and built a good reputation.

Though you have to be realistic about who will be available to your label (especially before you've established a solid track record), there's no reason you can't recruit artists who have been developing themselves and understand that there is still much work to do. Pay attention to artists who continue to take vocal, instrumental, and/or performance lessons throughout their careers. They understand the need to improve themselves, even after they've developed many of their basic skills. To gauge an artist's level of development, ask him or her the following questions:

How long have you been performing?

Have you been in other groups or bands?

Have you done any recordings?

Have you released any full-length recordings?

How long have you been writing songs (if the artist is a songwriter)?

Ideally, you'll find artists who, while not completely polished, have begun developing their skills and understanding of the music business. If you sign a teenager who has raw talent but no experience, you'll spend a lot of time helping this artist to develop, which will take away from the time you can spend trying to sell records. And chances are, you won't have the luxury of extra time. So the more developed an artist is when you sign him or her, the better. Someone with live-performance experience and an established fan base can help your label's promotion efforts and will require less direction from you to know—and do—what needs to be done.

Some labels also consider age when deciding whether or not to sign an artist. An artist's age may have no impact on your label's marketing efforts, but depending on your genre, it might. For example, labels that produce pop, rock, and hip-hop will market to younger audiences, so they will seek out younger artists. Labels that focus on other genres, such as blues, may actually look for older artists. It's difficult for young blues artists to be taken seriously. After all, it's the blues. What does a 16-year-old know about the blues? The artist may be very talented, and may become a great blues artist, but he or she will not be acknowledged as such until he or she is over 30. People who buy blues music can relate to an artist of that age.

Regardless of your label's genre, you want artists who take a professional approach to their live performances and public appearances, and in business settings. You want to have a constructive working relationship with your artists. You can't have that with someone who doesn't have a sense of responsibility for his or her conduct. Furthermore, the artist's professional attitude will help you promote the artist and sell records. This, obviously, helps the artist as well.

I've seen too many talented artists fall by the wayside because they couldn't, or wouldn't, accept that the music industry is, at its heart, just another business that requires professionalism. Artists who argue with promoters or producers, don't show up for recording sessions, come to live shows late or wasted, skip photo sessions and interviews, or insult radio personalities really hurt your ability to sell records. It's fine for an artist to cultivate his "bad-boy" (or her "bad girl") reputation, if that's part of the artistry and image. But that reputation needs to be put aside when it's time for the artist to do his or her job. If a bad attitude carries over to the artist's work, it can affect your label's mission, and you don't have enough resources to deal with head cases.

You're investing time and money in the artist. In return, he or she must understand the need for professionalism in this business. You may not know after one meeting if an artist "gets it" or not. But if you spend some time talking with him or her about some of these issues, and watching his or her behavior onstage and off, you can get a sense of the artist's conduct. On the other hand, never underestimate your first impression upon meeting an artist. It will be the same first impression everyone else has.

Sometimes, the skills, experience, and approach of the artist's professional team may factor into your decision as to whether or not to sign an artist. However, this shouldn't be *the* deciding factor, especially for a small label, because many new artists are unable to find managers or booking agents to help them. (For this reason, you should always keep an eye out for local managers and booking agents who work with developing artists in your label's genre. They may be willing to work with your artists, too.) By the time of a record's release, though, it can be very helpful if the artist has personnel in place to help coordinate the administrative and promotional efforts that follow.

Finally, I offer a cautionary note: Before signing a recording contract, it's critical for both the artist and label to understand clearly what the other is offering, and what will be expected in return. This is especially true for small record companies. It's good business, and it will help to avoid disappointment, bad blood, and lawsuits later.

I've seen the results of unrealistic expectations, and they're not pretty. Initially, the artist is thrilled to have his or her first record deal. Everyone is in love. But after this excitement fades, the artist realizes that a smaller label can offer only limited assistance in helping him or her to achieve immediate wealth and stardom. At this point, things can get ugly. Inevitably, the label will be blamed for failing to meet the artist's unrealistic goals.

To make sure the artist knows exactly what to expect, it's critical for you to explain up front precisely what you can and cannot do for him or her. This means that you must also be realistic with yourself when assessing the services your label can provide.

By accepting your place in the market, you can focus on what's important: Selling enough records to build your label. Most likely, the first artists you sign will never have recorded a full-length album or been in a relationship with a record label. What they have to offer is raw talent and enthusiasm. Their first label can offer a start to their careers, a solid record, and hopefully, some good publicity. If both sides are realistic and honest, and understand each other's roles from the beginning, the relationship will run more smoothly.

Examining and considering the factors discussed here will help you make more informed decisions about the artists you sign. It will also force you to sit down and talk with artists about their development, their goals, and their direction. Although it is not foolproof, this process will allow you to obtain information you need to decide if an artist is not only talented, but right for your label.

Things You Can Do Today To Build Your Label

1. Formulate and write down questions to discuss with each artist to determine if he or she is a good fit for your label.

2. Decide which characteristics and qualities are most important for artists who make the genre of music your label will produce, and recruit artists who possess them.

3. Prepare to discuss exactly what your label can and cannot offer to an artist, so that both sides are clear about what to expect.

WHERE TO LOOK FOR ARTISTS

*L*ike most people who start a label, you probably live in a city/region with many talented artists. It's your job to find them. There are several ways to go about doing this. But first, decide on the genre of music you wish to produce. This will help to define the places where you'll look for talent. It will also help you sift through the hundreds, if not thousands, of demo tapes and promotional packages you will receive from artists who want to get signed.

Some of the best ways to find talent are to see live music at local clubs, network with others at music-related organizations and seminars, and receive demo tapes and promotional packages from artists. You may also learn about promising artists through word of mouth, relationships with record stores, local newspaper and magazine critics, your distributor, and local radio and television stations.

Never underestimate the importance of these relationships and the "ears" of others in helping you to find talent. I've been contacted many times by major-label A&R representatives who had been transferred to Texas and were looking for talent. The first thing they did is contact key people in the region to get some insight into the state's music industry.

Obviously, local clubs are a great place to see and hear developing artists perform, and to familiarize yourself with the local music community. Clubs are the lifeblood of any city's music scene. Different venues feature different genres of music, of course, so you'll want to visit clubs that book artists/bands who play the kind of music your label wants to produce. Some clubs also have "open mic nights," usually during the early part of the week, when developing artists sign up to give a short performance (usually one to three songs). You may not discover anyone there who is ready to be signed, but you may see artists to watch. And any time you're in a club, you have an opportunity to network, inform people about your label, and learn about up-and-coming artists.

It can be very exciting, but draining, to go to clubs every week. It can also get expensive to pay all those cover charges. But if you hope to find talent, you have to get out and see bands. Over time, you can develop relationships with your favorite clubs by giving them free CDs, inviting them to your artists' shows, booking free promotional shows by your artists in their clubs, and giving booking agents merchandise from your label, like T-shirts, posters, hats, etc. Eventually, your networking and good-will gestures may help you to get into clubs free, and to learn about promising artists/bands from club booking agents. If there is a particular artist you want to see, ask to be put on the guest list for the artist's next performance. This will allow you to see and hear artists perform before you decide whether or not to pursue them.

As your label grows and begins to produce and sell records, you should work to develop good relationships with local record stores. Naturally, you'll want these stores to carry your label's releases, but they may also inform you about new artists. Many independent or "mom and pop" record stores sell records released by small labels and by artists themselves. Ask store managers and owners about independent artists who have been selling well, or whom they think are good. Relying upon someone else's opinions and "ears" can help you sort through many artists and find the ones who may be a good fit for your label. If your label is aligned with a local record distributor, ask the distributor about any artists who have been selling well and who might be ready to sign with a local label.

Another way to find artists is to read reviews in local entertainment newspapers and magazines. The opinions of local music critics can be valuable. Even if the artist does not receive a favorable review, he or she still may be worth checking out. Read the review carefully. Maybe the critic just did not like the way the artist's CD was recorded, the guitarist's style, or the sound in the club where the artist/band was playing. Focus on the things the critic did like (while keeping in mind that sometimes, negative reviews are accurate). Maybe your label can help this artist take the next step in his or her development. As you establish relationships with local critics and writers, you will learn which ones have a good eye for talent. They may like certain artists whom they think your label could help. If you end up signing the artist, the critic may write a favorable review of the artist's CD and/or performance.

You can also find talent by talking to other artists or music-industry professionals, and by attending seminars and music conferences. Listen to college or public radio stations in your city that play local artists. Sometimes, these stations can be your best resource for local talent. Get to know the DJs. They'll usually be happy to tell you about their favorite artists. They may also play the records your label produces. Local cable TV access channels may have music video shows. Many times, these shows play videotaped club performances by local artists. This gives you another way to see, as well as hear, local artists and to gain exposure for your label's artists.

Finally, you'll find artists through demo tapes and promotional packages submitted by artists, managers, producers, and attorneys. To avoid being inundated, you'll need to devise a system for reviewing the packages and tapes you receive. You may even hire an intern to go through the tapes and pick the best ones for you to hear. Then, you can contact artists you might want to sign. Your intern can call or send a post card to promising artists not yet ready for a record deal, thanking them for sending their package, encouraging them to continue to develop, and asking them to send more material in the future. You never know how an artist will progress. Keeping the door open and treating artists with respect now may yield a record deal with a talented, developed artist later.

Things You Can Do Today To Build Your Label

1. Make a list of venues where local artists perform and visit them regularly. Get to know the club owners who can tell you about promising new artists.

2. Each week/month, read local entertainment magazines and newspapers that review artists' shows and self-released CDs. Contact the music critics to learn how they decide which releases to review.

3. Find out which radio stations in your city play local artists. Make a list of the shows on which local music is played. Listen frequently.

What Is the Artist Looking For?

Most artists will never have record labels lining up to sign them. Most likely, only one label will be interested in signing an artist at any given point of his or her career. Despite their limited options, I recommend to artists that they sign *only* with companies that are reputable, experienced, and knowledgeable about the music business. It's far better to remain unsigned than to be trapped in a bad deal with a record label that can't (or won't) help to advance their careers.

A recording agreement does not guarantee success for an artist's record. The artist's entertainment attorney will attempt to negotiate the best deal possible, but if your label is not able or willing to deliver (i.e., produce a good record and then promote and sell it), it won't matter what the contract says. The artist will be out of luck, and his or her music career will be stuck in neutral. This can happen even to established artists, and it can be very damaging when the artist is just beginning.

Sometimes, even if only one label shows interest, I tell an artist that he or she might be better off not signing. Below I describe some basic issues that an artist will consider before deciding whether or not to enter into a recording agreement. Most of these questions are more applicable to independent labels, where many artists begin their careers, than to large record companies. However, they can apply to major labels, too.

First, the artist will want to know your label's track record in producing, releasing, and promoting records. The artist will be concerned, understandably, if his or her record is to be the label's first release. No one wants to be a guinea pig. If this is your label's first record, be prepared to demonstrate to the artist that you have a solid plan for recording *and* promoting his or her CD. This is good business, no matter how many records you've released.

Any label can pay for a producer and studio time to get an album recorded. But the artist also wants a label to have knowledgeable, experienced people who know how to promote and advertise a record properly. You may put out the greatest-sounding record of all time, but no one will buy it if they don't know it exists. You need to promote. This is what sells records. It's also a record company's hardest job. An artist will naturally want to know how you intend to go about doing it, and that you have the ability to follow through on your plans.

Consequently, it's important to have a marketing strategy in place—no matter how small—and to discuss this with the artist. Yours may be a new label with limited resources, but an artist will often overlook these shortcomings if you're honest, organized, creative, and aligned with experienced, knowledgeable people. In short, artists (and other professionals) are much more likely to take a chance on your label if you seem to have it together. This is why you should have a plan and vision for your label before you ever start looking for your first artist.

Second, artists will want to listen to other records put out by your label, so they can be sure you're making good-quality recordings and producing the kind of music they perform. Okay, your label is just starting up and you haven't produced a lot of records yet. Every label has to begin somewhere. Besides, a lot of the artists you talk to will also be new and relatively unproven.

But, to start off on the right foot, you must be able to dispel any concerns the artist may have about signing with a new label. Aside from a strong vision and sense of organization, you may have to demonstrate a willingness to work harder than other labels to ensure a high-quality record. You may also have to agree to allow the artist to make some demo recordings for your label before he or she signs a full-length recording agreement.

Third, an artist will check out the label's reputation and track record. Artists conduct their research by talking to other people in the industry—especially other artists—who have dealt with the label. Some people will always complain, but consistently negative feedback may be indicative of legitimate problems at the label, and may keep artists from signing. Obviously, you don't want that kind of reputation.

Every new label owner makes mistakes. Artists and others in the industry can overlook your mistakes, as long as you show a willingness to work hard to correct them and prevent them in the future. Naturally, you'll get better at running a label as you gain experience. If you take responsibility for errors and show artists that you're willing to work hard to fix any problems that arise, you can build a reputation as an imperfect, but professional business owner who treats artists fairly. Most new artists would be very pleased to sign with such a company.

Fourth, an artist will want the label to have an administrative staff, rather than one person to do everything. Your small label will have minimal resources, including personnel. But one person (no matter how diligent you may be) can't do it all. Your label should have at least a few people to coordinate marketing, promotion, and sales support for the artist's record. If you don't have your own staff, make sure the artist knows that you will use outside personnel to carry out these critical functions. Then explain your plan in detail.

Which leads to the final point: Good communication makes good relationships. Do your homework and strive to provide as much information as possible. No matter how big or small your label may be, always explain your goals and plans for the artist. Showing that you care enough to have— and explain—a plan, and that you understand how to produce, promote, and market the artist's CD, will build the artist's confidence in your label.

Further, if the artist has developed a fan base and achieved some success (e.g., through previous recordings, radio airplay, and/or regional touring), listen to the artist and be willing to work with him or her to build upon this success. Also, discuss the artist's goals to be sure you understand what kind of support he or she may require from the label. These steps will help get the relationship off to a good start.

The role of a small independent label in an artist's career is no secret. Unfortunately, many artists don't understand it. Being honest and realistic about what you can and cannot do for the artist will go a long way toward helping him or her to decide whether or not to sign with your label. If the artist does sign, he or she will know exactly what to expect from your label, which inevitably will make the relationship run more smoothly.

Things You Can Do Today To Build Your Label

1. Make your label's previous releases available for artists to hear. If you haven't released any albums yet, prepare a solid plan to discuss with the artist, so he or she will know your label is able to produce a good recording and to promote it.

2. Be conscious at all times of how you treat people within the industry. A good reputation is important, even if your label has no track record.

3. Start assembling a list of quality people who can work for your label. If you do not have the resources to hire employees, identify freelancers you can bring in to help operate your label.

IMPORTANCE OF A GOOD LIVE PERFORMANCE

Successful label owners know that an artist's performance can increase record sales. They understand that a strong live show can persuade the public to purchase an artist's records now and in future. Many times, an artist's live performance may be the most effective marketing and promotional tool available to a small label. This is why performance ability should be a major consideration (maybe even the most important one) when you're deciding whether or not to sign an artist to your label.

Marketing is simply getting the product to the market. However, it's not so simple for a new label like yours, which will have limited options for getting its CDs to people who want to buy them. Ultimately, you'll sign with a distributor to get your artist's CD into retail stores. But with your relatively small marketing and promotion budget, that CD could get lost in the sea of music available at a record store. For your label to achieve its primary goal of selling records, people have to know and care about your artist's CD.

Because you probably won't be able to flood the market with radio, TV, and magazine advertisements, and since your artist will probably not appear on Saturday Night Live any time soon, the best place to inform people about the artist's new CD is at his or her live shows. In fact, unless the artist is getting radio airplay, the only people who may know about your artist are fans who come to his or her performances. Therefore, this is a logical place to start selling CDs. You can set up a merchandise booth at the venue, or simply have the artist bring a box of CDs to each show.

I find that developing artists tend to sell more records at live performances than at record stores anyway. I attribute this, in part, to the motivational aspects of a good live performance. I have purchased many artists' records after a great live show. Moved by the performance and caught up in the moment, I want to remember the show and support the artist. I know I may not get to a record store in the near future, and by then, I may have lost the feeling. I might not find the record at my local retail store anyway. So I buy a CD at the show. Fans of the artists on your label will undoubtedly feel the same way.

There is another important reason to sell CDs at your artists' shows: Profit. (Remember, this is a business.) Direct sales at live performances will yield almost twice as much profit as sales at record stores will. If you've priced the CD at $14.99, for example, a distributor will pay you between $4.00 and $7.00 for each CD sold to a record store. On the other hand, you keep all $14.99 for CDs sold at shows. This definitely helps the cash flow for a new label. It even allows you to sell CDs for a little less at the shows (maybe $10.00 to $12.00), to reward fans who come to see the artist live. They're happy because they get a discounted price. You're happy because you'll still make a greater profit than you would receive from CDs purchased at the store.

Live performances can also be a vital component of your overall promotional strategy for the artist. If you plan to advertise the release of a new CD, include the artist's upcoming live show(s) in the advertisement. By notifying the public that the CD has been released and will be available at the listed shows, you get two advertisements for the price of one.

Many labels will also host a party to celebrate the release of an artist's new CD. Often, the artist will perform at this event, which the label will advertise as a "CD Release Party." Of course, you will sell the new CD at the show. You can also hand out promotional copies of a one- or two-song CD sampler, along with posters, postcards, and other promotional items. You might even ask the artist and venue to make the show free. This way, people can spend their money on the CD, rather than on a cover charge. Plus, free shows create a feeling of good will and always encourage more people to attend. Everyone at the event will want to support the artist (it's a party, after all). If the artist is able to give a great performance, people will want to buy the CD.

One additional benefit of strong performance skills is that they generate opportunities for an artist to get into (and remain in) the public eye. For instance, local radio stations often host live, on-air performances, and many record stores host live shows in their stores. Their goal is to attract listeners and buyers, respectively. These venues provide excellent opportunities for your artist to reach new fans and promote/sell his or her CD.

Aside from their immediate promotional benefits, these events can lead to even greater exposure. Many radio stations host music festivals where the artist may perform. And shows at record stores can help you develop a relationship with retail stores that will assist with future record distribution.

Things You Can Do Today To Build Your Label

1. Try to sign artists who are already performing live on a regular basis, have developed a good live show, and have a fan base. Look for artists who are able to play a scaled-down show using only acoustic instruments.

2. Make a list of promotional activities focusing on an artist's live performance, such as record-release parties, in-store shows at record stores, and radio station appearances. (The acoustic performance comes in handy for in-store performances and at radio stations.)

3. Make a list of local live music venues, record stores, and radio stations where your artist may be able to perform.

Signing the Contract

Eventually, you'll begin to speak with an artist about signing a record contract. At that time, you'll need an entertainment attorney to provide consultation and to represent your label in contract negotiations. I recommend that you establish a relationship with an attorney well before this point so you have time to discuss your plan of action and explain to the attorney exactly what you want and need from the contract. Obviously, you'll have to pay for the attorney's time, but it's a good investment, as this preparation will help you offer the best deal possible for your label. Also, once you and the attorney have created a basic contract for your label, you can use it again, with minor revisions, for other artists.

If your label and the artist decide to enter into an agreement, I suggest that you present a deal memo to the artist and his or her attorney before you sit down to sign the actual recording agreement. The deal memo is a brief document that sets forth the main terms of the agreement, such as the number of records the artist will record, the basic royalty rate, and advances. The deal memo saves time and money by allowing the parties to negotiate and agree upon the "big issues" before fine-tuning the smaller details of the contract.

The parties may or may not utilize entertainment attorneys during the deal-memo process. However, it's critical to include your attorney in contract negotiations. Inexperienced label owners sometimes get into trouble by using "one size fits all" recording agreements that aren't actually appropriate for all situations, or by adding to contracts that were poorly written in the first place. Maybe the label owner even deleted important phrases because he or she didn't understand them, and as a result, the contract doesn't serve its intended purpose: To create a legally binding agreement between the parties that is based on terms agreed to by both sides.

It doesn't matter what either side intends or promises to do. In the eyes of the law, only the terms described explicitly in the written contract govern the agreement. As the old saying goes, "get it in writing." If a contract is unclear, its ambiguity will favor the party wanting to break it—usually, the artist. Even worse, you might be setting yourself up for legal problems if you can't fulfill the terms to which you agree. I cannot overemphasize this point: Have an entertainment attorney assist you in making changes to the contract you negotiate with the artist.

Many times, record labels fail to sign the artists they want because the labels simply say "no" to contractual clauses they don't understand. Here again, an entertainment attorney can help. After you explain what you want or don't want in a contract, the attorney can explain which of your requests are realistic. Certainly, you don't want to promise more than you can deliver, or more than you feel comfortable offering, but some things you might have refused to allow in the contract may turn out to be fairly standard artist requests.

With this new information, you'll be able to offer a contract that meets your needs while giving you the best chance of signing the artists you want. Once you and your attorney have agreed to the general terms of the contract, the attorney will enter into negotiations with the artist (or the artist's attorney) to produce a final contract that is reasonable and fair, based on your label's level of success and how much you want to sign the artist.

It is your attorney's job to negotiate a legally binding agreement that is acceptable to you and the artist, *not* to push the artist into signing a contract that is unfair or does not conform to accepted industry practices. The contract you present to the artist will automatically be to your advantage. It's natural that you'd want what is best for your business, but if you intend to sign other artists in the future, you must also be fair. The objective is for both sides to be satisfied with the agreement and the results that the agreement will produce.

Also, understand that contract negotiations can take a long time. For major labels, it can take six months or longer, based on the schedules of the attorneys, label, and artist. Contract negotiations for independent-label deals are usually less complex, but they can still take days or weeks. Be patient. Through negotiation and compromise, a deal will be reached. In the end, you and the artist will sign a well-written recording contract with terms that are reasonable for both parties.

Things You Can Do Today To Build Your Label

1. Meet with an entertainment attorney to make sure your recording contract fits your label's needs. Be certain that you understand which terms of the contract are negotiable, and which are absolutely necessary to the operation of your label.

2. Draft a deal memo that you can present to artists before entering into formal contract negotiations.

3. Accept the fact that, to sign the artists you want, your new label may have to be more flexible than other, more established labels.

ARTIST RELATIONS

For me, one of the most exciting aspects of being in the music industry is getting to hang out with artists. It's fun and exciting to work in such a creative environment. If you're like most people who start a label, you want to help the artists you sign to have successful careers. And you *will* help them, simply by recording, releasing, and promoting their albums. In addition, your artists will develop as a result of going through this process.

But this doesn't mean you should become friends with your artists. Instead, I compare the label/artist relationship to a parent/child relationship. Not because the artist is a child (though some artists may be, or at least act like, children), but because you have to make some tough decisions regarding what is best for the label and balance that with the artist's wishes. When you put two or more people in continual contact and require them to make monetary and creative decisions, the initial love can fade sooner than you can say, "No, you don't get a private plane for Christmas." However, the three practices described below can help you build a positive relationship with your artists and avoid conflicts.

First, be honest. Be honest with yourself at all times about the level or size of your label. Then be honest with your artists about what the label can do for them. It's natural to be excited about your label, and it's great to have dreams of success and goals to help achieve those dreams. But you have to be realistic. I often hear the owners of small labels talk about how big their labels will become, rather than what they're actually doing on a daily basis to sell records now. They fear that if they're open about their labels' limitations, an artist will not want to sign. But believe me, if you're not up-front with an artist, you're in for a rough time later when he or she inevitably finds out that you created false expectations you can't fulfill.

Be honest early. Some artists will believe they should start their careers on labels larger than yours. That's nothing to feel badly about, and it's a mistake to try to convince an artist to sign if you can't meet his or her expectations. Simply discuss the artist's goals and explain exactly what you can and cannot do for him or her. If the artist decides to sign with your label, both sides will have entered into the relationship with similar expectations.

Second, be open to compromise. While it's natural to have opinions and take positions on different issues, you should never close your mind to new ideas. No business, especially a small record label, can afford to go through daily battles. It distracts from the job at hand and stifles the creative process. That's why I think it's good for record-label owners to approach every situation with an open mind. Yes, you need a vision for the label and should strive to do things right. But remember, your ideas aren't the only good ones. If you allow others, especially the artist, to have their ideas heard, considered, and, when appropriate, incorporated into your label's operations, you'll find that a good working relationship can develop.

Third, leave the artist's career development to the artist and other third parties, such as managers, agents, music coaches, etc. Most small-label owners really want to help the artists they sign. I'm sure you do, too. But daily involvement in an artist's development will consume a lot of your time and resources. Too many record labels become too involved with their artists. Label owners want to be the manager, booking agent, producer, merchandiser, publisher, publicist, stage and vocal coach, and finally, label owner. No small-label owner can do all these jobs, and such overlapping relationships are full of professional and legal conflicts. Furthermore, all the time a label owner spends as manager, publicist, etc. limits his or her ability to conduct label business properly.

Your label will be much better off if you focus on the label's only job—to release, promote, and sell records—and allow artists to develop themselves. As I have said before, staying in business is the best way for a small label to help artists. In the course of doing label business, you will meet managers, booking agents, venue owners, publicity firms, recording studio owners, etc. Introduce your artists to these experts. Let them do their job (helping your artists to develop), so you can remain focused on yours (growing your label).

You are helping an artist to develop by bringing him or her into a studio to record, and by providing opportunities for the artist to perform live and promote the sales of his or her CDs. Through this process, you are providing experiences that can improve the artist's recording, songwriting, and live-performance skills. Ultimately, though, it is the artist's responsibility to take the steps necessary to improve his or her musical skills and understanding of the music industry. When this kind of natural development happens, both the record label and the artist benefit.

Things You Can Do Today To Build Your Label

1. Accept that your small label has limited resources, and be honest with artists when discussing what your label can and cannot do for them.

2. Read a book, attend a seminar, or take a class that will help you to build skills in the areas of negotiation and compromise.

3. Start a list of reputable music professionals in your region—such as managers, booking agents, producers—who might be able to assist your artist.

PART
FOUR

PRODUCTION

CREATING THE RECORDING

There are three distinct, but equally important steps to making a record: Pre-production, production, and post-production. Most major labels rely upon the artist's management, the producer, and/or the studio to oversee and help the artist through the record-making process. But this can be expensive. To limit unexpected or unnecessary costs, and to ensure that studio time is used efficiently, I believe most independent labels, including yours, should manage these three steps themselves.

It's impossible within the scope of this book to describe every tip for making a better recording. And, despite my years as an attorney representing labels and as the owner of an independent label, I can't begin to explain all the technical aspects of the recording process. In fact, I've found that some of this can be learned only through experience, and from the talented people with whom you work. Nonetheless, I can share some simple, effective strategies that will help you make the best recording possible on a limited budget. That's my goal in this section of the book.

I'll start with some definitions. *Pre-production* is all the preparations made before you begin recording in the studio. It includes administrative work, such as creating your budget and finding/obtaining the studio, producer, side artists, and/or additional instruments needed for the recording. Pre-production also includes the artist's preparation, most notably rehearsing and perfecting all the songs to be recorded. This may be the least exciting stage of the recording process, but it's critical. The more work you do before getting into the studio, the less money you'll spend while you're there. I discuss pre-production in detail in Chapter 37, Pre-Production.

Production is the technical process of recording musical and vocal performances onto tape, CD, or a computer. (See Chapter 43, The Recording Process, for practical advice to help you save time and money during production.) Unless you own professional recording equipment, production will occur in a recording studio, with the assistance of a recording engineer who will be provided by the studio to operate the recording equipment. If you can afford a producer, he or she also will be brought in during the recording/production phase (I explain the producer's role in Chapter 40, What Does a Producer Do?). Most cities have a number of studios, each with different strengths and weaknesses. Chapter 39, Finding and Choosing a Recording Studio, will help you select a studio that's right for your label and artist.

Post-production is the final phase of the recording process. It includes two primary steps: Mixing and mastering. I discuss both in greater detail in Chapter 44, Mixing and Mastering. Mixing means combining all the individual pieces, or tracks, that were recorded during production (vocals, guitar, drums, keyboards, etc.) into one whole. You've probably heard recordings that were not mixed well. Maybe you couldn't hear the bass drum, or maybe there was too much bass. Maybe the vocals were drowned out by the other instruments. The goal of mixing is to make sure everything is heard at the levels you want. Mastering, the final step, is an enhancement process that will improve the sound of your mixed recording. A skilled engineer or producer can help you to mix and master your recordings.

Things You Can Do Today To Build Your Label

1. Learn more about the technical side of recording by taking a course at a local college, or by reading books such as *Quick Start: Home Recording* by Ingo Raven, or *Home Recording for Musicians* by Craig Anderton.

2. Listen to CDs by local artists, paying attention to the mix, to see what you like and don't like in a mix. Listen to CDs that have been mastered and those that have not to understand the difference mastering can make.

3. Research the recording studios in your city and begin compiling a list of the services offered and prices charged by each.

PRE-PRODUCTION

P re-production is what you do to prepare for recording in the studio. It includes the administrative work your label does to create the CD, as well as the artist's preparation to record. Whatever you do (or don't do) in pre-production will influence—sometimes dramatically—the rest of the recording process and the quality of the final product. Therefore, it's very important to be organized and thorough. The more you prepare, the less likely it is that you'll make costly mistakes in the studio. So take a little extra time during pre-production and follow the steps described below. They'll help the entire recording process run much more smoothly.

First, make a list of all the steps leading to the finished product—from consulting with the artist about recording, to selecting and booking a studio, to finding a company to manufacture the completed CD—and have a plan for completing each step before you go into the studio. I suggest creating a detailed checklist on your computer, so you can change it as needed. (A sample "Pre-production Checklist" is included in Appendix D.) After you've compiled your list, you'll need a thorough plan to work out all the details related to the studio, producer, artist, side artist(s), and manufacturing and packaging. I discuss these issues in detail later in Part IV.

Aside from helping you to get organized, the checklist can also serve as your budget. In other words, in addition to identifying the tasks to be completed, you should write down all costs and payments to be made to those providing services, such as a studio or producer. (As always, terms between you and third parties should be laid out in a written agreement signed by both sides.) Writing down the expenses involved in each step will give you a pretty good idea of what the entire project will cost before you start recording. This will help you to prepare, and to deal with unanticipated expenses that may arise during the recording/production process.

Second, when in the studio, reduce or eliminate any activities that aren't directly related to the recording. Studios charge by the hour or day, so while you're there, time is literally money. Unfortunately, there are a million distractions that can slow down the recording process, increase your bill, and possibly even result in a lower-quality record. The remainder of this chapter offers tips to help you avoid these distractions and make sure that everything gets done properly and on schedule.

Before you agree to put your artists in the studio, require them to rehearse all the songs they're going to record as many times as they can stand, until you're confident that they can perform them perfectly. This is a critical step. Chances are, an artist will have been performing live for some time before recording and will know the songs well. However, extra rehearsal can help him or her to work out final arrangements, side artist parts, lyric changes, newer songs, etc. This preparation will save time in the studio by limiting performance mistakes and artistic changes.

After the songs are perfected, make sure the artist arrives at the studio on time, awake, and ready to work. Help him or her to understand that it's far more important to get adequate rest each night before recording than to spend all night rehearsing one last time (or partying). Cramming didn't work the night before my Constitutional Law exam, and it won't help your artist to learn the songs any better, either.

Third, before recording begins, I recommend that both you and the artist visit the studio to meet with the engineer and producer (if you are using a producer). Provide these technical personnel with a demo tape or CD of all the songs the artist intends to record so they can get an idea of the artist's sound and the arrangements of the songs. Their familiarity with the songs can save time once you start recording the full-length CD. If you don't have a demo tape or CD, you might invite the producer and engineer to a live performance or a rehearsal.

During the meeting, discuss your goals for the recording, including the amount of money you've budgeted for the project. This will help the engineer and producer to estimate how many days you can spend in the studio and how much time you'll be able to spend on each song. It will also ensure that your budget is sufficient to achieve the goals you've set. You should also devise a plan for the recording session, deciding which songs to record first, addressing challenges you may foresee with certain songs, etc. The artist should be involved in this part of the conversation, so he or she is aware of your plan. With everything "on the table," everyone will be on the same page when you begin to record.

Believe me, there will be enough surprises in the studio even if you have a solid plan in place. Once you're there and the clock is running, you don't want to spend any more time than necessary figuring out what to do next, or how to solve a problem. If you've done your research, shopped for the right studio and producer, and involved everyone in the pre-production phase, the entire team will be ready to work the moment you turn on the microphones.

Things You Can Do Today To Build Your Label

1. Before you enter the studio, create a detailed checklist on your computer of all the steps leading to the completed CD, along with the costs involved with each step.

2. Meet with the studio engineer and producer to develop a plan for completing each step. Discuss the recording process, your budget, and your goals for the recording.

3. When in the studio, reduce or eliminate any activities that aren't directly related to the recording. Make sure the artist has rehearsed all the songs prior to going into the studio.

PREPARING A BUDGET

Most people believe a budget is restrictive, but unless you have unlimited funds, it can actually be liberating. When you know exactly what you have to spend and you accomplish the task within the budget you've set, you'll gain confidence in your ability to operate a label, even with limited funding. Sure, you'll visit studios that you can't afford and learn about all the high-end services available to record labels with larger budgets. Don't be discouraged. Enjoy the window-shopping and feel free to dream. Recording in a particular studio, or even owning a studio, can be a long-range goal. As you sell more records, this may happen. But no matter how successful your label becomes, there will always be new frills you can't afford, and you will always need a budget to help you put out the best product with the money you have.

How do you create a budget? Start by making a list of each item needed, and every step required, to produce a master recording, manufacture the CD, and do at least three to six months of promotion. Include the individual costs for everything, with tax. You'll probably forget a few items, and it may turn out that you don't need everything on your list, but you want to avoid surprises. Set aside 10% to 20% of your budget for miscellaneous, unforeseen costs, especially if you're not using a producer and/or have never been involved in the production or marketing of a recording. When unanticipated expenses do arise (and they will), you'll be prepared.

Of course, there will be times when you have to choose between what you must have and what you can do without. If you're working with a producer and/or an independent promoter, he or she can help you to create your checklist and make those potentially difficult choices.

In the Appendices, you'll find a Pre-Production Checklist and a Promotion Plan that can help you organize and budget the recording/manufacturing/promotion process. Use these lists as a guide while you're preparing your budget and calling around to obtain prices for various services. Once you have an estimate of the total cost for everything you want, you can begin to pick and choose the things you can afford, based on the amount of money you'll have available.

You may also realize that you don't yet have enough money for the project. My rule of thumb is not to begin recording until you have sufficient funds to complete the record, manufacture the first 1,000 CDs, and do three to six months of promotion. An artist recording on his or her own can work at intervals, when he or she has money to pay for studio time. But your label has a contractual responsibility to complete the record on time and begin promoting it and selling it. If you take months to finish a recording, your artist is going to be very unhappy. You may have heard stories about major-label artists taking six months to a year in the studio to make a record. (This is rare, but it does happen.) As the owner of a small label, you don't have the luxury of time or money to allow this kind of schedule. Plus, you have to prove to the artist that you can get the recording completed, manufactured, and promoted within a reasonable time frame. So, make your list of tasks, prepare a budget, and stay on schedule.

Probably the biggest variable in your budget will be the length of time spent in the studio. Studio rates are based on hours or full days, so you'll have to determine how many days your artist will need in the studio before you can know the cost. The studio owner and producer can help you here, so be honest with them about your budget. However many days you can afford for recording and mixing, you need to set a schedule and discuss it with the artist, engineer, and producer. I think it's worth spending a little extra for an experienced producer, who will limit mistakes, and therefore, limit the time required to complete each song.

Once you've determined the number of songs to be recorded, you can budget your time. If you have five days in the studio and 12 songs to record, you'll probably record three songs during each of the first four days and spend the fifth day mixing. (This compressed recording schedule reinforces the importance of rehearsal before recording. The better the artist knows the songs, the less time it will take to record them.) If you can afford more days in the studio, obviously, you can spend more time on each song.

Be as honest as possible with the artist about your budget. Eventually, you'll have to explain the expenses related to recording (as well as producing, promoting, and distributing the record), so it's best to be up-front about how much you can spend on the project. I have found that most artists are willing to work with a small, budget-minded label, as long as they feel they are being treated fairly and honestly. Many recording agreements even include the budget amount in the contract. However you decide to handle it, the budget is a big issue that should be addressed early and honestly. It really helps when you can discuss openly how you plan to record the artist, based on the budget available.

Yours is an independent label with limited funds. Maybe this is your first record. The artist will know this going into the recording studio. He or she knew it before signing the contract. It's nothing to be ashamed of or secretive about. You just have to do your best with what you have. People in retail and radio have often been impressed with my ability to produce a great-sounding independent record for $5,000 to $10,000. I can't afford the most expensive studios, but I've been lucky enough to work with some very talented engineers and producers. Through the years, I've learned that experienced, skilled professionals really can help you produce a great record, even if you can't afford the high-end facilities.

And because cash is king in this business, you can often get more for your money if you have cash on hand during the recording process. Remember this when creating your budget. Many times, I've gotten extra studio days or a better rate because I was prepared to pay in advance (rather than paying each day or being billed for the costs). By negotiating with small studios, and by working with an experienced engineer and producer, you can produce an excellent recording on a limited budget. If you can build a good relationship, some smaller studios may also allow you to use extra days when they don't have other projects scheduled. The last thing a studio owner wants is to produce a poor-sounding record that will make other artists hesitant to record in that studio. Even if you get extra studio time, though, you should budget your time to prevent the process from dragging on too long.

One of the most important benefits of a budget is that it helps you stay focused. Don't be intimidated by studio owners or others who say you can't make a good record for under $50,000. The fact is, they may be right: You might not be able to make a good record in *their* studios, with *their* producers, for under $50,000. And you can be sure these studios are not going to negotiate lower rates to meet your budget.

That doesn't mean you can't make a good record for much less than $50,000. Indeed, very few small labels can afford that price tag for one record. As with any new independent label, you're trying to create and market a good recording on a limited budget. And you know what? Thousands of excellent records are made every year for very little money. No, you can't buy a Mercedes when your budget will only cover a Honda. Even so, you can and should stick with your budget and negotiate to get the most for your money.

Things You Can Do Today To Build Your Label

1. Review Appendices A and D, and make a list of every expense related to recording, manufacturing, marketing, and promoting one full-length recording. Research the cost of each item/service by getting quotes from different businesses.

2. Talk to local producers or other experienced professionals to learn ways to cut costs and save money.

3. Be honest with studio owners and managers, producers, and others (including your artist) about how much you have to spend on each task. Discuss your budget and plan with them to determine if any cost breaks can be provided.

FINDING AND CHOOSING A RECORDING STUDIO 39

ecording studios are exciting and creative places to work. They can also be expensive. Because it costs money to make the master recording you're going to sell, the recording studio is an inevitable cost of doing business in the music industry. Exactly how high that cost goes depends on your budget, preparation, and efficiency in getting the recording completed. Your primary goal will be to produce a record of good songs that sounds good enough to meet consumer standards.

I'm not going to kid you. The record you make for $10,000 in a small studio with decent equipment won't sound like a $100,000 CD done at Ocean Way Studios in Hollywood or The Hit Factory in New York City. However, you *can* get a very good recording for $10,000 to $20,000. (You can also spend a lot of money and end up with a bad recording.) With a little forethought and experience, your label can save money, reduce mistakes in the recording process, and produce records that will be radio-quality and satisfy your customers. Small labels with limited budgets do it every day. Here's how.

One key is to take your time and be thorough during pre-production, especially until you have the experience of a few records under your belt. Do your homework and shop around for the right studio, and don't begin recording until you have several good choices on your list.

The right studio can provide a comfortable atmosphere during recording and facilitate a better final product. It's a mistake to select a studio simply because it's inexpensive. But if you end up in a studio that costs more than your budget allows, you may ask everyone else to rush to meet your budget. This will create tension and result in a mediocre recording. The goal is to find a studio that fits your budget and has an experienced staff with whom you feel comfortable. Although you need to keep moving forward to get the record done in a reasonable period of time, you shouldn't start recording until you've found a studio that meets these criteria.

Ultimately, you're shopping for a recording "system" that you can rely upon each time you record. This system will consist of a studio, engineer, and producer that consistently provide you with a really good recording at a cost your label can afford. Many times, the studio is the key. It must have sufficient equipment, experienced staff, and a comfortable environment.

How do you find a recording studio that meets your needs? The first step is to identify the studios in your area. Many, but not all, studios are listed in national music industry directories, such as the *Recording Industry Sourcebook* or *Musician's Atlas*, so you can start there. If you're in a large city, you shouldn't have much trouble finding a local studio to meet your needs. If you live in a smaller city, you may have better luck checking the local yellow pages first. And, of course, there is always the Internet.

After you've identified several studios, ask local artists, producers, labels, attorneys, music-venue owners, etc. for opinions and information about the studios on your list, or others you may have missed. Then call the most promising studios to obtain information about their rates, including discounts for reserving the studio for 24-hour blocks, and for non-prime time, or "graveyard" blocks. (I usually do not recommend starting your recording during "graveyard" hours, because most people involved with the recording will be tired.) Inquire about the number of recording rooms available. Some studios have more than one recording room, with different prices for different rooms. Also, ask about the kind of recording equipment they use and number of tracks available, the number and type(s) of microphones used, and any instruments and amplifiers that might be available. Finally, ask if they have mastering equipment or facilities. All of this information will help narrow down your list of potential studios.

During this process, you should consult with your artist. If he or she has recorded before, ask about studios he or she has used. You can learn a lot this way, especially when you're starting out. If the artist gave you a great demo and had a good experience making it, it may be worth checking out the studio he or she used. And obviously, everyone will benefit if the artist is comfortable in the studio. This doesn't mean you should choose any studio the artist wants, but he or she should at least feel that you're open-minded. If you're using a producer, which I highly recommend, talk with him or her about the artist's style of music and recording experience to make sure the studios on your list have the right equipment, people, and experience to meet the artist's needs. Some smaller studios may not have enough microphones, or a mixing board with enough channels, or sufficient space to record your artist's music properly. Having said that, it's important to recognize that, with all the new technology, recording studios are getting smaller, while producing bigger sounds. So don't rule out studios that are in someone's home or garage. The main goal is to find a place that meets your needs and fits your budget.

After doing your homework and compiling a list of potential studios, it's time to take the steps toward choosing one. First, you'll want to visit the studios on your list. If possible, bring someone with recording experience, preferably the producer you will use or a studio engineer, who can provide educated recommendations. Visit as many studios as you can, including the most expensive, even if you don't plan to record there. You'll get an idea of the options available and the things you like about each studio. Besides, you may end up using them in the future, when your budget increases.

After touring a studio, there's no shame in telling the owner you can't afford the studio's rates right now, or in asking for recommendations of other studios in your price range. You might even ask the engineer (in private) if there are smaller studios where he or she works and can recommend.

Your choice of studio may be based on the people who run it, or the engineers who operate the equipment, so be sure to ask about the engineer's experience and about the studio's previous recordings. (Every studio should provide an engineer as part of the price they charge. You shouldn't use a studio that doesn't provide an engineer unless you're hiring a producer who is also an experienced engineer.)

You may see gold records hanging on the wall in some studios. No matter where you visit, it's okay to ask to hear the studio's latest projects and/or to sit in for a few minutes on a recording session. At this point, you're networking and learning. Take notes during each studio visit for reference during your final decision-making process.

As mentioned earlier, I believe strongly that you should hire an experienced producer for the recording. This is a good investment that will save money in the studio and help you to put out a better product. You might find an engineer who is also a producer. He or she may work at a studio as an engineer for a regular paycheck and take on side projects as a producer. If you find such a multitalented person, you can save money by eliminating a separate producer fee. Just understand that an engineer with producer skills will not be able to spend as much time on the producer's job as a separate producer will.

Another good option, if it's available, is to work with experienced producers who have their own studios. They are doubly motivated to put out good products, because their reputation as a producer *and* as a studio is at stake. Another benefit of a producer-owned studio is that you may be able to negotiate a flat "producer/studio" rate for the entire project. Because the producer owns the equipment, he or she can be flexible in how much to charge. And while a producer/owner will not allow you to over-run your recording time, he or she will have a vested interest in making sure that things get done properly. If he or she chooses to spend an extra day or two re-recording or re-mixing, you won't have to pay for the extra studio time. These all are very good reasons to include some producer-owned studios on your list of recording facilities to visit.

Once you've narrowed your choice of studios down to two or three, I suggest having the artist record one song—the easiest one—at each studio before committing to a longer recording session. Consider it a test drive. The purpose of this exercise is to determine which studio is most comfortable for your artist, and to make sure each studio can meet your needs. After recording a song (which you may or may not have mixed), you might decide not to use a particular studio. Still, the recording may be good enough to include on your original master recording, so the day will not be wasted. You might even take a "test drive" in a more established and expensive studio. The recording from this studio may not sound much better than the one you make in a lesser-known studio. This will make you feel good about using the smaller, more affordable studio.

Finally, you'll have to select a studio. You've worked hard to gather the information you need to make this decision, so feel confident that you'll be able to make the right choice. Review your notes. Consider the equipment available at each studio, the experience of personnel, the studio's track record, and how comfortable the artist (and you) felt in each place. Listen to the demos you cut at the different studios. Talk with your producer to get his or her thoughts. Which studio feels good, meets your needs, *and* fits within your budget? Every studio will have strong and weak points, but by now, your choice should be getting clear. You may not be able to afford the perfect studio (few labels can), but hopefully, your research will lead you to a studio that will produce a solid recording of which both you and your artist can be proud.

Things You Can Do Today To Build Your Label

1. Consult music-industry directories, the Internet, or your local yellow pages to compile a list of the studios in your area. Ask local artists and industry professionals for their opinions of the studios on your list, or others you may have missed.

2. Call studios to obtain information about their rates (including block time), hours of operation, available equipment, etc.

3. Visit the most promising studios, even if some are out of your price range, to get a feel for what they can do for you now and in the future.

4. Have your artist record the same song at several studios so you can compare the sound and evaluate the working environment at each studio.

WHAT DOES A PRODUCER DO?

A producer oversees the recording/mixing/mastering process. Different producers participate in the process more or less, depending on their experience and ability, and on the skills of the other professionals involved. Some producers also have the technical expertise to be the sound engineer (the person who operates the equipment that records the songs as the artist performs in the studio). Producers with musical ability may even play a musical instrument on the recording and/or help the artist to write and arrange songs. But the producer's most important function is to coordinate the recording process. He or she directs the artist, musicians, and recording technicians, while attempting to get the sound and song arrangements that the artist, producer, and record label want.

A successful producer once told me that his job is not to change the artist, but to help the artist do what he does, and to do it right in three-and-a-half minutes. A talented producer can promote an artist's success by providing guidance, a well-produced record, and an innovative and new sound. He or she will usually have several traits.

First, it's no coincidence that many great producers are musicians, and have been—or performed with—recording artists. A producer with musical and technical skills can really help the production run smoothly. He or she will understand what the artist and the engineer are trying to achieve and will be able to explain or demonstrate how to obtain the desired results.

Second, an effective producer should have the ability to communicate and stay cool under stress. Long days and nights, disagreements, pressure to perform, and the desire to get just the right sound can lead to a lot of tension during studio sessions. When large egos mix with frustration and fatigue, sparks and beer bottles may fly. (One reason to limit alcohol consumption in the studio is to reduce the number of bottles available as ammunition.) The producer must work through these problems and keep everyone calm and focused. Sometimes, this is the most difficult job of all.

Of course, a producer must also understand the music business and the costs of recording. Your record label is paying the bills, and the producer should work with you to make sure the recording is done properly, on time, and within your budget.

Unfortunately, some producers won't care about your label's money. I know one who allowed a band to spend more than $500,000 recording an album that bombed, even after the band's previous album—recorded for much less—was successful. He showed up late for recording sessions and allowed the band to play video games while the clock was ticking. He knew that any part of the $500,000 not spent on recording could have gone into promotion, new gear, or something else to sell records and make money for the label and band. Evidently, he wasn't too concerned about that. I'm not suggesting he should have cut corners in the recording process, but this producer was irresponsible and unprofessional.

The point is this: Just as you must be honest and professional in all aspects of running your label, it is appropriate for you to demand honesty and professionalism from the individuals with whom you work, including producers. These people are working for you. Make sure they work in your best interest.

Recently, a new kind of producer has arisen in the rap, pop, and hip-hop musical genres. I refer to this type of professional as a "producer of tracks." He or she wears two hats: One as the creator of the music to be recorded by the artist, and one as the producer of the recording of that music. The producer of tracks creates and records the music. After that, the artist records vocals to go with the music. Some producers of tracks will help the artist to complete production of the vocals, but most will not. Instead, the artist will employ a different producer to mix the vocals with the music to obtain a final version of the song.

In any case, you want a producer who can capture the essence of the artist's songs and make the artist sound as good as possible. I once represented a band that had great songs and a huge regional following. With the help of a producer who understood their work, this band independently recorded and released a few records that really captured their sound. Unfortunately, on their first deal with a small record label, the label owner insisted that they use an inexperienced producer who was the owner's friend. (I urge you not to repeat this mistake. If you use inexperienced people—even friends—everyone will regret it.) Predictably, the band was not very happy with this producer. Worst of all, the record did not capture what the band did best. The CD was panned by critics and ignored by the band's fans.

After the record was completed and mastered, the band's singer and main writer told me that, in his view, "those songs were lost forever." It's sad that those great songs will always leave a bad impression on the band, their fans, music critics, and radio stations. A producer really can make that much of a difference.

Things You Can Do Today To Build Your Label

1. Read more about what a producer does in the books, *How to Become a Record Producer* by David Mellor, and *Behind the Glass* by Howard Massey.

2. Listen to good local records that match your artist's musical style. Scan the credits to find out who produced those albums. Contact these and other producers to determine if they might be available and appropriate for your project.

3. Start making mental notes and written lists of the qualities (volume levels, mixes, tone, etc.) that you like and don't like on records you hear.

HOW THE PRODUCER GETS PAID

*U*sually, a producer is paid by the hour, by the number of master recordings completed, or a flat fee. He or she will probably ask for a royalty from the sale of the record as well. "Producers of tracks," discussed in the previous chapter, will receive an additional royalty, because they create the original music to which artists add vocals. If you agree to such an arrangement, you'll have to account to the producer and make regular royalty payments, based on record sales. These issues must be agreed upon in advance and laid out in a written contract. As always, I recommend that you consult with an entertainment attorney to provide guidance in drafting and/or negotiating this contract. (You can find a variety of producer agreements at *MusicBusinessMadeSimple.com.*)

The producer's up-front fee can vary from $250 to $10,000 per song, based on his or her experience and success, your artist's level of success, and the number of songs to be recorded. The fee can also be influenced by whether the label is a local, national independent, or major record company. Ultimately, the producer you and the artist select will depend on the artist's musical style and, naturally, on your budget.

Aside from his or her fee, the producer, like the artist, will receive a record royalty. This is usually a percentage of the record's sales price, multiplied by the number of CDs or cassettes sold. The record royalty for a producer is usually 3% of the record's sales price. On a CD that sells for

$16.98, the producer's royalty would be about $0.50 for each copy sold. However, this 3% record royalty (or "three points," as it's called in the record industry) is not actually paid by the record company. In fact, it comes out of the artist's royalties.

How does this work? It's simple. If the recording agreement says the artist is to receive a royalty of 13% of the retail price for each record sold, the artist actually will get only 10%, or "ten points." The three points paid to the producer will be taken out of the artist's 13 royalty points, not the label's pocket. A record contract will refer to this payment system as "all-in." It means the label will pay a total of 13 royalty points (or however many points are agreed upon), and no more. All royalties paid to producers or anyone else will be deducted from the artist's royalties.

This is another reason why the recording contracts your label offers to artists must be perfectly clear. They should provide you with the right to hire a producer on the artist's behalf, to offer the producer a certain royalty percentage, and to pay the producer's royalties from the artist's "points." Your entertainment attorney will know about this aspect of the record business, and will be able to guide you. For a detailed explanation of record royalties, see Chapter 22, How Does the Artist Get Paid? and Chapter 23, The Record Royalty.

If the producer assists in writing or arranging the artist's songs, he or she will receive a mechanical royalty in addition to the record royalty. As described more thoroughly in Chapter 24, The Mechanical Royalty, this royalty is paid by the record company to songwriters for the right to record their songs. Some producers, namely "producers of tracks" who compose the music, are entitled to 50% ownership of the song, and thus, 50% of the mechanical royalties. The record company would pay the other 50% of the royalty to writer(s) of the lyrics, usually the artist. If the artist is the sole songwriter and does not want the producer to share in the song royalties, this issue must be negotiated in the producer's contract. Before you hire a producer, it's best to talk with the artist about the producer(s) you're considering, the role they will play, and royalty rate they'll receive.

As you can imagine, this system can get complicated if you use several producers for the recording. Consult with your entertainment attorney to determine the best way to structure a contract with your producer(s). In all cases, you *must* have a written agreement with the producer(s) to protect your copyright ownership of the artist's master recordings. The next chapter discusses the producer's contract in detail.

Things You Can Do Today To Build Your Label

1. Talk with local producers about their fees and royalty rates. Then do some math to determine who can do the best job, within your budget.

2. Read sample recording contracts at *MusicBusinessMadeSimple.com* and elsewhere to gain a better understanding of how royalties work. Include a provision in your recording agreement that allows you to negotiate a limited amount of the artist's royalties to a producer.

3. Obtain a sample producer agreement at *MusicBusinessMadeSimple.com* and tailor it to meet the needs of your label and to be consistent with your artist recording contracts.

The Producer Contracts

42

A great producer can be invaluable to your artist's recording. It's equally invaluable to have a written agreement with the producer. There's no option: If you're going to use a producer, you *must* have a written contract with him or her. The practical reason for this agreement is to ensure that both parties are clear about what the producer will provide, and what he or she will receive in return. The legal reason is to address various rights of the producer and record company. The three main issues to address in a producer's agreement are rights in the recording, rights to the songs, and payment.

Before addressing these issues, I want to review briefly the producer's role, as described more thoroughly in Chapter 40, What Does a Producer Do? Traditionally, a producer oversees the recording process. He or she may also help to write or arrange the songs to be recorded. In this case, the producer has some ownership rights in the recording he or she has produced. (These rights should be transferred to your label in the producer contract.) As described earlier, a "producer of tracks" will write and record a music track, over which a vocalist (your artist) will add his or her vocals. In this case, the producer has ownership rights to both the written song (which he or she will keep) and to the recording (which he or she will transfer to your label or the artist via the producer contract). A producer of tracks may help the artist to record his or her vocals and then mix them with the producer's music track, or the artist may hire an entirely different producer. In the latter case, the second producer will also own some rights to the recording, which must be outlined in a separate producer contract.

Regardless of the type of producer you use, the first issue to address in the producer's contract is his or her rights to the recorded versions of each song on the CD (as opposed to the written songs themselves). A recording's copyright is shared by everyone involved in making the recording. Therefore, vocalists and musicians whose performances are captured on the recording, as well as the producer who helps to create it, share the copyright. Though the studio engineer has rights too, he or she is usually an employee of the studio. His or her rights to the recording should be addressed through a contract with the recording studio (if he or she is an employee), or directly with the engineer (if he or she is not working for the studio).

It's imperative (and standard in the music industry) for your label to have complete ownership of the recordings, so you may use them in every way possible to sell records and make money. That's why your label's recording agreement transfers the artist's copyrights in the recording to the label. (The songwriter retains his or her rights to license or re-record the *written* song, but the label owns this recorded version.) Your producer agreement should be structured similarly, to transfer the producer's copyrights to the label—in writing. Without this written agreement, the law will consider the producer a co-author of the recording. As such, he or she will be entitled to a share of the overall profits from that recording, and not just a royalty or flat fee to which you may have agreed. (Note: If you use side musicians or featured artists who are not members of a union, you'll also need a separate written side artist agreement to obtain the rights to their recorded performances. You can find a sample side artist agreement at *MusicBusinessMadeSimple.com*.

If you've hired a traditional producer to oversee the entire record, a standard producer agreement will transfer ownership of the recording to the label by identifying the producer's contributions as a "work made for hire." If you're purchasing musical tracks from a producer, the process is a little more complicated. You'll need a producer of tracks agreement to ensure your label's ownership of the recording of each musical track. Both types of producer contracts can be found at *MusicBusinessMadeSimple.com*.

The second issue to address in the producer agreement is the producer's rights to each song (not just the recorded versions being made for this CD). Will the producer be considered a songwriter and entitled to rights and mechanical royalties as a co-author? As noted earlier, the producer may help to write, rewrite, or arrange the songs. Great producers can help to create new or better songs from existing material. Sometimes, the changes they make are substantial, and can even help the song to become a hit. In such cases, a producer may expect to be compensated not only for his or her production work, but also as an author of the song. Depending on the amount of assistance provided, the producer may be entitled legally to claim co-authorship, even if the original version of the song was written before he or she was hired.

There is usually no dispute about authorship with producers of tracks (see Chapter 40, What Does a Producer Do?), who write the music to which an artist adds lyrics. As authors of the music, producers of tracks are entitled to a credit in the song and half the songwriting royalties. If you wish to have a different arrangement with the producer, it must be explained clearly in the producer contract. In any case, it is important to address your producer's rights in the recorded songs—in writing—before the producer begins working on the record.

The third main item in a producer agreement is the payment schedule. A producer can be paid several ways: A flat fee for services, a record royalty, and/or a mechanical royalty (if the producer helps to write the songs). These payments are explained in depth in Chapter 41, How the Producer Gets Paid. Depending on the negotiations of the label and producer, these payment options can be combined in different configurations to satisfy everyone's needs (e.g. fee only or fee plus a record royalty). Whatever the parties decide, the producer's payment plan must be included in the written agreement. If there ever is a discrepancy over the producer's rights to the recordings or songs because you failed to address payment in the contract, the agreement may be declared void, or it may be deemed that the producer is entitled to more compensation than you agreed to provide.

Other issues, such as accounting, rights to use the producer's name, production or songwriting credit, etc., should also be addressed clearly in your producer agreement(s). The more detail you include in the agreement, the less likely you are to have a dispute later. Once again, an experienced entertainment attorney can assist in drafting and negotiating contracts that are most appropriate for your label.

Things You Can Do Today To Build Your Label

1. Study the different ways a producer is paid; make sure you understand the various payment options.

2. Obtain samples of the various types of producer agreements your label will need from *MusicBusinessMadeSimple.com*.

3. Meet with an entertainment attorney to ensure that your label's producer contracts include all the important terms you want to offer to a producer.

THE RECORDING PROCESS

*L*ike most other independent record companies, your label will probably be working on a modest budget. Therefore, it's important to manage the recording process and reduce mistakes so you can get the best recording possible with the limited funds and time available. I noted earlier that I'm no expert on the technical aspects of recording. I can't explain how to work a mixing board or the best way to set up microphones. (For advice and information on this side of the process, I refer you to *Assistant Engineer's Handbook* by Tim Crich, or *Basic Digital Recording* by Paul White.) However, the tips I provide in this chapter will help you to work efficiently, keep everyone focused, and get the best results possible.

Once you've completed all the preparations and you're finally in the studio, everyone will be excited and ready to celebrate. But before you send out party invitations and crack open the champagne, remember why you're there: To make a solid recording *and* stay within your budget. Recording is work, not a party. And you're paying for every hour. Therefore, my first suggestion is this: Do not allow any extra people (girlfriends, boyfriends, groupies, family members, etc.) into the recording sessions. Discuss this with the artist(s) beforehand. Sure, it might be fun, but I've seen many times how distracting and time-consuming friends and family can be. Wasted time will cost you money, and possibly a good recording.

Similarly, believe me when I say you must limit the consumption of alcohol during recording. Again, discuss this with the artist(s). That rock 'n' roll lifestyle may be appealing, but too much alcohol (or other substances) can slow down the whole process or become downright debilitating. I've seen ugly fights over an inebriated band member's inability to play his or her parts properly. That's the last thing you want in the studio. It's a waste of time (for which you are paying), and it distracts everyone from the job at hand. Just as sure as alcohol will not enhance your artist's performance, it can cloud your judgment and cause you to make bad decisions about the recording. It's far better to wait until after the day's recording to celebrate.

While everyone else sets to work, you may wonder, "What is my role, as label owner, in the studio?" Well, your job is to be supportive and unobtrusive, and to let people do their jobs. I know from experience, it's very difficult for a label owner to sit back and watch while everyone else is busy, especially when things go wrong. And yes, things will go wrong. The artist may be nervous and have a hard time getting started, or playing a certain part. Equipment will fail. The producer or engineer will make mistakes. You'll want to leap in with advice and opinions, but for the sake of the recording and everyone else involved, refrain from hovering and telling people how to do their jobs. Think of the sports franchise owner who never played the sport but still insists on telling the coach how to run the team. No one likes that person, and that meddling usually just distracts everyone from their jobs.

It's fine to be in the studio, but once you're confident that everyone understands the game plan, step back and trust them do their work. Rely on the producer and engineer to complete the recording properly. Trust your artist to perform as he or she has so many times in the past. It may take everyone a moment to get settled, but you know what these people can do; that's why you've decided to work with them. For best results, set your ego aside, intervene only in emergencies, and allow your team to make a recording for your label.

I suggest that you come to the studio each day with coffee, donuts, and a smile. Before the day's recording begins, meet briefly with the producer, engineer, and artists to discuss the previous day's session and how well the recording is adhering to the schedule devised during pre-production. Sometimes, you will find that things aren't going exactly as planned. At these times, composure is critical. Getting angry will only make everyone else unhappy and nervous. So remain calm, work with the team to make constructive decisions, and keep moving forward. You, the producer, and the engineer can discuss any deviations from the original plan and determine how best to complete the recording within your budget.

After making sure that everyone has arrived at the studio on time and is ready to go, you may need to leave. Ask the producer to give you an update at the end of each day. If you plan to stay at the studio, the best thing you can do is be quiet and observe. As long as everyone is at the studio and working, you're proceeding the best you can.

It's very important to avoid making suggestions regarding creative aspects of the recording. This will confuse the artist and open the door to changes that were not part of the songs the artist rehearsed and perfected. The goal of the recording process is for the producer, engineer, and artist to record the songs as previously rehearsed. Any alterations in song arrangements, structure, etc., should be made before recording begins. Although excellent creative ideas will often arise in the studio, you want to limit changes or second-guessing through preparation. Make sure your producer understands this so he or she does not enter the studio expecting to have freedom to experiment.

Finally, I learned from an experienced producer to take occasional breaks in recording and mixing, and to quit the session when everyone starts getting tired. After several hours of playing and hearing the same song(s) over and over, it can become difficult to tell what really sounds good. Artists and studio professionals alike need energy and fresh ears to get the best recording, so I suggest that everyone take a break from time to time. Stop when you're tired, and begin the next day rested and ready. Sometimes you might even stop working on a certain song for a while. There's no reason to force things if they're not going well. Instead, move to another song and return to the problem song later.

If you've done your pre-production properly, you will have prepared yourself, the producer, and the artist for a creative, exciting, and fun experience. Once you are in the studio, preparedness and organization must continue to rule the day. The label owner's most important and difficult task is often to keep the process moving according to plan quietly, while also keeping the artist and producer happy. Through the experience of producing several CDs, you'll begin to master this balancing act. What may seem overwhelming at first will become second nature after a while. If you follow the pre-production and recording tips described here, you will establish a good reputation among artists and producers, develop strong organizational skills, reduce mistakes, and establish an efficient system for producing quality CDs on schedule and on budget. Not coincidentally, these all are qualities of a successful record label.

Things You Can Do Today To Build Your Label

1. Review your plan for recording with everyone involved before entering the studio, so all parties will be on the same page when recording begins.

2. Before the day's recording sessions, meet briefly with the producer, engineer, and artists to discuss the previous day's progress, and how well the sessions are adhering to the recording plan devised in pre-production.

3. Remain in the background and allow the artist(s), producer, and engineer to do their jobs. Make sure everyone is staying on task, but avoid making artistic suggestions or getting upset when things don't go as planned.

Mixing and Mastering

After the songs are recorded, you will mix the record, which is the process of combining all the individual recorded tracks of a song (vocals, guitar, drums, keyboards, etc.) so that each can be heard at the volume you want. The idea behind mixing is pretty simple, but the task itself is anything but easy. It takes a special talent to get the mix right, and the right mix is crucial to the overall quality of a record. As you've probably heard on CDs in your own collection, records that aren't well mixed just don't sound good. Maybe you can't hear the keyboards. Maybe there is too much bass, or the guitar drowns out the vocals. Whatever the case, a skilled engineer or producer can make the difference between a decent-sounding record and an excellent one.

The exact process you use to mix the songs you record will vary, depending on the amount of studio time you can afford, the level of interest shown by your artist(s) in participating, and the skills of the people with whom you are working. Usually, the studio's recording engineer will mix the record first, with the assistance of the producer. If the producer has the technical skills to work the mixing board, he or she may mix the record without the engineer.

Sometimes, you and the artist(s) will sit in on mixing sessions. However, I have found that it works best for the engineer and/or producer to prepare the initial mixes. This will prevent you and the artists from wasting time scrutinizing every detail of the mix before it's ready to critique. Further, I have seen heated battles erupt between bassists, singers, and guitarists, all wanting to be heard above the others without regard for the quality of the final mix. It's better if all of you sit out the initial round of mixing.

Allow the engineer and/or producer to work his or her magic first. Afterward, you and the artist(s) can sit in and make suggestions for the final mix. The recording contract may give you the final say in these matters. However, unless you have previous experience in mixing sessions, I recommend that you remain as neutral as possible and allow the producer and artist(s) to work out the mix. Over time, you may develop a good "ear" for mixing, but until you do, it's best to let the professionals handle it.

After your record is mixed, the process moves to the next stage: Mastering. Mastering is an enhancement process that will improve the sound of your recording and set it apart from other CDs. You may be able to have the CD mastered at the same studio in which it was recorded. However, chances are that you'll have to use a specialized mastering facility. If your recording studio can't master your CD, ask the studio manager to recommend local mastering facilities. There are mastering studios all over the country with whom you can work via mail, but I always prefer to work in person, even if I have to drive to a larger, neighboring city.

Mastering costs can range from $50 to $1,000 per track, depending on the equipment used and the notoriety of the studio and/or the mastering engineer. You should be able to find a small facility to master your label's full-length CDs for $500 to $1,000.

Typically, you will give the mastering studio a DAT (Digital Audio Tape) or a CD-R (Recordable Compact Disc) of the master recording, which is provided to you by the recording studio. The mastering engineer will play back your recording through a sound system that is connected to the mastering processors and equipment. The engineer can adjust the overall sound of the mixed recording, but cannot alter the levels of individual tracks (vocals, keyboard, drums, etc.), because all tracks have already been mixed and now are combined into a single recording.

The mastering engineer will put the songs in order, place the requested amount of space between each song, and configure the CD-R for manufacturing. After the mastering is complete, the studio can provide you with a mastered DAT and a CD-R, from which a duplication company will manufacture and package copies of your compact discs and/or cassette tapes. The details of this process are described in the next chapter.

You'll pay the mastering studio by the hour. If you or the artist wants to sit in on the mastering process (which, in honesty, you probably know nothing about), it will take more time and cost more money. Therefore, I recommend that you allow the mastering engineer to do the work. Then, you can visit the mastering studio to approve or make suggestions for the final version.

I cannot overstress the importance of mastering. If you want your records to sound their best, they must go through this process. Therefore, you need to include the cost of mastering in your budget, even if you have it done at an inexpensive studio. As in every other phase of the recording process, do your homework about the mastering studios you're considering to be sure that they have the necessary equipment, and that their engineers have the requisite skills and experience to do the job properly.

Things You Can Do Today To Build Your Label

1. Learn more about mixing and mastering by reading books such as *Basic Mixing Techniques* by Paul White, and *Home Recording for Musicians* by Craig Anderton. Or, while shopping for recording studios, ask if you can sit in on a mixing session.

2. Ask recording studios for references on mastering facilities. Visit mastering facilities and ask to hear some of the recordings they have mastered, both before and after mastering.

3. After talking with various mastering engineers and getting a sense of how much they charge, be sure to include the cost of mastering in your budget.

MANUFACTURING AND PACKAGING

*A*fter all the songs are recorded, mixed, and mastered, it's time to create the product that your label will sell to the public. It's not practical to discuss all the details of the manufacturing process here. In fact, there are as many variables in this process as there are artists in your city: How many copies of the CD do you want manufactured? What kind of art do you want, and who will create that art? How do you want the CD/cassette packaged? Regardless of your answers to these questions (and others that will arise), the following five basic steps in the manufacturing process (explained below) remain constant.

1. Artwork for cover and booklet inserts are created by a graphic artist.
2. Computer files of the artwork are converted to a film negative.
3. The film negative is used by a printer to print the booklet inserts and back tray cards.
4. The master recording and artwork are sent to the manufacturer to duplicate the discs.
5. CDs/cassettes, inserts, and tray cards are inserted into a CD/cassette case and wrapped.

First, you'll need to employ an artist to design the artwork for your CD or cassette, unless you're going to do it yourself. You'll need artwork for the front and back cover of the CD or cassette package, the printed booklet inserts, and for the compact disc or cassette itself. Although many graphic artists may be able to create the necessary artwork, it is important to use one who is familiar with the specific requirements for compact discs or cassettes. For example, the artist must know the proper dimensions and configuration for printing on a CD. He or she must also be skilled on graphic art computer programs that are compatible for use in the filmmaking process. And he or she must understand the film and printing process to ensure that the design's colors and elements will print correctly. After completing his or her work, the designer should give you a computer disc containing all the art, which you will then give to the manufacturer and printer.

Before you print and manufacture the CDs and/or cassettes, make sure the artwork looks exactly how you want it to look. Once you get past this point, "do-overs" can be very expensive and time-consuming. I remember having 1,000 CDs manufactured, only to find that a computer problem had eliminated the bar code from the printed artwork. Because we failed to follow the printer's advice to get a printed "proof" copy of the art to review beforehand, we didn't catch this mistake until all the artwork for 1,000 CDs had been printed. We were lucky, though, as we were able to solve the problem by printing the bar codes on stickers and manually attaching them to each CD package. To avoid delays and expensive mistakes with your CDs and/or cassettes, discuss each step with your printer and manufacturer, and follow their recommendations. This is the best way to ensure that you get the product you're expecting.

I mentioned bar codes. You'll need them for your label's CDs and cassettes. They may not seem like art, but they're part of the artwork package. You probably have noticed that the bar code, or manufacturer's UPC code, is a unique series of black lines and numbers. It identifies and distinguishes all manufactured products sold in stores today, including this book. You or your graphic artist can generate UPC bar codes via a computer program by entering certain numbers assigned to you by the Uniform Code Council (UCC). You can apply for your UPC code on the UCC Website *(www.uccouncil.org)*. For most small record companies, the application fee is $750, with an annual renewal fee of $150. Once you have the bar code, your graphic artist can insert it into the artwork so that it appears on the back cover of your CD or cassette. From there, it can be scanned by computers in stores to register a sale.

Many good companies are available to assist in manufacturing and packaging your CD or cassette. Like every other decision you make for your label, do your research before committing to a deal. Ask artists, studios, other record companies, or whoever might be knowledgeable about which companies they use, and about their experiences with those companies. You can also ask manufacturers in your area for sample packages that demonstrate the quality of their work.

The terms "manufacturing," "replication," and "duplication" typically refer to the multiple duplication of the compact disc/cassette and all accompanying artwork by the manufacturer. "Packaging" is the process of placing the manufactured CD or cassette into a plastic case (the "jewel case"), along with the printed artwork. The CD or cassette is then covered in a plastic or cellophane wrap (this process is called shrink-wrapping), boxed, and shipped to your label. Sometimes this entire process, including the printing, is referred to as "manufacturing."

Many manufacturing businesses are turnkey, or "all-in-one" operations. They may also be called duplicators, replicators, or manufacturing and packaging companies. Some turnkey businesses will take care of everything, from printing the artwork and getting the CDs manufactured, to delivering the shrink-wrapped product to your door. Others may handle only printing and shrink-wrapping and send the CDs out to be manufactured by a different company. Still other businesses act as brokers. They don't have equipment or do any of the work, but they know the process and utilize different businesses to complete the project.

Whichever type(s) of service(s) you use, make sure you work with experienced companies that can show you samples of previous work. Get referrals from other independent record labels and shop around for the best deal. I recommend using companies in your city, or one nearby. This will allow you to communicate face-to-face, which can help you to avoid problems, especially when your label is just getting started. It's much easier to approve some aspect of the process, or to make changes, if you can meet in person. Working with a company in your city also allows you to establish a personal relationship with the individual who is overseeing this important step. You can find a list of manufacturing businesses, including "turnkey" companies, CD replicators, manufactures/packagers, and printers, in resources like the *Recording Industry Sourcebook, Musician's Atlas,* and *The Indie Bible.*

Things You Can Do Today To Build Your Label

1. Ask local record labels, manufacturing companies, or others in the industry to recommend local graphic artists who design CD artwork for the genre of music your label is producing. Speak with these artists and ask to see some samples of their work.

2. Obtain your bar code from the UCC Website *(www.uc-council.org)*.

3. Speak with local labels or artists to identify reputable manufacturing businesses in your area. Ask these businesses to send you samples of their work.

PART
FIVE

MARKETING

AND

DISTRIBUTION

THE RECORDING IS OVER,
BUT THE WORK IS JUST BEGINNING

*A*record company does two things: It creates a product, and then markets and promotes it. You might expect a label to invest equal resources and time in each of these tasks, but in fact, creating the product is only a small part of the work. The large majority of your efforts should, and must, be devoted to marketing and promotions: Finding consumers who want your product, making them aware that it exists, and getting the product to them so they can buy it. Many labels don't place enough emphasis on—or work into—these critical aspects of the business, which is why most of them fail.

As the owner of a record label, everything you do, and every dollar you spend, should be directed toward selling records. It may not sound very creative or artistic, but it's the only way to survive and succeed. Every time you consider a marketing or promotional strategy, ask yourself, "How does this help my label to sell CDs?" If you can't think of an answer, you should try another strategy. Quite simply, marketing and promotions are the most important aspects of running a record label. Without them, you can't sell records, no matter how good they may be.

So, what are marketing and promotion? As indicated above, marketing entails identifying your market (the buying consumer) and getting your product (records) to that market. This is done in a variety of ways, which I discuss at length in the following chapters. Promotion is anything you do to notify your potential market about your product. I discuss promotional strategies in Part VI, Promotion. There are infinite options for marketing and promoting your records (and for spending money in the process). Don't be overwhelmed. With experience, you'll get a sense of how all the pieces fit together and which strategies work best for your label. But right now, there's no need to get fancy. You'll do fine by keeping things simple and focusing your efforts on what you need to do to sell records.

Things You Can Do Today To Build Your Label

1. Learn more about basic marketing strategies in *Guerrilla Marketing* by Jay Conrad Levinson, and about online marketing strategies in *Making and Marketing Music* by Jodi Summers, and *This Business of Music: Marketing and Promotion* by Tad Lathrop.

2. Learn more about promotional strategies by reading *Ruthless Self Promotion in the Music Industry* by Jeffrey Fisher; and *Inside the Minds: The Music Business*, writings compiled by the Aspatore Books staff, in which CEOs and presidents of major labels provide a behind-the-scenes glimpse into recording and promotions.

3. Create a reminder to hang on your wall or place on your desk that asks, "How does this effort help my label to sell a single CD?" Refer to it frequently.

WHAT IS MARKETING

The market is typically the place where people go to buy the things they need. Think of street vendors bringing their merchandise to the city—where most people (consumers) live—and selling their products under a tent in the town square. For centuries, this has been marketing in its purest, simplest form. As a manufacturer and merchant, you'll follow the same fundamental marketing process: Identify and locate the consumers who want to purchase your products (CDs, cassettes, etc.), and then figure out the best way to get your goods to them. Of course, you'll need a plan to make this happen. This section of the book will help you to create that plan.

The best way to begin a marketing plan is to write down your ideas—the good, the bad, and the absurd. Until you get your thoughts on paper, it will be difficult to put them into action. Write everything down. Nothing is crazy or too simple. That's the point of this activity. Ideas that seem unrealistic or impossible now may turn out to be great later. Begin by making three lists: (1) Who is the audience for my artist's CDs? (2) Where can I find them? and (3) How can I get my records to that audience? Your marketing plan will coordinate your efforts to answer these three questions. If you keep things simple, at least at first, you can succeed. Here's a very simple plan.

1. Who is the audience for my artist's CDs? High school and college students.
2. Where can I find that audience? At the artist's live performances.
3. How can I get my products to that audience? Bring CDs to the artist's shows and sell them there.

Yes, this is very simplistic, but it's the beginning of a marketing plan. Now, these ideas must be developed to include more detail and broader forms of marketing and distribution. The following chapters will get you started.

Things You Can Do Today To Build Your Label

1. Attend live shows by your artist or by another artist who performs the genre of music your label will produce. Make notes about the general age, gender, race, economic status, and any other traits you notice about the audience.

2. Drive or walk around town, do some Internet research, and consult the phone book and local newspapers to identify as many live music venues as possible for your artist. Take special note of places that attract patrons similar to those who attend your artist's shows.

3. Prepare a preliminary marketing plan listing every possible method for getting your artist's CDs to the market—including distribution to record stores—even if you don't have the means or organization to follow through on every strategy at this point.

IDENTIFYING AND FINDING YOUR MARKET

The first step in writing your marketing plan is to identify the artist's audience. The most logical place to begin looking is among his or her fans. One reason I encourage you to sign artists with performing experience is that they come with a built-in market. If the artist has been performing at local clubs, bars, or restaurants, you already know where fans (consumers) gather to see that artist perform and to purchase his or her merchandise.

Of course, you or someone from your label should be at the show selling CDs every time your artist performs (a great job for a non-paid intern). Even before the CD comes out, you can do some valuable marketing research simply by observing and talking to the "market" of fans at your artist's performances.

When you go to see your artist perform, write down what you observe. Talk to the artist, talk to the audience. Ask fans to fill out a brief survey with questions about where they go to hear music, which radio stations they listen to, how and where they typically purchase CDs, and what they do and/or don't like, about your artist and other local acts. Give people a free band decal or CD single for completing the survey. Put them on your mailing list, if you have one (and you should have one).

Above all, pay attention to the demographics of the audience (age, gender, ethnicity, race, occupation, income level, etc.), and include questions on your survey to gather this information from your artist's fans. In my opinion, demographics are the single most valuable marketing tool for any record label.

To illustrate my point, I'll introduce Robert Earl Keen and Pat Green, two successful artists in Texas who write and perform music that's been designated as Americana or alternative country. You'll notice most of the audience at their shows consists of 18- to 30-year-old college students and young professionals (both male and female). Most are Caucasian. This is not the traditional country music demographic (usually, older blue-collar workers).

If your label was trying to market Pat Green or Robert Earl Keen, you would want to get their records into places where white college students and/or young professionals hang out. Given your demographic information, you would probably focus on the areas around the local university campus and college record stores. You'd also target local bars, clubs, and restaurants that are willing to display and sell CDs to the patrons who frequent their establishments. (Each location would take a cut of your sales, of course.)

If your artist is not yet performing live, you can conduct a different kind of marketing survey. Go to the local mall, coffee shop, record store, restaurant, club, or anywhere your artist's potential audience might congregate. Ask people to listen to your artist's music on a portable CD player. Ask if they would buy a CD of the music you've played for them, and why they like or don't like it. (Make sure to get permission from the businesses to conduct your marketing near their stores.) It's okay if you use a demo recording for this activity.

Even if you're shy like me, you can introduce yourself, explain what you're doing, and ask people to complete a simple form (keep it very brief and easy) that asks for age, race, gender, household income, and musical preferences. Ask them to list interests, where they like to hang out, and where they usually buy their music. Keep a separate mailing list on hand for people who want to know more about your artist and/or label.

Your marketing research can be completed at a couple of the artist's shows, or during a day or two at the mall, or outside of a record store. However and wherever you do your surveys, the information you collect will help identify your target audience. At the very least, you should be able to get a good sense of your market's ages, genders, ethnicities, musical interests, and jobs. For additional information, you can consult music business textbooks, like *The Music Business Handbook* by David Baskerville, which often include charts and graphs of the latest demographics for various genres of music. Add all of this information to your first list (Who is the audience for my artist's CDs?).

You may even be pleasantly surprised by your market research. You may expect to find that everyone listens only to commercial radio and buys CDs from the mall's giant record store chain, and that you'd need a distributor to get your products into that store. (See Chapter 51, Finding a Distributor.) However, your research might indicate that most of your target audience listens to college radio and buys CDs at artists' shows or online. In that case, you can focus your resources and energy on sending promotional CDs to college DJs (who are much more likely to play your CD than commercial radio DJs are), promoting your artist's shows, and advertising your label's Website, where you'll sell the artist's CDs. Armed with good information, you can make knowledgeable, confident decisions about where to distribute and promote your products.

Of course, professional marketing firms will be happy to collect this information for you, and to deliver it along with full-color charts and tables. They'll apply science and statistics to produce a very thorough report. They'll also charge a lot of money that you probably don't have. As your label grows, your marketing plan and goals will become more sophisticated, and you may decide to hire a marketing company. But until and unless your label requires (and can afford) detailed market studies, you can gather the information you need on your own.

The fact is, most market research is done through the kind of sampling I describe above: Gather responses and information from a small cross-section of people to make generalizations about the larger buying public. Your results won't be perfect or scientific, but with a little legwork and a basic understanding of marketing principles, your efforts will help you to target the audience for your marketing/promotion campaign. (I discuss promotion in Part VI.)

But your work isn't done yet. Once you have a handle on who your audience is, you'll still need a clear sense of where to find them. Reviewing the information gathered during your marketing research, and applying your own experience and instincts, write down every place you can imagine where your audience might be exposed to music. If your market includes college students (very common for independent labels), your list might include the college campus, the artist's shows, local live-music venues, festivals with live music, coffee houses, local record stores, the Internet, college radio or other local radio stations, and campus or local entertainment newspapers.

This list serves two purposes. First, it indicates where you might try to distribute CDs for sale to your "market" of consumers. (I address distribution in the following chapters.) Second, it identifies promising locations where your label can advertise and promote its CDs. It may not be feasible to get CDs to every location, or to advertise everywhere you'd like (on radio or TV, for example). That's okay. The point is to find the most effective places to begin your efforts.

Once you have identified and located your audience, you'll need to determine how best to get your product to them (distribution) and to make them aware of your artists' CD (promotion). I discuss these concepts in the next chapters.

Things You Can Do Today To Build Your Label

1. Conduct your initial marketing research by observing and talking to the "market" of fans at your artist's performances. Write down what you observe.

2. Gather more detailed information about your potential audience by asking people to fill out a marketing survey at your artist's shows, or at a local record store, coffee shop, or mall. Keep your questionnaire brief and simple.

3. Using the information you've gathered, along with your experience and instincts, write down every place you can imagine where your audience might be exposed to music.

Types of Distribution

The previous chapters explain that the goal of marketing is to identify your market and get your product to the consumers who want it. Those chapters provide strategies for identifying and locating your market. This chapter will discuss some of the ways your label can distribute its products to that market.

Traditionally, record companies have used distributors to get their goods (CDs, cassettes, etc.) to buying consumers, usually at retail record stores. Most labels still rely on distributors to get their records to the market. However, new technologies, such as the Internet, MP3s, and file sharing, are revolutionizing the business of distribution, and many independent labels are using these technologies to their advantage. (You can learn more about the relationship between a label and its distributor in Chapter 50, What Does a Distributor Do?)

Because distributors make money only if the CDs they distribute are purchased, they only want to distribute product that they know a record store will sell to the consumer. Quality has nothing to do with it. No matter how great your label's products are, you'll probably find it difficult to attract a distributor until your label has demonstrated an ability to sell records. Don't be discouraged. This is a natural part of starting an independent label, and your marketing plan should include provisions for self-distribution. Once your label is more established, you'll be able to secure deals with independent distributors. At some point, you may even be able to get major-label distribution.

But let's return to the present. Starting without a distributor, you'll have to develop creative strategies for getting your artist's records to the customers on your own. These strategies will probably include alternative types of distribution that don't rely solely (or at all) on record stores. Given the state of flux and uncertainty in today's music industry, this works completely to your advantage. And by creating self-distribution options and devising a strong promotional plan tailored to those options, you'll show potential distributors that you know what you're doing and that, with their assistance, you're ready to expand into a larger market. After you've sold a few records, they'll be ready to jump on board.

Most labels start self-distributing CDs and/or cassettes at their artists' live performances. This is a logical and effective place to begin. (You should encourage your artists to announce during their shows that they have CDs for sale.) It also reinforces the importance, or at least benefit, of signing artists who have live performance experience and the ability to play in local clubs and bars. A 13-year-old pop singer with lots of talent might make money for your label some day. Just remember, this artist's youth may prevent him or her from being able to perform regularly, and from being booked at certain clubs. Until your label has regular distribution (to get your label's product into record stores), live performances may be your best chance to sell product. Any limitations on those performances can impede your label's sales.

That's why I recommend waiting to sign very young and/or underdeveloped artists until after you have a distribution deal. With distribution, you'll have more options, and live performances won't be the only places to sell CDs. Even so, live-music venues will continue to be important points of sale for your products.

Another self-distribution method is to sell or consign your CDs to local independent record stores that are not associated with a regional or national chain (often referred to as "mom and pop" stores). This is a simple process. You approach the storeowner, introduce yourself, and ask him or her to check out the CD. If the store accepts your CD(s) on consignment, you'll provide several copies for display. The store will pay you an agreed-upon price after the records sell. If they need more, they'll ask. If your CDs don't sell within a certain amount of time, the store may return the copies to you to make room for other product.

While you're setting up self-distribution with local stores, ask for references on reputable local distributors. Conversely, if you sign a distribution deal later, you can tell your distributor about the independent record stores with which you have established relationships. Simply having these relationships might help you to attract a distributor.

Other methods of self-distribution are mail order and computer downloads through the Internet. Most distributors leave these efforts up to you anyway. Traditional mail order involved advertising in music magazines and providing a phone number (usually toll-free) or an address where customers could send payment and request the CD to be shipped. With the advent of the Internet, mail order has grown into a huge, but different, business. Websites such as *Amazon.com, Borders.com,* and *CDBaby.com* allow independent labels to set up accounts and sell product online. The sites handle all payment transactions, shipping, and handling in return for a percentage of the labels' online sales. Many small labels sell CDs directly through their own Websites, as well. And some distributors have Websites for Internet sales, or have accounts with some of the online stores. As technology and Internet distribution change, so will options for distribution. If you start now by embracing self-distribution, you'll be prepared for future developments.

Once your label has demonstrated its ability to market and sell records on its own, you should be able to establish a relationship with an independent distributor to help get your CDs into retail stores, including chains. "Independent" used to mean any distributor not owned by a major label, but now there are various levels of independent distributors, some with major-label affiliations. Therefore, even with independent distribution, you will progress from smaller, local distributors to larger distributors that have relationships with regional record stores and national chains.

After gaining widespread coverage and notoriety in your local market, your label will be in a position to move to a larger independent distributor. By this point, you will have built a strong business plan around local and regional distribution. Even if that plan is working well, you should move to national independent distribution only if you have the resources to advertise and promote on a national level. This is a big step, but not out of reach for a successful independent label.

To attract national distributors, you'll apply the same principles that helped you to reach this point. Incorporating lessons you've learned along the way, you'll develop a solid marketing and promotion plan similar to the one that allowed you to secure your first local distribution deal. But now, you have to explain how you're going to sell records all over the country.

When you consistently sell between 50,000 and 100,000 units per release, your label is on the path to obtaining interest from major-label distributors, which offer a network that reaches major markets all over the world. Major-label distribution is usually available to independent labels only if they are directly affiliated with the major label or one of the major label's distributors. Sometimes, major labels will approach independents that have shown strong national sales. They'll seek to work with the smaller labels on future projects and, thereby, benefit from their creativity and the niche they have created.

Finally, I want to mention the "Pressing and Distribution" arrangements offered by some distributors. In these arrangements, the distributor pays the up-front cost of manufacturing and packaging the CDs or cassettes. Some Pressing and Distribution arrangements may even pay advances to the label, to spend on promotion.

However, as part of these agreements, the distributors will usually pay the label less for each CD sold, or not at all, until all expenses for advances and/or manufacturing are recouped. Before entering into such an agreement, you also need to understand that manufacturing is not recoupable from your artist's royalties. Therefore, all the money you pay for manufacturing will come out of your label's pocket. And even if you're not getting paid by your distributor yet (you may be paying off the distributor's advances or manufacturing costs), you still have to pay your artist for each of his or her records that sell. If you spend your entire distributor advance before the distributor recoups expenses and begins paying you for sales, you'll have limited or no cash flow to cover operating expenses and artist royalties. As you might imagine, this can be disastrous.

Don't get me wrong. I believe Pressing and Distribution arrangements can be a good deal for small labels with a limited budget. But you have to be extremely careful, ask a lot of questions, and, as always, have an entertainment attorney work closely with you on the contract. It's critical to know exactly what you're getting into, what to expect from the deal, and how the arrangement will affect the daily operations of your label.

Things You Can Do Today To Build Your Label

1. Learn more about distribution by reading *Music Distribution: Selling Music in the New Entertainment Marketplace* by C. Michael Brae.

2. Prepare strategies for distribution that include your artist's live performances and consignment agreements with local record stores. Ask local labels or artists if they know of record stores that accept CDs on consignment. Visit the stores to speak with the owners about accepting your product.

3. Make a list of online retailers that accept product from independent labels and contact them to learn how to get your CDs sold through their sites.

WHAT DOES A DISTRIBUTOR DO?

T he most common way to get your label's product into record stores is to align with a distributor, a business set up to get CDs to retail outlets when there is a demand. In conjunction with your label's efforts to notify consumers—through advertising, promotion, and publicity—that the artist's CD exists and where it can be purchased, your distributor will seek to make sure the CD is delivered and available when and where people show up to buy it.

How does this work? The distributor will buy CDs from your record label and notify stores that the particular CD is available for sale. Upon request from retail outlets, the distributor will sell and deliver the CDs to the stores, with an average price markup of $2.00 to $6.00 per CD. (The retail outlets will then sell the CDs with an additional markup.) Distributors that are associated with major labels will distribute product created only by labels aligned with that major label. Other distributors, like Caroline, Select-O-Hits, or The Beggars Group, have no formal association with a major label and distribute only independent labels. Major-label distributors, and some independents, are able to distribute records nationally, while smaller distributors focus on a region of the country or just one state.

(Note: When I refer to "retail stores" or "outlets," I am including online stores. Traditionally, distributors only sold to retail record shops. However, with today's technologies, new electronic markets are developing rapidly,

led by online stores like Amazon.com, CDBaby.com, *etc. Even most retail stores, such as Borders or Tower Records, now have their own online stores.)*

A distributor will know the market and will have relationships with various retail chains, independent stores, wholesalers, online sites, and other distributors. The distributor's first objective will be to get your product into record stores, which, in turn, will rely upon the distributor for information about your label, the artists on your label, and your efforts to promote the artists' releases.

Some distributors may notify stores about your product directly. They have salespeople who work with the various record stores (independents, Tower Records, Sam Goody, etc.) and larger retail chains (e.g., Best Buy, Borders Books and Music, and Wal-Mart), attempting to convince these stores to buy your records.

Distributors may also notify retail stores about your record with a "one-sheet," literally one page of information about the CD you want the stores to buy. A one-sheet will include an image of the CD cover, information about the artist, media reviews of the CD and/or the artist, a description of the music, your record label's bar code, the distributor's name, and a telephone number to call to order the CD. Some distributors may require you to create your own one-sheet and to provide the information in a suggested layout. Others will request the information and create the one-sheet themselves. Regardless of who creates the one-sheet, there is no single format that everyone follows. A bit of creativity can be beneficial, as long as the necessary information is presented clearly, and in a way that will help to convince retail stores to buy your record.

Most distributors also publish a catalogue each year that provides information about your label's records (and all records that they distribute). Distributors make their catalogues available on their Websites, and mail them to targeted retail record stores and other outlets that may not have been contacted during your initial promotional efforts.

As your liaison with the record store, a distributor can suggest ways to increase a store's interest in purchasing your records. One way to do this is to participate in "payment for placement" programs, whereby you put up promotional posters, organize in-store performances by your label's artists, and/or get your CDs placed in listening stations or on special display shelves—called "end caps"—at the ends of each aisle. For this placement, you will have to compensate the record store (hence the name, "payment for placement"). Your distributor may work directly with the record store to arrange these things, or may simply provide contact information and leave the rest to you.

A distributor may also assist in promoting your label's CDs by creating and paying for advertising. One cost-effective way to advertise is through a "multi-ad," which promotes two or more artists' or labels' CDs. You see multi-ads most often in print advertising, featuring CDs from several artists and including information about the specific store(s) where the CDs can be purchased. If you are promoting a new hip-hop artist, for instance, a record store might contact you and other local hip-hop labels with the same distributor and ask if you want to combine your resources. By spreading the ad's cost among labels, the record store, and the distributor, labels may be able to purchase larger ads. (It's in the distributor's best interest to help pay for advertising, because the distributor will profit from the sales of your CDs.)

Finally, a distributor will bill and collect payment from record stores for the number of records they purchase. Depending on the relationship, retail stores will have thirty to ninety days to pay for the records. The distributor will take its cut before paying the label. Therefore, it's critical to find a distributor that has a good reputation for collecting from record stores *and* for paying labels in a timely manner. Quick payment from the distributor will help your label to maintain a sufficient cash flow to pay bills and continue to do business (i.e., signing and recording musical artists, manufacturing and promoting CDs). I discuss finding a distributor in the following chapter.

You will find that each distributor is different. Some provide more and better service than others. Like record labels, there are different levels of distributors, from independent operators that work in one part of a state, to major distributors that serve the entire nation and other countries. As your label becomes more successful, you can approach larger, more "full-service" distributors. But at first, all you can really expect is for a distributor to notify record store product buyers that your product is available for sale, deliver your records quickly to any retail outlet that requests it, collect money from stores, and pay your label as agreed.

No matter how large or small your label is, a distributor can help you sell (and get paid for) your artist's records. If the distributor is doing its job, you will have more time to promote, advertise, and publicize your artist's CDs, which will increase sales and, therefore, raise retail stores' incentive to buy more of your label's records. In turn, this means the distributor will get paid more and be even more motivated to sell additional CDs for your label.

To create this cycle of success, the distributor, retail store, and record label must work together, and you need to play your part. Invest the time to establish good relationships with retail stores and your distributor's sales representatives. Simple courtesy and small gestures of gratitude on your part (a hand-written thank-you note, free CDs for the staff, and a fruit basket during the holidays) can go a long way. When combined with hard work to promote your artist and participation in placement programs and multi-ads, these efforts can pay big dividends and strengthen your relationships with the distributor and retail stores.

Things You Can Do Today To Build Your Label

1. Talk with other label and record store representatives to get recommendations for reputable distributors in your region.

2. Contact these regional distributors to learn what they pay independent labels for the sale of the labels' records, and which services they do and do not provide. Ask them what you can do now to position yourself for their distribution in the future.

3. Create your own plan to market and sell records without the use of a distributor. You can find a sample business plan to help you with this task at *MusicBusinessMadeSimple.com*.

FINDING A DISTRIBUTOR

Most start-up record companies would love to have their CDs distributed by major labels. But as you learn more about the music business, you'll realize that, attractive as it may seem, this is not the best situation for independent labels. Nor is it the norm. In this chapter, I discuss some points to consider during your search for a distributor, and I identify resources to help you find and select the distributor best suited to your label (i.e., the one most able to help your record company make money).

In the previous chapter, I describe the various ways a distributor can help your record label to sell its product. I also explain that you must be willing to work with the distributor and retail stores to maximize sales, so you need to be realistic about how much your label can contribute to these relationships. For example, larger distributors that work with national chains will expect your label to commit to paying for multi-ads and in-store promotions, such as end-cap and listening station placement. Locally owned record stores that see you are working hard and selling some product may eventually give you a discount on their in-store promotions, but it will take time before that happens.

Consequently, I recommend that you start with a smaller, local distributor that can help you build naturally, establish yourself, develop in-store promotional efforts, and cultivate the relationships you'll need to grow. As your label becomes more successful and you demonstrate an ability to promote and sell your records in more and bigger markets, you can seek larger distributors to expand the reach of your label's product.

But I'm getting ahead of myself. At this point, you're just getting started, and with so many independent record companies and self-released records produced every year, it may be difficult at first to get your product into the marketplace. You can do some of this on your own. But to attract a distributor—any distributor—you must have a solid, detailed marketing plan in place to convince them that your product is going to sell. After all, this is how the distributor gets paid.

It doesn't matter how brilliant your artist and/or record is. If you don't have a thoughtful, detailed plan for advertising, promoting, and publicizing your product, distributors won't care what you're selling. Labels constantly contact distributors, promising the next smash hit. But in this part of the business, the only hype that matters is how you plan to promote, or notify the public about, this "smash hit" of yours. (See Part VI for information about promotion.) If you can't clearly demonstrate how you're going to do this, chances are, you aren't going to sell many CDs. You also aren't going to get a distribution deal.

Do not go to a distributor with just a CD in hand and expect any attention. It's a waste of your time and theirs. In fact, you should not approach distributors until and unless you have a solid business plan and are prepared to provide, at least on a minimum level, the promotional contributions I discuss above. You'll also need a promotional package for each artist on your label. I discuss the "promo pack" in Chapter 54, Creating and Using the Promotional Package.

Even if you have only one artist, a distributor might agree to work with your label if you're well prepared and make a convincing case that your records are going to sell. And if the distributor doesn't accept your single artist now, you will still have made a good impression by being organized and professional. If you're able to sell some records on your own and add a few artists to the label, you may get a distribution deal when you return to the distributor later.

One good way to find a local or regional distributor is to network within your music community. Talk to local record stores and other independent labels. Ask about the reputation and abilities of distributors in your area, and about their experiences with these distributors. Most important, ask if these distributors can get your records into the markets and stores they promise, and if they will pay you on time for the records that stores buy.

There are several helpful books and directories that list distributors, such as the *Recording Industry Sourcebook, The Indie Bible,* and

Musician's Atlas. The Internet is also a good place to begin your search for these types of resources.

When talking to distributors, ask for their thoughts about your label's goals and business plan. Listen when they describe what they need from you to help sell your label's records, and plan on providing what they need.

However, this is not a one-sided relationship. You may own a small label, and you won't have the luxury of choosing any distributor you want; but that doesn't mean you should accept a bad deal or sign with the first distributor that shows interest. The distributor must be a good fit for your label, meaning they can help you sell records. Be sure the distributor is familiar with the type of music your label produces and that it distributes to stores that sell a lot of CDs in your label's genre. Just as you need a solid plan to attract a distributor, you have every right to expect the distributor to have a plan and resources for getting your label's CDs into the marketplace.

Things You Can Do Today To Build Your Label

1. Prepare a marketing plan—for presentation to distributors—that demonstrates how you're selling records even without a distributor, and how you intend to promote and market your records once they are being distributed.

2. Compile a list of distributors in your city or region, focusing on those that distribute your label's genre of music.

3. Ask around your local music community for names of reputable distributors. Contact local and regional record labels to find out whom they use for distribution. Also ask small record-store owners which distributors they buy records from, and which ones they think might be good for your label.

RETAIL SALES

etail sales involves much more than just getting your label's CDs to the stores. You also have to manage the product once it gets there. Large record companies will have a "retail" or "sales" department to handle this responsibility. With your label's small staff, you won't have that luxury. Most likely, you will personally oversee all sales efforts by the stores that carry your label's product. Regardless of the label's size, there are three basic elements to retail sales: (1) obtain advantageous placement of your CDs/cassettes at strategic locations within the store; (2) promote your products at the store to encourage customers there (otherwise known as a "captive audience") to buy them; and (3) make sure your CDs/cassettes remain stocked.

Placement within retail stores is critical for any product. Whether you're selling soda pop or records, retail stores offer opportunities to place your product in high-visibility locations that are more likely to attract the buyer's attention. Of course, you want your CDs on the shelves with other CDs in your genre, but the average consumer is overwhelmed by the sheer number of CDs in the store. Most people are in a hurry, and they're not going to take the time to look through everything. Unless they've come specifically for your CD, they may never see it on the shelf among the thousands of others.

This is where your sales efforts are important. You have to figure out how to make your product stand out to the browsing customer who may not intend to buy it, or even know it exists. How many times have you walked out of a record store with more CDs than you planned to buy because something unexpectedly caught your eye? Your products need to attract consumers the same way. How do you do this? Maybe you can have your CDs placed on a special display shelf (usually at eye level) just above the CD bins. Some labels also add striking artwork behind their CD on that shelf to make the display even more appealing. There also are end caps (shelving at the ends of aisles), special shelves for new arrivals, a section for best sellers, etc. Your goal is to attract your artists' CDs placed in as many of these prime locations as possible.

The second key to retail sales is in-store promotion. There are several excellent strategies available to your label. First, you can try to get your CDs added to the store's listening stations (special areas that allow customers to listen to CDs, usually new releases, preselected by the store). If you've used listening stations in record stores as a consumer, you know they encourage sales by taking the risk out of buying a CD. The store may also be willing play your records over the in-house stereo system. Some record companies make giant cardboard cut-outs of the artist, or posters featuring the CD. All of these promotional efforts can help to get the consumer's attention and lead to additional sales.

Of course, you're not the only label trying to persuade record-store managers to place your CDs and promotional materials strategically around their stores. Sales representatives from other labels are making the same requests. So how do you do it? I doubt you'll be surprised to hear that some, if not all, of these placement and promotional opportunities will cost you money. The exact price and placement may be negotiable, which is another reason why it's important to establish and maintain good relationships with retail stores through self-distribution. As in any business negotiation, if the manager likes you, he or she may give you a better deal.

Smaller independent stores may welcome your efforts to help sell records and not charge you for special CD and promotional placement. In return, you can agree to direct traffic to their stores through advertisement. I discuss this kind of "multi-advertisement" in Chapter 50, What Does A Distributor Do? Your creativity in these negotiations will help you compete with larger labels that can afford simply to pay stores for all these promotional opportunities.

Finally, you have to make sure the record-store shelves are well stocked with your CDs. If you're using a distributor (as opposed to consigning product—see Chapter 49, Types of Distribution), the store is required to pay for the product up front. Therefore, if the store's buyer does not expect to sell many of your records, he or she may be reluctant to purchase many CDs from your label. In these cases, your sales call and marketing plan are critical. You must convince the buyer that you have a plan in place and are doing your part to ensure that the CDs will sell.

If you're providing CDs to the store on consignment, the buyer may be more receptive, because the store will not have any up front costs. Since the store can return any unsold consignment CDs to you without cost, you may be able to persuade the store's buyer to take a few more CDs than he or she usually would.

Before visiting a record store, set up a meeting with the store's buyer or manager while you're there. The purpose of this meeting will be to convince the person in charge that the efforts of your label and the artist warrant keeping the artist's records in stock. And how do you do that? By presenting a solid promotion and marketing plan, and by attempting to demonstrate that you will be or have been successful in implementing this plan.

The store does not care how good the record sounds or how talented your artist is. Sure, the manager/buyer will probably like you or your artist more if the product is good. But all the store's buyer really cares about is whether or not people are buying your records. Some distributors have a sales force that can help you to build relationships with local retailers, and to ensure high-visibility placement of your product in stores. After all, they make money when your records sell. But most distributors that will be available to your label do not have sufficient resources to promote your label within stores. Ultimately, the tasks described in this chapter are your responsibility, not the distributor's. If you show a willingness to take them on, and include them in your marketing plan, you'll have an easier time convincing potential distributors and retail stores that your label has a serious strategy and works hard to sell its records.

Things You Can Do To Build Your Label

1. Contact local retail stores and/or your distributor to learn how to get better product placement and promote your CDs within stores. Ask if there are ways to obtain in-store promotion other than by paying for it directly.

2. Begin building relationships with record stores, even if you don't have distribution and they don't take local records on consignment. Send a few copies of your records for their personal use. Ask what you could be doing to persuade them to take your records.

3. Prepare a section in your marketing plan that includes working with retail stores, even if you don't have a full sales staff. Accept that at first, you will probably be your label's sales staff.

PART
SIX

PROMOTION

WHAT IS PROMOTION?

The previous section explained marketing as the process by which you identify and locate potential customers and then get your product to them. But this is only half of the equation. The other half consists of promotion, or everything you do to inform potential customers about your product (and entice them to buy it). This section of the book will describe proven, cost-effective ways for your independent label to promote its product(s) without breaking the budget.

Promotion is divided into two categories: Publicity and advertising. The difference is that publicity is free, while advertising is not. For an independent label with a limited promotional budget, free is good. So although you'll certainly do some paid advertising, you'll also want to devise ways to obtain as much publicity as possible. This will teach you to be creative and de-emphasize a plan devoted strictly to money.

I stated previously that 10% of your label's effort and energy should be used to produce a CD, with the remaining 90% devoted to promotion and marketing. Now, I don't advocate spending 10% of your budget on recording and manufacturing, and 90% on marketing and promotion. That is not a reasonable split. But the fact is, many new labels focus too much on producing the CD and not enough on informing consumers and encouraging them to purchase it. As a result, many great CDs never get heard—or bought—and many dedicated labels go out of business before they ever get started. I don't want you to make the same mistake. That's why I emphasize from the beginning that you'll need to commit a considerable portion of your money, resources, and energy to promotion.

How much should you spend? Unfortunately, I can't say. There are just too many variables involved (e.g., whom you know, what kinds of deals you're able to make, the size of your budget). Plus, every market is different. Studio and promotion costs, the number and type of media outlets, and the size of the potential audience vary widely from one city to another.

One thing I can say for sure is this: Your plans to promote an artist's CD should be your main focus at all times, even before you begin to record. It might be the greatest record ever, but no one will buy it if they don't know it exists. You must have a solid promotional plan in place from the beginning, and you'll have to spend a lot of time and energy notifying the public that you have a new product for sale, and telling them where they can find it. The following chapters explain different types of advertising and publicity, and offer suggestions on how to combine these two elements to get the most bang from your promotional buck.

Things You Can Do Today To Build Your Label

1. Begin developing your promotional plan now, before you begin recording your artist's CD, and perhaps even before you sign the artist.

2. Accept that the music business is 10% recording and 90% promotion and marketing. Devise a business model that reflects this reality.

3. Study the promotional efforts of your competitors.

CREATING AND USING THE PROMOTIONAL PACKAGE

O ne tool you'll need is a promotional package, or "promo pack." Artists use a promo pack to gain the attention of music-business professionals like record labels, managers, and booking agents. You can help your label and your artist(s) by creating a high-quality promo pack to send to radio programmers, music publications, and distributors. Usually, the promo pack will feature a single artist—perhaps someone with a new record—who will appeal to your intended audience. In a sense, it's an advertisement for your label, using your artist and his or her music as a selling point. As you sign more artists, you can create promo packs for each one.

Your promotional package for each artist will include the full-length CD, a photograph, and a brief biography (or "bio"), along with favorable newspaper or magazine reviews of the artist's recording and/or performance(s). Some promo packs may also include a music video or a video of a live performance. However, I recommend not including a video unless it's of professional quality. (Many recipients won't have the time to watch a video anyway.)

Don't be overwhelmed by the thought of putting all this together. You'll just need to develop a system to compile the items, organize them artistically but simply, and replace old materials (reviews, photos, CDs) with newer,

better ones as the artist develops.

Hire a professional photographer to shoot several rolls of film (or a memory card's worth of images) of the artist in several locations and select the images that best represent the look you want. Use a photographer who can provide a computer disc of the photos you choose. This will allow you to e-mail photos to publications whenever they're requested. Black and white photos work best because they are easier for newspapers and other publications to print. They also tend to be more flattering to the subject.

Most often, the photos will accompany a story about the artist, an interview, or an ad for the artist's show in a newspaper or magazine. (It's important to have your own photos on hand, as a newspaper or magazine often will not provide a photographer.) You may also send the photos out to various media and to live-music venues to obtain publicity and/or gigs for the artist. The more original your photos are, the more likely they are to be used by the recipients.

Some commercial companies will create a professional promotional photo of your artist. These photos will come with a white border, which allows you to print the artist's name and your label's contact information directly on the photo. (The photos should be 8" x 10"; anything larger will not fit in a standard envelope.) These companies will duplicate the photos in large quantities relatively cheaply. Research several companies before deciding on one.

Reviews of your artist's shows and recordings will come over time. Starting today, collect copies of all comments about your artist's work from anyone other than a fan. You can use reviews from print or electronic media, or even spoken comments from a radio disc jockey. These clippings and comments give the promo-pack recipient some objective professional opinions of your artist's recording or performance style and abilities. It's acceptable to use a compilation of comments until your artist gets a full review in a local newspaper, or even better, a nationally distributed publication. If the artist has had some success before signing with your label, he or she may have some favorable clippings already.

A bio is a short personal history of the artist. A band's bio will include some information about each member (instrument played, important musical achievements, musical influences, etc.) and the story behind the group as a whole (notable performances, quotes by—or relationships with—national recording artists, etc.). If your artist doesn't have a lot of experience, there may not be much to write in his or her bio. No problem. Just be creative. The objective is to interest the people who read the bio and make them want to know more about the artist. Keep this in mind as you write. A well-written bio might prompt an article or an interview in the local newspaper, or a gig at a new live-music venue.

The overall quality of your promo pack will depend on factors like the artist's current level of talent, the studio and producer you use for the recording, and your photographer. Major labels spend a lot of money for polished promo packs with slick printing, fancy materials, and a music video. You may not have a major label's budget, but you can still build a solid, attention-grabbing promo pack with creativity and ingenuity. An excellent source for more information about, and examples of, promo packs and bios is *The Billboard Guide to Publicity* by Jim Pettigrew.

After you've collected all the materials for the promo pack, draft a brief cover letter. The letter should be addressed to the specific person to whom you're sending the package (not "To Whom It May Concern") and should be professional. Print it out on quality paper, preferably your label's letterhead. It should consist of only a few sentences. This is not the time to tell the reader about the accomplishments of your artist or label. The person reading your letter will be very busy and will appreciate your consideration in getting to the point. The letter's purpose is to get your package to the appropriate person, to identify yourself and the package contents, and to explain what you want (consideration for a record review, radio airplay, an opening slot for your artist on a national show, etc.). That's it. Close by thanking the reader for his or her time.

Given the technology available these days, many record companies are creating online promotional packages. This can be a very efficient way to reach a wide audience, while saving you the time and effort of sending out a hard copy promo pack. If a newspaper wants to write a story about your artist, for example, the columnist can simply go to your Website and download the artist's photograph, bio, and music.

But keep in mind, as you're trying to get established, it can be helpful to send out a traditional package to the people you most want to reach. Even in the digital age, the personal touch is still a nice courtesy that can help get your label and artist(s) noticed. When you send out a hard copy promo pack, you can mention in your cover letter that your label's Website provides additional artist photos and information, and maybe even downloads of selected songs.

As your artist builds his or her career, the promotional package will evolve with him or her. Over time, you'll replace older materials with new recordings, photographs, and reviews in more established publications. Think of it as adding new accomplishments to your artist's résumé. You want to demonstrate his or her growing abilities, notoriety, and experience in order to gain more exposure and, hopefully, sell more records. Never forget, this is your primary goal.

When you send the promo pack, don't ask for or expect anything more than consideration in return. If you sent it to a critic and continually harass him or her to review the CD, he or she may get tired of hearing from you and write a review just to get rid of you. The trouble is, the review will be negative, if not downright embarrassing. You won't be including *this* review in your promo pack. And you may never get another chance for a good interview from this person. The same goes with radio DJs. If they like the artist, they'll play the music; if they don't, it won't help to push them.

Instead of this non-productive (and potentially detrimental) approach, submit your promo pack with the idea that you're simply trying to make industry professionals aware of your artist and your label. Maybe they'll review it or play it. Maybe they won't. Even if they don't, they'll know who you are, and they will appreciate your professional courtesy. This often can pay off later. As your artist's career advances and your recordings improve (as demonstrated by the updated versions of the promo pack you send), you'll have a better chance of getting attention from these people.

The bottom line is, you have to be patient. There are no shortcuts. The first promo pack won't magically make your artist appealing to national radio stations and major distributors. But as your artist's and label's achievements add up over time, the promo pack will change to highlight these developments, and it will open new doors that may be closed to you right now.

Things You Can Do Today To Build Your Label

1. Create an interesting biographical sketch for your artist and begin to collect newspaper stories, quotes, and/or reviews to include in the artist's promotional package.

2. Have a set of professional photographs taken of your artist.

3. Compile a list of potential recipients for your artist's promo pack, such as distributors, radio-station DJs, and newspaper/magazine columnists. Prepare form cover letters to each of these potential recipients, so you will be ready when the time comes.

4. Get feedback from a friend or colleague on how to improve the

promo pack and cover letter.

PUBLICITY

P ublicity is free promotion. And for a small record label like yours, free is very good. Sometimes, you will use publicity to notify the public about a specific event, such as an artist's live performance, or about the release of an artist's newest CD. Usually, publicity will come through various local, regional, or national media, such as newspapers, entertainment magazines, radio, or television.

Most independent labels cannot afford to hire publicists or publicity firms to get stories about their artists (or about the labels themselves) into the media. Instead, they usually handle publicity themselves. This is fine, and probably necessary, at least during start-up. Just understand that publicity is much more than simply mailing promotional packages and sending faxes or e-mails. It can be a powerful, invaluable resource for your label, and it's so important that I recommend having at least one person focus solely on coordinating your label's publicity and other promotion. You and this individual (probably an intern) should conduct a full range of publicity efforts for each new record your label releases. You should also be constantly on the lookout for new opportunities to obtain publicity and incorporate it into your promotions. In the following chapters, I provide tips for approaching the "gatekeepers" of various publicity outlets and for creating an overall publicity strategy.

But before I get into details, here's a tip that applies to every situation: Be nice to everyone in media who can help your publicity campaign, from the receptionist and unpaid intern to the local radio DJ and music critic. Publicity may be free, but it's not guaranteed (unless you pay for it, in which case it's called advertising). That's why the old saying, "You catch more flies with honey than with vinegar," should be your motto. There will be times when people don't follow through on their promises to play your artist's CD on a radio show, or to write a feature about your label. This is justifiably frustrating, but remember, you need these people. Keep the big picture in mind and remain professional. Rather than slugging these people, or yelling at them (which will probably get you black-listed forever and earn negative publicity that harms your label and artist), follow the advice of another old cliché and kill them with kindness.

It takes time, work, and possibly some swallowing of your pride, to build relationships with the local media, club owners, record-store managers, etc. They have to get to know you before they're going to care about your label or do you any favors. But your patience and effort will help in the long run. If you can establish good relationships with these people, there's an excellent chance your label's releases and artists will be mentioned in print, and be publicized on the radio and at local venues. This kind of positive exposure can make a big difference in your label's success.

There's a sort of courtship that goes into winning these people over and getting them to publicize your label and artists. Send e-mails and/or faxes to update them on label news. Invite them to your artist's shows and various label events. Put them on your holiday card list. And, as in any other courtship, don't forget to send them gifts.

When it comes to gift giving, make liberal use of what the music industry calls SWAG (Stuff We Always Get). SWAG is an appropriate and effective tool for building relationships. Obviously, a copy of your artist's CD is always a good idea. Other SWAG can include T-shirts, pens, notepads, lighters, key chains, key-chain flashlights, refrigerator magnets, coffee mugs, etc. These items aren't free, of course, but they're a cost of doing business that should be included in your promotional budget. Many merchandise companies can produce this stuff inexpensively, based on the number of each item you order.

I happen to know that media get tired of receiving the same gifts over and over (after all, they're human too), so the more creative and useful your SWAG is, the more likely that it will be noticed and kept. I've gotten some excellent SWAG at music conferences, including earplugs, a CD package opener, a cool mouse pad, label compilation CDs, and interactive CDs. Sometimes, the best SWAG is edible (such as cookies, chocolate, or a small holiday fruit basket that has your label's or artist's name on the package).

Whatever you send, make sure it publicizes your label or artist and is fun and interesting. Then it—and you—will be remembered, and that's your goal.

> **Things You Can Do Today To Build Your Label**
>
> 1. Read more about promoting an artist and his or her records in *The Billboard Guide to Publicity* by Jim Pettigrew.
>
> 2. Understand the need to build strong, long-lasting relationships with people who can help your label obtain publicity. With each new employee you hire, stress the importance of being nice at all times.
>
> 3. Research various types of (affordable) SWAG that you can send out to publicize your label, artists, and/or new releases.

PRINT MEDIA

56

I'm sure you've seen plenty of paid advertisements in various papers and magazines, but have you ever thought about all the free promotional opportunities available through those print media? When you're seeking ways to publicize your label and artists, remember that newspapers and entertainment magazines rely heavily upon CD reviews, live-performance schedules, and concert reviews to provide content for their publications. Their needs create a prime opportunity for you to help them, while helping your label and artists, as well.

A good review of your artist's CD or performance is some of the best publicity you can get. A printed interview with your artist is just as good, if not better. Whatever form it takes, publicity is most effective when it's repetitive. People need to see something a few times before they begin to pay attention, and they need to continue seeing it to remember. So you should do everything possible to keep your artists and label in the public eye. Print media offers a great way to do this. You won't always have big news, but even small items like calendar listings and show announcements in local entertainment publications can help. If you can obtain regular publicity, it won't take long for people to learn your artists' (and label's) names.

To begin, review copies of all relevant local, regional, and national print media you can find. Your search should include entertainment and music magazines and newspapers, and local newspapers and newsletters, including online publications. The number of national magazines interested in receiving your artist's first CD will be limited, but some smaller genre-specific magazines might accept your product and give you a review.

Your review will indicate pretty quickly if these sources can be helpful in your quest for publicity. Do they have CD and/or performance reviews for artists on small labels? Do they provide entertainment/event calendars? If not, there may not be much point in contacting them.

However, it never hurts to send a promotional package to a magazine or newspaper music critic/journalist, just to familiarize him or her with your label and artists. Include a short note to introduce yourself. Offer to send additional information and/or copies of the CD(s), and leave it at that. They may never respond, and you should not expect them to. But this short, professional presentation is good public relations. You never know who might like your artist, or who will remember you later, when they're in a position to help.

Once you've identified the most promising publications, contact them and ask to whom you should send news regarding your label/artist. Also, ask how best to reach the contact person (mail, e-mail, telephone, or fax). Your communications with this person should be brief and to-the-point. Busy people will usually be a lot more responsive if you show a respect for their time. So after introducing yourself, stay focused on these questions: What format do they prefer (CD, email, hard copy, etc.)? How do they want information delivered (FedEx, U.S. Mail, e-mail, fax, etc.)? When are their deadlines? Once you have the answers, thank them for their help, tell them to expect your package soon, and let them get on with their work. As in all aspects of the music industry (and most businesses), your professional approach will make a favorable impression.

When you're working with music critics and reporters, send full press kits or promotional packages. (I explain how to assemble and use promotional packages in the previous chapter.) Keep in mind that music critics usually choose to review CDs that will appeal to their readers' tastes and interests. A critic may like your artist's record, but if the audience isn't interested in your artist's style of music, he or she usually will not write a review. Consequently, it's very important to be familiar with the publications to which you send your promotional materials. Otherwise, you may be wasting your time and effort (not to mention CDs).

You'll have the best chance of getting a review—a favorable one, at least—if you send promotional packages to critics who review artists similar to yours. Oh, and make sure you send your package well before the submission deadline. Finally, never, *ever* give a music critic a hard time or insist on a review. I have witnessed this, and the critic often gets so fed up that he or she writes a scathing review. Obviously, this is not the kind of publicity you want.

Over time, you will build a valuable list of print (and other) media contacts, along with the necessary contact information for each. With this raw information, you can go to work. On a regular basis (depending on the frequency of publication), send everyone on your list a press release to update them about your label and artists. Make your press releases informative, but concise.

When you have a specific event planned (e.g., a CD release party, in-store appearance, or label party), be sure to send an invitation to each of your contacts. When your artist books an important gig, ask your print media contacts if you can put them on the guest list. Always leave an open invitation for them to call you any time they want to attend a performance. (To avoid problems, inform the club in advance that you'll have a guest list.) This gesture costs nothing, but promotes good will and can help you make friends in the media. Of course, if the event or performance is related to a new CD from your artist, be sure to include a copy or two of the CD with your press release/invitation.

One of your primary jobs as a label owner is to inform the media about what your artist is doing and explain why the reading/viewing audience should be interested. To do this, you must provide information your media contacts can use, such as well-written press releases or your artist's performance schedule. Cool SWAG, as described in the previous chapter, never hurts either. It will take some time and relationship-building, but eventually, you should be able to show the music critic or reporter that your artist is popular among his or her readers. If you can do this, you'll have an advocate in the media, which just happens to be a key to getting good publicity.

Things You Can Do Today To Build Your Label

1. Make a list of local, regional, and national magazines and newspapers (including online publications) that review independent label CDs, interview independent artists, do stories on local and regional independent labels, and/or have calendar listings for music events.

2. Find out to whom at each publication you should send information, and request the address, telephone and fax numbers, and e-mail address of that person. Create a database on your computer to store this information.

3. Send out your artist's promotional package to each of your contacts, graciously requesting a CD review if the artist's music will be of interest to their audience(s). Notify media contacts of upcoming events by faxing or e-mailing press releases and event invitations.

RADIO 57

R adio is the best form of promotion any label can get. Having one or more songs in regular rotation on the local college or public radio station will introduce your artist (and label) to new fans and help you sell extra CDs. Plus, for a new artist and label, it's cool just hearing your songs on the radio. Commercial radio is an entirely different outlet. Depending on the city, an artist's exposure on commercial stations can account for thousands of CD sales. To grasp how this system works and where your record label fits within it, you must understand the business of radio. With a basic knowledge, you can design an effective radio campaign for your label.

There are three main types of radio stations: Commercial, public, and college. All three provide some form of content (e.g., music, talk, news, sports) to attract listeners. Commercial radio stations rely on advertisements—or commercials—for their funding. When a company pays for advertising on a particular station, it does so with the expectation that the station will reach large numbers of people in the company's target demographic (i.e., age, gender, economic status, ethnicity, etc.). If the station doesn't attract enough listeners in the advertiser's market, the company will move its advertising dollars to another radio station. To avoid losing those advertising dollars, commercial radio stations base every decision—including the genre of music (and even the specific artists) they play—on a single unwavering goal: Attract the maximum number of listeners/customers for the advertisers. The thought of finding and playing good new music is irrelevant. I don't mean to sound cynical; that's just how it is. That's also why your artists (along with those on almost every other independent label) will probably never be played on commercial radio.

Public radio stations operate differently. Instead of receiving money from advertisers, they rely on donations from their listeners to pay for operating costs. This is one reason why public radio stations tend to be much more flexible and listener-focused than commercial stations are, and why they are more likely to adapt their formatting to meet listeners' interests. After all, if they want to keep the donations coming, they need to please their listeners.

College radio stations are funded by the student fees collected by the university, and sometimes by donations from their listeners. Because most of these stations are small and broadcast from campus, they usually provide content geared toward students and the campus community. They often broadcast alternative, non-commercial music (traditionally referred to as "college" music), and/or the college's sports events. Though they do not rely upon funding from advertisers, they still must maintain a certain level of responsiveness to the student body and the community. Everyone has a boss, and in this case, it's the college or university, which oversees the station and may require changes in format. Overall, though, college stations are the most progressive and free when it comes to selecting music and playing what they like without any structured musical format or play list.

Understanding the roles of different radio stations can help you find ones that might play your artist's CD. As you may have guessed, it's highly unlikely that you'll get radio airplay on commercial stations, so you'll probably be working with public and college radio. Great! Pretty much every new label starts this way. The most important thing is to get the music out there. Don't waste time worrying about stations that won't play your artists. Instead, focus your radio promotional plan on stations that *will* play your label's CDs. If commercial stations in your city play local music on special programs, or even in regular rotation, by all means, add them to your promotional plan. Just recognize that these stations are the exceptions, not the norm. You can find a list of U.S. radio stations in references like Billboard's *Musician's Guide to Touring and Promotion, Recording Industry Sourcebook,* and *The Indie Bible,* and online at *www.radio-locator.com* or in the *Radio Mall Commercial and Non-Commercial U.S. Radio Station Databases* (the *Radio Mall* databases are expensive but can be found at most major city libraries).

Once you've identified stations that might be interested in your artist's music, you'll have to approach them about getting radio airplay. You can contact stations directly or hire an independent promoter to do it for you. In either case, remember that everything you do should be geared toward selling records. With that in mind, you'll want to seek radio airplay only in cities or regions where your records are available for purchase.

If your label is based in Knoxville, Tennessee, it does little good to get your records played on a college radio station in Rochester, New York, unless you have a way of getting your records to consumers in that city. Without distribution to Rochester, you can't sell any records to listeners there, even if they want to buy the CD. Therefore, your efforts—even the success in getting radio play—will result in zero sales, which means zero benefit.

Don't get me wrong. Radio exposure in other markets is always good, and it never will hurt you. But you have to balance the costs of obtaining that exposure with the rewards earned by it. Ultimately, the expense of creating and mailing the promo packs, and the time invested in pursuing airplay in a city or region where you have no distribution will outweigh any benefit you could hope to gain.

As you seek radio airplay, your label will have to make the important decision of whether or not to hire an independent promoter. A promoter will have a database of contacts at radio stations in your region that work with smaller independent labels, and will tell you if he or she can get your artist's CDs played on those stations. But be careful and pay close attention to what the promoter is saying.

Independent promoters make no guarantees. Many may tell you they can get your record played on 100 stations. What they don't tell you is that these spins will occur at 4:30 a.m. on that college station in Rochester. Sure, you can brag that your artist is being heard in 100 cities around the nation, but you're still not going to sell any records this way. Obviously, very few people will be awake to hear your artist's music, and even those who *are* awake will have no way of purchasing the CD, because it's not available in their cities. Again, this kind of radio play results in zero records sold. So make sure the promoter is specific about which stations he or she will contact, as well as when and how frequently your songs might be played.

You can avoid a lot of problems by doing your research ahead of time. Obtain referrals for promoters from other small labels that produce music similar to yours. If a promoter has succeeded in getting those labels' music on the radio at the right times and in the right markets, chances are pretty good that he or she will be able to help your label, too.

But before you charge off to hire an independent promoter, understand that most will command from $5,000 to $50,000 for their services. This price can rise as high as $250,000 for major labels conducting a commercial radio campaign. Even on the low end, this is a large investment.

Therefore, before hiring a promoter, be sure your distribution is solidly in place, and that your records are available for purchase by the audience who will hear your music on the radio. Otherwise, you're just throwing money away.

If you can't afford a promoter, you'll have to work with radio stations yourself. This means you'll have to do some research to identify the stations most likely to play your CDs, as well as the music or programming directors at those stations. You probably already have a sense of which stations in your city are the best candidates. If you have distribution to other cities, you'll have to do a bit more legwork to learn about the stations there, too. Contact the music or programming director at your targeted stations and ask if they would be interested in your artist. (At larger stations, you may only get to speak with the receptionist.) Be sure to ask which person(s) at the station should receive your CDs and promo pack (along with the address), and how many copies to send.

I encourage you to begin with this kind of limited, manageable approach before you hire a promoter. It will allow your label to establish relationships with small commercial, public, and college stations in your state, and to obtain radio airplay that supports and enhances your distribution and sales. Focus on breaking one market at a time, in places where you have distribution. Eventually, you may find that 100 stations in your state are playing your label's CDs, and that you've grown at a pace that allows you to distribute records to those cities.

Also, consider that most artists are still performing within a limited radius of their home cities (maybe they've gone statewide, or have started playing two or three states) when their first CDs come out. By working with radio stations in that region, you maximize the impact of your promotional efforts. Listeners can hear your artist's songs on the radio, see your artist perform live, and buy the CD at their local record store. Moreover, most college, public, and small commercial stations love to have artists do interviews and perform live in the studio when they are in town. Here is an opportunity for your artist to promote his or her CD, while building good will and fans at the radio stations. It can also lead to performances at radio-sponsored events.

The artists on your label may never be played on radio stations coast to coast. In fact, the artists on most independent labels never are. This doesn't mean that you can't reach a lot of people and sell a lot of records. You just have to apply your resources wisely. Start by covering your region thoroughly with radio exposure, live performances, and distribution. When demand for your product increases, your distribution opportunities will increase with them. Then you can extend your radio promotion plan to surrounding states, and maybe even the entire nation.

Things You Can Do Today To Build Your Label

1. Make a list of public, college, and small commercial radio stations in your city, region, and state.

2. Contact these radio stations by telephone or e-mail and ask if they play artists on independent labels. If they do, inquire about their submission policy.

3. Research radio promoters that might be able to help you obtain radio airplay on the stations, and in the regions, you want to reach. Inquire about promoters' costs, policies, and success rates.

ADVERTISING

A s I mentioned earlier, the main difference between publicity and advertising is that you have to pay for advertising. If you send a CD to the music critic at your local newspaper, he or she may listen to it, review it, and even write something good about it. The paper even may decide to do a story or interview featuring your label or artist. All of this costs you nothing, aside from one CD and postage for a promotional package.

This kind of free exposure is wonderful, but it's not guaranteed. The critic may never listen to the CD, and the paper may never write a story about your artist. And even if they do, it will only happen once. Fans and customers will forget even the best review in a short time, so you need to keep your artist in the public eye. If you can't obtain continuous publicity for free, you'll need to consider paying for advertising. Naturally, your budget will determine what kinds of ads you run, and in which media. Appendix A lists a variety of promotional options that may be helpful as you consider publicity and advertising possibilities for your label. I discuss a few of these options below.

Like any other company selling a product, you can advertise via magazines/newspapers, radio, television and/or the Internet. If you have unlimited funds, you can pay to advertise in all of these media. However, you probably won't have that luxury, so you'll need to be selective and efficient. A

$2,000, full-page ad on the back cover of a major monthly entertainment magazine will reach a lot of people for one week. However, this fleeting, high-visibility attention generally will not have as much long-term impact as will more modest, but consistent and well-placed ads.

Because it takes awhile for consumers to become familiar and comfortable with a new "brand," promotion is most effective when it's sustained over a long period of time. So instead of spending $2,000 for an ad that fills the magazine's entire back cover for one month, you might consider investing $500 for a series of quarter-page ads that will run for four months. Some magazines come out once a month, some every three or six months. Obviously, your advertising dollar goes further in publications that are published less frequently. In some cases, you might be able to stretch that $2,000 over an entire year. So do some research, try a variety of approaches, and pay attention to the results. Over time, you'll learn what strategy works best for your label.

Depending on your situation and goals, some media may be more cost-effective than others. Commercial radio and television can be expensive, but you may find affordable ways to advertise in these media. For example, your label might be able to underwrite a program on the local college or public radio station. As long as the station plays the type of music your artist performs (at least during the program on which your ads appear), you can feel confident that your ads will reach your target market.

Another relatively inexpensive advertising option is cable television. You might be surprised to learn how inexpensive it can be to run a television ad in your local market on MTV or other cable channels that appeal to your market. A local public-access channel (usually a cable channel operated by a college or a city) might even allow you to sponsor a video show or music-related production that it plans to air. TV ads cost more to produce than radio or print ads do, but they can reach large numbers of people at one time, so you may want to consider this medium in the future.

In the beginning, though, print and radio ads will probably be the most cost-effective options for your label. You might pay $500 for a magazine ad that will reach a predictable number of subscribers for an entire month. And because it's in print, people can refer back to the ad. This gives print advertisements an advantage over those in electronic media, which won't make an impact until you've run them at least a few times a day over an extended time period.

Of course, the big benefit of advertising on a radio station (as least one that plays music like your artist's) is that consumers listening to the station are likely to be interested in your artist's record. Furthermore, if the radio station plays records from independent labels, it might become aware of your artist through your ads and eventually begin playing his or her record.

Regardless of the medium, I have found advertising to be most effective when coupled with a performance or event. In a sense, you get two advertisements for the price of one. The initial announcement of your artist's new CD, for instance, could also advertise your record-release party or an in-store performance by the artist. In addition to alerting fans about the CD's availability, this approach can help attract more people to your artist's shows, which creates goodwill between you and the artist and helps to promote his or her success at area clubs.

It will take some time to determine the most effective system for incorporating advertising and other forms of promotion into your label's overall plan. Like everyone else starting out in this business, you'll make mistakes. While you're learning, you'll certainly hear from advertising sales reps at local publications and electronic media. Beware. They can be very helpful, but some may try to talk you into buying advertising that you don't want, or won't help your label. Remember, they're salespeople seeking a commission. Most don't know enough about your business to know (or care) what is best for you.

When I owned a live-music venue, I battled constantly with radio sales reps determined to convince me that I needed to advertise during weekday drive time (the most expensive time to advertise). Their rationale was that more people would hear my ads then than at any other time of day. That might have been true, but I didn't believe the people listening during that time were my club's target audience. It doesn't matter how many people hear, see, or read your ad if they are not interested in your product.

Instead of paying for expensive "drive time" ads to reach people who probably wouldn't come to my club anyway, I chose to advertise at 12:00 a.m. to 3:00 a.m. on the weekends (which also happens to be the cheapest time to advertise). This was "drive time" for my market: People who were leaving clubs and listening to the radio on the way home. I reasoned that these were the people who would be most interested in my club. The sales reps never understood, and they never stopped trying to get me to spend more money. But I didn't care because this strategy worked for me without breaking my budget.

I believed, then as now, that, rather than being your sole source of promotion, advertising should support your publicity efforts. Too many labels accept the old saying, "it takes money to make money." I prefer the phrase, "it takes creativity to make money." Ultimately, I suggest that you do as little advertising as possible. There are times when advertising is absolutely necessary and appropriate, but it should always be viewed as a supplement to your promotions. Use your creativity and concentrate on obtaining publicity rather than paying for advertising. This will teach you how to promote your artists through the free avenues. No matter how successful your label becomes, this will always be a valuable skill. And in the beginning, it may be the key to your label's survival.

Things You Can Do Today To Build Your Label

1. Review Appendix A for a list of promotional options that may help you develop a publicity/advertising campaign for your label. Identify all local media outlets available to your label and contact each to determine the cost of advertising with them.

2. Research the feasibility of cable-television advertising in your city. Seek a college student or intern who has some television-production experience and might be willing and able to help you create an inexpensive television advertisement.

3. Create a promotional plan and budget in which advertising supplements publicity and your other promotional efforts. Even if you don't have money for advertising right now, include advertising in your plan, so you'll be prepared to incorporate it when your label starts making money from sales.

OTHER PROMOTIONS

T he great thing about promotion is that it allows, if not requires, a creative approach. Creativity is especially important for a small label on a tight budget (like yours). With some imagination, you can develop great, inexpensive promotions that increase your sales and create a positive image for your label and artists among consumers and industry professionals. The traditional promotional outlets discussed in previous chapters are crucial to your campaign. But this is just the beginning. A number of less conventional (and less expensive) options, such as club promotions, record release parties, artist's live performances, Websites, and record label promotions, can also be very effective. These alternatives will reinforce and broaden the scope of your label's promotional campaign, often with little or no expense to you.

For instance, most labels kick off promotion for a new CD by holding a record release party at a local club. The party usually consists of the artist's record being played over the venue's sound system, followed by a performance by the artist. You'll want to invite local media, retail store buyers and sales people, radio and club DJs, and distribution representatives. Give everyone a free copy of the CD, and provide free food and libations. A well-planned CD release party presents a great opportunity to schmooze and promote goodwill within the industry, while setting your label apart from other small labels.

In conjunction with the CD release party, you can also schedule a free performance by your artist, open to the public. By foregoing a cover charge, you encourage fans to spend their money on the record instead. (Of course, you will sell the CD at the show.) This kind of event can gain a lot of exposure for your artist and label, and attract new fans who have not seen the artist before.

Your artist's musical genre (dance, country, R&B, rock, etc.) will determine the type of club where you should hold the show. When selecting a location, consider venues where your artist draws especially well, and/or that have been particularly helpful in your artist's development. (By bringing in a good crowd, this event can be a great way to repay venues that have been especially supportive.) Before the show, put up posters, set out postcards, give away CD singles, and do whatever you can to create a festive atmosphere. If all goes well, the audience, a captive market, will like your artist's music, be caught up in the enthusiasm of the moment, and want to buy the CD. Even after this initial wave of promotion, though, you should always have CDs available for sale at all of your artist's shows.

One bit of advice: Do not schedule your record release party or the free performance until you have the CDs in hand. I have seen many labels and artists waiting nervously for their CDs to be delivered on the day of the party. On some occasions, the CDs did not arrive, spoiling most of the good will and enthusiasm that had been building. In fact, these kinds of mishaps can make your label and artist appear unorganized and unprofessional. So before you send out the invitations, make sure you have all the pieces in place.

Another good way to promote a new CD is through live "in-store" performances by the artist at record stores that are selling the CD. What you make of this event is up to you. The goal is to expose people to the artist and have them buy the CD. Some record stores may allow you to bring in food and libations for the customers who are at the store during the event. You'll need to speak with your record store contacts to work out the details. But usually, they'll be open to "in-store" shows, as these events often draw additional customers to the store.

If you advertise these events, be sure to mention the new CD in your ad. For example, in a print ad announcing your artist's free live performance, include a picture of the CD cover and inform people where they can buy the record. If you don't have retail distribution yet (i.e., your records aren't available in stores), advertise that the new CD will be available at the event, or lead readers to your Website.

I also suggest printing posters that feature the record cover. Send these posters to clubs, record stores, and other locations in advance of your artist's performances, and ask them to display the posters. You can send the same poster to everyone. Just leave some white space at the bottom of the poster, in which the club or record store (or your artist) can write in the location, date, and time of each performance. The poster effectively advertises both the show and the artist's new CD.

In addition to these efforts, send a press release to inform all local media about your artist's performances and any events your label will host. Most radio stations and newspapers have a club calendar that lists upcoming events at various venues around town. As always, free press is best, and even small notices like this add up over time.

After you've released a few albums and hired a couple of people, you can have a holiday or "industry appreciation" party. Invite your employees, label partners, venue owners, record store representatives, and media contacts. It doesn't have to be extravagant. Just some libations and hors d'oeuvres at a small restaurant, or even at your office, will generate good will for your label and artist(s). Although promotional in nature, these parties can be very pleasant, as there is no pretense of trying to sell a particular record. And everyone likes to be appreciated.

Finally, your label must have a Website. These days, there's no way around it. A Website is a powerful and relatively inexpensive way to provide information about your artist(s) and your label to a global audience. If you don't have distribution (or even if you do), your Website can serve as an alternative marketplace where people can order your artists' CDs. In addition to basic information about the label, the Website should include a promotional package for each artist (see Chapter 54, Creating and Using the Promotional Package). This will make it easier for media to get the information that will help publicize your artist's performance or record release. Be sure to include your Web address on all label-related advertisements, business cards, and promotional materials.

All of the promotional strategies described in this chapter have a common characteristic. They engender personal interaction that will leave a lasting impression on media, venues, music-industry professionals, and your potential market. In a competitive and challenging business like music, a little face-to-face contact goes a long way. So, as you brainstorm to create innovative promotions for your artists' CDs, always try to include some kind of personal contact with your label and your artist.

Things You Can Do Today To Build Your Label

1. Plan a record release party for your artist. Contact venues where your artist has drawn well to determine which ones are most receptive to hosting the event.

2. Begin calling record stores that distribute your label's product and discuss the possibility of an in-store performance. Make sure to work out details regarding the availability of (and space for) sound equipment and the possibility of serving refreshments at the event.

3. Begin thinking about a Website for your label. Review the sites of other independent record labels to determine what features you like and don't like. Seek a Website designer (many are listed on the Websites themselves) who can create a site that matches your label's vision.

A Final Word

60

There's been a lot of talk lately about the demise of the music industry. And it's true that recent developments involving the Internet, commercial and satellite radio, music downloading, and copyright laws have many major-label executives scratching their heads and wringing their hands. But don't feel too bad for them. The music business is a multi-billion-dollar industry, and as you read this, each major label is planning a new multimillion-dollar ad blitz to push its latest cookie-cutter artist (who probably looks and sounds exactly like the last one did).

In fact, the music industry is doing just fine. As David Baskerville reports in *The Music Business Handbook*, Americans spend more on CDs and videos than on tickets for movies or sporting events. Musicians in this country spend more than $5 billion annually on instruments, sheet music, and related items. And perhaps most amazing, the annual sales of cassettes, discs, and videos, combined with income generated from their prime delivery medium, broadcasting, exceeds the gross national product of more than eighty countries in the United Nations. So, despite all the wailing and worry by major labels, I believe there has never been a better time to start an independent record label.

Technology does have an important impact on the music industry. But hey, it always has. Look back over the past 100 years, and you'll find a long list of groundbreaking advances. Vinyl records may seem like a quaint idea today, but once, they were quite revolutionary. And what about FM radio, CDs, and MP3 files, not to mention all the devices invented to record and play these different formats? As your favorite philosopher, Heraclitus, wrote, "Nothing endures but change." Somehow, though, the music industry always manages to adapt and survive.

And usually, independent labels lead the way. Small labels like yours are more nimble, more comfortable with change, and more creative in meeting challenges than major labels could ever hope to be. Unlike the majors, independent labels don't have the luxury of sitting around high-rise office suites complaining about how tough things are. To survive, they have to be proactive. This places independent labels in a natural position of leadership.

Yes, the music industry is shifting. The Internet and other technologies really have opened things up, creating new ways for small labels to get their music heard and to sell records. Eventually, all labels, even the majors, will have to adapt to the new landscape. Because you're just getting started, you don't have to adjust. Simply embrace developments and changes, incorporate them into your business plan, and use them to your advantage. As always, creativity is your best asset.

Major labels have blamed the Internet, the digital format, MP3 players, and the Man in the Moon for declining record sales. And while illegal downloading certainly has had a negative impact on record sales, it isn't the biggest cause of the labels' problems. The main culprits are the major labels themselves.

For far too long, they've been signing mediocre artists who have one good song with commercial radio appeal. Unfortunately, that one good song doesn't make up for the twelve other crummy ones on the CD, for which major labels have been charging $15.99 or more. That's a very high price to charge for one track. It's bad business, too, and labels are now paying for their greed. They've driven consumers to find new ways of getting the good songs without all the filler. Technology now allows them to do just that. I wholeheartedly condemn illegal downloading, but I'm a big fan of legal, pay-to-download sites that allow consumers to get exactly what they want without buying a bunch of extra crap.

You'd think major labels would take heed and start working to put out better records. Nope. Instead of rethinking their approach to signing and recording artists, they've responded by lowering CD prices. (And not all majors have taken even this step.) A bad product at a cheaper price still is a bad product, and $10.99 is still far too much to pay for one good song. Major labels complain about Internet downloading, but apparently they still haven't figured out why it's so rampant, or attempted to address the root cause. If they don't get it by now, they must not be listening.

Part of the problem is that major labels are locked into a business model that relies very heavily upon commercial radio. They've set a terrible precedent by paying hundreds of thousands of dollars to promoters, who, in turn, pay radio stations those hundreds of thousands of dollars to play the label's music. You might have heard of this before. It's called payola. There's a federal law against it, but the law only prohibits record labels from paying radio stations directly. A loophole in the law allows a promoter to pay stations on a label's behalf. Maybe you've wondered why you hear certain artists so often on commercial radio. Well, someone is paying to make sure you do.

This practice, coupled with the loosening of laws that used to limit the number of stations one company can own in each market, has had a significant negative impact on radio. Now, most commercial radio stations in the U.S. are owned by a few very large corporations that dictate what you're going to hear. This is why radio sounds the same no matter where in the country you travel. The parent corporations aren't concerned about the health of the music industry, the towns and cities in which their stations are located, or what the listeners want to hear. I often wonder if they even listen to music. Sadly, commercial radio has become little more than an outlet for advertising. It's all about the bottom line and the science of selling widgets. I don't mean to sound cynical; that's just the way it is.

Major labels built this system to eliminate competition and limit consumer choices (all in the name of maximizing profits). Now that the monster they've created has turned against them, they complain about losing money. I have no sympathy, and neither should you. They've done this to themselves. Given their reluctance to evolve, I don't expect the system to change any time soon. This means that for the foreseeable future, major labels will continue to monopolize commercial airwaves in a misguided effort to sell mediocre music.

That's okay. You have other outlets for your label's music, as described in this book. And as consumers become more fed up with the inferior products being put out by major labels, they are looking for alternatives. Now more than ever, music fans have options as to where and how to acquire what they want. This causes trouble for major labels, but creates opportunities for independents. I believe things can change. In fact, I believe the industry is changing—for the better—even now.

For example, more and more artists who were on major labels are moving to independent record companies, or starting their own. The number and success of Internet and satellite radio stations are exploding. The options for acquiring exciting new music—legally—continue to grow. Consumer awareness of, and demand for, these alternatives is growing, too. This isn't just a trend; it's the future of the music industry. And you can be a part of it.

By embracing and supporting public, college, AM, Internet, and satellite radio stations, we can change the industry from within. As an independent-label owner, you can be part of the cutting edge by producing new, influential, and ground-breaking music for these stations to play. Instead of trying to create product that you hope can be sold to, or distributed by, a major label, focus on the forgotten element: Quality. Yes, you have to sell records to survive, but you can succeed as a label *and* advance the independent-music industry at the same time.

The modern music industry was built by energetic, innovative people who cared about music. They were businesspeople, sure, but they had a vision and something important to say. You can't measure the impact of small record labels like Chess, Decca, King, Roulette, Sun, and many others just like them. Even today, their legacy and influence endure. And you know what? By current standards, they all were independents. I'm not saying your label will ever reach that stature, but you can take comfort knowing you'll be in very good company as an independent.

I encourage you to attend a music conference like SXSW (South by Southwest) in Austin, Texas; NXNW (North by Northwest) in Portland, Oregon; or CMJ (College Music Journal) in New York City. Similar conferences are held all over the country. Hundreds of bands play at these conferences. You'll be amazed by the energy, diversity, and quality of these artists' songs and performances. Sadly, you will never hear these artists on commercial radio. Most aren't on major labels and never will be. But if you ask, you may be surprised to find that most are quite happy with their smaller, independent labels. You may also be surprised by the enthusiasm and size of their audiences. Yes, people *do* want independent music, and they're willing to search—and pay—for it.

Whenever I attend one of these conferences, my faith is renewed. They display the music industry at its finest: Entire conferences supported by unsigned artists and those on independent labels, along with their fans. As an independent label owner, this is your world. Enjoy it.

The music industry is based on a simple objective: Produce good songs and find a paying audience for the artist's live performances and recorded music. This audience is never far away. People crave and pay for music because it evokes an emotional response and satisfies a need that nothing else can. The beauty is, they always want more. This ensures the future viability of the music industry. As the owner of an independent label, you can be part of that future and play a role in defining this industry for years to come. Instead of looking up at the tall buildings where major labels are developing a survival strategy, look ahead to what you can do in your own city, state, and region. Get started today. To quote the Red Hot Chili Peppers, "There's never been a better time than right now."

Appendix A
Promotional Efforts

BASIC ADVERTISEMENTS

Place co-operative ads with record stores and clubs.
Advertise CD release parties.
Advertise CD with in-store performance.
Advertise CD with artists' live shows.

RECORD STORE PROMOTIONS

Create and display posters.
Set up end caps.
Arrange in-store performances by your artist.
Print stickers (include label name and slogans).
Obtain listening stations.
Put up posters for ongoing live shows.

PUBLICITY EFFORTS FOR PRINT MEDIA

Send out CDs.
Send press releases about label and artist events.
Line up interviews.
Make follow-up calls.
Fax information about the artist's live shows.

PUBLICITY EFFORTS FOR RADIO

Mail out CDs.

Organize on-air performances.

Ask radio to conduct ticket give-aways for the artist's shows.

Fax out press releases about label and artist events.

Make follow-up calls.

Fax information about the artist's live shows to concert calendars.

LABEL WEB PAGE

Provide label info.

Provide artist info.

Post artist photo.

Post CD cover.

Link to artist's Website, or create a site for the artist.

Set up sales on *Amazon.com* and/or *CDBaby.com*.

Link your site to *Amazon.com* and/or *CDBaby.com*.

LIVE PERFORMANCES

Advertise the CD with artist performance.

Place posters in record stores.

Distribute flyers and label bumper stickers.

Fax radio and print media show dates

Fax information about the artist's live shows to
radio and print media contacts.

Place your poster throughout the venue.

Give clubs a copy of your artist's CD for their jukebox.

Sell CDs at the artist's shows.

LABEL IDENTITY

Throw parties; invite industry contacts and leaders.

Sponsor festival stages.

Purchase a booth to sell your label's CDs at music festivals

RECORD ROYALTY ACCOUNTING STATEMENT

All royalty calculations shown below are based on the sample sales figures, royalty rate, advances, and deductions listed here.

Number of CDs sold:	32,000
Recording costs (recoupable):	$20,000.00
Other recoupable costs:	$10,000.00
Suggested Retail Price (SRLP):	$15.98
Artist royalty rate:	13%
Free goods:	15%
Packaging deduction for CDs:	25%
Reduced Rate for CD configuration:	85%
Return reserves:	25%

$	15.98	SRLP
X	.85	Configuration reduced rate
	13.58	
-$	3.99	Packaging rate x $15.98 (SRLP)
$	9.59	Price artist's royalty is calculated on.
$	9.59	Price artist's royalty is calculated on.
x	13%	Artist contracted royalty rate
$	1.24	Artist royalty per CD sold
	32,000	Records sold
	4,800	Free goods (32,000 CDs sold) x .15 (free goods rate)
	27,200	Number of records royalties are paid on
x$	1.24	Artist royalty per CD sold
$	33,728	Gross royalties payable to artist
-$	8,432	Return reserves (.25 return rate x 33,720 royalties)
$	25,296	Artist royalties payable this statement
-$	30,000	Recoupable costs (deducted from artist's royalties)
$	(4,704)	Recoupable costs still owed to record company
+$	8,432	Return reserves released 1–2 years later
$	3,728	Artist record royalty paymnt on the first 32,000 CDs sold

MECHANICAL ROYALTY ACCOUNTING STATEMENT

All royalty calculations shown below are based on the sample sales figures, royalty rate, advances, and deductions listed here.

Number of CDs Sold:	32,000
Statutory Mechanical Rate (cents)	8.50
Reduced contractual rate	75%
Number of songs on CD:	12
Number of songs on which royalties are calculated:	10
Free goods:	15%

$	8.5	Statutory rate
x	.75	Reduced contractual rate
$	.063	Negotiated rate paid to artist
x	10	Negotiated number of songs paid on
$	.63	Total mechanical royalties paid for each record sold
	32,000	Records sold
x	.63	Royalties paid for each record sold
$	20,160	Gross mechanical royalties payable to songwriter-artist
-$	5,040	Return Reserves (.25 return rate x 20,160 royalties)
$	15,120	Artist royalties payable this statement
+	5,040	Return reserves released 1-2 years later
$	20,160	Mechanical royalties paid on the first 32,000 CDs sold

PRE-PRODUCTION CHECKLIST

1. STUDIO

_____ Studio Rate (Hourly or Day Rate)

_____ Number of Days (Number of Hours)

_____ Recording Format (Digital, ADAT, Tape, DAT)

_____ Recording Equipment Available (Including Microphones)

_____ Musical Equipment Available (Piano, Electronic Keyboards, etc.)

_____ Additional Musical Equipment Needed, and Cost

_____ Engineers

_____ Other Amenities (Kitchen, Lounge, Vending Machines, etc.)

_____ Band Approval (Visit by Band)

_____ Mastering Process (Costs, Expected Time)

_____ Session Cancellation Policy

_____ Demo Rate (If Doing a Demo of Songs)

_____ Contract

2. PRODUCER

_____ Experience (Artist and Label Approved)

_____ Fees (Mixing Mastering Included)

_____ Contract

3. ARTIST
_____ Costs (Per Diems, Union Fees)
_____ Recording Schedule

4. SIDE ARTISTS
_____ Fees and Per Diems
_____ Rehearsal Fees
_____ Contracts or Union Forms

5. MANUFACTURING & PACKAGING
_____ Bar Code
_____ *Graphic Artist*
　　_____ Band Approved
　　_____ Samples of Artwork
　　_____ Experience with Printer
　　_____ Photographs (Costs, During Recording, Contracts)
　　_____ Contracts
_____ *Printer*
　　_____ Configuration Needed
　　_____ Provide Print Proofs
_____ *Manufacturer*
　　_____ Configuration Needed (CDR, DAT)
　　_____ Artwork/Print Configuration Needed
　　_____ Days to Complete

RESOURCES

MAGAZINES FOR INDUSTRY PROFESSIONALS
Alternative Press
The editors cover everything with an eye toward alternative music and
   culture.
(800) 339-2675 x 115
www.altpress.com

Billboard
The industry tip sheet for musicians and record-company executives.
(800) 745-8922
www.billboard.com

Billboard's Musician's Guide to Touring and Promotion
Printed twice a year, this magazine lists all the necessary information for
   a band or booking agent to book a national tour.
(615) 321-4250
www.themusiciansguide.com

CMJ New Music
For new music, there's no better resource.
(917) 606-1908 Ext. 248

Uncut
Published in the UK, for the best of the music of yesterday and today. A
   passionate look at music.
+44(0) 845-676-7778
www.uncut.net

RESOURCE DIRECTORIES
   Commercial U.S. Radio Station Databases by Radio Mall
   www.radio-mall.com

   Non-Commercial U.S. Radio Station Databases by Radio Mall
   www.radio-mall.com

   The Indie Bible by David Wimble
   www.indiebible.com

   Musician's Atlas
   www.musiciansatlas.com

   Recording Industry Source Book
   www.artistpro.com

MUSIC BUSINESS BOOKS
   All You Need to Know About the Music Business by Donald Passman

   The Billboard Guide to Publicity by Jim Pettigrew

   Guerrilla Marketing by Jay Conrad Levinson

   *How To Register a Trademark: Protect Yourself Before You Lose
       Your Priceless Trademark (The Entertainment Industry)* by
       Walter E. Hurst

   Making and Marketing Music by Jodi Summers

   *Making Music Make Money: An Insider's Guide to Becoming Your
       Own Music Publisher* by Eric Beall

   The Musician's Business & Legal Guide by Mark Halloran

   Music Copyright for the New Millennium by David J. Moser

Music Distribution: Selling Music in the New Entertainment Marketplace by C. Michael Brae

Music, Money, and Success by Jeff and Todd Brabec

Music Publishing: The Real Road to Music Business Success by Tim Whitsett

Ruthless Self Promotion in the Music Industry by Jeffrey Fisher

Self-Promotion Secrets for Musicians by Michael Gelfand

This Business of Music: Marketing and Promotion by Tad Lathrop

The Music Business by David Baskerville

They Fought the Law: Rock Music Goes to Court by Stan Soocher

MUSIC BUSINESS BIOGRAPHIES

Exploding: The Highs, Hits, Hype, Heroes and Hustlers of the Warner Music Group by Stan Cornyn and Paul Scanlan

Hit Men: Power Brokers and Fast Money Inside the Music Business by Frederick Danner

Inside the Minds: The Music Business by Aspatore Books Staff

The Men Behind Def Jam: The Radical Rise of Russell Simmons & Rick Rubin by Alex Ogg

Mansion on the Hill: Dylan, Young, Geffen, Springsteen, and the Head-on Collision of Rock and Commerce by Fred Goodman

What'd I Say: The Atlantic Story by Ahmet Ertegun

MUSIC RECORDING BOOKS

Assistant Engineer Handbook: Gigs in the Recording Studio and Beyond by Sarah Jones

Assistant Engineer's Handbook by Tim Crich

Behind the Glass: Top Record Producers Tell How They Craft the Hits by Howard Massey

Basic Digital Recording by Paul White

Home Recording for Musicians by Craig Anderton

How To Become a Record Producer by David Mellor

Producing Hit Records by David Farinella

Quick Start: Home Recording by Ingo Raven

MUSIC BUSINESS VIDEOS
The History of Rap: The Russell Simmons Story MTV Productions

Takin' in to the Streets MTV Productions

Hype! Sub-Pop/Warner

MUSIC CONFERENCES
CMJ Music Marathon
Held in New York City in October
www.cmj.com/marathon

Nashville New Music Conference
Held in Nashville in September
www.2nmc.com

NEMO Music Conference
Held in Boston in September
www.nemoboston.com

North by Northwest (NXNW)
Held in Portland or Seattle in September
www.nxnw.com

South by Southwest
Held in Austin, Texas in March
www.sxsw.com

Winter Music Conference
Held each spring in Miami Beach, Florida
www.wmcon.com

MUSIC BUSINESS CONTRACTS
www.MusicBusinessMadeSimple.com
www.musiccontracts.com

MUSICIANS' UNIONS
AF of M (American Federation of Musicians)
www.afm.org

AFTRA (American Federation of Television and Recording Artists)
www.aftra.org

PERFORMANCE RIGHTS SOCIETIES
ASCAP (American Society of Composers, Authors and Publishers)
(212) 621-6000
www.ascap.com

BMI (Broadcast Music, Inc.)
(212) 586-2000
www.bmi.com

SESAC (Society of European Stage Authors and Composers)
(615) 320-0055
www.sesac.com

GOVERNMENT RESOURCES
U.S. Copyright Office
(202) 707-3000
www.copyright.gov

U.S. Patent and Trademark Office
(800) 786-9199 or (703) 308-4357
www.uspto.gov

OTHER HELPFUL WEBSITES
Universal Code Council
Provides UPC Codes to businesses.
www.uc-council.org

RadioLocator.com
Resource for finding information on radio stations.
www.radio-locator.com

The Harry Fox Agency
Agency that grants mechanical licenses for most songs.
www.harryfox.com

INDEX